Juana la Loca

Linda Carlino

VeritasPublishing

ISBN 978-0-9555980-6-7

Juana la Loca

By LINDA CARLINO

VeritasPublishing

Queen Juana of Spain was the daughter of Ferdinand and Isabella and sister of Catherine of Aragon. She was contracted to marry Philip the Fair, a known womaniser and political schemer, and fell passionately in love with him at first sight., The marriage proved to be short lived but very passionate and stormy When her mother died she should have reigned as Queen of Castile but Juana was callously denied power and status throughout her life, most of which she spent imprisoned, by the three men in her life who sought power for themselves: her husband Philip, her father Ferdinand and her son Charles. She faced their relentless physical and mental cruelty with courage and determination, her spirited resistance earning her, unjustly, the nickname by which she is remembered; "Juana la Loca" (Joan the Mad.)

CONTENTS

MARRIAGE

Chapter 1

Juana's head was a confusion of the hopes and fears of a young girl just turned sixteen. The pulse in her throat tugged at her breath.

She left her room to hurry along the first floor gallery her ladies and her slave girl Zayda close behind. Her thoughts were on the council chamber. The courtiers and guards with their exchanged glances, their sympathetic head shaking went unnoticed. The pleasing scent of lavender, her favourite perfume, rising from the freshly waxed oak floor and the heavy chests held no charm today.

She knew why the queen, her mother, had sent for her. Of course she knew. She had longed for and yet feared the arrival of this moment ever since the contract was signed only a short while ago, yet she had still dared to hope that this moment might not be for some years.

But on this cold January morning of 1496, a day she felt would be engraved on her heart for ever; she had been summoned to a formal audience. There was no doubting its purpose. It could be nothing other than to inform her that all the marriage negotiations were concluded and a date set for her departure.

A painful tightness crushed her ribs. It was as if she had received her death sentence. Gone were all the harboured, delicious dreams of a handsome prince, sad and joyless, yearning to see her beautiful face that he might be returned to happiness.

'Zayda, I will be exiled from Spain – banished.' Choked words tumbled between gasps. 'How can I possibly live in a country so far away? It is too far and too dangerous a voyage to get there. I know I will be separated from everything I hold so dear. I will never see my family again. I know it. I will be lost and forgotten.'

She stopped close to the corner where the stairs rose from the courtyard below and gulped in the icy winter air that crept stealthily upwards. She brushed at her green velvet skirt, her fingers fidgety and nervous.

Zayda took her hands in hers to steady them. 'Courage, my lady, courage,' she urged her beautiful mistress.

And Juana was beautiful, in every way: in appearance, in the grace of her movement, in the music of her voice. She was of medium height, slim, and perfectly proportioned. Her oval face was crowned with luxuriant copper-gold tresses. Hazel eyes that sparkled readily with intelligence, a joy of life, with warmth and love glistened today with threatening tears. A mouth more accustomed to smiles and laughter was pinched with fear.

Her ladies waited a few feet away.

'What am I to do?' Juana pleaded with them. 'I am scared. Can you promise me that I will be happy in Flanders, and if so for how long? And if not, what then?'

'My lady, no one can know. We must put our trust in God.'

'I hope He will take pity on me. My sister Isabel says she wants to retire to a convent. Do you think I should tell my mother that I intend to become a nun too? Impossible! That is not the life for me. I say my prayers, go to confession and mass, and that is more than enough for me!'

Shocked gasps from her ladies stopped her. 'I only said that because Flanders really is so very far away. You would say exactly the same if you were me! But how dare I stand here tarrying! My parents will not be slow to accuse me of reluctance or disobedience.'

Juana raised the heavy skirts of her dress, bobbed and made a hasty sign of the cross before the triptych tucked in the corner then made her way towards the Rich Salon to be told of her future. Her ladies followed pausing for only the briefest of seconds to cross themselves.

She had known for a year of the proposed union and of all the various negotiations surrounding her marriage to the Archduke Philip, son of the Holy Roman Emperor. Naively she had supposed that it would be several years before the actual wedding took place, but it became apparent all too soon that this was not to be. There had been constant comings and goings of ambassadors throughout the year. The wedding by proxy earlier in the month and her signature declaring her bound by all the clauses in the wedding contract screamed the imminence of her departure. Then there were all those rumours of the special fleet being assembled in the north.

She now stood before the doors of the Rich Salon. What awaited her on the other side? All she did know was that she had no choice, there was no alternative.

Her ladies busied themselves carefully tucking wayward strands of auburn hair back under the green ribbon that crossed the crown of her head; checking the neatness of the single coiled braid that reached down her back to her waist; fussing over her bodice; turning back the voluminous sleeves to reveal their red satin linings; smoothing the folds of her skirts into place.

Zayda smiled, 'My thoughts are with you to give you strength, even when I am not beside you.'

Juana jumped as the doors snapped open. The time had come. Her breath now came in short and painful sobs. She willed herself to enter the room, to take the first steps into a bewildering future.

The salon was a blaze of red and white and gold; from the walls to the painted cornices and the painted carvings on the ceiling. Rich tapestries added to the splendour. Down the entire length of this council chamber stood the grandees, prelates and ambassadors; almost the entire court was in attendance.

Juana was completely overawed. After several steps she stopped; her legs unable to carry her further.

Beyond this brilliant gathering of invited witnesses Queen Isabel and King Ferdinand were seated on thrones under a scarlet velvet canopy bearing the shield of Spain, its coat of arms proudly declaring the power of the united houses. The monarchs were dressed, not in the everyday simple attire they preferred, but in gold brocades, red satins and silks.

Juana shot a nervous glance in their direction before lowering her head, desperate to avoid so many inquisitive eyes. As she studied the floor tiles it all became suddenly very clear. This was to be a farewell audience. She pouted, quietly grumbling her disappointment that this certainly didn't compare in any way with the extravagant displays of tournaments and banquets arranged for her sister. It was all so unfair! How much easier it would have been to lose herself amongst a throng of merry-makers than to have to stand alone subjected to the scrutiny of so many.

Queen Isabel looked down the length of the chamber and wondered how long her daughter intended to remain standing there looking so out of place. It was beginning to annoy her that Juana should be overwhelmed by this occasion. Regrettably Juana had as yet developed no regal bearing and was still so easily daunted. This child with the bowed head, the fidgeting fingers at her girdle, was surely not the same girl with the stubborn chin, the wilful daughter she so recently had cause to severely reprimand?

Juana's lack of dignity wasn't Isabel's only concern. There was the question of her increasing tendency to shun company, (alarmingly similar to her grandmother's and one which sadly led to her mind becoming confused); hopefully it was nothing more than another symptom of a rebellious phase and not uncommon in girls of a similar age.

Finally Juana raised her head; she curtsied to her parents and began the long walk towards the thrones. From the corner of her eye she saw some friends including her favourite, her Latin tutor. Their warm smiles offered encouragement and she held her head high, until she saw Cisneros standing close to her mother. He was the newly appointed Archbishop of Toledo and Primate of all Spain. Juana was terrified of him. He was much more than the leader of the Church, he was a powerful man of piercing intellect and tireless zeal for the faith. This priest was able to influence, persuade and guide the queen, even daring to address her as his equal. Remarkably, the queen was never offended by his audacity; proof enough of his power, proof enough to make Juana quake in her shoes even before daring to look at his long cadaverous face with its deeply set eyes. She was well aware that Cisneros had seen deep into her soul and had found her wanting.

Her lips began to tremble. She knelt quickly at the feet of her parents, lowering her head lest anyone witness the welling tears. She pressed her jewelled medallion of the Virgin, a gift from her mother, close to her thumping breast.

Isabel and Ferdinand rose and together descended the three steps to greet her. They were both in their mid-forties. Years of unremitting struggle to forge a new nation had taken their toll, especially on Isabel who had also had the burden of the rigours of six pregnancies. She was no longer the tall, slim, graceful young woman who had charmed Ferdinand. Her fair complexion had turned sallow, her long face with its firm jaw had become puffed and slack. The chestnut tresses had dulled and were now always covered with a fine veil; for today's audience a small crown nestled on top.

Ferdinand had been more fortunate. His face, bronzed and weathered in the fields of battle, was still strong and handsome. His continued riding and hunting had helped him maintain his firm, muscular frame.

Together they took Juana's hands to raise her up. She saw their smiles and was convinced they were of self-congratulation at having successfully completed the marriage contracts for both herself and her brother Juan. The bond between the Holy Roman Empire and Spain had been reinforced twice over by this double marriage, tightening the circle around the enemy, France, thwarting any expansionist ambitions.

Juana was to marry Philip and her brother would wed Philip's sister Margaret. With the treaties that these marriage contracts brought and others with England making steady progress, (these contingent upon the marriage of another daughter, Catalina, to the son of King Henry VII), France would find herself completely surrounded.

King Ferdinand spoke, 'Sweet daughter, all the necessary arrangements for your wedding are now complete. All waiting and uncertainty are at an end. You are to marry in October. Then you will become the wife of Philip, Archduke of Austria, Duke of Burgundy, Count of ...'

It took all her strength not to scream back at him that she knew all this, that it was unimportant. What she wanted to know, but dreaded knowing, was when must she leave. Words from a song repeated themselves in her ear as if to taunt,

They say that I must marry,
I do not want a husband, no.

Polite applause filling the room and Queen Isabel's voice, seemingly from somewhere far away, interrupted her thoughts.

'You are to leave for Flanders in July.'

Juana panicked; it could not be July, that was too soon!

'Such an adventure for you; and it will be upon us in no time at all. We must choose some faithful servants to accompany you. We will also have to determine which priests would be most suitable for your confession and spiritual support.'

She would be leaving in a few months and with servants and priests of her mother's choosing, her own preferences ignored. Hot tears began to sting her eyes. She considered running away, hiding somewhere; or perhaps even throwing herself at the mercy of her parents, begging to be allowed to remain here, at home, in the bosom of her family.

Words finally formed saving her from such embarrassments. 'Your royal highnesses, I shall do my best to please you, to be worthy ...' She was choking, her whole body aching with despair.

Everyone's attention was suddenly focused on the doors. They swung open to reveal a young man of seventeen years. It was Juan, a fair skinned and sickly looking youth, who for the whole of his childhood needed to have doctors in constant attendance. He was the special child in the family, the one so very dear to Isabel. Was this because he was the only son God had granted her? Or was it because as an infant he had had such a tenuous hold on life? Was it because of his determination to overcome his disabilities? Perhaps it was his kind words and deeds. It may have been a combination of all these things. Whatever the reason Isabel saw him as her *angel* and always addressed him so.

Juana watched her slight, fair haired brother walk slowly towards the dais, his long gown of red velvet and his studied walk disguising his rickety limp. She loved him and wished she could be like him, finding pleasure in so much around him and drawing friendship from everyone he met. He always sought to please and was always cheerful.

Isabel and Ferdinand, disciplined diplomats expert at showing no emotion, could not disguise their joy in their son.

'Your m-majesties,' Juan knelt on the cushions placed at their feet. He rose and first kissed the hand of his mother then that of his father.

'Dearest son, our beloved prince, we have good news. The

11

Archduchess of Austria will be coming here in the latter part of this year. She will sail with the returning fleet that will have escorted your sister to her new home.'

Juan was delighted, his eyes shone, and he nodded his head, looking about him inviting all the court to share in his happiness. 'G-Gentlemen, l-ladies, is this not w-wonderful. It will not be too long before we have my wife Margaret here among us. How f-fortunate we are to have s-such a prize.'

His audience bowed. Very few had understood him; the words coming from his scarred and twisted mouth were virtually unintelligible and it was impossible for most people to make any sense of his mumblings.

Ferdinand nodded a command and trumpets and sackbuts heralded in a procession of standard bearers to take up their positions on either side of the two thrones and on the steps to the dais. First was Isabel's device of five bound gold arrows on a field of green, this was followed by Ferdinand's gold yokes on a black field. Next were the Knight Commanders of the three Military Orders, wearing white capes and carrying banners showing their distinctive crosses. Last came the royal coat of arms; quartered to represent Castile, Leon, Aragón, and Sicily, with the added stylised pomegranate of the recently reconquered Granada.

A pause, then with music from the minstrels' dulcimers and lutes the courtiers filed past the royal group to kiss hands, to offer their congratulations, and to bid Juana farewell. They moved on to view copies of the marriage contracts, written in Latin and French, the names of the betrothed in gold. In a border of entwined leaves was the inscription: *Et qui quispiam praevalent contra unum, duo resistant ei* ..."If one is prevailed against, two shall withstand him ..."

The ceremony was over and most of the court dismissed. It had not been terrifying after all; in fact Juana had actually enjoyed it.

Ferdinand took Juan, one arm lightly resting across his

shoulders, to the fireplace with its cheery fire. They stood together talking and laughing so at ease with each other, their mood matched by the lively crackling of the logs.

Juana looked on until her mother beckoned, 'Come my child let us sit for a while, over here.' Isabel lowered herself onto a divan and Juana arranged some cushions around her, one or two of these made by Isabel's own hands in snatched moments of leisure.

'Tell me, mother; tell me all you know about Philip, have you any further news? Remind me of his looks. Tell me, will he like me? Am I pretty enough for him?'

'Slowly, slowly Juana, not so many questions at one time! Sit down and we shall talk.' Isabel waited until she was sitting comfortably at her feet. 'Philip, as you already know, is tall, is fair of features, has blue eyes, and his looks are enough to have attracted the nickname, *Philippe le Beau*, Philip the Handsome. You have his miniature, Juana; that says it all.'

'Oh, yes,' Juana closed her eyes, rocking herself gently on her cushion. She was to marry a prince called Philip the Handsome, just one year older than herself, tall and beautiful. How she wished she could be with him this minute. She saw herself in a gown of fine white silk, with a mantle of dark green. She was running in silver-slippered feet over dew-kissed lawns bearing gifts of roses and lemons, and a small golden cage of song birds. He turned to welcome her with outstretched arms.

'Tell me more. What does he do? What does he enjoy? What is he good at?'

Isabel paused. The tales and rumours from Flanders of the young man's philandering once more raised her concerns for her young daughter. 'I think it can be said that Philip enjoys life to the full. He has a passion for hunting, dancing and sports. He shows great talent in the game of pelota. He also loves convivial evenings spent with his many friends.' She omitted the fact that he was an obnoxiously arrogant youth with a fiery temper that was easily roused.

'Mother, how wonderful it must be to be someone so exceptional, so popular. And to think he is to be mine, all mine. I dance gracefully, I have a good singing voice, I play several instruments well, or so my teachers tell me. But am I pretty

13

enough? Such a man must have a pretty wife. Am I pretty, mother?'

Isabel was alarmed. Did Juana still not realise the true nature of royal marriages? How could she not after all their discussions? It worried her to see the mind of her innocent sixteen year old continue to be filled with foolish romantic notions; the result, no doubt, of having her nose forever buried in books.

But all serious misgivings about this union had to be set aside. Her son, as the inheritor of all Spain and its dominions was central to the negotiations; but truth to tell, and it was a very painful truth, his health was not good. Spain's security had to be maintained and its power increased. It was vital, therefore, that the contract with the Emperor Maximilian should be for the two marriages, lest that of Juan should come to nought. A match with their eldest daughter Isabel had been refused. Maria had to be held in reserve for any contingencies which might arise. Catalina, their youngest, was promised to the Prince of Wales. Unfortunately, it had to be Juana.

Juana tugged at her hand, 'Mother, I am waiting for you to tell me if I am pretty enough. It is taking you quite a while to decide.'

'Oh, you are pretty enough, my child,' Queen Isabel stroked her daughter's head. For just a moment she felt a wave of guilt at the sacrifice of this the prettiest and weakest of her lambs.

Chapter 2

Queen Isabel had predicted that Juana's departure would "be upon us in no time." The intervening months since that cold, January day had sped by and now Juana found herself sitting with her mother making the final checks of the various itineraries; and she was not in the best of moods.

The whole business had become most aggravating. It had started well enough discussing the inventory of furnishings and the materials for her new and splendid wardrobe. Then she had been delighted with the contents of the jewellery box, her parents' gift. What fun she had had modelling the ropes of pearls, the gold chains, the exquisite earrings; making her be-ringed fingers dance like butterflies about her mother each and every finger sparkling with a precious stone set in its golden circle. They had been like two young girls together. More serious matters had followed starting with the allowance she would have for herself and her household. This would come from her husband, just as Juan would provide a similar amount for Margaret. It was an astonishingly generous annuity of twenty thousand escudos, but there was little need for her to bother her head with details as she would have a treasurer to deal with boring accounts.

The choice of ladies-in-waiting had irritated her to the point where she had insisted they defer making some decisions until later when perhaps, just perhaps, some sort of compromise could be reached.

So it had come as no surprise to either of them that on hearing her mother's nomination for confessor Juana rebelled, refused, shouting, 'No! I will not have him. He is your choice not mine. I would never confess to him. I neither like him nor trust him. Mother, I insist I have someone I know will stand by me and not someone put there to spy on me. You have chosen him because you do not trust me!'

'Juana, remember who you are, and what you are …' Isabel began.

A clattering, skittering of hooves on cobblestones setting the courtyard ringing mercifully brought their dispute to an end.

'That must be Juan,' cried Juana, and Isabel, with a nod, agreed that it probably was and that it would be a blessing since they were not going to make any further progress today.

Juana made as if to stand but her mother's restraining hand on her wrist demanded she remain seated. She glowered at her mother, her face a mixture of anger and misery so Isabel relented, removed her hand and nodded her approval. Like an animal freed from a trap Juana leapt to her feet.

Below in the courtyard Juan and his steward were dismounting and handing over the reins to stable lads who had raced to claim the honour. Other members of his household were still arriving, each to be similarly greeted and attended to. Juana hurried along the open gallery, snatching quick glances of the excitement below her. Then, too impatient to wait any longer, she leaned over the balustrade and clapped her hands, calling down to him. He looked up, saw her, and gave her a huge smile. He waved his large travelling hat making a great show of having to avoid the cloud of dust from its immense brim before making her an absurdly deep bow. She laughed, her fingertips held to her lips, and she ran back to the room, to her mother, all arguments forgotten.

Isabel was standing waiting, resolute. She cautioned, 'We will continue this another time, Juana. There is still much to talk about. And, in the light of your behaviour this morning, I am even more determined you have good counsellors about you. But for the present let us go down to welcome our angel.'

'Dear, blessed angel indeed,' agreed Juana.

The courtyard remained pleasantly cool in the July sunshine. Isabel, Ferdinand and their family found the summer months in northern Spain far more to their liking than in the south where the intense heat and searing sun made life almost unbearable. This year it suited them to come to Almazán. From here Isabel would find it more convenient to attend to the details of the fleet for the Flanders voyage, while Ferdinand could visit his court in Zaragoza as often as was required, especially during this time of unrest between Aragón and France.

It was here only a few days earlier that they had invested Juan, heir to the throne, as Prince of Asturias, granting him the cities, lands and revenues pertaining to the title. This castle, set on a hilltop and looking out over the most beautiful of valleys, was a part of the gift and Juan was already beginning to furnish it to his liking, a summer home for himself and his bride.

The two ladies stepped from the shadows into the warmth of the early afternoon sunlight and into the sweetest of summer perfumes from the jasmine and roses twisting and turning about the columns of the arcade.

Juan and his steward were supervising the unloading of rolled up tapestries, huge chests of silver and gold plate and enormous candelabra. Isabel grasped the opportunity to stroke the chestnut neck of her son's mount. Her thoughts skipped back over the years to remembered damp, earthy scents of the days when she went hunting for wild boar in the dark, dank forests shot through with flashes of autumn gold. She could still hear the earnest thud of the hooves, the creaking leather, jingling harness and bridle, the snorts of horses eager for the chase. There was nothing to equal the exhilaration, the excitement. Now she was too old; sighing, she patted the horse's flank.

Juan saw his mother and came to kiss her outstretched hands. The servants stopped, heads respectfully bowed, until all the greetings were over and they could resume their unloading of carts before leading away the oxen.

'Welcome, welcome, my angel. It warms my heart to see you organising a home for Margaret.'

'Dearest mother, that is exactly what I want. I want a home, not a castle, for my bride. S-sister Juana, you too must be finding these days exciting, and not so many more b-before you l-leave ...,' his voice trailed off noting how quickly her welcoming smile was fading and the corners of her mouth were beginning to turn downward, 'You are n-not sad are you Juana?'

'Not now my dearest,' Isabel warned, 'we all have much to tell, but later, please. You are tired, dusty and thirsty.'

She placed herself between her children, wanting no further display of temper from Juana and she certainly did not want

Juan disturbed by any outburst from his sister when he was already exhausted. This uncontrollable stammering signalled his weariness, and it worried her that a half-day's journey should have taken such a toll.

'We shall prepare ourselves for lunch and afterwards everyone will rest.' It was not an invitation, it was a command. 'This evening will provide all the time we need for everyone's news and by then we shall all be refreshed. Come.'

'Bruto, take up your station!' Juan commanded a rather scraggy-looking black and white hound, which immediately lolloped, its ragged tail crazily scything the air, to stand guard beside the queen.

Juan offered his mother his hand, his arm first tracing a huge arc before her. She accepted it, inclining her head with exaggerated grace, delighting in precious moments such as these, happy to see that he was not so tired after all. Juana received one of his understanding smiles. She gave his hand a squeeze of gratitude.

'Bruto, forward march!' With great pomp and dignity humming a fanfare he and Bruto escorted the two ladies, who in no time at all were both laughing. The morning's bitterness was forgotten - for the moment.

❖   ❖   ❖

Late in the evening, when dinner was over, the family gathered in their mother's apartments, hastily seating themselves on their floor-cushions, impatiently awaiting her first question that would then permit theirs. Isabel was in her favourite leather chair with her four girls and her beloved son forming a circle around the brazier, brought in to offset the chill that often crept into the room even on summer nights.

The room was a comfortable size sufficient for their family and not too large to lose its intimacy. Flemish tapestries transformed the stone walls into vast tracts of peaceful woodland. The flickering of torches in their sconces and heavy curtains drawn against any intruding draft lent an added cosiness. Juan sat at his mother's feet prepared for her first question.

'Are you well pleased with your steward?'

'Oh, certainly. We have a great understanding of one another. Of course your careful training has helped me tremendously. I am confident I have the ability to run a household. I rarely need to ask him for advice. And you know, mother, he is a most likeable person, very well mannered and friendly and an excellent riding companion.'

Isabel stiffened, 'Take particular care Juan to see that he is not permitted to be friendly. You must remember that you are the prince and he only the steward. There should never be an occasion when you can be friends. As I have said you are the master and he is the servant. I would wish you both never to forget that. He must never expect anything from you other than that which you demand. After that it is at your discretion when and where to grant favours.'

'Yes, yes, dear mother, I understand and believe me he does know his place and always will, but please let us not be so serious.'

'No mother, not so serious. And I have something to ask Juan,' broke in Catalina, who with all her ten years felt that her question was more urgent than anything her mother or the others might wish to concern themselves with. 'I want to know if you feel any different now that you are the Prince of Asturias.'

'It certainly sounds very grand, Catalina, and I admit I think it does make me feel older if not wiser.' He pretended to whisper a special secret, just for her, 'What is even better, I now have more money for myself and my bride.'

Catalina giggled. 'I would feel so proud to have a title. I know what I shall be known as. Just imagine having to call me Catalina, Princess of Aragón, the Princess of Wales. Does not that have such a pretty ring to it?' She stood up, hastily straightening her skirts, to walk proudly around the circle, nodding her head acknowledging her humble subjects. She bobbed a curtsey to her mother before hugging her and returning to her cushion, a rosy blush creeping across her cheeks.

'Yes dear, and one day you will have a title all of your own; when the time is right. Then you will be able to tell us just how it feels. At the moment it is not fitting for you to assume a title, even in jest. I will forgive you this once, my child.'

'Yes, yes, sorry,' she hurried on, 'but Juan, is it not quite wonderful that you are to marry a beautiful girl? I think that must be the best news ever.'

'You are right dear Catalina, it is good news. But what I hope for most of all is someone who is happy and can discover happiness in the most ordinary of things. What do you say dear sister Isabel?'

'Without doubt what you say is true.' A smile flickered for a moment then died leaving tragedy written deep in her gaunt young face. 'Finding happiness together in everything, no matter how mundane, is important; but of more importance is that you both share a deep love of God, that is when you will have joy beyond ... forgive me.' She lowered her head to hide the tears from her family and fingered the embroidered pattern on her girdle as though hoping to discover comfort there. Seven years had passed but still the pain of the premature death of her most devout Christian husband lingered.

Her mother shook her head, 'Isabel you must try harder, you really must. You do so disappoint me!'

Isabel's answer was a fit of coughing; a cough that racked her thin frame, about to break it with its violence.

Juana mused on her mother's arch comments, Isabel's misery, Catalina's refreshing innocence, and on her own daunting future

'You did not answer me, Juana.' Her brother was bending over her, 'We thought you had fallen asleep. You were in a little world of your own.'

'Sorry, I did not realise you had spoken to me,' she looked nervously from her brother to her sisters and finally to her mother. How often had Juan tried to attract her attention before he had got to his feet to come over to her? 'I beg your pardon ... I was thinking ... forgive me; what were you saying?'

'We were wondering what your ideas might be for a happy marriage.'

'Well,' she began, biting back the desire to say that given any choice in the matter probably no marriage at all would be by far the best, 'I think a happy marriage depends entirely upon the couple both being good looking making it easy for them to love each other with the whole of themselves not just with their minds but with their bodies. To share …'

Queen Isabel could not believe her ears, she was astounded that any lady would speak so, she was furious that her daughter dared. 'Juana I think you forget yourself, you have gone too far, much too far this time.'

Silence, complete and unbearable silence; they could scarcely breathe.

'No mother I have not gone too far,' she boldly replied, knowing full well she had done, but at the same time hoping that an inspired thought might just render her safe from severe censure, 'for I have in mind you and father, the perfect partnership.'

Audacious it might well have been but it worked. Her brother and sisters, freed from their dreadful apprehension of yet another conflict between their mother and Juana, applauded in nervous agreement, while the queen looked searchingly at her daughter. Was this a sign of her daughter's growing worldliness and precociousness, and if so did it spell further worries for this marriage with Philip?

Juan invited Maria to say something, 'You have not had your say; come, what are your views?'

Maria knew he would remember that she had not yet been asked. So often in these family *tertulias*, discussions, she was the one left until last, but she was never left out, Juan saw to that.

'I think you must be philosophical about it,' she paused for effect, waiting until her audience had fully appreciated the new word so recently acquired, before continuing. 'With this approach you are bound to find happiness in all things generally and in marriage in particular.' Her eyes shone and she coloured to the roots of her hair while she repeated her profound statement to herself with delicious satisfaction. She looked to her mother for confirmation of the wisdom of her fourteen years.

Clapping his hands and laughing Juan invited her to explain.

'I mean you must be positive: do not go searching for troubles and difficulties, discuss misunderstandings. Something

21

of that nature.' She turned again to her mother this time seeking support, which she received in the form of a warm smile and a sigh.

But Isabel had no heart for a family gathering tonight, or for the direction in which the conversation was apparently headed, and she desperately needed to talk to Juan. She would hear no more; she bade her daughters goodnight and dismissed them.

The moment they left Isabel bared her heart, 'My angel, I realise that you must be exhausted from your journey and this tiresome evening, but bear with your poor mother a few moments more while she begs a favour.'

'Dearest mother you do not need to beg of me, I am your most willing and obedient servant. It would give the greatest joy to do anything to please you. I see the worried look in your eyes. How can I help?'

'Do talk to Juana; appeal to her better nature. It concerns the choice of members of her household. She is convinced that I am imposing my will at every juncture and only for my own self-interest. This is not so. I seek only to offer her the best support. This morning when I suggested the Dean of Jaen to help her with her prayers and confession she refused vehemently.' She stood up and began to pace about the room, 'In any other circumstances I would concede. But Juan, we hear such disturbing rumours of Philip and his dissolute ways. These and Juana's, shall we say, less than heartfelt dedication and commitment to the faith, and her tender youth convince me that the people I have chosen, especially spiritual advisers, are essential. They will provide some stability in what may well be extremely difficult times.'

'Yes of course I will talk to her. I know she will tell me what her objections are, and I am sure I can dismiss them as being totally unfounded and unjustified. They certainly are with regard to the Dean who is such a kind and gentle priest. I shall then offer my suggestions. She always respects my ideas so it will not take much to persuade her. If you would give me a list of those you wish to accompany Juana you can leave the rest to me. Never fear, she shall not know that I am your emissary. I will be nothing more than her concerned brother.'

'If you could possibly do this for your mother; you are the only one to dissuade Juana from her own misguided choices.'

'I will do everything in my power to bring you peace of mind and I, like you, want nothing less for Juana than she have the people around her who she truly needs.'

'God bless you my angel.'

Chapter 3

The brisk morning sunshine stole into the courtyard without offering any hint of warmth and travellers and well-wishers alike were thankful for their cloaks at this early hour.

Everyone had been assembled for some time anticipating an early departure but Isabel and Ferdinand had still to appear. Horses and mules fidgeted impatient to be off, servants and soldiers shifted their weight from one weary foot to the other; and Juana agonised.

She stared fixedly at the still empty doorway. 'What can be keeping them, Zayda? All this waiting. I want it over and done with.'

Juana was desperate for her journey to commence since it was now obviously inevitable. Her trembling fingers fidgeted with her red velvet travelling hat tugging all around the enormous brim, nervously undoing and redoing the ribbons. She pulled her red cloak about her but finding no soothing warmth wrapped her arms about herself hoping they might be of comfort.

A giggle from her younger sisters made her look up. Bored with the lack of activity they had decided to practise their dancing steps and had got into such a dreadful muddle, hence the laughter.

Juana envied them, jealous of their carefree joy, and quickly switched her attention to her brother who was talking most earnestly with their sister Isabel. Bruto, sitting at his heels, had his head cocked to one side listening attentively to every word. He was gazing up at Juan, paddling the ground with his forepaws as if impatient to join in the conversation.

'Dear Bruto,' she called to him, 'you darling mongrel. You may not be very handsome but you are very clever. I shall miss you and all your funny tricks.'

Juan and Isabel came to join her with Bruto tagging along behind.

'Be brave Juana,' Isabel took her hands in hers, 'believe me you will soon make Flanders your home.'

24

'But I will be all alone!'

'You will have a full Spanish court, almost a hundred; a small Spanish kingdom of your own!'

Juana was not persuaded so Isabel tried once more, 'Juana, do not be so anxious. It will not be the ordeal that you imagine. Do not be so pessimistic. I think it is unkind of you to suppose that Philip and the Flems are all monsters. And have you forgotten your romantic ideas about a happy marriage? You and a handsome young gentleman called Philip must surely meet your requirements.'

'Oh, Isabel if only I could be brave. I am so frightened I think my heart is about to stop beating. Feel how it thumps wildly. Dear God, I feel ill.'

Juan interrupted, 'You are talking nonsense, Juana! We were just saying how we envied your strength. When have you ever been ill?'

She was ready to protest but Juan stopped her short, 'Never! So come now, dear sister, we will have no more of this.'

'But I am ill, truly ...'

'This is not illness, it is a refusal to face facts,' Juan continued, ignoring her. 'You have no choice as to whom you wed and where you will live. There is nothing further to discuss. I must also point out that you are making everyone miserable with these melodramas, and quite a few are growing weary of it all. You know I love you dearly and do not intend to be harsh, I speak so only for your own good.'

'But Juan, I thought at least you would understand.' She was devastated, she had been confident of his support.

'Dear sister, I said you had such tremendous stamina, which I have been denied.' He raised her chin to have her look at him then teasingly played his fingers over her lower lip that she had pushed into a huge pout. 'You also have the strength and the spirit to counter all adversities,' he brushed aside her denials. 'Show me the Juana who will never give up the fight. Show me.'

She looked at him sadly. It seemed no one could understand the depth of her misery at leaving her family; of not having a single friend by her side. The ladies-in-waiting were passable enough, she supposed, but she had only accepted them with great reluctance; and as for the priests, they were not of the sort to raise anyone's spirits. And not one tale of love, not one image of a joyful union with her handsome prince could be summoned to rid her of her desolation. Through sniffles she mumbled something about her head agreeing with everything he said, but her heart being too bruised and broken to follow suit.

'God bless you.' Holding her face in his hands, his thumbs gently smudged the tears on her cheeks then he kissed her forehead, 'I wish you a safe journey and of course Godspeed; the sooner you arrive in Flanders the more quickly will the fleet return with my Margaret. Forgive my selfishness.' He laughed, hugging her tenderly.

She hugged and kissed him in return, clinging to him; it was their last embrace, she would never return to Spain.

A sharp rapping of the chamberlain's rod halted her grief. King Ferdinand and Queen Isabel made their way across the courtyard towards Juana.

Ferdinand drew her to him, 'We wish you well dear child. You must always keep in mind that your duties as wife and confidante to Philip will be of the utmost importance to your parents and to Spain. We rely upon you to be steadfast in your support for our country, expecting you to take every opportunity to further her cause. Never let it be said of you that you were negligent.'

And that was it; there was nothing more. Where were the words of warmth and affection from the father she loved?

She whimpered, 'You still cannot come to the port of Laredo?'

'Juana you know I cannot. I have to be with my troops, my presence is imperative. I cannot shirk my duty. Duty to our country must always come first. I should be gone already, but I stole some days to say my farewells.'

Juana sobbed into her cloak, some tears finding their way onto her father's gloved hand to settle like diamonds amongst the jewelled rings. She found her way to her mule to be assisted into the saddle by misty, tear-blurred figures. There she sat hunched, her wretchedness hidden under the large brimmed hat, willing her mother to signal their departure.

An untidy scuffling and slithering of horseshoes and the

horses and mules were off, quickly settling into a steady rhythm, taking the riders away from the castle, wresting Juana from the bosom of her family.

'I will wave to you from the gallery,' Juan called out over the clamour of clattering hooves.

They made their way between the two huge towers guarding the Herreros gateway, leaving Almazán behind and heading for the waiting mountain pass.

Juana bit her lip, head down, looking neither to left nor right thinking only of her hurt. It pained her that she was nothing more to her parents than a pawn in their political game of chess; how could she ever recover from the blow of that farewell scene?

And yet in a little while she remembered Juan's words, and she resolved that from this moment she would be more positive and assertive, after all she was no longer a child to be reprimanded or manipulated. As of now she was a woman, a princess, an archduchess, with whom the world must deal.

She took a deep breath and straightened in the saddle glad to have been reminded of her other self. She turned to look back at the castle with the church tower clinging to it, and waved several times. Perhaps there were some figures gathered in the gallery, and perhaps one of them was Juan.

Her spirits lifted, she looked around at the mountains through which their trail would take them. The views were astonishing with sweeping hills, one followed by another, all clad in folds of green velvet, with here and there dashes of browns, greys and purples. Juana's eyes moved upwards tracing wooded slopes, stony outcrops, cliffs and shadowy secret hollows. A fine silver ribbon of water reached down into the valley, growing wider on its fall, until finally disappearing through an iridescent veil into the bluest of lakes. Eagles soared, they dipped and dived, they rose again effortlessly. There was probably a lesson to be learned from their watchfulness, their waiting, their ability to swoop, to snatch and hold their prey with such tenacity; but she doubted she would ever have such patience.

Chapter 4

The port of Laredo had never known so many people, animals and ships. It had never heard such noise, had never been so busy.

The view from the cabin window offered ever-changing scenes of comings and goings. Young boys staggered under sacks of urgent last minute supplies. Corpulent masters hurled oaths at fidgeting oxen and their carts that refused to remain still. Against the angry groaning of winches and hoists, officers bellowed out orders to their sailors below. Curses at spillages and bursts issued from everywhere. Meandering seamen, who had found the wine jugs too early, wove their drunken way amongst barrels and chests that littered the wharf, merrily slurring tuneless shanties. Soldiers whose responsibilities had yet to begin strolled about enjoying soldiers' hearty laughter and back-slapping camaraderie.

Juana, delighting in the hubbub and determined not to miss any of the activity, ran from one window to the next pressing close to the glass. Her cabin at the stern of this newly built galleon stood so high it made an excellent vantage point and by using the windows on all three sides she could see quite a distance both to left and to right.

The royal party had arrived in Laredo several weeks ago but could do nothing until they had a fair wind, and this was finally promised for tomorrow, August the twenty-second, 1496, hence the frenzied activity out there.

She stopped to look at the letter for what might be the hundredth time. It was from Philip and dated the seventh of July. It had been sent to her mother who had given it to her to keep. Yes, it was a letter from her future husband impatient for his bride. The bold tone had annoyed the queen but it had wooed Juana. To her it spoke of a lover's desire to be with his loved one. Her heart leapt every time she read the words demanding she sail immediately or he would send the Spanish ambassador to bring her to him, for he would wait no longer.

She kissed the letter before handing it to Zayda inviting her to read it again. The priceless treasure was then returned to her jewellery box.

'Now we shall attend to these.' Juana picked up the documents the admiral had left with her that morning. Her mother had insisted that she be involved with some of the preparations for the fleet and here was the latest and, hopefully, the last for her perusal. The other papers had been of no interest whatsoever, merely listing the types and names of ships: their tonnage, their captains, their crews, the number of soldiers and whether they were cavaliers, infantry or archers and on and on; *ad infinitum,* or *ad nauseam*, as she had remarked to her uncle, the admiral.

Nevertheless Juana had dutifully read them, and it was reassuring to know that France would be so intimidated by the power and size of the fleet she would never dare consider military involvement. Also, it was beyond question that Philip and his countrymen would be profoundly impressed by this show of Spain's wealth and power.

Today's lists were of provisions. She glanced down the neatly drawn-up columns then began reading them to the assembled council or, rather, to Zayda and one or two empty chairs. 'Sirs, I see we have biscuits from Seville; excellent. Olive oil, yes that is important, we will certainly require olive oil. Salt-fish and dried meat; wonderful, we should never be without them. What was that? Not to your liking, Zayda? Here it says peaches, jams and flour, now that sounds much better, think of the lovely cakes, pies and fresh baked bread. Now what do we have on this sheet? Why, enough for a feast: chickens, eggs, butter and wine.'

'My lady, I think we may congratulate the admiral on such fine choices to suit our palates.'

'Of course, you are so right. I thank you all, gentlemen.' She dropped the papers onto the table dusting her hands free of her duty. Not yet accustomed to the subtle motion beneath her feet she took a few timid steps out onto the deck and grasped the rail to steady herself. Zayda placed a shawl about her shoulders.

The morning rain had given way to afternoon sunshine. A breeze toyed with flags, and pennants were curling and snaking, their colours cutting across the forest of masts and rigging that rose, fell and rocked gently in the languid swell. Juana continued to be amazed at the number of vessels. The admiral had told her that there were more than a hundred, and twenty of them were newly built this year. They all looked new with their sparkling fresh paint and varnish. The gentle deep groans of the timbers and the higher pitched moans of the hawsers were rudely interrupted by the angry screaming of ill-tempered gulls. Everything was crying and tugging to be free, impatient to seek adventure.

She breathed in all the sights, sounds and smells, the strangeness of it all.

A neighing and a clattering of hooves made her look back to the quay. Juan's horses, his gift to Philip, were being taken aboard a ship moored nearby. Their hooded unseeing eyes made them nervous and they fought against being moved. Servants cajoled and encouraged them on to the unsteady ramp with pats, strokes and kind words, while others held firm on strong tethering ropes. Other horses neighed out their fear as they were unceremoniously winched aboard in slings.

'Poor beasts. I commiserate with them Zayda, that is exactly how I feel. I am being taken blindfold onto unsure ground; but what can we do? We must do as we are bid.' Her eyes searched beyond the horses anxious to find her mother who ought to be on her way by now. 'My mother is unfeeling. Here am I ready to be despatched to extend Spain's influence westward, while she sits at her desk writing letters to England to seal the fate of my sister Catalina. It is all so callous.'

'Not so, my lady. It is the way of things with royalty. Indeed any person of substance would not countenance anything other than an arranged marriage.'

'It would be marvellous all the same if, instead of writing to England, she is writing to Flanders saying she has recognised her error in supposing I would make a suitable bride.'

'Where would all your tales of love be then? Consigned to a fire, unwanted? And what of Philip's letter almost in pieces with the number of times it has been opened and read, the words smudged by moist lips endlessly caressing them?'

'Dear Zayda, of course you are right.' She began to sing,

'this girl who is in love
no longer cares to sleep alone...'
'How wicked of you, ma'am!'

Chapter 5

'A double tragedy ma'am,' the Admiral of Castile, Don Fadrique, broke the silence of horrified disbelief of all those gathered along the ship's rail. They were watching the pitiful writhing of the Count of Melgar's huge Genoese galleon. The giant lumbering ship had found her way onto a sandbank and now lay twisting and heaving like an animal trapped in a snare, her sails flapping like useless broken limbs. Sailors leapt from her sides into the churning waters to swim to the awaiting safety of the surrounding smaller vessels. Others sought to launch boats from the stricken craft.

Without taking her gaze from the drama before her Juana asked; 'A double tragedy? What could be worse than the loss of lives and that magnificent ship after travelling so far, and through seas far worse than these?'

It was true, they had experienced the most terrifying journey imaginable. The Bay of Biscay had been in a sour mood, the fleet mercilessly pounded by its gales and mountainous waves. The travellers were held prisoner in its howling, grey, drenching grasp, and tormented by the alarming sounds of crashing and splintering wood; captives in a world of chaos and disorder, a world of disorientation and nausea.

Nine days later, most of the fleet had managed to limp to shelter in friendly English waters, for some the battle was lost and they were now laid to rest on the ocean bed.

They rested for two days in Portsmouth, a welcome respite and pleasing interlude where she was feted as Princess Juana of Castile; treated as a princess in her own right and not as the daughter of the monarchs of Spain, nor as the wife of the Archduke Philip. Then blessed by the return of a favourable wind they were able to set sail once more, this part of the journey taking them up through the English Channel and on towards the Low Countries.

Now, six days later, the voyage was finally reaching its longed-for conclusion. Land was in sight and it was only a matter of hours before anchoring and putting the weary but grateful passengers ashore. Yet it seemed that even their arrival was not to be without incident; another ship lost, and this time a major one.

She turned to the admiral, one hand on the rail to steady herself, the other clutching at the collar of her cloak as it tugged in the wind. Her face, framed by her scarf wound securely around her head and neck, for the moment, had lost much of its fresh bloom. 'But Don Fadrique, you *still* have not told me; why "A double tragedy"?'

'Much of your trousseau was in that ship, and many of the jewels belonging to your courtiers. I am afraid that there will be no way of retrieving any of it, she will soon be ripped apart and sunk, her contents scattered over the sea bed.'

'So, there we have it, the proud flotilla bearing the Princess of Spain has been transformed into a raggle-taggle fleet bringing a pale and sickly looking pauper with few belongings. What will Philip think when he sees this pitiful waif before him.'

He smiled, 'Ma'am, if you will allow, he will think you the loveliest of beings. And as for the loss, well, I am sure that it will not be long before everything is replaced by even better. It is just a sadness that it should happen now when we are so close to our haven. Aye,' he sighed, 'but, no matter, it cannot be undone. We will not dwell on sad events, rather let us think about how you will charm all who come to meet you. How all their eyes will feast on this sweet vision from Spain.'

'Don Fadrique, you are the kindest, dearest of uncles. But for you I do not know how I could have endured such a dreadful journey. And now you say just the right things to encourage me. Oh, would that you could be by my side always.'

She had said this once before, to her brother, and now as then she knew that this could not be. This part of her uncle's task was almost completed and the next, to escort the Princess Margaret to Spain, would be all too soon; and he would be gone, lost to her forever.

She would miss him sorely; she would miss his kind face, his merry eyes and the gentle smile in that comforting, depend-on-me beard. Who could replace such an expert chess opponent, who else could entertain her with such amusing tales, and who else could be such a caring guardian to her? No one. She reached to touch his arm, as if in doing so she could hold this moment and him forever.

The admiral's words put paid to any wild fancies. 'And now my Princess Juana of Castile, Archduchess of Austria, your maids are waiting. It is time to prepare for your grand reception.'

He took her hand, held it to his lips, then let her go, watching her cross to her cabin, thinking of what might have been. He thanked God he had had the foresight before leaving England to transfer Juana from that stricken vessel yonder to this smaller galleon which was far better suited to negotiating these dangerous shallows and notorious sandbanks. She might well be amongst those even now struggling for survival, despite her earlier insistence that royal folk never drowned. She was a plucky young lady, true enough, and she would not go down without a fight, not she.

'Take a hold of yourself, man,' he wiped his eyes and blew his nose into a large handkerchief. 'You must be getting old, indulging yourself in imaginings fit only for womenfolk. You have done the job your queen entrusted you with. So far, so good. That is enough to think on.'

Juana and three of her ladies stood in a luxurious billowing rainbow of silks, satins and velvets, a glorious heap of skirts, bodices, sleeves, chemises, underskirts and mantles.

'The blue, your highness?'

'I think not, Ana. After so many days at sea I shall feel I am drowning in those brocade waves. We shall put that colour away until we have rid our minds of a frightful journey, and until blue will only remind us of skies, rivers and gentle lakes.'

Beatriz held up a white velvet skirt embroidered with hundreds of pearls, 'Perhaps white, ma'am, white for a new beginning. Like paper before it is written upon?'

'What a lovely thought and so poetic. But today I think we need a strong colour.'

'Then, a red dress?' suggested Ana, 'I do so love red, it is my favourite colour.'

'No, too bold,' replied Juana before deciding upon the yellow. 'A yellow dress will be perfect. Yes ladies, we will dazzle the Archduke Philip with the golden warmth and brilliance of the Spanish sun. And it will raise our spirits too. Let us begin, Maria.'

Maria was her favourite lady. Juana felt most at ease with her; she had, after all, chosen Maria herself and therefore would have more confidence in entrusting her with any of her private thoughts. The others were of her mother's choosing.

Maria directed the complex task of dressing their mistress. They busied themselves, chattering and fussing; concentrating. Today, more than ever, they had to dress Juana with extreme care. As they worked, their shared giggles and exclamations released the nervous tension.

Maria inspected the brocade dress very carefully, a little pull here or a tuck there, so that just enough but not too much of the chemise showed in the front openings running down the sleeves. She inspected the stitching, just this minute completed, attaching the sleeves to the bodice. She checked the fit of the bodice over the skirt. Then she turned back the wide sleeves to show six inches, no more no less, of yellow satin lining and the gold and red embroidered cuffs of the chemise. She then fitted a modesty vest of fine gold thread, delicately woven and set with rubies, across Juana's breast, tucking and pinning it carefully to the chemise. Finally she fastened the clasp of the necklace with its enormous ruby; a farewell gift from Queen Isabel.

'Your highness, you look radiant. You will astonish and delight all who see you today.' Maria spoke for all, 'And now for your hair. Beatriz, the hairdressing cape, if you please.'

The yards of travelling scarf were unwound from her head and her auburn tresses tumbled free in scented waves; the handiwork of her slave who possessed all the secrets of the mysterious world of perfumed oils and their powers. They were brushed then braided with a ribbon into a long single plait down her back. A gold hairnet was pinned in position and over this Maria placed a black velvet hood with its trim of gold flowers, each one with a tiny ruby at its centre.

Maria gave their work one final inspection, running her expert eye over every detail before allowing Beatriz and Ana to arrange the gold velvet mantle trimmed with ermine over Juana's shoulders. She gave the hood a tiny adjustment, ensuring that it neatly framed Juana's face and gracefully curved out to rest on her shoulders, then stood back to admire their work.

Juana looked at them, anxiously awaiting their judgement, 'Well, what do you think? How do I look?'

Their voices tumbled one over the other telling her just how exquisite she looked: how the dress was so perfectly made and fit her just so; how the embroidered border of her hood so cleverly repeated those of her bodice and skirt; how the ermine of her mantle and the white of her chemise peeking through the sleeves so delightfully completed the dazzling picture.

No one would see her white stockings, her yellow shoes made of the softest leather, nor her black slip-on mules, but Maria knew they were there and she was proud of the overall effect and completeness. This was to be Juana's first public ceremony, and one open to the greatest scrutiny. Maria felt they were all to be congratulated for a task well done.

Before they could exhaust all the praises a tapping on the door interrupted them; now there was silence where only seconds before there had been such commotion.

The moment had finally arrived; the moment when Juana would set foot in this new country, her new home.

Her laughter was gone, 'Blessed Virgin Mary, on this your special day, see fit to protect this humble child before you. Guide me through these next few hours. Help me to do and say the right things. Help me, as you did in England, to play the part of a royal princess. Help me to hide my nervousness. Please make them like me. Be there when I meet Philip. Make him glad when he sees me; make him happy that I was the one chosen to be his wife. *Hail Mary, full of grace, the Lord is with thee: blessed art thou ...*'

Her prayers finished, she counselled herself to take courage, to count to ten then give her orders.

On the count of ten she raised her head. 'Open the door, Maria, we are ready to leave.'

36

❖   ❖   ❖

The captain and his crew had lined the decks, waiting on bended knee to say farewell to their precious passenger. Their cries of God's blessings warmed her heart and with a smile she turned to thank them. They cheered and tossed their bonnets high in the air.

The ship had been brought in and moored alongside the quay at Bergen-op-Zoom. A broad gangway had been prepared and Don Fadrique led Juana down onto the cobbles. How good it felt to step on the reassuring strength and solidity of those stones even if they did seem to rise and fall like gentle waves. Her attendants merrily fussed around her. Her uncle stood at her side admiring her.

'Here we are at long last, safe and sound and with firm ground beneath our feet, and you looking quite beautiful. Unfortunately they are not ready for the reception. We will know when it is time to proceed when our heralds, followed by theirs, have formally announced your arrival.'

'It took them no time at all in England.'

'This is all very different; this must be done in a formal manner according to the rules of protocol.' He didn't add that he could not understand the delay, and that he was concerned. 'You enjoyed our stay there?'

'It was marvellous; every moment. Everyone was so kind and generous in their welcome with cheering crowds wherever I went, and the mayor and the magistrates so hospitable.'

'Unfortunately the English hospitality proved too much for many of our sailors.'

'The good folk of England made allowances, blaming the strangeness of their beer for causing such drunkenness.'

'The "good folk" almost fought one another for the chance to see you; except for one admirer who had no need to use force,' he smiled, shaking his head.

'Ah, the king's representative.'

'As you say, my lady, the king's representative. His majesty of course was forbidden by protocol to meet you.'

'Rules, rules, rules! He was certainly a good listener. I have never known anyone show such interest in everything I had to say. I felt so wonderfully grown up.' She had basked in the warmth of his attentions. The memories of that day were something quite exceptional to be guarded forever.

'I shall tell you a secret. When he took his leave to return to London he said, "If Catalina, the young sister of this dear lady is but half as beautiful, half as charming, half as graceful, half as intelligent, then I will have chosen the best possible bride for my son Arthur."'

Juana's eyes opened wide, 'No! You cannot mean that he was not the representative after all, but King Henry himself? And no one knew?'

'And no one knew,' he chuckled, enjoying her astonishment, tapping his lips with a finger. 'Ah, but I see we have action at last, and about time too.'

The heralds with their trumpets and banners bearing the quartered coat of arms, the castles and lions of Castile, had moved to the head of the group. The soldiers were forming two splendid ranks of scarlet and silver. Priests and courtiers were assembling, determined to arrange themselves according to rank and position.

A fanfare, then another in the distance signalled the beginning of the procession.

At a slow, stately pace they made their way towards the gates of the town.

As they walked Juana gripped Don Fadrique's wrist, whispering, 'Do you see Philip amongst those waiting?'

'No ma'am, as yet I do not.'

'Oh, Don Fadrique.' Her grip tightened.

'Wait, wait, hush now, be patient a little while,' he urged, having to control his growing disquiet.

A little further on and her heart began to pound mercilessly. She had tried so hard to be brave, to summon up enough courage to see her through the reception, but things were not going to plan. Something was wrong. She knew it. Why was it that they had been kept waiting for so long before commencing their procession? Why, too, were there so few people gathered to meet her? What little courage she had was dwindling fast.

From the midst of a fairly meagre reception committee an

even smaller group stepped forward. Juana gazed at the four figures in dismay. Four people: two bishops, some sort of priest and a young lady.

But there was no one else. No one else came to join them. Just those four; no Philip. He was not there.

Philip was not there!

Juana's fingers dug into Don Fadrique's arm.

'*Ma chère Jeanne, nôtre soeur, sois bienvenue,*' the young lady smiled and reached out her hands to take Juana's in as warm a welcome as possible. Juana released her grip on her uncle's arm to respond to the greeting, returning the smile; a weak and miserable effort.

They kissed hands, one princess to another.

'Dearest Juana it is so good to see you at last, so safe and well after your long journey. Welcome to your new home.' After an awkward silence she continued, 'I am Margaret, and I am here to greet you on behalf of my brother Philip. He is still at Innsbruck with my father. I understand that their negotiations are not yet finalised. But of that later, we must get you properly rested. We shall take you to a beautiful house not too far from here. It used to belong to my Grandfather. I love everything about it, and I am sure you will find it greatly to your liking. Everything there will be to your satisfaction. You will be able to rest in comfort while all your belongings are brought ashore. And you will have time to recover from your travels. I am so looking forward to hearing all about you and your family, especially Juan, my betrothed. I want to know everything there is to know about him ...'

Juana knew that Margaret was babbling, trying to conceal her acute embarrassment. As for herself, it was taking every ounce of strength to maintain her dignity, to hide her hurt. The insulting lack of honours; and as if that was not humiliating enough the public slight from her future husband, showing no regard for her arrival, was almost more than she could bear.

Philip knew she was coming! He should have been here to meet her! She thought of his letter; all those words of impatience; were they nothing but lies? Why was he not here? Why was he with his father? Where were the lords who should have been here to represent him?

She stood valiantly fighting back her tears, holding her head high, nodding and smiling as various people were presented, and deep inside there was an overwhelming loneliness.

❖   ❖   ❖

She had no recollection of how she had got there, but she was alone in her bedchamber. As soon as she had heard the door close she abandoned herself to total despair. She sank to the floor weeping, howling, sobbing, until her tears and energy were spent and she lay there exhausted.

Maria had remained in the next room, listening sadly. She understood how the day's cruel events had so wounded her mistress, and was desperately sorry for her.

The ever faithful Don Fadrique paced the floor, he too was thinking of the events of that afternoon. He was furious. He swore, 'By all that is Holy, what is going on here? I knew something was amiss right from the beginning. That is why I had the soldiers delay their formation. I hoped that between times that miserable little group of town clerks would have more nobility arriving to swell their ranks. But no, nothing better than a few priests, a scattering of gentlemen and ladies and the Princess Margaret,' he growled his anger. 'Heavens above I have known more lowly folk be offered more than that!'

'It was not the reception we were expecting, that is for sure,' agreed Maria.

'And where, in Heaven's name, is Philip? What game is he playing? He has no right to be anywhere else but here. Right here; right now! How dare he show such blatant disregard, and after building up her hopes so. I know what I would like to do to the young scoundrel.'

'When Queen Isabel and King Ferdinand hear of what went on today they will have something to say.' Maria commented.

'Have something to say? Their anger will know no bounds. I was so proud of Juana keeping her dignity throughout. That must have taken some doing, poor lass. She has every right to give way to her emotions now she is alone; and I say no one could blame her. But I am here, I will protect her. I will not leave her side until I see her safely married to her prince; and soon, let me tell you. By God but he has put us all in a difficult situation!'

Zayda slipped by them, passing silently into the bedchamber. She knelt beside her mistress, drawing her close, to cradle her in her arms.

Chapter 6

'But the very next morning they brought
letters from abroad.
Inside the words were written in ink,
but on the outside in blood.
And they told that her Roldan had died,
hunting at Roncesvalles.'

'Oh, the poor lady; that is dreadful. That is exactly what happened to your poor sister Isabel's husband,' Maria took the book and snapped it shut. 'I thought it was going to have a happy ending. Why did you not read that one about the lady's beauty captivating her beloved, how he wanted its fame to be spread far and wide?'

Maria looked at her mistress, resting so pale among the pillows of her sick bed. 'Is it that poem,' she spoke more brusquely than she intended, 'or has the room taken on its afternoon chill too soon? Whatever the case the book shall be put away and I will have someone attend to the fire. No more melancholy stories and more warmth in the room; that is what we need. Truly ma'am, I do not know why you should want to go making yourself so sad with dismal tales. You are downcast enough as it is. If I were your mother I would never have allowed such books in your hands, ever.'

Maria was no longer addressing her mistress, she was grumbling at the world. She bustled about the room thrusting the offending book out of sight, crossing to the door to demand someone come to build up the fire then hurrying back to the bed to fuss over her patient.

She made bows in the broad red ribbons that fastened the neck and cuffs of Juana's night shift and straightened her white holland cap and red wrap. This done, she gently re-arranged the pillows and smoothed the fur-lined coverlet before sitting down once more by the bedside.

A servant busied himself piling extra logs on the fire, pushing here, poking there, pulling and shaking them causing sudden bursts and showers of noisy red and yellow sparks. After he left the room all was quiet save for the comforting crackling in the fireplace, the ticking of the clock and the sound of rain blown by a petulant September wind spattering against the windows.

The Royal Court of Princes was as magnificent as its title. The apartments for Juana were breathtakingly splendid; and this room, her bedchamber, was no exception. It was warm, it was comfortable; but it was more. It was luxurious, the like of which she had never seen before. The walls were hung with sumptuous tapestries all showing legendary knights returning in triumph from various feats of valour. Every piece of furniture was intricately carved. The tables held beautiful vases, bowls or figurines of exquisite porcelain. Most spectacular of all the decorations was the gold clock on the marble mantelpiece. It was in the form of a castle. Gold pennants flew from the tops of its towers and on its roof. Some knights stood idly resting on their shields; others were on guard at the doorway. Fair damsels leaned from the windows. The minute details on each tiny figure were exquisite.

When Juana had first entered this room several days ago she had been astonished by its splendour, visiting each part of it with little cries of delight. But it had all paled to nothing with this dreadful cold.

'I feel so miserable. I want to go home. Maria, I have never known so many grey days of rain, no wonder I feel so ill. I think I do still have a fever. Oh, everything here is so different and confusing. I feel so lost, and so lonely.' Her eyes welled with tears and she let them roll down her cheeks.

Maria dipped a corner of a napkin into a bowl of cool water and placed it gently on Juana's temples and forehead. 'I know ma'am, colds always seem so much worse when we are in a strange place.'

She couldn't help observing that in fact her mistress had not had a temperature in days; that while not denying the fact that she had indeed been indisposed, many of the cold symptoms most certainly were now imaginary. More than likely Juana was in her sick-bed seeking refuge from any further disappointments. She had never truly recovered from that dreadful business of Philip's absence from the welcoming

43

party. That had been a dreadful shock, turning her whole world upside down. Nor had it helped matters when his sister Margaret had not been here to receive her in Antwerp. On the other hand, perhaps her mistress felt that news of her illness might reach Philip and cause him to hurry to her bedside.

'But the worst is over,' she continued, soothing Juana's brow, 'I am positive you have no fever today.'

'Are you sure? My head hurts so.'

Maria would hear no more of it. 'I think we should talk about our arrival here, that would make far more sense.'

'You mean when Margaret failed to appear at the reception?'

'No, nor do I intend to concern myself with that. I am thinking of you and how you astonished everyone with your beauty.'

Juana did remember those events of a week ago. 'You are right. It was all rather wonderful. Sit next to me, here on the bed. Remind me.'

'I doubt if I shall remember all of it,' replied Maria making herself comfortable without causing discomfort to her mistress, 'but I am sure you will help me if I forget anything.'

Juana settled back amongst her pillows and waited as a child waits for a story to begin.

'Well, we had made our way here. We made such a fine picture all right, our long and most colourful train had ribboned its way through the countryside.'

'And nothing went wrong on the way. There was no calamity. That made a change!'

Maria tut-tutted, 'No calamity. Well, it was about seven o'clock in the evening and daylight was giving way to dusk. We stopped as the city officials, the priests and the bishop approached. They came in perfect procession with the burgomaster coming last.' Maria laughed, 'His welcoming speech was awful. I had to be so careful not to catch your eye or I should have laughed. That had to be the longest, most boring speech I have ever heard.'

'It was interminable! My mule, the laziest of beasts, fidgeted and fussed, eager to gallop off. It was quite dark by the time he had finished.'

'Then our entrance to the city, no one ever saw the like. The rich velvets and brocades of all colours draped from balconies, roofs, windows ...'

'You are right, Maria,' interrupted Juana, the dreadful cold forgotten. 'There were trumpeters and drummers to lead the way, followed by judges, guildsmen and merchants all in their superb liveries, their hats and robes of red, blue or green.'

'And the knights of the Golden Fleece, ma'am, each with their heavy gold chains with pendant gold sheep; every knight with his own little page boy. And all those gentlemen, lining either side of the procession, lighting our way with torches.'

'Our court was splendid too.'

'Oh yes indeed.'

'My dress of fine gold tissue, with its precious stones and pearls was just perfect, and my white velvet tabard was draped in such a way that it revealed the full splendour of the skirts. Yes I felt every inch a royal princess that day.'

'And so you should. But where were we? Ah yes, I followed you with six of our nobles, all in the richest of brocades, and, of course, all our mounts were draped in red or blue velvet. What a sight to behold. It was perfect, so it was; perfect.'

'And the crowds, Maria!'

'Yes, all lining the streets, they were, or leaning from balconies and windows, all cheering and shouting, "Long live the Princess *Jeanne de Castille*."

'I do remember, how could I forget? It all took so long that by the time we got here it was quite late. The rooms were all brilliantly lit with hundreds of candles, their lights multiplied by huge mirrors on almost every wall. You are right, it was a wonderful day. I had not really forgotten, Maria, I was just feeling too sorry for myself to care to remember.'

Maria was delighted that she had lifted her mistress's spirits, 'And more good cheer; the Archduchess Margaret and her grandmother, Margaret of York, are on their way to see you, and ...'

'And?'

'And I believe they bring good news of Philip.'

Juana's fingers made little pathways across the velvet bedcover. 'So, he has found time to write to them, but not to me. All I have is this one letter speaking of such impatience.' She reached for that beloved paper, its folds all in tatters. It was tossed impatiently onto the bed as she pouted, 'In any case he should have set off immediately once he knew we were in Flanders.'

'There will be a good reason.'

'And I know he is not with his father now. I have been told he has gone hunting.'

'Sometimes men need to seek some diversion following difficult negotiations.'

'How can he leave me here all alone for so long? We are foreigners; unprotected.'

Maria changed the subject, 'You do have his sister's visit to look forward to.'

'But I do not want to meet his grandmother. The very thought of her fills me with dread. See how my hand trembles.'

Margaret of York, Philip's grandmother, had for years been vigorously conspiring to have the English Crown wrested from the Tudors and returned to the House of York. She had also been tireless in her efforts to have Philip marry her niece, Anne of York. There could be little doubt that she would find Juana an undesirable substitute.

'Do you know what she looks like? I expect she is tall and grand and will make me feel this big.' Juana made the tiniest gap between her thumb and forefinger.

'I have never seen her but I am told she has a slender figure, is most elegant and was considered an exceptional beauty in her time.'

'I might have known it,' groaned Juana, 'a busybody who is forever interfering and is forceful would have to be beautiful too; typical. I shall melt to nothing before her, like wax beneath the candle flame.'

'For shame; you with your youth, your beauty, your intelligence and all the rest? You will come to no harm with Margaret of York. Besides, she is so old now I should think her flame is already spluttering and almost ready to go phut.'

'Oh Maria, really, what a glorious picture.'

Chapter 7

It was early evening in mid-October. One or two of Juana's court were playing chess, others games of cards, while some preferred just to talk. The musicians were playing one of her favourite ballads. Recorders, a vihuela and a viola de gamba accompanied two singers, filling the room with their rich melody. As she sat listening to the tender tale of unrequited love her gaze strayed lazily about the room, one of the most beautiful in the Berthout Mechelen mansion. She had been here for six days during which time her own mood and that of her court had been slowly lightening. An air of expectancy had replaced the despondency of earlier days. The waiting and uncertainty was soon to be over.

Juana's thoughts drifted from the music to the delightful events of that morning.

Margaret had brought such splendid news. Philip was to arrive later in the day. He would come to see her tomorrow and their marriage was to be officially blessed in the cathedral two days hence.

Philip was arriving today! She would see him tomorrow! She had been so excited that she had hugged and kissed Margaret.

Margaret and she had become almost like sisters. She smiled recalling their excited talk about their forthcoming marriages, and how they had tried to outdo one another in singing the praises of their dear brothers. Juana felt uncomfortable knowing that she had not been entirely honest with her new sister-in-law. She could not tell all, would not tell all about Juan.

Juana swallowed hard remembering her words both said and unsaid. She had spoken of Juan's stammer but without mentioning it was often disturbing for those who knew him, and extremely embarrassing to those who didn't. But worst of all she had been less than truthful about his other speech difficulties; not mentioning that he was tongue-tied, that his lower lip was set so far forward of the upper malformed one that it made it ... no, she had carefully avoided all this by saying merely that his voice was thick and his way of speaking very ponderous.

She excused her actions with the conviction that as soon as Margaret met him she would discover what a wonderful person he was and that was all that mattered. She would be loved and cared for by someone very kind and compassionate. Her new life with him would more than compensate for all those years she had spent in France waiting for a marriage that had failed to take place, then the years of being held and treated little better than a prisoner before being allowed to return home. As the chosen bride of the *angel* she would also have all Queen Isabel's love and affection.

Having shaken off the twinge of conscience she settled back into her seat only to be overcome by another; she had not yet written home and it was now three months since she had left Spain. That must be attended to soon; definitely; but not when she was listening to some of her favourite songs.

The tambour, tambourine, and tenor and bass recorders were now playing a jolly little song about a young girl looking after her goats and being teased by young goatherds.

Oh maid that looks after your goats
Your skirts drawn up to your knees,
Say, sweet maid of the pretty hose
You'd care for us goat boys, please.

She sang along with the music, merrily tapping out the rhythm with her fingers on the arms of the chair.

The music faltered. The courtiers closest to the doors had been the first to hear the urgent, hurried footsteps approaching, the voices growing closer and louder. Don Fadrique, sword drawn, was there immediately.

Fear had returned and spread among them. They were rudely reminded they were foreigners in a strange land and as yet their mistress was not married to its ruler.

Juana sat rigid, terrified. She could only think of Margaret's imprisonment in France when her marriage contract was broken. Was this wedding to come to nought; were those ominous sounds the clatter of soldiers' boots?

48

The doors were flung open. A very relieved Don Fadrique sheathed his sword and went down on bended knee.

'Don Fadrique, Admiral of Castile, my lord.' He had recognised him from the many portraits he had seen and not by the rain and mud-splattered youth now offering a dirty gloved hand for him to kiss.

'Welcome, Don Fadrique. Indeed, a warm welcome to you all. I am pleased to welcome you to my lands. I hope that your stay here will be a pleasant one.' He motioned Don Fadrique and the rest to stand then strode into the room his eyes searching.

The courtiers looked at the admiral, hoping for some explanation. He shrugged his shoulders, shook his head, stared at the heavens then whispered to Juana's head steward, 'Well this beggars belief. He has now defied all the rules of protocol. Hopefully he will only remain here for a short while, inasmuch as he has decided to dispense with a formal audience. How many times since our coming here have I been thankful that Queen Isabel has not had to witness such impertinence at the hands of this arrogant young fellow? I tell you I can feel it in my bones that he will be intent on insulting us with every action he takes.'

Juana had heard Philip's welcome. His voice: such a strong and self-assured voice; so hearty and vigorous a voice. What did the owner of that voice look like? What would he think of her? She panicked, the moment for their meeting had arrived and she wasn't prepared.

She tugged at Maria's sleeve, 'We are supposed to meet tomorrow. Tomorrow I would be wearing the gown made especially for the occasion. Here I am in the plainest of skirts and bodice. He will think I am nothing more than a serving maid.' She looked anxiously down at her clothes; the green velvet skirt with its full-length matching green satin apron, a simple laced black bodice trimmed with only tiny emeralds and pearls. There was not another jewel to be seen. 'And my hair, drawn back into the most ordinary little green roundel!'

The admiral spoke, desperate to bring some formality into a disastrous situation, 'Sire, with your permission, allow me to introduce ...'

'Where is my bride? Where is my Spanish princess? Why

surely this must be she?'

The voice, that wonderful voice, was standing before her.

She rose unsteadily to her feet. She clasped her hands firmly together, her head lowered, her eyes fixed intently on her white knuckles, the pounding of her heart so loud the whole room must hear. A slender hand appeared, she closed her eyes, her head was slowly raised by long gentle fingers.

'Juana? Can this beautiful maid be my Juana?'

The voice charmed her. She looked up at him. She caught her breath. He was incredibly handsome. He was so tall, so athletic. He had the most beautiful face she had ever seen, ever dreamed about. He was fair skinned with rosy cheeks. His light brown hair was almost blond. He had the largest, softest and bluest of eyes. And his proud mouth with its full lips was sensual and inviting.

'Juana, they never told me you were so beautiful! I never expected a treasure such as this for a wife. Kind sirs you may now withdraw.'

Don Fadrique's patience was once more put to the test. This action of the prince was defying all codes of honour. Juana's good name was at stake. He was powerless before this young man and the frustration was hard to bear. He looked towards Juana and coughed aloud his displeasure.

Juana watched them all leave the room catching snatches of their whisperings: 'unacceptable', 'reputation', 'compromised', 'lovebirds', 'captivated', 'under her spell'.

They were alone.

'Forgive me my dear Juana for my disgracefully long absence. What a fool I have been. And you left all alone. Say that you will forgive me.'

How many weeks had she spent lonely, homesick, desperately unhappy, and yes even afraid? Had he not terrified her even more but a few moments ago with those sounds of spurred boots coming ever closer? And now he asked her to forgive him.

'Forgive, my lord? There is nothing to forgive.'

'Not "my lord", Juana, let me hear you say "Philip". Your pretty voice with its charming accent is music to my ears. Let me hear you speak my name. Say, "I forgive you Philip".'

'I forgive you, Philip.'

'Oh what bliss. This is heaven.' He held her face up towards him and kissed her. He kissed her once, twice so lightly then the third time he lingered long on her trembling lips. He held her at arms' length to look at her once more and was enchanted by all he saw and he could not believe his good fortune.

He had never wanted to marry a princess from Spain; in fact the very idea of being connected in any way with that country was anathema to him. He had strongly objected to being pushed into this marriage as part of his father's treaty with Ferdinand and Isabel. Surely his sister's marriage with their son was sufficient to seal the bargain?

His own sympathies lay with France and always would. He had been educated in the French Burgundian fashion. His mother tongue was French. It was only natural, therefore, for him to feel only contempt for that land beyond the Pyrenees continually at loggerheads with his French friends.

But this was something he had not dared to hope for. A pretty damsel for him to bed with; it certainly sugared the pill. It would make his royal marital obligations to the Austrian and the Spanish Royal Houses so much easier.

And Juana? Her timidity melted away. She took more and more delight in his looking at her, stroking her hair, gently touching her cheeks, running his fingers over her lips, then covering her face and lips with more kisses. She was emboldened by his seductive ways to raise her hands to caress the curves of those enticing lips, tracing the mouth that had covered hers awakening in her new and unknown sensations.

She knew they should not be doing this before their marriage was blessed, but she did not care. Not too long ago she had desperately wanted to return to Spain. All she desired now was to be kissed again and again. She was impatient to be folded once more in his arms, desperate to return his kisses with even better kisses of her own.

'What are you thinking, Juana?'

'That I must be dreaming.'

'Juana, bless your dear heart, this is no dream. All that we lack is the blessing, and as soon as we have that we shall be man and wife.' He kissed her again, the kisses becoming hungrier setting alight untold fires within her.

She broke away from him, gasping, 'And only two days to wait, Philip, and then ...' she dared not think further.

'Two days, Juana? What is this about two days?'

Puzzled, she replied, 'Margaret told me only earlier today of the final arrangements for the ceremony in two days time. I cannot have misunderstood.'

He laughed at her, 'Yes I know those are the plans. But why wait? That is only a public ceremony, to satisfy others. We can decide for ourselves when to have the blessing. In fact, let us do that right now.'

Philip knelt down before her, a child earnestly begging a special favour.

Her mind raced. To marry now, to become man and wife this very night; she wanted that more than anything. But what would people say? It was of no matter. This was Philip's land, he it was who decided, and all were at his bidding; like them she was at his command. She smiled down at him and nodded.

He leapt up and taking her by the waist lifted her high, 'Darling Juana. Precious Juana. Now all we need is a priest.'

Juana threw back her head in mischievous laughter, 'I have the ideal priest, my chaplain, the Dean of Jaen. He is so serious and so very strict. My mother insisted I have him for my confessor, though I would rather have had someone more congenial. Little could either of them suspect what would be his first duty.'

He laughed with her, thinking what an excellent signal this would send to Spain, letting them know that he was master in his own house and would brook no interference from that quarter. He rejoiced once more; this political union had brought him a warm and vibrant mistress instead of a cold wife. He kissed her again as if to seal the agreement, then strode to the door to beckon the court to return.

Once they were all assembled he asked for the Dean of Jaen to be summoned to read out the holy blessing on their union. Now! Immediately!

This was unacceptable. Don Fadrique registered his strong disapproval, loudly clearing his throat. It was a lost cause. Juana saw and heard no one except Philip. She followed her prince's every move, drinking in every movement. He turned to her his eyes speaking his desire; and she wanted him to draw her to his breast with those strong arms, to hold her there forever.

Chapter 8

It was a world of bewildering wealth and merrymaking. Life was one long celebration. The feasts, balls and tournaments held at every stopping point on their travels, each one more splendid than the last, declared that expense was no object. Compared with Castile, where pleasures were kept simple and always under the critical eye of the ascetic priest, this new lifestyle was a revelation to Juana and she threw herself into it with joyous abandon.

Philip was more gallant than any knight Juana had read of in her romance poems. He had chosen new jousting colours, green and yellow, to make public his love for her. Everyone would recognise that green represented courteous love; young love filled with hopes. Yellow was for contentment, but more than this it was a play on words; Juana = Jeanne = Jaune or Yellow. It was especially for Juana and no one else. She was immensely proud, her heart bursting with love for her knight in his gilded armour as he rode to the tribune to present himself to her. And it proved beyond doubt to his grandmother, Margaret of York, who sat at Juana's side, (she was always sat at Juana's side), that Philip could not be happier with his Spanish bride. A delirious happiness filled their days, weeks, months, where nothing else mattered.

But after a few months cracks began to appear in the euphoria. Problems raised their ugly heads.

Juana paced about her small salon. She was to meet with the admiral. In her hand she clutched a letter from her mother. The first part was a reprimand from her mother, because she still had not written home. She had been too busy, far too busy, having fun; until recently.

The latter part of the letter was a repetition of her mother's command to the admiral, ... *to tell Duke Philip to give Juana the twenty thousand escudos that was established and agreed upon and which is necessary for the upkeep of her house and her state. We are aware that this has not been done.*

It was true; she had been unable to pay her courtiers. Those with rooms within the royal palaces were not too severely disadvantaged but for those who had had to find their own accommodation life was becoming very difficult. Lodgings had to be paid for and it meant selling clothing and jewels. She had asked Philip on several occasions for some money and each time he had said he would attend to it in due course, but nothing had come of it. Admittedly she had not pursued the matter with any vigour, mostly because it slipped her mind, but also it was so embarrassing to have to beg for what was hers by right. The disdainful looks from Philip's secretary and treasurer reminded her, should she need reminding, that she had no authority in this royal court. It was best, then, to ignore the problem.

Unfortunately her uncle was waiting to be admitted; she was now obliged to discuss the financial affairs of her household, like it or not.

Maria opened the door and there stood not only her uncle but also her head steward. This was definitely going to be a very serious meeting; two very experienced and knowledgeable men and her so young, and so ignorant, of practical matters.

Formal greetings were exchanged then they waited, each one looking to the others to open the discussion.

Juana swallowed hard, the letter refusing to keep still in her hand, 'I know why you have requested this interview, gentlemen, my mother mentions it here.'

'Indeed ma'am. We are come to inform you that we are to meet with the archduke this afternoon,' replied Don Fadrique showing her the letter he had received from Queen Isabel.

'Yes ma'am,' continued her steward, 'This cannot be allowed to persist. It is unacceptable for good and noble folk to suffer deprivation and hardship, to live in conditions far beneath their station. It is not seemly, ma'am. We have certain standards to maintain. Our very honour is at stake. I beg your pardon for my boldness, but something must be done and without further delay.'

He was right, and Juana hoped that in his position as head steward he would have some success with Philip. A steward was, after all, the very one to deal with financial matters and not she, nor would he burst into tears when Philip became angry about being asked yet again.

'You are right. I have often broached the subject with my lord. It is my belief that Chimay is not carrying out his instructions.' Did that sound convincing, or did everyone know that Philip and his court were flagrantly ignoring her requests? 'It is best that you as our head steward remind my husband of the marriage settlement and insist on the allowance being paid forthwith into our treasury. Then it will all be settled and we can get on with our lives.'

Don Fadrique was not in the least bit confident, 'I hope you are right; but I have grave doubts. It may well be that I am too readily suspicious of all things Flemish, but I have the feeling that from the start we Spaniards have never been welcome here. We are snubbed or there are sly whisperings and sniggering behind our backs.'

So, her uncle had noticed, too, 'Oh, I am sure you are mistaken. Why, we are all having such a wonderful time; hunting, feasting and dancing. Everyone is joining in merrily together. I have only seen happy faces and lots of laughter.'

'There is a serious matter I must speak of.' His tone was harsh. The turn of the conversation to the court's idle pastimes had made him angry, and he wanted her to know it. 'I was hoping not to have to tell you about this. My fleet should have been long gone, and safely arrived in Spain.'

'Yes, I know that Margaret should have left weeks ago but Philip is loath to part with his sister and will not let her go. It is my poor brother I feel for, having to tolerate this lengthy wait, pining for his bride.'

'I cannot bother myself about what Philip wants or what Juan wants. It is more important that I speak plain about what I want,' he stormed. 'I have to ask Philip for the umpteenth time to provide for our sailors. Whilst you have been dancing and singing and playing your silly games, good Spanish sailors have been dying. They are freezing or starving to death or dying from God knows what diseases! Our provisions are long gone and our allotted funding exhausted!'

'Don Fadrique, do please calm yourself,' she smiled to console him, 'Why, you have turned quite red. It worries me to see you so cross. Of course I am saddened to learn that we have lost some of our men. But you know as well as I that death cuts men down all the time with famine and disease; everywhere, not just here. Perhaps you are getting old, dear uncle, and that is why their deaths are affecting you so.'

It was time she knew the truth. 'No one can remain unaffected by the deaths of nine thousand men!' He nodded his head, confirming the appalling toll.

Nine thousand men were dead because Queen Isabel had wanted to impress the world with the power of Spain and so had sent a ridiculously large fleet. Nine thousand men were dead because Philip had arrived more than a month late and then could not bear the thought of his sister leaving. Nine thousand men were dead because the winter weather had become so foul it was impossible for the ships to set sail. And many might still die.

'What can I say? I am so dreadfully sorry. If only ...'

'I should learn to curb my tongue, stupid man that I am. You could do nothing about it. But the archduke must help.' He took her hand in his, 'Dear girl, I should not have burdened you. Off you go, you worry about what you will wear to the ball tonight.'

Was he being cross with her? Was he mocking her? Was he trying to tell her it was time she shouldered some responsibility? She was uncertain, but found it preferable to suppose that he really was concerned about her continued happiness and sorry that he had let slip the gruesome news.

She listened and agreed with every point they would put to Philip and told them she was certain of their success. She wished them well and watched them leave the room. For a few moments she remained pensive. Matters were serious, but Philip would be honour bound to respond generously to all their requests.

It was with a heavy heart that she called Maria to accompany her to her dressing room to prepare her for the ball which now seemed so mistimed. However, all unpleasant thoughts disappeared as petticoats and chemise, blue skirts, a fitted bodice, and finally sleeves were tied, buttoned, laced or sewn in place. By the time the dressing process was complete she was happily anticipating all the fun of the banquet and the dancing that was to follow. Margaret had arrived and would be joining them. That would ensure a lively evening; she was always such fun to be with, Margaret always had the best riddles and could tell the most entertaining stories.

❖　　　❖　　　❖

Juana and Margaret were sitting together resting from their dancing and one or two ladies and gentlemen of the court were gathered around them, all vying to tell the best riddle.

'My turn,' insisted Juana,
> 'White is the field,
> Black is the seed,
> The man who sows
> Is one who knows.'

Madame Halewyn, that woman of stone who Philip had recently placed in her household, looked scornfully down her chiselled nose, 'Everyone knows that one,' and without giving anyone the opportunity to guess fired her own riddle at Juana.
> 'Next to an ox it is small,
> Next an egg tinier yet is.
> 'Tis more bitter than gall,
> Yet sweeter than any lettuce.'

Juana was totally perplexed; she could not begin to think. Was it Halewyn's intention to make her look stupid? Margaret took Juana's hand, laughing, 'Why is it that she chooses to tell such difficult riddles, when she knows full well none of us is clever enough to guess the answer. Where does she get them from? So, tell us Halewyn, what this tiny thing can be.'

'I think that you just pretend not to know. I did think, however, that the princess with all her book learning would have recognised an almond immediately,' Madame Halewyn sniped.

'No, no, that simply is not good enough, is it?' Margaret enquired of the company, encouraging their groans, 'That was far too obscure and not the least bit clever. Anyway, I want to tell you all an interesting story about that very tall gentleman over there, the thin one with the very serious expression.'

They followed her look until they found him and Juana whispered, 'That is Don Francisco de Rojas, my parents' ambassador to your father.'

'Exactly, and my story is all about him.'

They drew closer together, the gentlemen to sit at the ladies' feet, some lounging on their elbows amongst the trailing skirts, everyone desperately hungry for gossip.

'Well, when he was the proxy for our weddings, he arrived with only the simplest clothes, totally unsuitable for such a grand occasion. The story was that a friend of his offered him a beautiful brocade jerkin and gown. Imagine that tall man with his dark hair and dark eyes wearing olive green, the very colour to enhance those handsome features. Back to my story, the best part, when we both had to lie down on the matrimonial bed,' she began to laugh and they huddled in all the closer not wanting to miss a word, some taking an extra peek at the tall, thin ambassador dressed this evening all in black. This was going to be one of Margaret's best stories and about someone right here in this room.

'So, his friend may well have seen to it that his outer garments were in order and suited to the occasion but, dear me, when he removed the gown and the jerkin to come to the ceremonial wedding bed, I tell you I was bursting with laughter. Every movement was so deliberate, demanding my attention, that there was no ignoring his hose which were too loose on him, that they were not properly tied to his doublet allowing his chemise to hang out between the laces. There were yards of it, like a ship in full sail, billowing linen everywhere; and he all the while slowly advancing towards me. I thanked God that the chemise was sufficient to protect my innocent eyes from something even more outrageous than underlinen. I bit hard on my lip so as not to laugh then closed my eyes to deny myself this vision.'

They laughed helplessly, sneaking glances at Don Francisco, a vivid picture of his escaping rampant linen firmly engraved on their memories.

The angry voice of the equerry responsible for the safety of the horses on their journey from Spain stopped their laughter. 'Sirs, this kind of behaviour is not to be tolerated. In Spain no gentleman would be so discourteous as to sit so close to a lady's person. And you, count, instead of behaving like these ... these Flems, you should be setting an example of court manners. What would the king and queen think of you sitting on the skirts of Princess Juana and with your head almost touching her royal person?'

'Why you young pup, how dare you!'

'I dare because I defend my lady's honour.'

'In which case I shall be only too glad to offer you the opportunity to do just that!'

Juana swallowed hard. She had been borne merrily along on the wave of thoughtless, carefree and indecorous behaviour, intoxicated by the ready acceptance of the normality of permissive ways. Now it had been brought sharply and publicly to her attention and to her conscience by one of her fellow countrymen that it did not accord with her Spanish upbringing. She was ashamed.

Philip left the side of the young lady whose charms he had found most captivating, her trim little figure exciting him, her warm lips demanding yet more kisses. He was not best pleased by the interruption and strode angrily across the room. 'Gentlemen, who has caused this, and why?'

The Count of Chimay detailed the series of events, his fat fingers enjoying the fox fur collar of his short gown, before spreading themselves wide in dismissal of the whole silly affair, 'You know what these pathetic Spaniards are like, they do not know how to relax and enjoy life.'

Philip did not dismiss it so flippantly, 'I see, young sir, that you share the same concern for the ladies and their honour as you did for the horses you brought me. I commend you for your high degree of sensitivity. You are quite right about men lounging on the skirts of our fair ladies. It suggests a lack of respect. See to it gentlemen that I never witness it again.' He turned to Juana, 'Will you accompany me in the next dance?'

He had not been cross with her! She was blameless! Her blushes of shame became those of desire. She could now hold his hand, gaze into her lover's eyes. She was returned to her small island of complete bliss.

'Your lackeys came to see me today,' he announced coldly as they passed and bobbed to each other in the dance. 'They brought all their tiresome problems with them. I tell you I have had enough. You have far too many servants, that is the root of the trouble. They cost too much. I will not be continually pestered about their wages. The time has come to dismiss the lot of them and replace them with good Burgundian folk; I have been concerned for some time about my money going into the hands of foreigners. However, I will instruct Chimay to make some interim payments until arrangements can be made to ship them home.'

'I will keep my personal servants?'

'Some, we shall have to see how many. Chimay tells me that most are here to spy for Spain, and that must be rectified immediately.'

'Sir, you do them a grave injustice, but if it makes you more content then I will accede to the changes.'

'I would remind you that it is not your place to accede or no. In Flanders a wife does as she is bid.'

What was she to do? There would be more "Madam Halewyns" about her. Cold and contemptuous voices would be waiting, hanging on her every word, ready to ridicule. Her uncle was right, too many of the Flems were mean and spiteful, resentful of her presence. She had to be protected from them; a Spanish court whatever its size was vital. The pulse in her throat was choking her, she bit back threatening tears. A way would have to be found to persuade Philip to be generous.

The dance ended.

'And will you come to my bed tonight?' she coaxed, looking up at him from beneath her lashes, toying seductively with his sleeve.

'We shall see, we shall see. I cannot visit you every night.' He kissed her hand, brushed her cheek with his lips and escorted her to her seat next to Margaret before going off to the far corner of the room to find that lady whose seductive ways were beginning to excite, before he was torn away to deal with those quarrelsome Spaniards. He was not overly concerned if she wasn't there, for he was minded to visit Juana after all.

Juana was impatient for the ball to end that she and Philip

61

might lie together. She would have Zayda bathe her in perfumed water, brush scented oils through her hair, dress her in a wide-necked nightshift that would readily fall from her shoulders; or perhaps place only a robe over her nakedness. Then Philip would come to her bedchamber throwing off his clothes as he approached her bed; and then their love-making would begin, slowly at first, their passions heating as one, until … She blushed with anticipated pleasure; she had learned so much in so short a time.

Chapter 9

The twelfth of April, 1498 would always be for her a very, very special day Juana thought and she was not prepared to allow anyone else to bring the news. She rushed along the corridor linking her apartments on one wing of the building to those of Philip's on the other.

An enormous cloud of grief caused by the sudden death of her beloved brother had lifted. The huge gulf separating her from her family at a time of immeasurable sorrow didn't exist; she had received other, more important news that morning.

The two guards lowered their halberds across the door.

Juana laughed, 'I think the archduke will be quite safe. If you would step aside.'

For some time now she had been known to vent her fury on her unfaithful husband, and whichever woman of easy virtue happened to be in his bedchamber at the time, pounding on the door hurling abuse of the sort more usually heard in back alleys and not fit for the ears of those of noble birth. This behaviour had earned for her the nickname The Monster. Philip had been the first to call her a shrew, a monster, and it hadn't taken long for the Flanders' court to take it up; she had heard them whisper it often enough, it followed her wherever she went.

'You may open the door.'

She could barely wait until the door was wide enough for her to pass through, 'Philip, I have such news!'

He emerged from his dressing room, surprised at her presence.

Juana kissed him, 'I am with child! The doctors are certain!'

He returned her kiss, hugged her then held her up high. 'I am going to be a father. My clever Juana. Will it be a boy?'

'They cannot tell yet; they must wait a while to see which of my breasts becomes the larger, if it is the right one it will be a

63

boy.'

'I am to be a father! Celebrations are called for. We shall have a tournament for my beautiful wife who is going to have our child.'

'But what of the mourning?' The cloud had returned.

'Life is for the living, my pet. I should think that even your mother would rejoice at this news. No tears, Juana, I insist.'

'But it would be wrong with my brother dead, and what of poor Margaret?'

'I will not allow you to dwell on such things, you must think only happy thoughts. We shall take a walk in the garden and make plans for the celebrations. The banquet will be bigger and better than any you have ever known: roast swans, pheasants, partridges dressed in their feathers ...'

'Meat pastries made to look like castles ...'

'Fish on huge salvers, silenced by a circle of jelly sirens.'

They laughed as they tried to outdo each other with new ideas as they walked back to Juana's rooms for her to dress for outdoors.

She held a much read letter close to her breast as Maria removed her shoes to replace them with a pair of buskins, tying the side laces once they were firmly in place.

'Why did God have to take him from us?' She wept again for the beloved brother she had confided in so often, who had entertained her with his humour, who was always there to comfort and reassure. 'Juan was the best person the world has ever known. It broke my heart to leave him, to leave my best friend. And he was married to Margaret for such a short time.'

She opened Margaret's letter and read, '... *I am with child! A grandchild for Queen Isabel! She is overjoyed and of course has much counsel for my welfare. We are all so happy.* Yet within weeks of this letter he was dead.'

Zayda took the letter from her mistress to return it to the jewellery box, gently admonishing her, 'Today is not the day to indulge your sadness.'

'And,' Maria added, 'I do not think the archduke would like to take his good lady out walking when she has a long face and red-rimmed eyes. We must find a way to repair the damage.

You must wear the green cloak today with its special brooch.'

'Maria I think you are becoming a romantic.'

The diamond brooch was Philip's gift; their initials standing side by side held together with a love knot.

'When you return from your walk we can discuss what you should wear for the celebrations. This is going to be such fun! We have been a long time without any.'

'I wonder what Margaret of York will have to say about my good news.'

Maria giggled, 'Plenty, without doubt.'

Chapter 10

She caught them! They were locked in each other's arms, standing at the head of the old spiral staircase close to his apartments.

'You harlot, you whore, what did he offer you to let him rummage in your bodice, to pull up your skirts and push himself inside you, and you standing there against a wall like a woman of the night?'

Juana pulled at Philip's arm, trying to drag him away, 'You think you can poke at anything in skirts. How dare you fornicate in your wife's home!'

She turned back to face the embarrassed lady-in-waiting, 'Get yourself to a whorehouse where you belong. You can spread your legs there as much as you like, and wash away the filth ready for the next man who wants to get his prick ...' she continued her language deteriorating throughout her tirade.

'Shut your filthy mouth,' Philip hissed.

'If this is all the respect you have for your wife, I would rather be damned than ever have you known as the Prince of Castile. You are contemptible!' She hurried from the scene of her humiliation.

'I decide what happens here!' Philip announced to her back. 'I am leaving. When you have learned to control your harridan's tongue I shall return.'

Laughter and cries of, 'The Monster, The Monster is back to her old ways.'

Maria appeared from somewhere and swept down the corridor shooing them away like errant stubborn sheep who had wandered onto her land.

Juana fled into her apartments, slamming the door on the world, shutting out Philip's voice calling out his intentions, and startling Zayda as she arranged her mistress's dressing table. Hot tears of hurt and shame scalded her cheeks, she brushed at them with the back of her hand then reached for her box of letters.

Zayda watched her with alarm, 'You are upset enough

without adding to it.'

'This is all I have of my family, the only way I can feel close to them, and I need them.'

She read them all, quietly sobbing, until she got to the last one. 'Dear God is there no end to it? *Margaret was delivered of a child, a girl, but dead. My heart is broken and can take no more pain.* My poor mother; she lost her dearly beloved son, and now his child, the last of the male line, is dead. As well as the crippling pain of her loss all her hopes and aspirations are gone.'

While it was necessary for her mistress to have some time for grieving, today of all days was not the day. She had an important visitor and would need every ounce of fortitude. Zayda therefore gathered up the letters and put them away offering words of comfort, 'Out of the bad always comes good. This tragedy means that Margaret will be coming home and you will have your friend and confidante beside you once more.'

It was as if Juana had not heard. 'Please love me, Philip.' Her cry had broken free delivering her from the depths of her dejection. 'When he is with me I know he does. If there were just the two of us in our land of passion or nestling embraces, or if there was no ugly toad called Chimay whispering in Philip's ear, or no Busleyden insisting on what Philip may or may not do, we would be the happiest people in the world.' She pulled and twisted at the handkerchief Zayda had offered.

'You will have to wait until Archbishop Busleyden dies, the same applies to Philip's grandmother. They have both hovered over him since he was four years old, attacking anyone not to their liking who gets too close.'

'They hate me, Zayda.'

'Try to forget them.' She laughed, 'They would make an ideal couple: both ancient walking skeletons, both adoring Philip, both loathing Spain. But I was talking of good always coming from bad and I haven't told you the best one, the gift from your brother; *that other Juana*, the one who will fight for that which she believes is just or rightly hers. Now show me that Juana.'

'Of course, *that* Juana. I swear this Spanish priest my mother has sent had better come as a friend and not an enemy, for that is when the other Juana will make her first appearance. Thank God you were here to remind me. How fortunate I was that day in Granada when they said you were to be mine.'

'I am more fortunate. Who else would allow me to keep a Moor's name rather than the one given me when I was made a Christian. I can retain my identity, and,' she laughed, 'I fear Blanca was not a good choice. But perhaps you have something far more important to thank God for?'

'You are right.' Juana gave her cheeks a final dab with her handkerchief then let her hands follow the increasing fullness of her belly. 'I pray you will be a little boy, for Philip, and please be strong and healthy. Only three more months of waiting.'

There was a tapping on the door and Maria entered with a servant carrying fruits and juices.

'Brother Tomas has arrived.'

'A few more minutes wait will do him no harm. I have to make sure that *that other Juana* is quite ready.'

Chapter 11

Her coat cut in the French style, a long fitted coat reaching down to her hips, emphasised rather than disguised the stage of her pregnancy. She adjusted the crimson mantle about her shoulders and checked that her black hood with its border of gold and ruby flowers, last year's but of little consequence to a priest, was straight upon her head. She touched her mother's ruby at her throat, then pinched her cheeks to lend them colour. At last she was ready to meet Brother Tomas, her mother's envoy, sent from Spain to discuss The Rumours.

She stood by the hearth, decorated with sweet perfumed summer flowers, and watched the friar approach like an ominous black cloud heralding a storm.

'Welcome to Brussels, Brother Tomas. I hope your stay here continues pleasant enough.'

'Your royal highness. Good day. I thank you, I suppose it goes reasonably well,' was the thin-lipped rancorous reply. 'May I say that it is a joy to see you looking so well,' he hurried on without altering his tone, 'your family were most concerned lest you were not receiving the very best of care for this your first pregnancy. They are also most desirous to know that you are caring for yourself while you are carrying the child.'

'And why should things be otherwise?' Juana smarted at the implied criticism. 'I can assure you that the doctors here are as good as any in Spain. Look at me Brother Tomas; do I not look better than most women who are with child?'

'Yes, but on the other hand we have heard that you tended to be too often alone, and sometimes for days, not caring to be present in the court; this cannot be good for you or the child.'

Maria and Zayda exchanged glances, what did this priest know or think he knew?

'Gossip; gossip that gets exaggerated as it travels. It could only be the insensitive who do not realise that I have found mourning for my dearest brother very difficult without my

family. So I withdraw; my letters and drawn curtains help me.'
It made her cross that she need explain her bereavement to, of
all people, a priest.

'And your quarrels with your husband, do they play some
part in this?'

'I cannot believe that my mother would not sympathise with
me in this, my father's fidelity being as reliable as Philip's! My
sisters and I heard many an argument, believe me,' she was
truly ready for battle.

He was taken aback by her boldness so changed his tack,
'Your spiritual welfare is equally, nay, more important.'

Juana bristled, this meeting was decidedly not one of
solicitude; it was, as she had suspected, a grilling like those
conducted by a panel of priests sitting in judgement.

'Ah, but we have got to the crux of the matter rather
quickly, Brother Tomas,' she challenged. 'Do you have
concerns for the safety of my soul? I understand there is
malicious talk about me on that issue too. So, you are here to
confess me because there are rumours that I have been remiss
in my devotions, putting my soul in jeopardy and requiring
your intercession. Perhaps I do not confess as often as I should,
but my confessor is most understanding.' She was quite proud
of her courage; yes, she could and would stand her ground; and
because she lived in Flanders she felt free of any fears of the
Spanish Church.

'Ma'am let me assure you I am not here as an Inquisitor.' He
attempted a fatherly smile. He would have liked to start this
interview again; it was not going to plan; she was not, as he
had envisaged, the contrite child and he the priest ready to be
benevolent at the right moment.

Juana was furious, 'An Inquisitor no less! Things have come
to a pretty pass that they send an Inquisitor. Brother Tomas, tell
me what my dear family and countrymen say of me. Tell me of
my bad reputation.'

'The good name you enjoyed when you left Spain can never
be lost by any idle words being said there.'

'So it is true. They do gossip. What do they know about
what happens here? How dare they presume to pass

70

judgement!' She heard her voice getting ever louder, perhaps too loud.

He would be gentle. 'It is their heartfelt love and care for you that causes people to question ...'

'For instance,' she snapped.

'For instance it has been brought to our attention that you and the archduke go beyond the church's rulings on procreation.'

'Meaning?'

'A priest should not have to remind you that God only expects carnal knowledge for the purpose of procreation; beyond that it is wilful indulgence and a sin.'

She laughed, 'So, that is my crime; I enjoy the pleasures of the marital bed, and am not haunted by the spectre of a priest looking down on me and glowering in disapproval. Do not concern yourself, I have confessed it. I have been absolved of my sin. I have done my penance.'

Her audacity was too much for him; his eyes narrowed, his lips tightened, 'You have not confessed to your Spanish chaplain. You choose instead to confess to dissolute French priests. This is not acceptable.'

'Dissolute? Because they do not spend their entire lives buried behind their missals?'

'Worse, because they are gluttons and drunkards and far too eager to participate in all worldly pleasures.'

'What do you know?' she flung at him. 'Spanish priests have no tolerance, no understanding of the world beyond your Bibles and your masses. There is no compassion in your icy frames. It is little wonder that I choose to bare my soul to those who can listen with sympathy.'

'I shall ignore your intemperate outburst. You are young and obviously still immature. But I do want you to consider this; surely it is better to confess to a priest of the Church who can give a good account of your soul to God, than to one who walks the streets of Paris visiting taverns. I know of a young Spanish priest, without a penny to his name, living in a nearby monastery. He is far better suited to listen to the problems of your soul. And at least your money would go to the monastery and not into drinking houses. I suggest you give this your most earnest attention. I shall return another day when you are of a better disposition then I shall confess you, or if you prefer you may confess to this younger priest.'

'What makes you think that God will listen any differently to you or your kind. I have no need for any Spanish priest. You have neither heart nor ...'

He blazed at her, 'You are the one without a heart. You are the cold one, callously neglecting your dear parents. Not one, let me repeat, not one letter have they received from you. You are the one who has no respect, no honour for the Church, indeed no reverence for God. I fear for you. You are in grave danger of eternal damnation. My letter to your mother will do nothing to lighten her already burdened heart. You should feel deep shame!'

'How dare you speak to me like this!'

'I dare, madam, because I have the authority of my sovereign lords, Isabel and Ferdinand.'

'Get out! Get out! And never come back! Do you hear? You are a cruel old man!' She ran after him, hurling abuse at the door he had slammed shut behind him. She leaned against this barricade protecting her from the brutal world. 'Dear God, everywhere I turn I find hatred and lies. Am I then to have no one to love me?'

'Philip loves you, you said so yourself,' Zayda's answer was immediate. 'He always returns to you because he does love you, he is drawn to you. He is only unkind and hurtful because Chimay and Busleyden are clever at poisoning his mind. And I am always here.'

'Ma'am you look quite pinched with the cold,' Maria put down her sewing and drew a chair close to the fire for Juana, 'this January snow and frost bite straight through to the bones.'

'It was colder still in the church; how fortunate I had these,' she waved her old fur-lined gloves before tossing them onto the cloak hastily dropped over a table in her eagerness to reach the welcoming hearth.

As she warmed her hands she smiled down at the wooden cradle, its huge, solid bulk boldly decorated with the family coats of arms, so preposterously over-protective for so tiny a baby.

The Lady Leonor, two months old, healthy and quite, quite beautiful was sleeping soundly.

'Not a murmur since nurse brought her.' They were both taking delight in the little face as eyebrows knitted, nose twitched and lips smiled their way through dreams.

Leonor had been a good baby ever since her arrival into this world; and she had done that without any fuss. Maria had been present at the confinement, restored to Juana's court. Her dismissal had followed shortly after her chasing away the heckling Flemish courtiers. Chimay had demanded it. Juana, however, had thrown such tantrums in the later stages of her pregnancy that the doctors, fearing for the safety of the unborn child, persuaded Philip to insist on the reinstatement. Maria was now chief lady-in-waiting for the baby; apparently it was of scant interest to anyone who was in the baby girl's court.

'Oh, Leonor, if only you were a boy.'

'This is but your first of many babies; and you are most fortunate, childbearing is easy for you. All you did was to say the Hail Mary twice and there she was, born. The doctors just stood there with nothing to do.'

'Unlike my sister, dying within the hour of the birth of hers,' she gently turned back the white satin coverlet. 'So, Leonor, you have lost an aunt but you do have a little boy cousin; Miguel. Finally there is a successor for the thrones of

Spain. And you can be sure that grandmother, very relieved to have a boy heir, will see to it he is raised as a true Spaniard.'

Zayda brought in a tray of silver jugs, the aromatic steam of the infusions inviting them to drink.

'Brother Tomas is here ma'am.'

'Then bid him come in. He too must be in some need of comforting heat.'

A black habit and cape winged their way through the doorway, halted for a moment then rapidly brought their owner to the feet of Juana.

'Your highness,' the friar fell to his knees before her. He took her hands to kiss them. He had not seen her for some time and what he saw today was alarming. Juana looked ill, very ill. He prayed that she didn't have the same wasting sickness that had robbed his sovereign lords of their eldest daughter Isabel. Juana was painfully thin, her face had a deathly pallor, her eyes were sunk and had a feverish stare, all the symptoms of the dreaded consumption; and dressed from head to toe in unadorned plain and faded black velvet did nothing to relieve the disturbing picture.

'Brother Tomas are you not to get up?'

Exaggerating his difficulty, he rose, a hand comforting his knee. 'It is the cold,' he moaned, 'making my bones feel much older than they are. My lodgings do not offer much comfort either, fuel here is so expensive and I cannot afford the luxury of ...'

'Then do warm yourself by the fire. Zayda, we will have our hot drinks.'

They were poured and offered, the priest's cold fingers eagerly clasping the warm goblet. The swaddled Leonor was lifted from the cradle to be presented. He gazed at the tiny face, so peaceful in its slumber, a picture of perfect innocence in this oh so sinful Flemish land. He blessed her, she rewarding him by opening her beautiful blue eyes, her father's eyes.

'You are indeed fortunate.'

'Not fortunate enough, Brother Tomas, Philip is sorely disappointed. The child is not a boy.'

'You will have others. Do not distress yourself. At this moment you need only think about regaining your strength.

God in His mercy will keep you and guard you.' He made the sign of the cross and smiled his blessing, rejoicing once again at his success at having made Juana accept the full guilt of her disobedience both to the Church and to her parents. 'It has given us all great joy to have you back in our Spanish Mother Church. Why, my lady; it was not my intent to make you weep.'

'These days I spend much of my time in tears. You welcome me back and I do believe my return pleases God, but it does not please Philip. He says I am betraying him when I confess to Spanish priests, telling them things that could be secrets. I have been made to suffer many harsh accusations. He distrusts you and says it is becoming too difficult to trust me. And I love him so much!' She sobbed, reaching out to him for comfort; to the priest who but a few months ago she had considered an enemy. 'And then the days spent with my mother come flooding back and I think that I will never hear her voice again, never see her, unable to tell her that I am sorry for causing her such unhappiness because of my selfish words and deeds.'

'Hush, sweet child. Do not torment yourself so,' Brother Tomas congratulated himself once more for getting this stubborn child to recognise her sins and to beg forgiveness. 'If you wish we shall sit together quietly for a while. Later, if you would care to talk I am here to listen.' He set down his drink to take her hands in his as she wept.

Her problems were well known to him, he had not been standing idly by since his arrival; quite the opposite. He had been very busy gathering news, items of gossip, anything, from anyone prepared to talk. Evidently the gulf separating her from her family and those who had been her friends seemed to her to be growing ever wider. That and the apparent increasing hurts and threats she was made to suffer often pushed her into periods of black despair.

He had also discovered that her handsome, dashing husband, so expert in sport and hunting, showed himself a mere child in the hands of those seeking to advance their own interests. He had foolishly signed a peace treaty with the new king of France swearing his lifelong homage. King Louis joked about Philip being more French than any Burgundy wine; but the truth was that this treaty was an insult to Spain.

There was also talk of Philip insisting that his favourite, his old tutor, Busleyden, a Francophile and arch enemy of Spain, be made a Spanish bishop. That avaricious power-seeker wanted a base there. Brother Tomas was disappointed that Juana was never allowed to become involved in any matters of state because that ruled her out as a source of information.

She interrupted his thoughts, 'And there is no money, and I am to lose even more of my Spanish ladies. Chimay gives me only a meagre pittance.'

Brother Tomas nodded his head. Juana and her court's privations at the hands of the Flems had become notorious throughout Europe. King Henry of England was well aware of the situation and had given him a purse of gold towards his upkeep knowing full well he would get nothing from Philip. He was continuing to nurse the coins through the winter months providing himself with nothing more than bare essentials.

Juana brushed at the tear drops on her drab skirts, 'I am reduced to wearing old dresses, and never have any money of my own, not even a coin to give to the poor.'

Brother Tomas continued stroking the hand of this poor child at the mercy of the powerful in a dangerous and uncaring world; this young woman, a victim of her passion, so desperately seeking love. He, with his reputation for whining and whingeing about the smallest inconvenience, was almost humbled. It would be with mixed emotions that he would soon be saying his last farewells before returning to Spain.

The doors were flung open and in strode Chimay pulling his fur-lined gown across his huge belly. Next came Madam Halewyn as white and as cold as the weather. Last, but not least, the obsequious Spaniard Moxica crept in, hunched over with one hand wrapped about the other. There had been no announcement, no courtesies. They moved directly across the room to prepare a table with pens, ink and sand.

Moxica, his hands impatiently tapping the back of the waiting chair, summoned Juana. 'We have brought these for your signature.'

Juana moved mechanically, head bowed, to the table. She began to read the paper before her, but Moxica's hand came down flat over the words while the ringed fingers of his other hand pointed to the waiting space. 'Sign here.'

Each paper was placed before her and she signed. They were dried and passed to Chimay.

She swallowed hard before making her one request. 'My mother has sent me one thousand escudos, knowing I am in desperate need. I would like to have them now.'

'No doubt you would, but there are greater needs,' Chimay replied not even raising his eyes from the last document.

'But I have signed four thousand over to you already, and besides, this money is meant for me, for my sole use, you cannot keep it.'

'That is how things are.'

'I thought I might have it in lieu of the grant you have so cruelly withheld from my baby daughter,' she whimpered, her voice barely audible.

They ignored her; but before leaving they did remind her that she had still not written to her parents on that matter of the Spanish bishopric for Busleyden. They were gone as swiftly as they had arrived.

'Next time Brother Tomas I shall refuse to sign away any more of my money,' her voice lacked all conviction for *that other Juana* was not to be found. 'I shall tell them I want to know who is getting all my money, and why. I truly will.'

Chapter 13

'Come along, come along,' Philip called over his shoulder dashing into the room and silencing the music.

Juana calmed the rushing storm of desire always awakened by his presence. She handed her vihuela to one of her musicians to return it to its red velvet case, and in a satiny swish of white and gold she hurried to her beloved, her radiant smile of welcome glowing warmer than the August sun that had sent her and her ladies indoors.

'My Juana, my dearest heart, such news!' He took her hands, kissing her fingers greedily, noisily. 'Oh where has the man got to?'

A gauche young man slowly stepped into the doorway, embarrassed by his dusty malodorous clothes, nervously turning his hat in sweaty hands, shuffling his feet in discomfort and wishing he were anywhere but here.

'This gentleman has brought us wonderful news, my love. Wine for everyone, a celebration is in order. And give this poor, choking devil something for his parched throat.'

He held Juana close covering her face with kisses. This was the Philip of her bedchamber; he had not caressed her publicly like this since the first days of their marriage. It was delightful, if puzzling.

This year, 1500, was so splendidly different for Juana. The pain of separation from her family had disappeared; so too had the cowering and flinching from the hurts of Philip and his vicious courtiers. Those weeks spent withdrawn in her darkened room not caring to wash or bathe or change her linen and refusing to eat, were something of the past. She was deliriously happy.

Yes, a new life had dawned with the new century for she had given Philip his longed-for son. Favour had been found by providing a male heir, better still, a robust male heir. They had a son; Charles, Duke of Luxembourg. He was born in February, his hasty arrival interrupting her dancing at the St. Mathias Ball. Only one warning pain and there had been barely enough time to flee the ballroom, red brocade skirts raised above feet frantically hurrying, finding privacy in her nearby withdrawal room, before he launched himself into the world. Oh, how Philip had joked with her about the impatience of this little warrior prince.

Her husband was now so tender and affectionate. It was she he loved and not those temptress whores of the court with their long blond curls. They were but playthings of the past.

Margaret was with her again, for a little while at least, before leaving for Savoy and her forthcoming marriage, and they had quickly resumed their shared pleasures and diversions.

Juana's happiness was complete. Yet Philip had said there was indeed more to add to her bounteous cup of blessings. The kisses were repeated; on her eyes, her nose, her cheeks. Curious courtiers brought here by quickly spreading rumours appeared in twos and threes.

'I propose a toast to Archduchess Juana, Princess of Castile, the Princess of Asturias and heiress to the thrones of Spain.' He raised his cup and sipped just a little wine, not caring for its bitter taste. The toast was echoed by everyone.

'My lord,' she urged him, whispering, 'I beg you not to ... please, not that again.'

For months now Philip had been telling everyone that Queen Isabel's grandson, Miguel, was dead and that Juana was to inherit.

'Philip, my lord, do not continue with ...' This was embarrassing.

He hushed her, his finger resting on her lips. 'My Princess of Asturias, successor to the thrones of Castile and Aragón,' he insisted, turning to the dishevelled traveller at the door. 'This fellow has brought us the news direct from Granada. Here, what does it say in the letter? ... *Miguel died on the twentieth of July*. There is no doubt my pet. We are the Prince and Princess of Asturias, heirs to all those lands presently your mother's and, because of our darling son, heirs to all that belongs to your father.'

She gripped the stem of her glass. Not one drop of wine had passed her lips yet she was heady, dizzy. She was in ecstasy. Any sadness for the dead child drifted over her like a brief summer's cloud. Miguel not two years old was dead; making her free. His death was her liberation. She could leave this foul place, taking her beloved Philip with her to Spain where her handsome prince would be welcomed and loved. Oh, there would be such wonderful changes to their lives.

She reached for the letter, hungrily searching for those so important words. The writer had once been her carver, a trustworthy servant, and presently employed as their informant in the royal court in Spain. There was no doubting his words.

'It is good news, is it not, my dear heart?' Philip's hands were on her waist drawing her tight against him.

'The very best of news, indeed it is wondrous news. I could not have wished for better,' and she threw her arms about him spilling her wine in her reckless joy. 'But remember, this is not an official document. We must wait for that before we make public our plans for the journey. There will be so much to organise. Where shall I start: what to wear, who to take with me, what to take with me? Oh, Spain, here we come! Just listen to me,' she giggled.

She could not resist glancing at some amongst the gathering and savouring the thought that their days were now numbered, especially Moxica, Chimay and Halewyn. It would not be too long before she chose her own household and had people about her that she could trust; who would carry out her orders.

Philip was drawn from her side by Busleyden and some other senior ministers. She saw worry writ large on their faces, and secretly rejoiced that they, too, would have no place in Spain; and she twirled, laughing, an unrestrained child finally stumbling against Philip.

'I beg your pardon, it must be the wine. This is all too wonderful, am I truly awake?' She stood on tiptoe to kiss him.

'It is more than wonderful,' he said planting a kiss on the tip of her nose, 'but my ministers say there is much to discuss and they are determined to tear me away from you this very minute. We shall continue our rejoicing later, privately, I promise you. May God give me patience till then.'

His mouth was on hers, a promise of much more to come.

She was still in a high state of elation when Fuensalida, a Spanish envoy, was announced.

'Greetings, your majesty. May I say how well you look.'

Fuensalida was more than surprised. He had expected her to look ill, miserable, sour, and meanly dressed. Instead he saw before him a radiant young woman; splendid, both in her bearing and attire.

'I feel admirably well. God and the world are being most kind to me these days. You have seen my little ones, the Duke Charles and the Lady Leonor?'

'God has granted you two beautiful children.'

'God has indeed been most benevolent. But your news is good sir?'

'Your sister Maria is to marry King Emanuel of Portugal this year, the final depositions have been made.'

'He is most fortunate, Maria will make him a good wife,' she recalled the "philosophical" young girl of that evening four years ago when they had all sat at their mother's feet. 'And Catalina?'

'That has been rather more difficult, but at last that is also concluded. So much time was lost as I chased back and forth in pursuit of King Henry to finalise the contracts, forever arriving in the town that he had just left. Yes, Catalina will marry the Prince of Wales next year.'

She remembered how, on that very same evening, Catalina had posed as Catalina the Princess of Wales. 'I hope she will find everyone pretty and happy in England.'

'Ma'am?'

'Those were the wishes of Catalina when she was ten years old. And how is my mother the queen?'

'As well as can be expected, she has not enjoyed good health since the death of your sister. And because she is plagued by the possibility of yet further tragedies lying in wait she has been loath to part with Catalina. Fortune has indeed dealt Queen Isabel more than her share of bitter sorrows.'

'May both my sisters have long, happy and fruitful marriages,' Juana would not be involved with tales of woe.

'Amen to that. I understand by all accounts that the christening of the Duke Charles was a spectacular occasion.'

'Quite breathtaking. You cannot begin to imagine the splendour of it all. Philip and I watched the procession from the balcony. Charles was carried by his great-grandmother.' Juana pulled a face, 'The ancient Margaret of York, Madam la Grande, still lives. The news of Catalina and Arthur will infuriate her. You have no idea of the extent of her hatred of the Tudors! But see here, my gift from Philip,' she touched the huge tear-shaped pearl at her neck, 'and you are not to be superstitious! Pearls, whether they look like tears or not, do not always mean sorrow or no one would wear them, would they? But I cannot wait any longer, I must speak with you,' she drew him aside. 'I have heard that Miguel is dead.'

Fuensalida was taken aback. 'Ma'am, I had thought I was to be the bearer of these sad tidings and was waiting for a more appropriate moment, until after we had exchanged happier news. Who told you?'

'There are more ways than one for news to travel. I mean no disrespect to baby Miguel or my mother but his death is a blessing from God upon me and I humbly and gratefully thank Him for it.'

Perhaps the reports reaching Spain of an abused Juana had not lied. He must make discreet enquiries. 'The queen will be sending instructions. She wishes you meanwhile to become involved in the running of your household and to show more active interest in government in readiness for the weightier burdens that one day will rest upon your shoulders.'

'They believe in Spain that I have no interest in either. There is far too much gossip! The truth is my views are blatantly ignored. I am kept apart from any discussions or decision making. But when we are in Spain it will be completely different, of that my mother may rest assured. I, with Philip's support, will dedicate myself to continuing my parents' work. But I am not of a mood for such matters today. Tomorrow, perhaps.'

Juana dismissed him and the possibility of any serious discussions with a charming nod.

Philip and his counsellors almost collided with the departing

82

priest.

'Another Spanish priest in our midst? No matter.'

'He is the bearer of the glad tidings,' she clapped her hands. 'But you are returned so soon. I thought these people would detain you for some while.'

'Tut-tut, "these people", Juana really you must not ... No, it took little time to bring my feet back to the earth. It will take longer to prepare for our departure than I anticipated. There are insufficient funds in the treasury so I must visit my states to raise more. I will also have to ask for financial help from Spain. But, it still means that we are talking about months of organisation by which time it will be winter and the weather will be far too treacherous to attempt a sea journey.'

Juana's lower lip quivered in bitter disappointment. She blamed Philip's counsellors for this situation; they had never shown any restraint, allowing the profligate squandering of money. 'Are you saying that it will be next summer, a whole year before we leave?'

He laughed, cupping her face in his hands. 'I tease, because my counsellors have the solution. We will travel by land, my sweet. We will go via France.' He continued with increasing enthusiasm, 'Do not forget that King Louis is my friend, and I am his liegeman. And, listen to this, to seal this bond of friendship my counsellors advise that we offer our son Charles in marriage to his daughter Claudia. An excellent move!'

She could not believe what she was hearing. Not only had he failed to take a stand against France, which was a part of their own marriage treaty, he was now seeking ties with that country which were too outrageous to contemplate. Their son Charles would inherit all the states belonging to Philip, would one day inherit Austria and the Holy Roman Empire from Maximilian, and all the Spanish lands would eventually be his too. Incredibly Philip was seriously suggesting a marriage alliance between Charles and the daughter of the king of France. In one step he was offering most of Europe to Louis on a platter; and France was supposed to be isolated, denied the opportunities of extending her power.

And still he went on! 'Meanwhile Busleyden and de Veyre will go to Spain as our ambassadors ...'

Juana was already in such a wretched turmoil over the

proposed marriage treaty that when she heard the name Busleyden cited as an ambassador she rounded on Philip, 'You do not know what you are considering, do you? Have you taken leave of your senses? That you could knowingly hand over all that power and wealth into French hands lies beyond any sane person's comprehension!' Her words came as a volley from enemy arquebuses, her burning eyes reinforced the attack; that other Juana was in control. 'And, my lord, I wonder how you would dare send someone so openly hostile to the Spanish Court. Is this your idea of diplomacy? Can you not see the transparency of the insult or is that beyond your capabilities?' She wagged an angry finger at him, 'I will tell you this; I will not be party to any marriage treaty with France. You will never have my signature. Nor will I set my seal upon a recommendation for two men who have consistently harboured ill will against Spain.'

His hand came down hard across her cheek, 'Do not tell me what you will or will not do!' He barely paused as she crumpled at his feet, her fingers comforting the stinging pain, 'However, do give this some serious thought before making any final decisions. While I would obviously prefer your cooperation I do not need your signature on any document. In the first place I am the Archduke of Austria; second, I am the Prince of Asturias, the heir apparent of Spain. May I remind you that you are nothing more than my wife and it would be more than generous of me to allow you to put your name to anything.'

He turned on his heel and walked away.

It took but moments and a few deep breaths of undaunted determination for Juana to rise to her feet. Well might she be no more than a chattel in Flanders, but Philip was misguided if he thought that in Spain she would serve as nothing other than wife. He, and his counsellors much to their cost, would learn very soon that it was she who was heir; the Cortes of Castile and Aragón would make it abundantly clear that she was to be queen and Philip the king consort.

Now she would send for Zayda to soothe her painful cheek with one of her special balms.

Chapter 14

'Voila un beau prince.'

The patronising voice made Juana want to retch. She imagined the scene in the French king's throne room; Philip, his three obligatory bows of homage with the required five steps between, moving slowly towards the dais where King Louis, his Burgundian overlord, sat watching with glorious satisfaction.

And Philip would fail to see that each time he humbled himself he emphasised his position as the king's vassal, encouraging Louis to use him to further his own cause.

Philip and his closest counsellors had been led directly into the king's presence. Juana and Fonseca watched them strutting as they went; vain peacocks resplendent in their velvets, satins and jewels.

'See how they swagger?' she had whispered, 'and they are penniless, desperately hoping to have a share of Philip's future wealth.'

Juana sat in an ante chamber awaiting her turn to be presented. It had been this way for the whole of their journey through France. Her status as Princess of Castile and, more importantly, the true and lawful heiress of all Spain had never been recognised. It was Philip who was feted. Not once had they afforded her the respect and honour that was her right.

She leapt from her chair shaking with indignation, muttering to the Bishop of Córdoba, her companion for the long journey to Spain. 'I will not tolerate this much longer. Philip is so stupid. Does he not see that he is playing into Louis's hands? And has he forgotten that this is the country where his sister Margaret was held prisoner for years after the French reneged on her marriage contract? How can he have any truck with them at all after that? My God, there are times when he appears to have no brain whatsoever!' Her voice hardened, 'I tell you this, they will see how I, a princess with Spanish pride will present herself to this French king.'

Fonseca, Bishop of Córdoba, invited her to walk with him to

the other side of the room distancing her now loud voice from her ladies and anyone else who might overhear. It would give him time to quiet her.

Queen Isabel had sent Fonseca to Flanders because she had heard that Philip proposed to travel alone to take the oath of succession despite his contempt for Spain. Isabel was insistent that Juana must make the journey too, after all she was the future queen, with Philip no more than consort. She further suggested that only Juana's attendance was required at the ceremony. This was firmly rejected by Philip's counsellors.

Within days of Fonseca's arrival with Isabel's despatch he discovered that Philip was making no secret of the fact that he had as much desire to go to Hell as to go to Spain. He saw that Juana was being denied all respect, suffering many indignities. He was alarmed at the power that Chimay and Busleyden had over the archduke. As for the rest of Philip's court he found them despicable, and that was the most charitable observation he could make. His brief to hasten the departure of Juana and Philip had been difficult, but finally successful.

In the intervening months he had been Juana's Chaplain, adviser and friend; and had also helped her to rebuild her pride and dignity. He offered her understanding and guidance in learning to manage her anger, supported her against hurt and injustice. Now once again he had come to her rescue offering his arm to accompany her in a calming stroll.

As they walked she unburdened herself as though in the confessional, 'What has become of me? Philip strikes me as though I were a common serving wench. I realise now that he has no love for me. He has fooled me for the last time, never again. How well I remember that day. I had been ill for several days after our dreadful row over this journey. He visited me in my darkened haven of peace. He came whispering honeyed words against my cheeks about making amends, saying he would come to my rooms later and we could dine together and then we could … that was sufficient for me. The curtains were thrown back, the shutters opened, the sun poured in waking up the silver bowls and plate, making motes dart to and fro in a glorious dance. Zayda, singing songs of love, prepared a bath, washed my hair and wrapped it in a perfumed towel. The air was heavy with the scent of musk and oranges. That night

Philip and I were in each others arms again ... but, you see bishop, the truth is he came to my bed not because he loved me but because he was advised to. It was a precaution against my mother's insisting on my presence only. His counsellors were afraid! And, we have another child. I pray God keeps her and her brother and sister safe in Margaret of York's hands.'

It had torn at her heart to say goodbye to her precious little ones; Leonor was only three years old, Charles eighteen months and baby Isabel just three months. Her mother so desperately wanted to see them, but Philip was persuaded that she would find some way to keep them in Spain, especially Charles, to ensure he was raised a true Spaniard with Spain's interests at heart.

After a moment or two she looked up at Fonseca. She could probably never thank him enough for helping her get well again. Philip's contemptuous use of her, the undisguised hatred of the Flems, Philip's sister gone to Savoy, her pregnancy, all had combined to make her ill. She had fainting bouts; she spent days in her rooms wrapped up in her misery with the curtains drawn to hide her from the light. The bishop's patience had been tireless.

'Your company on the journey has been a blessing. I am only sorry that I have no Spanish gentlemen courtiers to ride with you in my retinue but the archduke refused my request. You have been left with only ladies. You must find it very dull at times.'

'Not at all, ma'am, it has been a pleasure and privilege to ride with you. And it stirs the pride in my old bones riding behind the banners of Castile.'

The train of Juana and Philip was enormous. There were more than three hundred attendants. Juana, flanked by the waving pennants with their proud lions and castles, rode at the head of her retinue of forty ladies. Behind the riders stretched an endless line of heavy carts. They lumbered along creaking and groaning under the weight of furniture, kitchenware, tapestries, gold and silver dining services; everything that was necessary for the journey.

A guard of hundreds was sent by Louis to meet them at the

French border. Juana had definitely feared the worst when this multitude of pikemen and archers galloped towards them.

The enormous cavalcade had made its way slowly through France and a few hours ago arrived at Blois, the birthplace and now the court of Louis. This evening a torch lit procession of hundreds of soldiers and pages had escorted them through dark and cold December streets.

'*Ecce quam bonum et quam jocundum est habitare reges et principes in unum,*' boomed a voice from the throne room.

Juana and Fonseca exchanged grins, 'Indeed, "How good and joyous it is that kings and princes live in unity", especially if you are the king and have the prince at your feet.'

'Precisely. But once we are in Spain, you will see it will be very different. A few lessons from the Catholic Monarchs and the archduke will understand everything. And when the time comes Spain will be safe in your hands. You and Spanish ministers will steady Philip.'

'I thank you for your confidence. I shall see to it that when I do assume that awful role, you will be one of my chief counsellors.'

He kissed her hand and bowed his gratitude.

The Duchess of Bourbon approached, she was to escort Juana into the king's presence.

Juana's ladies gave some last minute attention to her Flanders style décolleté dress; the fall of the blue velvet skirts, the satin-lined sleeves, the puffed chemise sleeves gathered into a cuff at the wrists, the low-cut bodice that flattered her milk-white shoulders, neck and bosom. A final inspection of the ropes of pearls with amethyst and diamond flowers braided into her hair and she was ready.

The Duchess led the way, Fonseca taking his position slightly behind Juana on her right.

Once inside the throne room she paused astonished at its splendour. Huge chandeliers suspended from silver chains and bearing countless candles cast their light over white and gold wall hangings, crimson curtains, enormous mirrors, velvet cushioned chairs and stools. Pike men's breastplates and helmets shone boldly. The robes and sparkling jewels of the courtiers completed a picture of consummate wealth, and how unlike that other throne room in Madrid that she had once considered so awesome.

But this was now! She made a deep curtsey and with head held high she moved slowly towards Louis taking pleasure from the gasps of amazement; Zayda had said that this would be quite a surprise for the French following the rampant malicious rumours about her.

King Louis came towards her, his arms outstretched in welcome. He was a veritable mountain of crimson velvets. He drew her to him and she, remembering Fonseca's council on French etiquette braced herself for the event, thinking how disgusted her mother would be were she to witness such impropriety. Two wet kisses were planted on her cheeks by very fat and very moist lips. He stood back and beamed.

So, this was the "Lord and Master". This was the person Philip would "serve until death to procure his good and avoid his hurt". He was a flabby forty year old, and were it not for his fine clothes he would be mistaken for a merchant, perhaps even a tradesman. The nose and chin were bulbous and the large mouth, that huge mouth that had kissed her, had thick lips. His hair was poor, sparse, and reluctant to curl under as fashion demanded. There were probably many to be thanked, even rewarded, for their endeavours to make this heap of flesh look like a king.

'Welcome, welcome, noble princess. We hope you will make your home with us for many days.'

Juana thought she would rather not, despite the warmest of welcomes at the home of her fellow countryman, the Count of Cabra, where she was lodging. She wanted to be on her way.

'Her majesty, my dearest wife, will provide many diversions. Alas, the archduke and I must occupy ourselves with the serious burdens of state; with some time, of course, for sport and recreation,' and he poured his fat, ugly smile on her. 'But you must meet the queen and our little princess. Duchess, escort the Princess Juana.'

Anger flooded her. She was to be pushed to one side again. That Philip would still dare discuss anything without her was too preposterous. Her eyes challenged Philip but he looked away. A firm hand, that of the duchess, pressed on her elbow telling her she was dismissed. Juana shrugged it away, deliberately taking her time to curtsey, before following her. She would not be rushed!

The walls of the queen's apartments were hung with cloth of gold and white damask; there were heavy red curtains and drapes; chairs and stools were furnished with green velvet cushions. Ana of Brittany, queen of France, was seated on her chair of state under a canopy of red velvet; her ladies-in-waiting were grouped at either side of her throne.

The scene had been set meticulously to make this visitor feel lowly. But Juana had a mission. Spain relied on her. She advanced to the dais to curtsey as protocol demanded when the hand of the Duchess once more appeared, this time grasping her by the forearm, pushing her to her knees, reminding her she was no more than the wife of a vassal.

Juana breathed very slowly. She would be patient. Her time would come; one day she would be a queen, queen of a country far more powerful than France. Taking a moment to calm herself she then rose.

This was not going to be an easy visit. How was she going to survive the next few days, or however long her husband decided they were going to remain here? There would be the constant torment of suspecting Louis of conspiring against Spain with Philip only too willing to serve his master like some loyal dog. She meanwhile would be in the company of ladies who would be either intensely boring or seeking the attentions of her husband. She was not going to be happy. Her hand rose involuntarily to her brow.

'Ladies,' the queen clapped her hands, 'before it becomes too late we must bring our darling Princess Claudia to meet her mother-in-law.'

Juana dug her fingernails deep into her palms and forced a smile.

The child was brought to her, a tiny bundle of white silk skirts all ribbons and bows, a frothing of frills and lace, festooned with amulets. Claudia, this little creature, was the cause of such discord between Spain, Flanders and Austria. This tiny thing at her feet who was contracted to marry their son Charles had ignited such a fierce argument between her and Philip.

As she looked down at this innocent, unable to find any affection for it, the child gave out a great howl and set itself to scream and bawl burying its little red face amongst the skirts of its nurse.

'This is most disturbing. Princess Claudia has never behaved so before.' Queen Ana, angry that her moment of glory should be so short-lived, hastened the departure of her daughter. Her little showpiece princess, destined for such riches and the key to vast wealth for France, had become nothing more than a mixture of blubbering mouth, snotty nose and wet cheeks.

Juana raised her hands seeking forgiveness for the infant, 'Do not concern yourself, ma'am. I have three children of my own and I well understand these things. But I see you are upset. With your permission I shall retire.'

Without waiting for a reply she curtsied, and walked from the room thanking Claudia for her timely outburst, for a moment quite liking her.

Chapter 15

Maria combed and braided Juana's hair, as she sat stroking the red velvet handle of her clothes brush indulging herself in reveries of her beloved Toledo where she longed to be.

It was Monday and they were all going to church; again.

'How often have we attended church since we arrived? I shall tell you. We went twice on Wednesday then once on Thursday, Friday and Saturday. Yesterday we attended the wedding of some marquis or other and today, as a special treat, I must attend a solemn mass; and always with these silly women. Every day it is the same; go to church, return to listen to idle gossip, dine with them and listen to more of the same. I am so weary of being cooped up with these cackling hens.'

She threw down her brush and began stabbing at a pincushion with one of her jewelled pins, 'Dear God what a senseless delay, such time wasting; every day puts us deeper into winter.'

Maria had finished and Juana studied herself in the mirror, a proud young woman in a dark green brocade dress in the French style. The red lining showing through the slashed sleeves matched her floor-length mantle and her soft leather buskins. She nodded her approval.

'The bishop is waiting, my lady.'

'Good, then please send him in.'

'Your majesty.' He closed the door behind him and bowed.

'Ah, Fonseca, I needed to see you as soon as possible; I did not sleep well last night.'

'I hope I am not the cause, and that you are not angry with me for yesterday.'

'Angry? You probably saved me from choking when you slapped me on the back. I will never, ever, eat another damnable French candy. No; I am worried about Louis and Philip possibly conspiring to crush Aragón should my mother die before my father.'

'Rest assured that Philip could not possibly sign a pact with

Louis; The Cortes of Castile would never put its name to it. But I have no doubt that Louis will be doing his utmost to exact all kinds of promises from Philip, and we should be away as soon as possible. I shall pray for our early departure.'

'Amen to that. I might just offer the same prayer too. If God is not too distracted by a congregation more concerned with fashionable robes, and the choirs of France and Flanders intent on trying to outdo each other in their quantities of lace and the volume of their anthems He may hear my tiny pleas.'

Fonseca shook his head; would she ever conform as a dutiful daughter of the Church?

Mass was as she had told Fonseca; the service went very much unheeded. The congregation was more interested in appearances than worship, and the choirs almost rent the air asunder in their rivalry.

It was not until the service was over that even Juana paid any attention to what was taking place. She became intrigued by the activity directly opposite at the foot of the altar steps. A young server carrying an alms box on a velvet cushion approached the king who placed his offering in the box. One of his courtiers then opened his purse and handed Philip some money. Philip accepted the coins, bowed to the king and put them into the alms box.

Juana stared first at the smug look on Louis's face, then at her naive husband being made to look again as nothing more than a faithful subject.

The server crossed to their side of the church to stand before the queen. She, in like fashion turned to one of her ladies who opened her purse and turned to Juana.

But Juana shook her head, first at the lady in waiting then at the queen. She spoke through a smile, her voice indignant, 'Should I wish to put something in the poor box I will do so. I am neither poor nor your servant. If, and when, I make an offering it is always my own.' She then removed one of her diamond and ruby earrings, a wedding gift from Philip, and dropped it clinking into the box.

The eyes of the queen narrowed in fury and she hissed at her between clenched teeth, 'Duchess, it is your duty to do my bidding. How dare you refuse!'

'Ma'am, how dared you presume?' returned Juana.

Queen Ana rose; a shimmering, shaking, rustle of white satins and hurried from the church, her ladies in close pursuit.

Juana's ladies gathered about her eager to whisper their congratulations and praises, but she hushed them. 'The queen in her anger has unfortunately committed a gross error of etiquette. Guests should always leave the church first. If the crowds outside are waiting to see if we hasten after her they will be disappointed. We shall take our time as we leave and once outside we shall go directly to my apartments.'

They strolled slowly down the nave giving carvings, triptychs and polychrome statues long and earnest attention.

Maria came to whisper that the queen was indeed waiting in the street presumably having remembered her manners, and that the townsfolk would not move until their curiosity was satisfied.

'Then if we are all quite ready ladies, let us proceed.'

They emerged into the December sunlight, Juana and her little army of ladies striding forth like crusaders against the infidel. With not a glance to right or left and with heads held high they walked straight past Queen Ana and on to the count's palace. As soon as they were indoors they fled, a flurry of skirts and laughter, to Juana's apartments.

'I think we must all wear something quite distinctive for dinner.'

There was such a hustle and bustle of ladies. Skirts, sleeves, chemises, stockings, bodices were everywhere, some waiting to be selected, others thrown aside. From out of the chaos Juana emerged, a perfect metamorphosis. She had been a Flemish beauty; she was now a radiant Spanish princess.

She looked in her mirror and saw that every item of her dress; the black hood, the high-necked chemise, the waist-length bodice, the panelled skirts all proclaimed her a Spaniard.

Juana and her ladies were ready for the banquet. She was ready for the enemy. Relishing the idea that one of the secrets of success in battle lies in the element of surprise, and had she not proved that at least twice today, she set off for what she knew would be an evening with a difference.

And Juana was to be proved right in every respect. Her satisfaction could not have been greater when the French queen came face to face with this personification of Spain. Queen Ana struggled to maintain her composure as she demanded an explanation; growing increasingly uncomfortable in the too royal gown and mantle of crimson velvet and ermine. These had been deliberately chosen to command respect and due deference from this little Spanish madam who, it would appear, must be reminded was merely a princess married to a common duke.

Juana would have replied but Louis and Philip entered. The king's flabby features quivered with rage; her husband's shock turned to fury. Unperturbed, with chin thrust forward, she announced, 'There were two breaches of etiquette this morning, for which I have as yet received no apology. I thought it time to remind everyone that I am not just the Archduchess of Austria, not merely the Princess Juana of Castile. I am the Princess of Asturias, heiress to all Spain and its vast dominions.'

She curtsied, aware that the situation was difficult although not entirely of her making. It was now the turn of King Louis to employ all his diplomatic skills; who might he anger most, Spain or Philip? Preferably neither, she thought, for both were vital to his plans.

Quietly content at having victoriously completed her mission for Spain, she waited for King Louis to lead them into the banqueting hall.

Chapter 16

The war of pride she had waged against the French queen with the consequent hurried departure caused greater disharmony than ever; nor did the following difficult months help.

Torrential rains and storms of sleet and snow made their passage through France completely miserable. Yet there was worse to follow.

To prepare for their journey through the Pyrenees all their goods and chattels had to be transferred from the huge ox drawn wagons to the backs of Spanish mules. Kitchenware, tableware, furniture and furnishings, and clothing had to be organised into small, balanced packs. This was carried out as the heavens descended on them in an icy and relentless downpour hampering their every move. Mud-slopped gold and silver ware, protected in sodden straw was wrapped in equally soggy canvas. Boxes and chests slipped from mud-slimed hands into squelching brown puddles, often spilling their contents, some never to be found, others to discover new owners. Exquisite silk tapestries in waterproofed rolls lay slumped like dead bodies across mules' backs and dripped forlornly. Tempers frayed and frustrated swearing joined the anguished cries of the animals no happier than the rest to be a part of this chaos.

One by one they were readied and added to the lengthy train to splash their way towards the mountain passes. Ahead of them rode Juana and Philip with their retinues, everyone enveloped in furs, scarves and waterproofed cloaks, a long dismal column trudging its way into a nightmare journey of narrow goat tracks and battles against biting winds and blinding snow storms.

Mercifully they eventually reached Spain alive and well but thoroughly exhausted and totally wretched. There were further delays; waiting while fresh wagons were sought in local villages along their route, as roads were repaired and bridges were reinforced to take heavy loads. The reception committees at each of their resting places feted them with hitherto unknown Spanish luxury, a dispensation granted by the frugal Queen Isabel in an effort to impress her son-in-law but which did little to cheer.

It was still all so very far removed from those idyllic plans Juana had nursed in Flanders so many months ago. Her husband was not impressed with her country, in fact he had found very little to please and much to aggravate, and he complained a great deal.

It was now April and Toledo, where the swearing in ceremony was to take place, was only two leagues away.

Juana was sitting on a large, hand worked, floor cushion in Philip's chamber. Although her Book of Hours was open she was keenly alert for any sound from her patient and willing him to awaken from his slumbers. She was eager to be his nurse, eager to shower her devotion on her beloved husband who only a few days before had been stricken down by a very nasty attack of measles. Her book rested on her knees as she only half-read, *Deus in auditorium meum intende* ... , only half-looked at the little shepherds and the angels tightly enclosed in the illuminated letter D, and the tiny animals hiding amongst leaves that traced the margin of the page.

'Yes, that is the reason for this illness'; she whispered to the page, 'God wanted us to have some time together, free from the domineering Busleyden and his evil influence; just the two of us, learning to love each other once again, like we did at the very beginning.'

But this would be going too far, for she knew Philip would never love her, not in the way that she loved, but so long as he allowed her to love him it would be enough.

The worst of his illness was over. The high temperatures were gone thanks to her insistence that he drink every drop of his medicine; a mixture of stinging nettle, plantain, celery and pepper. Happily for Juana there was still some nursing to be done; attending to his itching spots, his dreadful cough and those wonderful eyes that still hurt.

A groan followed by a fit of coughing issued from behind

the heavy gold brocade. Juana motioned to the two doctors standing by the window to remain where they were, to do nothing, she would attend to Philip. Her book was put to one side. She ran to partially close the shutters before drawing back the bed curtains.

As she removed the soothing cloth from over his eyes she brushed his forehead with her lips, 'And how does my patient feel after his sleep?'

'Juana; you are still here?' He reached for her hand but a fit of coughing made him seek out his handkerchief instead.

'My poor darling. Here, I have the very thing. Open wide,' she poured a spoonful of syrup of violets from a phial. 'It is so delicious.' She cleaned the spoon with her tongue.

'Are you my nurse, or just a greedy child?'

'Both; and now I think it is time for a bowl of clear chicken soup.'

He pleaded, 'No more chicken soup.'

She nodded to the chamber boy to take the order to the kitchen.

She fussed over her darling Philip; first bathing his face with cool water and gently dabbing it dry with an embroidered towel, then combing his hair and giving him a fresh sleeping cap. She plumped up his pillows and tucked the covers around him.

'I am so much better today, Juana. I will soon be well enough for another game of reed spears. Oh, I do not take kindly to illness; I want to be up and about.'

'The game of reeds that will have to wait for some time yet; in any case, throwing canes at each other does not appear to me to be a very sensible pastime.'

'The sport is lost on you.'

'Indeed it is. But here is your lunch. I shall leave you for a little while and take some air in the gallery. Be sure to eat it all, the doctors commend it highly.'

'I know that well enough, I have had nothing else for days, do not be surprised if on your return you find me clucking.'

Juana laughed.

'Your laughter is the best medicine of all.'

'But not as good as chicken soup,' she called back to him.

Outside she drank in the delicious April air. She walked slowly along the gallery's four sides thoroughly enjoying her new life.

There was a growing commotion; surprised voices; the courtyard below suddenly filling with riders. There were yelled commands; some of the horsemen immediately throwing themselves from their saddles to dash to a gentleman who remained in his saddle awaiting their attendance. Pennants bearing the arms of Castile and Aragón were held aloft by guards at the gateway.

Six years ago Juana had looked down at a young dusty rider; today she gazed down on an older but equally dusty traveller.

'No, you cannot be ... You are ...'

Juana kicked her feet free of her mules to let her fine leather shoes carry her swiftly in a scurrying, billowing cloud of red velvet along the gallery, down the stairs and across the paved courtyard to a gentleman dressed entirely in black.

'Father, father ...' she kissed him, threw her arms about him, then pressed her cheek against his breast.

Ferdinand kissed her forehead. 'Our dear Juana, returned to us at last.'

'Oh, father, father ...' She kissed him again and again, tears spilled down her cheeks.

'Juana, princesses do not behave thus.'

'This one does!'

'Let me look at my daughter; a young woman, the mother of three healthy children.'

'You will make me blush examining me so,' she giggled. 'My turn.'

Her father was much heavier than she remembered, and she noticed that as he removed his travelling hat and scarf he carefully checked that his wig was in place. He wore a wig! And he had lost one of his front teeth. For all that he was still her strong and handsome father. As for that cold farewell of the past, she dismissed it, for had he not just shown how impatient he was to see her again? He could not wait until she arrived in Toledo!

He asked the all important question that had brought him

here.

'I must know, Juana, how serious is this illness?'

'There is nothing to fear, believe me, he is over the worst and is mending quickly. Philip is strong, the doctors say he will soon be fit and well. But you must come and see him,' she took his hand to pull him towards the stairs.

'Dear child let us be calm. Of course I will come to see him, although it ignores protocol. I should really wait until your arrival in Toledo, but your mother and I had to know if the illness was as serious as we feared. That is the reason for my being here. Our joy at having you here in Spain was quickly turned to anxiety when we received the news. You must excuse our pessimism.'

Arm in arm they made their way to Philip's apartments Juana barely pausing for breath, wanting to tell everything at once.

Ferdinand strode across the room to his son-in-law. Philip strove to remove his cap as a sign of respect.

'No, my boy, you keep it on. You have need of it.' He offered his hand for Philip to kiss, thought better of it remembering the measles, quickly withdrew it and moved several feet away. He had a chair placed for him at what he considered a safe distance.

They were busily exchanging formal greetings until a squeal of laughter from Juana interrupted them. 'Forgive me, father, but I have before me the two men whom I most dearly love talking away, and neither has realised that the other cannot understand a word that is being said! If only you could see yourselves.'

'You must be our interpreter Juana. You can begin by telling Philip what a fortunate man he is to have such a wife; pretty, charming and so very intelligent. Who could ask for anything more?'

Chapter 17

A cornflower blue sky and a warming sun stretched out across the valley and up into the hills.

She and Philip, each under a canopy bearing their coats of arms and accompanied by their huge retinue, were within a league of Toledo. Her father with his entourage of noblemen, churchmen and guards had come to meet them; it was a welcome beyond her wildest dreams. The only disappointment was the absence of her mother, who remained at home still indisposed.

They rode together up the hill, entering the city through the horse-shoe arch of the ancient Bisagra Gate. Then they continued along narrow streets, all spread with rosemary and thyme, up to the Gateway of the Sun. Their cavalcade was a splendour of colours and a sun-flashing glitter of gold and silver. Townsfolk leaned from balconies draped with cloths of every kind and colour to cheer them on their way up towards the Cathedral, 'Long live the Catholic Monarchs. Long live Princess Juana and Prince Philip. God bless your little ones so far away, may He grant them long lives.'

Juana waved and smiled, feeling that her heart would burst with pride, loving every minute.

The tambours, bugles, horns and cornets added to the clamour. Flower petals fell in thick profusion onto the canopies, onto the heads and shoulders of all those in the cavalcade.

At last they entered the large square in front of the cathedral. Crowds thronged this area too, squeezing into spaces that before seemed not to exist, clinging to walls and window grilles, so determined were they to see the princess.

The broad front of "her church" with its three enormous portals was even grander than she remembered. The stone saints atop their columns and those standing in arched niches looked out as if rejoicing at her home-coming; some were definitely reaching out their arms in welcome. This Cathedral, where she had been christened, in a few days time would

101

witness the proclamation of her hereditary rights to the crowns of Spain.

Juana, Philip and Ferdinand dismounted and approached the steps. A hush settled over the crowd. Archbishop Cisneros came forward carrying his magnificent crosier of gold encrusted with jewels.

Was this the man who had at one time intimidated her? These eyes were not the eyes that pierced the soul; this mouth was not harsh and ready to criticise. Juana decided he looked much more like a kindly uncle than a disapproving priest. Perhaps in the past she had misjudged him.

Inside the Cathedral the pillars, the arcade of chapels, the screens and statues, all basked in the sunlight flooding in from the many windows. Their procession took them past the column marking where the first altar had stood those many centuries ago when the Virgin Mary had come down to earth to bless the monk Ildefonso for defending her virginity against the doubters. Juana knew that Philip wouldn't be interested but she still had to tell him. They finally passed through the silver choir screen to be directed to their seats.

The Solemn Mass was too long; the singing from the Introit onwards, although faultless thanks to an excellent cantor, was frustratingly so. Philip inspected his beautifully manicured fingernails more intensely as each minute passed. Juana let her eyes drift beyond the curling blue clouds of incense to the side chapels until they rested on the life-size weeping heralds in their gloriously coloured tabards watching over the tomb of Catherine of Lancaster, her great grandmother; and she began to think of Catalina and what life was like in England.

The choir sang the *Kyrie Eleison, Christe Eleison.*

At last it was all over. Now she could go to her mother.

❖   ❖   ❖

It was only a short distance from the Cathedral to the home of Beatriz, the Marquesa de Moya, where they were all to be lodged during their stay in Toledo.

Ferdinand, Juana and Philip came from the intense

102

brightness and warmth of the sun and the noise of the crowds into the sombre throne room. The walls were hung with tapestries depicting the imprisonment of Christ, Christ washing His disciples' feet and Pontius Pilate tormented by his indecision; not the most cheering of atmospheres to greet the elated young couple.

On a dais at the far end an old woman sat hunched on her throne. Juana swallowed hard. Isabel, looking old and infirm, was dressed entirely in black, except for a collar of tiny sheaves of gold arrows set with rubies and pearls.

Only two ladies accompanied her mother: the life-long friend Beatriz, and Juana's namesake, the natural daughter of Ferdinand.

Juana looked at the mother she had thought never to see again. Time and events had had their savage sport with this once indomitable queen. Her body was heavy and bloated; her face flaccid and deeply lined; her hair quite grey. She reached for her mother's hand to offer the customary kiss, but Isabel stayed her and rose awkwardly from her seat and painfully descended the steps.

'My dear child.' Isabel hugged her pulling her into her ample bosom, kissing her and weeping. 'And our son Philip. Prince you are most welcome.' She beckoned him to her to receive her welcoming embrace, 'I hope you are quite recovered.'

He too offered to kiss her hand but she withdrew it that she could grasp his arms in a show of affection.

Juana translated their brief conversation.

'Now then, Philip must stay with the king while I have you to myself, my child. My child, dear me, no longer a child but a mother. Let us go to my apartments.'

They walked together, arm in arm, slowly; every step for Isabel an agony.

Once in her room and settled comfortably with Juana at her feet she began her questions. She was eager to know about the three little ones left behind in Brussels. Were they healthy, who did they look like, when was she to have their portraits and, most importantly, when were they coming to Spain?

Then came the searching questions. Isabel was demanding

the truth: about Philip's behaviour towards Juana; Juana's religious obligations; Juana's isolation, self-imposed or otherwise. She detailed the many rumours she had carefully stored over the years.

Juana was thrown onto unsure ground, the information was unnervingly accurate. She dared not attempt answers, so shrugged off the queries. 'You concern yourself too much. Those things, many of them exaggerated, are all in the past and should be forgotten. Tell me of yourself, for you have suffered far more than I.'

Isabel decided not to press the matter; and her daughter did, after all, look well and happy enough. She spoke instead of the tragic deaths in the family, of how each had plunged a dagger deep into her heart.

'And my sisters, Maria and Catalina?'

'They are both wed and in good health, and it brings me comfort to read their letters; but I feel very much alone. There is no loneliness to compare with the loneliness of an empty hearth. I have a tremendous ache in my heart which can never be eased and nothing can remove this dreadful weight of sorrow.'

'Not even me mother?' she asked playfully, knowing she had been and always would be a poor substitute for her sisters in her mother's heart.

'But only for the briefest of time Juana. If only we could persuade you and Philip to live here. Or have you send us our darling grandson Charles that we might raise him as a true Spaniard. Spain must be ruled by one of its own, someone who cares, someone to ensure that it maintains its identity, its dignity,' Isabel's voice had an edge, 'and sees to it that it does not become little more than a part of Austria.' She shuddered her distaste for such an eventuality.

'Not now, please mother, not now. 'But I have a gift for you. Page, send for Madame Halewyn to bring me my red casket. Mother I have brought some exquisite cloth.'

'Juana you know full well that fineries hold no interest for me.'

'But this is fine Brussels material, perfect for your veils.'

'In that case I suppose it will be acceptable.'

Juana fought back the hurt. She jumped up, 'As soon as you have seen it we shall go to find Philip and father. And it must be almost time to dine.'

❖   ❖   ❖

Dinner, by Isabel and Ferdinand's standards was a most sumptuous affair. A grand show of gold and silver plate, most of it belonging to Beatriz, decorated the table and the sideboards.

Juana's heart went out to them. She applauded their efforts in arranging such a dazzling display, and she sympathised with them as it could not begin to compare with the excesses of France and Flanders. She knew too how it rode counter to their philosophy of austerity so firmly entrenched as a part of their permanent mourning.

She was delighted with the meal. It was, unfortunately, chicken. Scrawny Spanish chickens had been dipped in rice flour then cooked in goat's milk and rose water and finally garnished with a topping of grilled cheese.

Philip clucked at her before whispering, 'Good God, more chicken; scraggy birds barely meriting the title of sparrows in Brussels.' He picked and poked at the food on his plate.

Isabel and Ferdinand were shocked by his singular lack of table manners.

'Pay no heed,' Juana laughed nervously, 'Philip only complains about more chicken after a chicken soup diet for days, and he also has a strong aversion to garlic although I have told him it is beneficial. In truth any food not prepared for him by his own cooks is always regarded as suspect.'

'Our apologies for the chicken,' Isabel's reply was icy. 'Do assure Philip that there is no garlic lurking in his dish, so he may stop inspecting it as if what he has before him is something not fit for human consumption.'

When they had finished their first course the table cloth was removed and replaced by a fresh linen cloth delicately embroidered with country fruits. Servants carried in dishes of pastries, biscuits, doughnuts, marzipans, fudges and cream.

Juana was wide-eyed with delight, 'Philip, you must try these pine nut treats.'

'First you try to turn me into a chicken, now you think I am a squirrel. What are these others?'

'Almond fudges, marzipans, these are bishops, and over there are saints' bones ...'

'Go no further, the church gets its nose in everywhere. Tell your parents that tomorrow I will entertain them with a Flanders' dinner.'

'That would not suit at all. It would be far too much, too animated, and too noisy.'

'Exactly! They could do with a bit of life around here. Speaking of which, how soon can we make our excuses to leave and go to your bedchamber. I have in mind a far better dessert than any on this table.'

'What is Philip saying?'

'That he wishes to treat you to a Flemish banquet, mother. But I must warn you it will be very different to anything you know.'

Isabel and Ferdinand smiled acknowledging the invitation.

But Philip's other words were burning deep into Juana and nothing existed except a huge hot wave of desire. It was overwhelming, she could think only of Philip's naked body next to hers. Feigning tiredness after a long day and a desperate need to rest she left the table, commanding her feet to walk not run.

Philip said he thought it his duty to accompany her to her apartments.

Chapter 18

The December chill that swept through the castle at Alcalá de Henares was nothing to the chill that seized Juana. She held her head. She swayed.

The Marqués de Villena hurried to assist the princess, now in her sixth month of pregnancy.

'I need time. I must have time to think. This cannot be true,' she stared at the paper in her hand.

'Ma'am, the queen knew enough of Philip's determination to leave Spain to summon him from Zaragoza to caution him on his behaviour, to impress on him why he should remain, why he should make an effort to understand this nation which he is to inherit. As you can see from the letter she was unsuccessful; the prince has expressed his resolve to leave immediately. She is now relying upon you to persuade him to delay his departure. She regards it as a matter of great consequence.'

'Of course Philip is impatient to return to Brussels, and I long to see my little ones again, but my mother must be mistaken thinking Philip means us to leave now. This is not the time to travel.'

Disquieting thoughts insinuated themselves: was Philip so discontented as to want to hasten his departure, regardless of the outcome; would her mother encourage him to leave, to rid herself of what she regarded as a shallow, thoughtless son-in-law while she kept Juana here?

Villena continued. 'Nonetheless Queen Isabel thought it best that you be advised ahead of the prince's arrival.'

Philip was no more that two hours ride away so he would be here very soon. She had not seen him in weeks and had missed him so. Her heart leapt, at last her lonely days would be at an end; Philip was coming.

'Take your letter, Marqués. I thank you for your concern, all will be well I assure you,' she smiled, confident that once she had Philip close to her she could charm away all his ill humour, as she had done successfully so many times recently.

There was the untimely death of Arthur, Prince of Wales,

putting an end to their pleasurable stay in Toledo. Isabel had ordered nine days of mourning. Wisely Juana had granted Philip nine days of hunting although she knew she would be miserable without him.

Then, too, there was much about the oath taking ceremony, already postponed because of the mourning, to rankle; and when he was named only as consort and that in the event of her death Castile would pass directly to their son Charles, that was an insult too outrageous to bear.

He had been put into the foulest of rages by the fire that had destroyed so many of his household's priceless treasures. His prized Flemish cooks were guilty of careless negligence, although they strenuously denied all culpability and pointed the finger of blame at some Spanish servants.

But these problems were nothing compared with the loss of Busleyden. Throughout the summer there had been a number of Flemish deaths, all victims of the heat or the food, and his dearest friend and counsellor was one of them. It was no tragedy for Juana; she saw the counsellor's demise as nothing less than Divine Retribution for his many evil deeds. Philip, of course, had suspected poisoning, and it was a possibility as there was a rumour circulating about some stolen letters allegedly confirming his part in intrigues against Spain. True or not a young chamber boy was tortured into confessing to the theft and the murder.

Whatever the misfortune, Juana had played the sympathetic role to perfection, always returning Philip to his usual carefree self; with the exception of that disastrous oath-taking ceremony in Aragón when they were confronted with an amendment to include the possibility of a future aragonĕs heir. Ferdinand so desperately hated the idea of a Hapsburg wearing his crown he went so far as to state his intention to remarry should Isabel die. Philip's blind fury still frightened her, and she hurriedly pushed all thoughts of that day to the back of her mind.

'Marqués, do you suppose that Philip was merely giving the queen advanced warning of our departure? Immediately, as we all know, can still involve months of preparation.'

'That is what everyone is hoping.'

'I must wear something very special to welcome him. Maria, I think the purple velvet.'

Maria gathered up her sewing and made ready to leave the room when Philip stormed through the doors bringing with him an icy wave of winter air. He threw down his mud-flecked cloak, his hat and his gloves.

He spread his hands to the welcome warmth of the fire. His face was thunderous.

'They are not going to tell me what I may or may not do, nor what I should or should not say. I will not be preached at further.'

'Philip my love you are cold and weary from your ride. Warm yourself, rest awhile, we shall talk later,' she went to him her arms outstretched. 'My poor love.'

He thrust aside her arms. 'We will talk right now. I am leaving. I said at the start that I would return to Flanders within the year, and there is no one going to dissuade me.'

'Of course, my love, and I agree with you; but obviously we have to be patient, we need to wait a little …'

He grabbed at the hand that had ventured to smooth his cheek, '"Obviously", madam? "We need to wait", madam? Do you intend to preach too?'

'Philip, allow me. We must wait until after the birth of our child, only a matter of weeks. By that time it will be the beginning of spring …'

'I did not come here to ask your opinion, just as I did not go to Madrid to seek the counsel of Isabel. Neither she nor anyone else is going to tell me to choose between Louis and Spain, nor is anyone going to tell me where I should live. What I intend to do is this; I will set off for Flanders within the week.'

'Dear heart you are only saying this because you are cross, because my parents have upset you. When you have had time to consider, my love, you will concede …'

'Be quiet, for God's sake! Now listen and listen well. I hate this country; I hate its people; I hate its weather; and God knows I hate its food. But worse, I find your parents the most duplicitous people I have ever met and I refuse to stay to be made to look a bigger fool than they have already made me.'

Juana was shocked, dismayed, and anxious. What could she say?

'My lord, I am sure …'

'I said be quiet. Shut up and know your place,' the words

hissed from tight lips. 'I must get back to Flanders. I shall travel through France. There is nothing further to be said.'

'Going to France would be ...'

'You have either not heard or you are too dull-witted to understand what I am saying. Look at me and listen. I am leaving Spain. I shall begin the journey within the week.'

'But Philip I must stay here, I cannot travel in my condition.'

'That, madam, is your problem and not mine.' Philip was so blinded by his fury he never considered the possibility of Juana having a son and Isabel, because of her total contempt for the archduke, naming the child as heir, thereby denying him of any rights whatsoever to the throne of Castile.

'As soon as the baby is born we will leave. We will leave the child here, and we will go by sea.

'I mean to travel through France; to see King Louis, to clear my name.'

'Spain is at war with France.'

'I shall go as your father's ambassador. Two can play at the same game. I will negotiate a peace for Spain – on my terms, a timely reminder that I will never forgive him for making me chair a meeting funding his army against the French.'

So it was true. He meant to go and he intended travelling on his own, leaving her behind. She could not, would not bear it, 'You? You negotiate with Louis? How does a vassal negotiate with his master? From what I have observed you would do no more than lick his boots and snivel in agreement with anything he demands; a sordid picture of grovelling.'

'You vicious little ...' He grabbed one of her wrists in one hand while with the other he slapped both sides of her face before pushing her to the floor.

She crawled, howling, to his feet, 'The devil take my tongue, Philip. I did not mean it. Forgive me. Oh God, what have I done?'

Philip turned to Maria and Villena, the embarrassed witnesses, 'Look at this. This is the woman they would make queen and I merely her consort; and she speaks of grovelling!'

Juana knew that if he were to go without her she would lose any remaining hope of his being hers and hers alone; he would go straight to the arms of the first Flemish damsel he met. She had been protected from his philandering in Spain. The young women here were "cold fish", he had lamented, unreceptive to his amorous advances. Once back home and she not there she would be lost.

'I beg you. You see me on my knees begging you. Please Philip do not abandon me.'

He looked down at her; at the tear-stained face so ugly and swollen, at the inflamed finger marks across the cheeks.

She whimpered in abject defeat, holding fast to his boots, 'Will you not stay for Christmas?'

'You disgust me!' he flung at her kicking himself free.

Chapter 19

La Mota Castle glowered down from its grim hilltop isolation onto the bustling market town of Medina del Campo. With their bills of exchange folk from all across Europe thronged the market place at the Fairs buying and selling their woollens, silks, satins and velvets. The town square, disproportionately large for so small a town, was a riot of colours and sounds.

But the castle stood aloof; solemn, cold, with damp and mildewed apartments frequently flooded by the spring water feeding the moat.

On this bleak and blustery day in November the castle's enormous bulk looked more inhospitable than ever.

A slight figure in black, holding her skirts and cloak against a determined wind, made her way along the battlements, stopping occasionally to peer in the direction of the town.

'They should be here by now. What can be the delay? Oh, my Philip, I am coming. I am coming,' Juana called out into the harsh blasts. Her face was drawn; her eyes dark-rimmed, staring.

Her return to Philip's side had been the focus of her thoughts every waking moment since his departure almost a year ago. From the day he left she had gone into mourning; weeping for hours, speaking only of her darling Philip; how she missed him, loved him, wanted him, had to get back to him. After weeks of ignored pleas she had sunk into a deep melancholy.

This had persisted throughout the entire eight months since the birth of her son, Ferdinand, yet still she had not left Spain.

But there would be no further delays, no more deceptions. Excuses for promises constantly broken would be unnecessary because this time she had made her own arrangements. Margaret, her dear Margaret, and even Queen Ana of France had promised that carts would be ready and waiting for her at the frontier. She would go despite her parents withholding her license to travel. A peace treaty had been signed with France and that, so far as Juana was concerned, was enough to guarantee her safe passage to Flanders; to her husband.

As of today she would no longer be a prisoner. She was leaving.

But there was still no sign of the horses. She hurried down the steps, summoned half a dozen of her guard and with grim determination set off over the drawbridge to walk down the hill the short distance to the town, intending to deal personally with those responsible for the delay.

She had not travelled far when she met Fonseca. Neither was happy to see the other.

'Your highness, may I enquire as to why you have left the castle?'

'I am on my way to the town to discover why the pack horses have not been sent. Everything is ready to go, and now this waiting. I cannot understand what can be amiss. Someone will be brought to task if there is not a good explanation. But we waste valuable time. Good day, my lord.'

'Ma'am, you should not be going to the town alone.'

'Then you shall accompany me.'

'There is no need. The problem has been attended to. But we should not be standing here in the cold, let us return to the castle and I will explain.' He led her back through the castle gateway.

Juana stopped, suspicious, 'Tell me about the horses.'

'Will you not go inside?'

'I will not go another step. The horses!'

'They are in Medina.'

'Of course they are in Medina,' she snapped, 'that is why I was on my way there. Do not treat me like some fool.'

'They will not be coming here. I have stopped them.'

'How dare you. By what authority?' She screamed, choking on her anger.

'Queen Isabel has charged me with your safekeeping, and I am asking you to remain here.'

'No,' she howled, 'how could my mother do this to me again? But I will have no more of it. You have asked me to remain. I have refused.' Juana made to walk past him.

Fonseca stepped ahead of her, 'Their majesties only seek to have you remain here a little while longer until they are able to come to bid you adieu.'

'Hah! I beg you not to insult my intelligence. Move aside, I would pass.'

'Lock the gates! Bring down the portcullis!' Fonseca commanded.

The heavy slam of reinforced timber and the rattling of chains tore into her soul. She was listening to all her dreams, all her hopes, being crushed.

'I have received orders that you will not stir from this place until their majesties give their permission. You are not allowed to visit the town, nor are you to even consider travelling. They would remind you that it would be highly dangerous for you to travel without a permit. I am to take all necessary precautions to prevent you taking any action against their will.'

'You villain! You foul despicable villain! I thought you were my friend. You have gone behind my back to reveal all my plans and then you have schemed against me. And now you imprison me. I trusted you and you betrayed me. Now I have no hope.' She spat on the ground by his feet. 'You are not worthy of the robes you wear. Let me tell you that when I am queen I shall see that your deeds are justly rewarded. Before I do anything else I shall have you hanged. Unlike most people about me, I keep my promises, Fonseca. I hate you! I will have your vile tongue cut out!'

He had bowed and hurried through the postilion's gate, issuing urgent orders on the way. He was gone some time before Juana realised how abusive she had been to the very person she had insisted would always remain at her side when she became queen.

She raised her skirts and ran up the steps to the battlements, calling down to him, 'My lord bishop, please come back, I did not mean those words, I am so sorry.'

'No, I think it is best that I inform Queen Isabel of the situation. She will advise me what is to be done.'

Juana came down unsteadily, sick with apprehension, 'I only want to go to my Philip.'

For the remainder of the day and throughout the night she wandered the narrow path that ran alongside the wall, drowning in her unhappiness. Maids came and went unheeded, guards were changed unnoticed, offers of extra cloaks were ignored.

114

At some time the following morning she heard a voice addressing her.

'Two visitors, your majesty.'

Juana looked up, instantly brightening, there might yet be hope, 'My lord archbishop Cisneros and my dear uncle; please forgive this less than hospitable reception but as you see I am expecting to leave at any moment.'

'So we had heard, ma'am, but would it not be more comfortable indoors?'

'You are right,' she invited them to follow her. They scented an easy victory.

'Juana, these are but the kitchens. We thought to go to your apartments,' Don Fadrique whispered.

'Uncle, this is good enough for me. I shall do my waiting outside and my eating and drinking here until it is time to go.'

'Juana I am come from the queen to beg you for the good of your health to return to your apartments. You must take more care of your person so that when spring comes you will be well enough to travel.'

'Why did I imagine you came with good news? My mother talks of spring, does she? She intends me to stay here forever, I know it. You are sent here bearing a pack of lies. Uncle, all I want is my Philip, why will she not let me go to him? Why does she torture me so?'

'Juana, dear child, of course you want your prince and you shall go to him; eventually. You must remember that you are no ordinary lady seeking to return to her husband and children; caution is called for in all the actions that you and we undertake. Let us look at the situation carefully.'

Over the next hour or so Don Fadrique sought to encourage her to accept that the advice he offered came from the great love he had for her. It pained him to see her so desperately unhappy. Cisneros looked on, avoiding all comment.

Juana brought the interview to an end. She was resolute, her determination like iron, 'Go back to my mother and tell her that I am not going to listen to any more lectures from any of her messengers. Inform her of my intention to return to Flanders.

115

You have been at pains to emphasise my need for her permission to leave, so you may report that I will give her no peace until I have it. Tell her I will wait for it, for as long as it takes, at the castle gate. Farewell, may God speed your journey.'

She led them to the gate and as they left she took up her position at one of the guards' lookout posts that they should see she was in earnest. She held fast to the bars and stared out in what she thought must be the direction of Flanders.

She would not be moved. Guards brought her a brazier to lend some warmth and someone placed a fur cloak over her shoulders.

❖   ❖   ❖

She remained at her post for five bitterly cold days and nights resting only rarely in the guardroom.

On the sixth day her mother's baggage train arrived. Juana sent it back to the town stating emphatically that no one could possibly stay at the castle when everything was packed to go.

Later, when the litter bearing her mother entered the outer bailey Juana did not move, she ignored its presence gazing determinedly out across the countryside. Isabel hobbled her painful way to her side, but Juana did not turn to greet her mother.

Isabel was ill; her failing health further impaired by this unwanted journey. She had dragged herself from her sickbed to come to try once more to reason with her daughter.

'Juana, come with me that we might talk,' she summoned quietly.

'No. I will not take one step away from Flanders.'

'This is quite absurd. I have come to explain the reasons for the many delays, understandably disappointing, and how we intend to organise your journey.' The voice was tired and laboured.

'I will not be tricked again. Say what you have to say right here,' Juana answered still looking into the distance.

116

'I will not be spoken to in this way, nor do I intend to take any orders from you. I shall await you in the guardroom. I will give you a few moments but if after that time you have not joined me I shall assume you do not wish to hear what I have to say and I shall leave.'

Juana reluctantly joined her. She remained in the doorway suspicious, obstinate.

Isabel looked at this dishevelled and unkempt creature with its dirty, tearstained face. This was her daughter; this was the heiress of all Spain.

'I am ready to hear your reasons for keeping Philip and me apart.' Juana flung the words at her mother.

'We never sought to …'

'Lies, all lies,' she snapped, 'so why am I not allowed to leave? Why did you order Fonseca to have me held here?'

'To shield you from the inevitable shame you would have brought on yourself, demonstrating to the world your singular lack of respect for us and our country.'

'There is precious little respect for me, making me look foolish with the gates locked and me in the midst of my baggage with nowhere to go.'

'Do not interrupt. We have to be sure that the peace treaties are acceptable to all parties.'

'I am surprised you can keep track of them, changing them as often as you do. And who is to say you will not break them? You did before, betraying my Philip when the ink was barely dry on the peace treaty he had negotiated for you with France. He was seriously ill for weeks. You are keeping me hostage to prevent his making any fresh alliances or treaties with France; I know it.'

'Juana, listen to me.' Isabel fought for breath. 'I had hoped that during this period of waiting you might come to see your role in a different light.'

'Now we come to the crux of the matter. You do intend me to remain here. You want me to rule Spain while Philip rules his lands. You do not want us ever to be together again. Allow me to tell you that I am not interested in ruling any country. My only desire is to return to my husband.' She brought out a folded paper from her bodice, 'Read it, read that part there

117

where he tells me how much he wants me, how much he needs me.'

'Juana, I do not need to read his letter. I am sure he wants you by him. He certainly does not want you here on your own when my death cannot be too far away. That letter is the result of the advice of his counsellors, who have pointed out the danger of your being crowned in his absence, and with your baby son Ferdinand as heir.'

'How dare you try to besmirch Philip's letter. Do you see nothing beyond crowns? Do you never see people with feelings; or is that too much to expect?'

'Your father and I have fought hard to build this nation. It was God's will to take Juan, our beautiful son, who would have been its king. So too did God decide to take darling Isabel and the tiny Miguel. It has fallen to you, Juana, to be the guardian of these lands, and it is breaking my heart to think that they might become nothing more than an appendage of Austria because you do not care enough to protect them. Oh, Juana, I would be lying were I to say I had not prayed constantly for you to realise where your duties lie.'

'Stop it. Stop it. You do not care about me, or my feelings; you are obsessed with your Spain. I give you one last opportunity to prove that you have a heart inside that calculating body of yours. Here is a letter from my little Charles; *I want my mother to come home, because my father is very lonely without her. The Princesses Leonor and Isabel, my sisters, send a thousand kisses to their dearest mama.*'

'I am already aware of this letter Juana. Child, I thought you had more sense than to be so easily fooled. Do you not see the hand of the schemer in this? It ends ... *please forgive the discourtesy of not writing this myself.* These are the tender bleatings of a four year old? Do not delude yourself; these are the evil machinations of your beloved Philip and his counsellors.'

Juana moved towards her mother as if to strike her, screaming, 'I hate you!'

Isabel stood and looked deep into Juana's eyes, 'Were it not for your state of mind I would not have tolerated the way you have spoken to me today. Your father will soon be joining me then all the necessary arrangements will be made for your journey to Flanders. The infant Ferdinand will remain with us.'

'Another of your schemes? To have him inherit?'

'Enough, Juana, I am tired of this. I have brought Zayda with me. She will prepare a perfumed bath for you and get rid of those stinking clothes. She might just be able to make you look and smell like a princess even though you are unable to behave like one.'

Chapter 20

Juana passed from the sun-drenched gardens, through the orangery, and into an unfamiliar corridor.

'This way, my lady?'

'Why not, Maria?' Juana replied not caring where her steps took her. She was in a world of bliss, a never ending bliss, and had been since her return to Brussels in May.

In her year's absence Philip had apparently forgotten her beauty and vivacity and he was completely intoxicated by her loveliness. He called her his "young bride" and "my Juana". Her wonderful, god-like husband loved her. Their days were a euphoria of romantic chivalry. There were tournaments, with Philip wearing her yellow and green favours, and always unseating the opposing rider. The banquets and balls were better than any she could remember. And their nights together were of unrivalled passion and ecstasy.

She froze. 'Go!' she whispered her command. She had heard voices. A sickening suspicion raced through her; an ice cold, searing hot suspicion of something she didn't want to put a name to.

As soon as she was alone she tiptoed forward and listened again leaning in the direction of a nearby door. It was Philip's voice. She moved closer her head resting against the panelling.

'Reasons of state insist that I be with her, your uncle must have explained. But Beatrice, my darling Beatrice, I have still been such a fool to neglect you so cruelly. Please say that I am forgiven.'

'I forgive you, my lord.'

'Not "my lord"; say "I forgive you, Philip".'

'I forgive you, Philip.'

Juana covered her ears and turned away to escape the stinging treachery of words that belonged to her, words spoken when she and Philip first met. She should have left but it was impossible. Nor could she throw open the door to put an end to this infamy. She was driven by something, compelled, to hear more.

'... tomorrow night, most definitely. And by that time I will know of the final arrangements for our week's hunting and where we shall stay.'

'Do you promise?'

'My word of honour. Dear God, if only we had met years ago, how different our lives would have been.'

'It is silly to look to the past, Philip, to what cannot be changed. Instead, let us be grateful to my Uncle Charles, Prince Chimay for bringing me here when he did.'

There was a silence. There was no doubting they were in each other's arms. Juana crumpled against the wall. This was Chimay's niece! Why had she been sent for? By whom? When? How many knew of this, and for how long? Why had no one told her? What was she to do? She felt sick; her world, that gloriously happy world, had crashed, irreparably broken.

Somehow she pushed herself free from the wall. Trance-like she moved back along the corridor Philip's teasing voice echoing in her ears, his rich laughing voice speaking of a love note he would hide somewhere in the garden for "beloved Beatrice".

An iron will carried Juana past courtiers and their hurtful gossip all the way back to her apartments where she collapsed to her knees, sobbing.

Zayda rushed to her side. 'My lady, whatever can have happened?'

'Ask Maria,' Juana sobbed.

Maria said nothing.

'Tell her, Maria, you must know, probably have known for some time.' Juana continued, rocking backwards and forwards in her grief.

'I was unsure. It was best for me to say nothing when I was uncertain; and I was warned not to.'

'By whom?'

'Madam Halewyn.'

So it was Halewyn as well as Chimay. Who else was in this conspiracy? 'And you would follow her instructions to further

121

betray me?'

'My lady I humbly beg your pardon, she assured me it was nothing, that the affair would be over soon enough, that it would do you more harm than good to hear of it.'

'The liar, this is no affair! Philip is in love; he loves her, prefers her to me! I heard him say so!' Juana howled.

'No, no, no, my lady, this cannot be. I am so sorry.'

'Who is she?'

'A widowed baroness. Chimay brought her here to recover from her husband's death some months ago.'

'And Philip wrote to me begging me to return. He said he missed me, wanted me. Lies, all lies! My mother was right; it was the heiress of Spain he wanted to return to Flanders, not his wife. While I quarrelled so bitterly with my mother he was in the arms of Chimay's niece. What am I to do, Zayda? I am lost.'

'Never!' Zayda knelt down by her side and took her hands. 'You are not lost. You and I will find a way to win this battle. Remember your brother's words about Juana the fighter.'

'They cannot work this time.'

'They have not failed you yet. And I have many ways of helping.'

'I must be in the garden tomorrow. I have to be there, there will be a letter.'

'Of that later, my lady. First you must sleep and gather your strength for the challenge that awaits you. I have the necessary philtres and potions. I will go for them immediately.' She shot a furious glance at Maria before leaving. 'It is barbarous that anyone, anyone at all, should dare insult the Princess Juana like this.'

There was enough sun to make sitting outdoors quite comfortable, while the shadows from the trees and bushes in the arbour protected Juana and Maria from its rays.

Juana broke the silence, 'No more sewing today, my fingers are too unsteady.' She took a final look at her embroidery. It was Philip's motto with her romantic response *QUI VOULDRA – MOI TOUT SEUL*. A bitter laugh escaped her, '"Who wants me - only me". How wonderful if that were true.'

She rose from the bench and brushed her sleeves. Maria returned the sewing to its basket before seeking out stray strands from amongst the patterns of Juana's brocade skirts.

'A short stroll, ma'am?'

They wandered along the pathway edged with box, a row of white roses beyond. Juana drew their velvet petals towards her to drink in their perfume. 'The white rose of York. The old witch finally died. Madam la Grande is one less to mock or whisper against me.'

Their skirts brushed over stone flags as they sauntered towards a cluster of red roses clinging to a wall and basking in the sunshine.

'These are my favourites, ma'am. Such a deep red, so soft to the touch and with a far superior perfume.'

'The red rose of love; its blood coloured petals at once fiery and velvety soft.' She cupped one in her hand. 'The lovely Beatrice will find the note,' she snapped off its head, 'I will find her,' a second head was snapped off, 'and then we shall see what we shall see.' The petals were ripped and tossed away.

They retraced their steps to the arbour to wait.

Within minutes Juana heard hurried footsteps. She could see perfectly without needing to move an inch from her concealed vantage point. A young lady ran towards one of the decorative urns set close to a myrtle arch and pushed her hand deep inside, drawing out a folded piece of paper. Juana watched the broad beaming smile of delight as the note was raised to her lips.

'Dear God in Heaven, You have granted her everything: beauty, a trim figure, pretty hands with slender fingers, tresses of gold, a noble birth; and now my husband.'

Juana looked on, drowning in her anguish, as the note was unfolded, greedily read then tucked inside her bodice. 'Yes, put it next to the milk-white breasts that Philip knows so well,' she screamed pouncing on her quarry, roughly snatching the note. 'I will have that. What does he say?' Her hands shook, the pulse in her throat strangled, *'My dearest Beatrice ...'*

Beatrice tore it from her grasp, hurriedly tore it and pushed the pieces into her mouth.

Juana grappled with her, snarling, 'Go ahead, I hope you choke. You harlot, how dare you steal my husband. Keep away from him, do you hear?' She pushed and pulled starting with her clothes then finding her hair.

Somehow Juana got her to the ground and sat astride her. Then her sewing scissors were in her hand. She began to cut and hack at the golden curls ignoring the terrified eyes staring at her and the open mouth unable to utter a sound. The frenzied scissors scratched and tore at flesh as well as hair and blood streamed from each new wound.

Her task completed Juana stood up to consider her work.

'You may go, baroness, this lesson will serve as a reminder to stay well away from Philip.'

Maria had not moved. She was like stone unable to go to the aid of either lady. She remained as if paralysed as Beatrice struggled to her feet to go stumbling blindly over the flagstones. She stood motionless watching as Juana left the garden as serenely as she would a ballroom floor.

'Maria, I think it would be marvellous to have one of Zayda's special baths. The perfumed oils will work their usual magic on Philip.'

Chapter 21

The water was ready and Zayda was adding the first of the oils when Philip arrived accompanied by some friends. He looked with distaste at the slave before going to her collection of phials to send them crashing to the floor.

'Get out! I am tired of this sorcery. I want you out of the palace, out of Flanders, now!'

Zayda slipped quickly through the group of gentlemen and ladies gathered in the doorway.

Philip turned on Juana, 'You damned fool. Whatever possessed you? She could so easily have been blinded. The doctors are with her now. For your sake I pray her face will not be scarred permanently,' he raged. 'God knows when she will recover from the shock let alone the wounds. You are crazy, can you even begin to think of what you have done?'

This was not how Juana had planned it. She had expected the girl to flee the court, embarrassed, to find a place to hide far away never to return. That, she knew from experience, was what always happened in Spain. Every time her mother discovered one of Ferdinand's mistresses, the girl was quickly dismissed from the court; offered a palace somewhere far away; found a husband; and the whole business forgotten. Nor had Juana considered the possibility of this woman making the incident public knowledge, or of herself being called upon to account for her actions, Queen Isabel had never been faced with such an obligation. Nevertheless; if she must, she could.

She took a deep breath and began, forcing her words above the deafening noise of her pounding heart, 'My lord, I would say two things. First, you have changed the rules of the game; you were not supposed to love. You have played me false with this strumpet. Second, she dared to defy me, refusing to give me, Princess Juana, the letter. Naturally I had to punish her.'

'No hint of sorrow madam? No repentance for your actions?' he snarled.

'No, and I wonder you should ask. She got no more than she deserved,' she replied head held high.

He took her by the shoulders and began shaking her violently, yelling his hatred for her and his love for his mistress.

Her strength, her conviction in the rightness of her actions, her refusal to accept any culpability, was crumbling, 'I will share your body if I must, but please do not ask me ever to share your heart,' she pleaded.

'I tell you now that unless you go and apologise to her immediately, you may forget my having anything whatsoever to do with you ever again.'

'Never! The little whore got no more than she deserved, and royalty never apologises to harlots,' she retorted, her courage returned.

He swung his fist into her face. She crumpled to the floor. With a voice still strong and determined she continued, 'No matter what you do or say, I will not apologise. I will not have any woman try to take what is mine. And let them all be mindful that I would do the same again, or worse, should they dare.'

'Such fitting behaviour for a queen, you see what I have to tolerate? A wild beast in my home. Well, unless the beast is tamed it will not be permitted any freedom. Take her to her room and lock the door. I will decide who is to be allowed in or out.'

He watched her with undisguised loathing as she rose, wiped the blood from her mouth, stood tall and raised her proud chin.

Philip beckoned to Moxica, 'Come here my man. I have decided that there is something far more important for you to do than keeping the household accounts. Yes, I think from now on your duty will be to keep a detailed account of this mad woman's behaviour. It should make good reading in Spain. It will help them make a fair judgement on the mental state of their dear princess, the person they would have inherit the throne.'

Juana wiped more blood from her mouth before taking a long, icy look at Moxica. 'Ah, the turncoat; I have no doubt you have been longing for just such an opportunity. I know you will carry out the task to perfection. You choose well, Philip, since such a professed enemy of mine will surely lack neither inspiration nor dedication in the words he writes.'

She curtsied to Philip and walked proudly to her chamber.

'Lock the door, and see it remains locked until such time as I order otherwise. Gentlemen, ladies, you will report any incident, however trivial, to Moxica. That is a command. Now I must get back to Beatrice.'

Chapter 22

On a cool spring morning of 1505 Juana formally received an important delegation from Spain.

'Your royal highness; Fonseca, Conchillos and Ferreira.'

The three gentlemen came from King Ferdinand with instructions to discuss matters of grave urgency with Juana, and only Juana. He had chosen his emissaries with care, she knew them and would trust them: his personal secretary, Conchillos; Fonseca; and Ferreira, who had escorted her on her return journey to Flanders.

They entered, bowed then knelt one after the other to kiss the hands of their new queen.

Fonseca under his priestly demeanour carried troubled thoughts of their last encounter in Medina when Juana had threatened him with torture and death once she was queen. 'Your Highness, Queen Juana of Castile, we come to swear allegiance and to offer our condolences on the death of Her Highness, Queen Isabel.'

'She died in her beloved town of Medina,' she looked at him, raising her eyebrows. 'Not a favourite of ours, perhaps?' There was lightness in her voice telling him that the incident was to be forgotten and their friendship restored. 'I said such dreadful things to her, things a daughter should never say to her mother; her last memory of me would be ...'

Fonseca interrupted, 'She fully understood your problems ma'am. And notices received in Spain since your return here increased her sympathies towards you. However, it still remained her fervent prayer that she could rely on you to continue her mission for Spain, to strengthen it, to protect it, to preserve it ...'

'How is my son Prince Ferdinand?' Juana would hear no more; as far as she was concerned everything had been arranged according to her mother's will.

'He is well, and doted upon by his grandfather.'

'And here come my other children.'

The three little ones moved slowly towards their mother and the important visitors, their steps a mixture of studied dignity, awe and, for the tiniest one, shyness.

Charles, walking with measured step, so proud of all his five years, was dressed in a red velvet tunic, black hose and a black velvet bonnet with an upturned brim. He was every inch a little prince.

His sisters followed. Leonor seven and Isabel almost four were dressed alike in dark blue, but while Leonor walked demurely and quite grown up with her hands resting on the front panel of her dress, her little sister toddled along firmly holding a doll, which should have been left in her room, but instead was half hidden behind her. Tears misted Fonseca's eyes as he watched them. These were the fruit of a stormy marriage, the offspring of a tormented young woman who was the gossip of every court in Europe. Leonor, so gentle, perhaps too serious for her years, Isabel a delight with her plump little cheeks and sparkling blue eyes, her face framed by a white coif; the doll held by its neck and pushed into the folds of her skirt.

He turned back to Charles, the leader of this enchanting group, a young version of Philip including the arrogance. This little fellow would one day be the ruler of all Spain, the Holy Roman Empire, Austria, the Netherlands and more; he might also marry the French princess; and he walked as if fully aware of all the riches and power awaiting him.

When sufficient time had been given for the various expected compliments and by almost too much time pretending to understand the young Charles' speech, which was virtually incoherent, the children were ushered from the room.

Fonseca asked, 'Ma'am, why is it that you so often refuse to see your children?'

'Because I am embarrassed to see them; they know I am a prisoner.'

'A prisoner? With respect, my lady, you have often sought solace in seclusion, finding peace in the quiet of your chamber.'

'My only useful strategy, you mean?' Juana shook her head, 'No, I am talking about Philip having me placed behind locked doors. I am talking about a guard at the door lest I escape.'

Fonseca, along with most of Europe, knew of Philip's infidelity, of his violence towards her, of confining her to her apartments because of the attack on a lady of the court. He knew the contents of Moxica's infamous diaries diligently despatched to Spain detailing her refusal to eat, change her clothing, sleep in her bed, and flying into rages against those who were her oppressors.

'But we do not find you a prisoner ma'am. There are no guards at the door.'

'Very easily explained; because my mother is dead and Philip has seen fit to set me free, to pretend that all is well between us. Without me he cannot inherit, so he has decided that my health is of the utmost importance. He also seeks to show the world that we live in harmony; hence my pregnancy.'

'It grieves me to hear such bitterness.'

She took his hands and squeezed them reassuringly, 'Do not be so sad my friend, I am a survivor. Gentlemen, you have other business?'

It had fallen to Conchillos to urge Juana to give her father her unqualified support; in writing. He withdrew a paper from his leather pouch. 'King Ferdinand has sent me to seek your written support.'

Juana read the letter, 'I see no problem. The Cortes has already sworn allegiance to my father as governor, stating he may even hold the regency, if necessary until our son Charles has reached his twentieth year.'

'Unfortunately there are those who are beginning to show dissent. Some of the grandees are still angry about the confiscation of their land.'

'Land that belonged to the Crown!'

Conchillos hurried on, 'Be that as it may Philip's envoy is offering to return their lands if they support Philip against Ferdinand. And their number is growing. You will vouch for this Ferreira.'

'It is true.'

'How could they be so mercenary? What must I do? There must be no doubting my intentions to have my father rule as regent.'

Conchillos sighed with relief. Juana would comply with

Ferdinand's request, and he would be unequivocally recognised as regent. 'We need a signed affirmation of King Ferdinand's regency and a mandate granting him any additional powers he deems necessary.'

'It shall be done immediately. My father must have the authority to protect the crown and the country for me and for my son. I expect nothing less than the full support of the Cortes.'

She wrote swiftly, the quill scratching her determination vigorously across the page. Conchillos beamed his satisfaction; he sanded the ink then carefully folded the paper and put it deep into his pouch.

Juana was curious, 'My lord bishop do you not have something to say?'

'No ma'am, I do not. I am saddened by so many recent events, wearied by so many rumours, sickened by endless politicking. My heart aches for quiet.'

'And am I to be turned comforter while you are to be comforted?' She put her hands out towards him.

He knelt to kiss them, 'Pray God that Spain will soon be at peace with itself.'

'Amen to that.'

'We must be on our way,' Conchillos sounded agitated. 'The sooner we are gone from here ...'

Ferreira tut-tutted, 'I hope you were not thinking to leave before having an audience with King Philip?'

'Why no ...' he blustered.

'King Philip is returning from his hunting trip and should be here later today.'

'Well then, all the better.' Juana knew that while haste was important protocol demanded that they have an audience with Philip, so his early return was fortunate. It was odd, nonetheless, that he should cut short his beloved hunting.

131

Chapter 23

It was early evening when they were informed of Philip's arrival and told to await him in the small reception salon. Their conversation was awkward, kept alive by Juana describing and explaining the features in the backgrounds of the several portraits of Philip, herself, and the three children. Then she talked of the books in the growing library, of which she was very proud, covering an entire wall, inviting them to look at whatever was of interest be it music, poetry, nature.

Then Philip appeared and walked very slowly towards them leaving guards posted at the door.

Juana's confidence, already weakening, vanished. 'Sir, you have returned so soon, I had no idea ...'

'My lady, there are several things about which you have no idea. For example you probably do not realise that I know why these men are here,' he advanced on Conchillos, 'and that I know that you are Conchillos, secretary to Ferdinand. I am also reliably informed that you carry on your person a very important letter.'

'Letter my lord?'

'Ferreira. Remind him of the letter.'

Juana gazed at Ferreira in disbelief.

'My master requires the letter you carry,' Ferreira held out his hand.

Juana stepped towards him, 'I would remind you Ferreira that the letter under discussion is mine. Philip, I have written to my father reaffirming the mandate he was given by my mother's will. I also give permission for him to take any additional measures as and when they are needed; my father has my complete trust and support. There is nothing more to be said.'

Philip's harsh laughter filled the room, 'Dear God, the famous will. Ferdinand has repeated it often enough to the Cortes, especially that part ... *if Juana is incapable of understanding how to govern.* You see, that and the extracts from Moxica's diary of your bizarre behaviour have done an excellent job of convincing the Cortes that you are indeed totally unfit to rule. You fool, you have written a letter of abdication; duped by your own trusted father into handing him Castile!'

'You are wrong. I am his daughter and I know he intends nothing more than to keep the country in good order. There are some who would bring it to ruin, and those few dissidents must be defeated; to do so my father requires absolute power and I will provide it.'

'One or two dissidents?' Philip snorted. 'It is quite the reverse. He can only rely on one or two friends. Ferdinand is lost without your support. More importantly we will be lost if you give it. The letter, Conchillos.'

Conchillos unbuckled his pouch and handed over the letter.

'Burn it, Ferreira. Guards, take Conchillos to the cells; see that he gets the punishment appropriate for traitors.'

Juana watched the flames devouring every word of her royal command.

'We will not lose Castile,' Philip grabbed her wrist. 'I have another letter that you have written to the Cortes.'

Juana looked for Fonseca. She needed his help; she didn't know what to do. But Fonseca had gone. She hoped he had rushed away, to return to Spain without delay to tell her father what had happened.

She sat in the chair and listened to "her" letter.

Philip read, '*Sirs, I am writing to defend myself against those who accuse me of lacking in mental powers. Moxica's diaries were sent to my father to justify my husband's actions against me and the contents should have remained private; it is a family matter. People who continue to believe that I am unable to rule can rest assured that should this be true I would transfer the government of all the realms that I possess not to my father, but to my husband, and to him alone because of the love I have for him. Also I have no intention of granting any land or power to my son Charles so long as my husband lives. Dictated in Brussels this third day of May, 1505. I, the Queen.* Sign it,' Philip ordered.

She snatched it from his hands and tore it to shreds. 'I refuse. You betrayed me to the world with your infamous diary and now you are worried that because of it you will lose Castile. And you would have me lie to help you? Never!'

'No matter, I have another. You will sign. You have just begun to enjoy your freedom. It would be sad to lose it again. You have the choice of joining me and sharing in my fortunes, or disappearing, locked away for good.'

Again she refused, so he picked up the quill and forged her signature.

'You win, my lord, but the game is not over yet, take care you do not celebrate too soon.'

'We have done well, Ferreira. This letter and my instructions to the Cortes not to make any decisions until our arrival leave us free to concentrate on the organisation of the voyage. Juana,' he shook his head at her, 'you have proven yourself untrustworthy. From now on no one who speaks Spanish will be allowed anywhere near you, apart from your chaplain; and you will be confined to your apartments. I also think that more isolated accommodation for you would be appropriate.'

He left her desperately trying to cope with "disappearing, locked away for good" and "more isolated accommodation".

Chapter 24

Juana, her chaplain and Madam Halewyn sat in the intense quiet of her salon as they had done every evening for the last two weeks.

Night was gathering beyond the group of three arched windows and the candles and flickering firelight did their best to add a gentle glow to a room too dark with its sombre tapestries. So often her refuge in the past, this time her room offered no comfort. These walls were no longer her protection; they were her prison as she awaited her final sentence.

From time to time the chaplain turned the pages of his missal; Madam Halewyn's needle stabbed its way along a length of linen; Juana glanced from one to the other then down at her still unopened book. The silence suffocated her.

'Father, do you suppose that Philip's words were no more than idle threats?' Juana's voice shook as she asked the question she had asked every day.

'Put your trust in God as I do, my lady.' The priest removed his spectacles and his eyes smiled kindly at her.

Madam Halewyn thrust her sewing down onto her lap, furious that she could not understand their Spanish.

'And what is the news on my father's secretary?'

'Conchillos is recovering and may soon be well enough to return to Spain.'

'What they did to him is unforgivable. He is crippled for life. If they treated him so ill, what might they do to me?' She ran to the window, pulling it open, inviting a wave of cold air to wash over her.

In the street below, lit by a row of torches in their iron sconces, a group of men, some with torches, were making their way to the palace gates.

'Come quickly, Father. Who are those men?'

He came to join her, as did Madam Halewyn.

'I see soldiers and …'

'Ah, Chimay! At last!' Madam Halewyn sounded relieved.

Juana threw her hands to her head, 'So, they have come to

take me?'

Madam Halewyn nodded, looked down her long thin nose and announced with a certain satisfaction, 'It could well be they have found a suitable place of seclusion. You will then be declared mad, leaving Philip free to marry.' She walked briskly across the room to open the door.

The priest fell to his knees; and Juana, after a moment or two, shrugged off both her fear and Halewyn's vicious words and walked with purpose to the fireplace to take up a defiant posture.

Chimay and the Captain of the Guard appeared in the doorway and stood for a moment before advancing into the room. Chimay bowed.

This was Juana's moment. She grabbed a poker. 'Get out of here!' she shouted, cleaving the air about her before finally bringing her weapon down hard on his shoulder. He screamed and was gone, the captain retreating with him.

'I will kill them all if necessary! Help me, Father.'

Soldiers filled the doorway, but she held them at bay as brave as any knight. 'Am I such a bad woman to warrant so many guards?' she demanded wielding her "sword" in defiance.

'Bad woman?' Chimay's voice issued from a place of safety behind the soldiers where he nursed his injury, 'The world will judge. But you can be sure that all Spain will hear of this.'

Juana called back, 'I think not, for you would be accused of treachery, daring to enter the presence of the queen with armed soldiers.'

'Well done, my lady, your fighting spirit has returned!' The chaplain, still on his knees, looked absurdly jubilant.

Chimay, holding his painful shoulder, pushed his way through his men and glowered down at him. 'Get out priest! In future you will only come here to say mass, nothing more and then you will leave. Out!'

'Ayeee …' Juana doubled over, her hands clutching at her belly. 'My baby, I am losing my baby. Halewyn get me Maria, immediately, I need her returned to the court; she must be at my side.' She writhed, her face contorted with pain, 'Someone tell Philip. And I need the doctors, quick! Oh, no, I must not lose my child.'

Heavy boots and relayed orders were heard echoing down corridors. The priest dragged himself to his feet to come to her aid, Juana stumbled towards him, and they fell to their knees together.

'Pray for me, Father.'

The chaplain began, 'God have mercy on us, hear us ...'

Juana interrupted, 'First you must know what to pray for. Ask God to forgive my lies. There is nothing amiss with the child in my womb. I simply could not think of anything better.'

Chapter 25

'Get those whores off the ship! We do not sail until every last one of them is ashore!' she screamed; and she meant it.

Juana stood on the quayside fuming. Philip had dared to appoint "ladies-in-waiting" for her.

'These are your ladies,' Philip insisted.

'Maria will suffice until I am in Castile when I can choose decent, honest ladies. I refuse to suffer the indignity of having your Flemish mistresses anywhere near me.'

Swallowing his ire, and conforming to his counsellors' advice to pander to her every whim until once they were underway (he had already dismissed Moxica for this very same reason) he agreed; although swearing his innocence, insisting he was being misjudged.

With undisguised disgust she watched them disembark then she boarded the Juliana. She was going to Spain to be crowned Queen of Castile. Never having wanted the crown and indeed still not wanting it, the fact that it was hers promised deliverance.

Watching the coastline shrinking and disappearing she waved a last farewell to the country that had brought her happiness but even greater sadness, misery, and finally fear. Ten years ago she had arrived here as a young bride, come to meet her husband, and her silly romantic notions had tricked her into falling in love with someone unworthy. Today he was her enemy, finding her very existence so unspeakably intolerable that he entertained thoughts of imprisoning her, having her declared mad, divorcing her and remarrying.

Her only sadness at this moment was that her children, including the new infant Maria, were not travelling with them. Hopefully it wouldn't be too long before they would be sent to her; in the meantime her widowed sister-in-law Margaret would take great care of them.

She thought of Maximilian and how she would be forever

grateful to him for spending the last few months with her. If only Philip had been granted but half of his father's understanding and compassion, she thought, then chided herself for even contemplating the idea. There was no way of salvaging so ruptured a relationship however much she loved him. Maximilian; she brought her thoughts back to her father-in-law. She was still riding high on a crest of happiness from the many delightful times shared with him.

First there was Maria's christening in November. She smiled, remembering how Maximilian having finally consented to be godfather regretted it the moment the child was put in his arms. Maximilian, with the stature of a Greek warrior, shook in fear and trembling lest this tiny baby in its billowing masses of lace and silk be crushed in his arms or slide through them and crash to the floor.

She remembered her brilliant performance at the soiree for her twenty-sixth birthday that same month. Resounding applause erupted when she came to the end of her programme of pieces for the vihuela. Maximilian then brought the Venetian ambassador forward to be presented, who, at the end of the evening exclaimed his amazement that one so young and beautiful should be so accomplished, have such intellect, wit, prudence, grace, charm. Everyone knew how Venetians loved to flatter, and the ambassador excelled them all with his superlatives. But no matter; he had praised her in the presence of a large gathering. It had been so long since anyone had done so.

'So much for my being crazy, Chimay,' she announced to the faint indigo strip of land which was all that remained of the Low Countries.

January was not the best month to be travelling by sea but a journey through France had been ruled out as Philip and Louis apparently were no longer allies and, sure enough, within hours of their departure they were ploughing through the wind and heavy seas of a very wintry English Channel.

Juana was in her cabin choosing the rings and brooches that best suited her green velvet dress.
She studied herself in her hand mirror. Despite the storm Maria had succeeded in making her look as if ready for some grand

139

function rather than simply to join her husband for a few moments. That was Juana's plan, to let Philip know that neither he nor the storm would intimidate her.

She made her way unsteadily to the door. The wind was relentless; the waves buffeted the sides of the ship, hurling drenching showers over her as she made the few steps to her husband's stateroom.

The hot, vile stench that burst from Philip's cabin as the door opened made her reel and she hurriedly found a handkerchief to hold over her nose and mouth. The pride of Flemish manhood were vomiting and pissing themselves in their terror; jerkins, breeches, boots and floor were all splattered and stained. There were groans, weeping, retching.

In one corner two gentlemen slapped each other's face trading blow for blow with ever increasing ferocity. Juana briefly took the handkerchief from her face to inquire about their strange behaviour.

'Your highness, I thought that by trying to be like Christ, who turned the other cheek, God would have mercy on me in this dread hour, so I invited my friend to strike my face, then I turned my cheek to invite the second slap. Then I thought that he would like to seek God's mercy in the same way, so I hit him. He, not caring to be slapped, retaliated so to speak.'

'And there you are,' she laughed, 'a more perfect pair of fools I am never likely to see.'

The ship shuddered, heaving violently to one side throwing everyone and everything into turmoil. Juana held on to a stanchion to steady herself, watching the gallants sink to their knees, slithering in their own filth, howling, 'Sweet Virgins of Guadalupe and Montserrat, pray for us ...,' making outrageous promises of monies and miraculously reformed characters if God would spare them.

A sailor pushed the door slightly ajar to shout that the yardarm and sail of the main mast had broken free and were pulling the ship down, but that a brave lad was fighting to cut the sail free and the disaster might yet be averted.

Philip roused himself from his state of paralysing terror, releasing his white-knuckled grasp on the leather pouch containing farewell letters to his children to tuck it securely inside his doublet. 'I offer the Virgin of Guadalupe double my weight in gold in return for my salvation,' he called out. He removed his hat, put several gold coins in it then ordered his page to go amongst the company for their votive offerings.

Eventually the hat was brought to Juana, she studied the heap of gold and silver then pulled open the strings to her purse. It was so long since she had carried a purse or indeed had ever possessed any money to warrant having a purse at all. With the utmost care she sought amongst the coins. Once discovered and retrieved, one very small silver coin was placed gently in the hat. There was incredulity all around her.

'It will be enough. You see, royal people never drown.' She had told her uncle that many years ago, and it was true. 'I shall have need of my money when we reach land.'

Philip, her cruel gaoler was by now reduced to a whimpering, frightened child and she longed to cradle him in her arms. Instead she could only watch as two servants busily fitted him with a life jacket. It was an entire goatskin sealed with pitch and covered in cloths of yellow, red, green, and white. It had bells, it had ribbons; no popinjay ever looked so fabulous. Across the back written in the boldest of letters was *King Philip*. Once inflated by his two men all red-faced and puffed-cheeked, the thing looked completely bizarre.

'Oh, Philip, what little faith you have.' She pulled her cloak tight about herself and left the cabin, stumbling through the driving rain and the seas breaking over the gunwales; struggling against the heaving deck covered in surging water; finally fighting the buffeting wind to climb to the forecastle. Once there she took her stance, to face the storm – and defy it.

After a while from out of the din of the gale and the thunderous cracking of timbers she heard cries of, 'He's done it.' Cheers joined forces with the roar and racket of the storm. Juana peered through the lashing rain and could just make out, silhouetted against the boiling seas, the damaged yardarm freed of its sail being heaved down onto the deck.

Then the wind seemed not to blow so loud or hard, the seas perhaps not so high and men willingly set themselves with renewed vigour to their tasks. Juana returned to her cabin content that order was being restored.

By dawn more benign winds were directing the dispersed

flotilla, not towards the Bay of Biscay but towards an unwanted but necessary refuge; England.

Everyone was on deck; never had land looked so beautiful, so solid, so inviting. About the Juliana in the gentle swell other ships hove into view. A sense of victory and rejoicing pervaded.

Philip, much recovered but still pale and drawn, publicly decorated the young lad who had saved their lives by so bravely risking his own. He pinned the badge of his elite group of bodyguards on his very proud chest. The young Scot could barely believe his good fortune; his future would be secure and extremely well paid.

A newly appointed counsellor emerged from the crowded deck to engage Philip in an urgent conversation. Juana recognised him; it was Juan Manuel, once her mother's envoy. He was another of those eager to join Philip, undoubtedly seeking gifts of land once in Spain. She drifted towards them, curious. He seemed to be repeatedly insisting that Philip refuse to surrender someone to King Henry; to consider the consequences. Philip was looking increasingly uneasy with every word. She brushed closer wearing the broadest of smiles.

'I know I must be in Spain as soon as possible, but this is a heaven sent opportunity for me. I can visit my dear sister Catalina. And yes, I can renew my acquaintance with Henry!'

That stopped their conversation, which pleased her not a little; and she moved on.

Their landing at Weymouth still had to be negotiated. The coast was lined with terrified Englishmen and their womenfolk; everyone armed. Mounted soldiers with pikes, men with arquebuses raised, farmers with scythes and pitchforks, women with brooms, all were ready to stand fast against the threatened invasion.

The foreigners' presence was fortunately successfully explained and they were allowed to disembark. Firearms were set aside, brooms leaned on and the good people of Weymouth gazed open mouthed at the elegant gentleman, his beautiful wife and their equally splendidly dressed friends.

Horses had to be found and a small group of worthy citizens chosen to accompany a delegation from these foreign visitors to Windsor, to inform the king of their presence, to seek his protection, and be given permission to remain in England whilst repairs were carried out to the damaged ships.

Chapter 26

Juana was summoned to the king's presence in mid February. Philip had been there for several days. He had lied about her health, saying she was too ill to travel, while he, of course, had been enjoying his role of king of Castile.

Her small party rode into the courtyard of Windsor Castle. Lord Mountjoy, her host for the past week or so helped her down from her horse. He kissed her hand then moved aside; Maria gave her mistress a swift inspection; she was ready.

The king and his family, and Philip, were gathering on the steps. Henry left them to come down to welcome her. Her eyes lit up for she instantly recognised the gentleman who, several years earlier, was "the king's representative" in a town called Portsmouth. He was still that same gentleman neither tall nor short, neither fat nor thin, with dark eyes; but he looked tired, older. He had sunken temples, his lips seemed thinner, and his eyes had lost their lustre and had narrowed into a myopic squint. He offered her his bony hand and smiled a smile of welcome, the warmest of welcomes; a smile of pleasure in seeing her once more.

'I thank you my lord king for the honour of being called to your presence.' Juana curtsied deeply and kissed his hand.

He kissed her hands as one monarch showing respect to another. 'The honour is all mine, Queen Juana, having your grace and beauty adorn our home.'

'Ten years have passed since last you flattered me. Your words, now as then, are music to my ears.' She surprised herself at her boldness but instantly excused it, it was the excitement of the moment.

'And is your health quite restored? I have been concerned.' Henry obviously knew that Philip had ordered her to be detained somewhere far from Windsor, hence this royal command for her presence.

'If ill health was the reason for my absence, then I must admit to being completely recovered.'

They exchanged smiles.

'Now you must meet my family.'

Prince Henry, a handsome, elegant youth clad in scarlet was introduced. He was tall, much taller than his father and only fourteen years old. This was Henry, Prince of Wales, the future husband of her sister Catalina.

Next to him was his sister, Princess Mary, ten years old, and beside her ... how her heart leapt as Henry introduced her as Catherine, Princess of Wales. Just to hear her name gladdened her. Catalina; her little twelve year old sister was now a woman of twenty-one, with an English name; Catherine.

They hugged then looked at one another crying tears of joy; two sisters dressed in black, holding hands, reminded for a moment of happier times before there were any tragedies, rough justice, and maltreatment.

Last of all there was Philip. Juana gave him but a hint of a curtsey. He bowed nursing his displeasure at seeing her.

The following evening Philip ushered her through a side door into a room of dark oak and grey stone walls covered with shields and banners.

Henry was taken aback when they were announced, 'Is this meeting to be a secret?'

'Probably only so far as certain Flemish counsellors are concerned I would suggest,' Juana replied. 'But that story would take too long to tell.'

He led her to a large table littered with documents. Her name was added to several agreements drawn up and signed by Henry and Philip while she was "indisposed" at the home of Lord Mountjoy. As she wrote *Yo, la reina, Juana* she could feel Philip's irritation that Henry had insisted on her signature.

To her the papers were of no great importance. The first two were marriage treaties: their son Charles was now offered as husband to Henry's daughter Mary (the contract with Princess Claudia of France now abrogated); Philip's recently widowed sister Margaret as bride for King Henry. As anyone knew treaties of this nature were usually broken at some point or other, that of Charles being a prime example, and no doubt these would suffer the same fate. The other agreements were mostly to do with trade and their only interest for Juana lay in the aggravation it caused Philip. But there was one not requiring her signature which did give her some degree of pleasure. Philip was surrendering to Henry a pretender to the English throne; somebody or other belonging to the house of York who Madam la Grande had apparently been sheltering and grooming for years, and who, since her death had remained in Flanders. This would be a wonderfully bitter blow to Juan Manuel after all those earnest words with Philip on board the Juliana.

And that evening they celebrated with a grand banquet in the great hall. The royal green and white Tudor livery dominated the magnificence of the tapestries and wall hangings. The silver and gold dishes gleamed their brilliance on the whitest of damask tablecloths covering the long tables set out on three sides of the room. The hundred guests in their various coloured robes added further to the splendour. The minstrels in the gallery filled the air with a majestic fanfare.

King Henry led Juana on his arm, enjoying the moment. This was the first time since the death of his wife that he had had the opportunity to escort a lady, and such a lovely lady too. Juana was an excited mixture of pride for the recognition of her status and the sheer delight of being in Henry's company.

During the meal she was given the honour of granting approval to each dish as it was ceremoniously presented before being carried to the serving boards: chicken pasties, venison in orange sauce, roast pork in spiced wine, and huge meat pies with pastry cases in the form of birds or animals. Subtleties were carried in, some borne aloft, as table cloths were changed between courses. And finally the desserts: the pastries, fruits, almond lumbarde, pine nut candy and marzipan; all crafted as castles, lions, eagles. Best of all was the one resembling their own ship, the Juliana.

She clapped her hands with joy and was starting to thank Henry, when Philip's voice could be heard rising above the music and all the other conversations. He was telling such a tale of his heroism throughout those terrible storms at sea. His listener, the young prince, was sitting wide-eyed and open-mouthed in awe and wonder.

Henry laid his hand on hers whispering, 'I must admit that it is a most interesting tale, that of the Juliana; I do like the way it improves with each telling.'

Dancing followed but Juana declined all requests, preferring to watch, occasioning Henry to ask if she was perhaps still a little unwell. She explained that there were times when she found the crush and noise of large gatherings overpowering, but that she was more than happy to watch others.

She remarked how well Catalina and Mary danced together.

Henry answered, 'True, but wait until you see Mary dance with her brother, they make an extremely fine pair.'

Mary asked her brother Henry to dance with her in the very next dance, and Catalina approached Philip to invite him to partner her.

He looked icily at Catalina and answered, 'What you see before you ma'am is a simple sailor. What makes you think a humble man of the sea would know anything of dancing?' And he had walked away leaving her sister standing alone; embarrassed.

Henry had also witnessed the rebuff and urged her, 'Do go to Catherine.'

Juana and Catalina were at last together. 'Look at us, two sad looking crows amongst the gay songbirds.'

Catalina replied, 'At least you have chosen to wear black, I wear it because it is the most serviceable colour. This is my only good dress, and it has cost me several bracelets. You see, King Henry has stopped my allowance. I used to get one hundred crowns a week but now I receive nothing. I am reduced to selling my silver plate to pay for my small household.'

Juana sighed and shook her head. 'And yet Henry is so kind. I know of many instances of his generosity, he even gave brother Tomas money when he travelled to Flanders.'

'Since the death of Arthur it is as if I am a nobody. Henry and our father argue continually about my unpaid dowry. And now father never answers my letters.'

'The first thing I shall do when I get to Spain is to speak with father to arrange for whatever is outstanding to be sent immediately, I promise. And should there be any delay I will personally arrange some help for you. Oh, Catalina, how things have changed since that evening in mother's apartments when your view of a grown-up's world was all "prettiness".'

147

'I shall be forever grateful. But tell me of yourself. I think you should know there have been many unkind stories about you.'

'There is nothing you could say that would surprise me. The stories are not only unkind but untrue. The problem for my enemies is that I am a survivor. I admit that sometimes I have to resort to strategies frowned upon, usually passive resistance but on occasions, shall we say I become more actively involved.'

'The gossip which excited people the most was with regard to your bathing.'

'My refusal to bath certainly was a part of my campaign, but …'

'Lord, no, the English were disgusted by the frequency of them. You may not know, but in this country bathing is actively discouraged. They say it weakens a person's whole system.'

They burst into laughter at the absurdity of the notion. Henry looked at them, his attention arrested by Juana's radiant face; and his anger increased. Philip and his followers, especially Juan Manuel, were all liars; Juana was not the half-crazed creature they repeatedly referred to.

Juana was still laughing; remembering. 'You may be too young to remember the time when mother refused to change her chemise until the Moors of Granada were defeated. Perhaps it was the smell that made them surrender!'

Catalina joined her in her laughter until Philip interrupted, 'You seem to have plenty to laugh and talk about.'

'Indeed we do,' Juana answered. 'I would invite you to join us, but your manners are in sore need of education. In fact until you have learned how to behave towards a lady I think it best that you remove that blue velvet ribbon from your leg. Had King Henry realised that a real "humble sailor" could show far more respect than you he may have thought twice about creating you Knight of the Garter. My sister awaits an apology.'

Chapter 27

Catalina and Juana stayed on at Windsor for a few more days then one bright Saturday morning they left, going their separate ways. Catalina travelled to Richmount, Juana to Lord Arundel's home to be close to the reassembled fleet in nearby Falmouth.

It was now April, and Juana still awaited Philip's arrival that they might be on their way. She was impatient to be with her father, with her own people. But not before she had made Philip aware that there were some things she was no longer prepared to tolerate. And she promised herself that she would not lose her argument by raising her voice; she would be dignified, reasoned. She had waited a month for this confrontation and would not have it ruined by losing her temper.

In the early hours of the evening she heard the horses.

She and Maria were apparently absorbed in their reading. Juana's book rested open on her lap; she would at least give the appearance of composure even if she did not feel it. When he stormed through the door complaining, as she knew he must, she would at least look calm riding the wave of anger until it was her turn to speak.

Predictably, he fumed his way towards her followed by friends as angry as himself. 'Well, this time your father really has upset the apple cart. Gone and married the French king's niece after all. Put himself in a sorry situation in Castile. Not many friends left there now, for sure; and he is very misguided if he thinks that he and Louis can do anything about it. If they start anything I have two thousand skilled soldiers with me and expert advisors ...' he spat out.

'Philip, we will not comment on events we only know from a third party, or which may be purely speculation. I prefer to wait until we are in a position to assess the situation at first hand.'

'Dear God,' he scoffed, asking of Juan Manuel, 'You hear the voice of wisdom?'

'A gem of intellect and diplomacy as ever, my lord ...'

Juana interrupted quietly, ignoring the insults, 'I refuse to hear more of it. But I would speak on matters of more immediate importance which must be taken very seriously. These friends of yours, and that includes you Don Manuel, did right to press you with their concerns about your promises of titles and pots of gold. Their worries were justified; I shall not permit any more of Castile's wealth to pass into their hands. I would also warn you that plans to have me locked away ...' she continued to address them quietly, 'yes, I have heard them all, would not be tolerated by my people. There is no one outside your own circle who believes a word any of you say, and to dare to repeat such treason will be punished accordingly.'

She closed her book, laid it down on the table at her side, rested her hands on the arms of her chair, and still speaking with measured tone she continued, 'I also want you to know that I will not go anywhere near our fleet until those Flemish whores are returned to Flanders. It was unbecoming of you, my lord, to conspire to deceive me so. I had assumed, obviously incorrectly, that they had been dismissed before we left Flanders, yet you had merely found accommodation for them aboard other ships. How can my people have any confidence in a foreign sovereign who has proven by acts of falsehood that he is untrustworthy? Sir, they will see you as a cheat and a liar.' Her chin was thrust forward, her head held high, her hazel eyes burning with indignation as she rose and approached her offending husband.

He had been caught completely off guard; he was supposed to be the accuser not the accused. He was about to thunder, to strike, then stopped. He dismissed everyone from the room.

'This requires immediate attention,' insisted Juan Manuel waving a large piece of paper in his direction.

'And that is my intention. Patience, Manuel. Go.'

The document was left on a table. It was a promissory note for the two hundred thousand gold crowns borrowed from Henry to meet the expenses of their stay in England, for repairs to the ships, and to pay the wages of Philip's soldiers. It required Juana's signature as Queen of Castile. Until it was signed they would not be permitted to leave.

He approached her with a voice he knew would captivate. 'Read this note Prince Henry has sent me. While you charmed the old Henry, I impressed the young one. See where it says ... *let me know of your returned health which with all my heart I desire* ... and here, ... *I pray God give you, most high, most excellent and mighty prince, a good life and a long one ... your humble cousin* ... If only my Juana would be so warm towards me. I received no word from you while I was ill.' He brought his face down to hers, pressed his cheek against hers, 'I know I have ignored you my dearest. Perhaps I have even been a little unkind to my darling. But these have been difficult days for me Juana; I have had much to concern me. King Henry is a cunning negotiator. I have been made to wait until the pretender Suffolk was safely landed from Flanders and handed over, as if Henry thought my word was not to be trusted. I think that was what made me unwell. I was also unwisely counselled to appear as a hard man, a man of iron. Henry was right; I should have shown you more consideration. I have been such a fool, but I shall make amends, my dear heart.'

Juana turned from him and returned to her chair, not wanting to be tricked by the voice she still loved, 'You offended me with great discourtesies at Windsor. You have kept me waiting here for a month. You lied to me about those women.'

He drew her towards him, 'You are right, and I know I am unworthy of you, my precious one. But now I have had time to think and realise I am completely in the wrong. Can you find it in your heart to forgive me? I beg you to; I have been too long without you. Will you allow your prince ...' he murmured, kissing the words into her ears, around her mouth, unbuttoning her bodice, untying the ribbon at the neck of her chemise.

His hand slipped slowly under the yielding silk to caress her breast. His sensual mouth enclosed her lips.

Her body stirred; waking, aching for him.

Chapter 28

A Castilian June sun flooded the inner patio of the castle giving a golden glow to the walls and the stone well at its centre. Its warmth suggested a morning of indolence and languor. Juana strolled under the arcade enjoying its shade and the heady perfume of jasmine.

Men's voices put an end to the peace and silence. A snatched word or two sent her deeper into the shadows behind a tangle of dark green leaves and tiny white flowers cascading from the balcony above.

She could have stayed to greet them for she knew them well enough, they were her "guardians"; or she could have gone indoors, but she did neither. She pressed herself as close to the wall as she could; pulling the twisting, leaf-laden branches about her.

Benavente, the castle's owner clapped his friend on the back, laughing, 'A most impressive display, eh, Villena?' He rested against the stone of the arcade.

'And that is how you saw it?'

'How else? All those German lancers? Hundreds of our own men in full armour? More than two thousand in all? That would put a halt to any plans of Ferdinand to rescue his daughter.'

Villena was sceptical, 'That is probably nothing more than another of Juan Manuel's stories.'

'No matter,' Benavente continued, 'so, there we were hundreds of us, a magnificent display of power when along comes Ferdinand, all in black with a few followers, and him riding a mule, no less!' He clapped his friend's back even harder before wiping away his tears of laughter.

'Ferdinand is beginning to appear to be the peacemaker,' grumbled Villena, 'and Philip a foreign youth with his foreign army come to invade. Support is beginning to drift away. And, by the way, I have yet to see a single ducat of the thousands Philip promised me for joining him. You?'

'Nothing. Hopefully when Philip is crowned. Although I

find it galling the way he has been very quick to reward his Flemish friends.'

'God in heaven, I hate to be associated with them.'

'We had to accept that when we switched our allegiance,' Benavente shrugged.

'And what about her?' Villena motioned towards the gallery above.

'No one will be interested. What has she done since she landed in this country? Nothing to show she should be queen. She will quietly fade into the background, disappear, be forgotten.'

Juana bit hard on her knuckles. Her passive resistance, shutting herself away, had played right into her enemies' hands.

'That was an embarrassment to everyone, that scene about the Flemish women!'

'All that ranting and raving about Philip's whores as she called them!'

'Then there was the tantrum because no one would go into mourning for her mother. Good lord, we had done that already!'

'All very pathetic really; unimaginable that an adult would go into a grand pout like a child,' Villena added, 'refusing to see anyone, listen to anyone – even from the other side of the door, and howling and throwing things.

'And now she is not allowed out to play,' laughed Benavente.

Juana wanted to shout that there was much more to those stories than that; much, much more. But it was all so trivial compared with what had been happening while she sat stubbornly wallowing in her misery. She had allowed Philip to surround her with his own guards and with Benavente and Villena her guardians, not permitting any possible friend anywhere near. These same guardians, Judases seeking their filthy twenty pieces of silver, along with other turncoats had accompanied Philip to meet her father. To discuss what she wondered, and how could they discuss anything without her presence? She hoped she had wakened up in time, that it wasn't too late. She urged herself into action with an almost forgotten resolve. She would show them all she was the queen and not to be ignored. Head held high, chin thrust determinedly forward; she left her hiding place prepared for a confrontation with her husband.

'Good day,' she threw at her guardians as she swept by.

'Can she have heard?' whispered Villena.

'Not a word, and if she did it would be of no interest to her.

The doors to Philip's apartments were opened for her. Philip looked up from his breakfast.

'You have met my father!' she stormed, marching towards his table.

'I have indeed.'

'To what purpose?'

'Some new agreements had to be reached.'

'The others were good enough.'

'They did not suit me.'

'Nothing can go ahead without my consent.'

'I would remind you that a short while ago you decided you wanted no part in these affairs, you shut yourself away. Now it is too late; Ferdinand and I have managed admirably without you. In any case look at you: your person, your behaviour. You are not fit to be involved in governing this country, and believe me we shall see to it that you are not.'

She looked down at herself. It was the first time in days, perhaps weeks that she had even thought about the clothes she wore. Her dress was a little soiled, perhaps; her hair not brushed and re-braided, but still tucked inside a gold mesh coif and black hood. It could also be said that she had not washed; but these things had all been part of her strategy. As for her behaviour, she had done nothing more serious than show her anger at those who warranted it, her husband in particular. She had never heard one word of criticism regarding Philip's behaviour towards her: his lying, his malicious slander, his verbal and physical abuse.

As he stood up a servant brushed crumbs from his sleeves, another pulled back his chair to turn it to face the wall.

'Since you are interested, read this, it will save me the effort of explaining,' he shoved a document across the table.

Let it be known that Queen Juana is by no means required to involve herself with any type of administration, government

154

or any other matter. If she did, it would mean the total destruction and loss of these kingdoms because of her illness. And should she, either of her own volition, or induced by others, desire or be desired to become involved in government we, Philip and Ferdinand, will not consent to it. This is agreed upon. And we will support one another against any who align themselves against us ... June 27, 1506.

This was Juan Manuel's doing; he was the one cunning and evil enough to have conjured up this vile document tying her father's hands. How dared he! 'You have used coercion and intimidation. My father would never have willingly signed this,' she challenged.

'How clever of you Juana! Yes, Ferdinand does as I say and he gets paid: his rents, his share of the riches from the New World and so on. If he refuses or decides not to leave Castile, or shows the least sign of enmity towards me, he will lose everything. I have had to caution him already. Juan Manuel uncovered some plans to "rescue" you. Ferdinand will not attempt that again, and if he is sensible his gossip about my holding you prisoner will cease forthwith. His disclaimer of this treaty, saying it was signed under duress is also null and void. All in all I am well pleased. Now I am on my way to celebrate with friends. Bullfights and banquets. I bid you farewell.'

Philip was gone. She hesitated, but only for a moment. There was only one option, she had to get to her father before he left Castile; they would seek out those who were sympathetic to her cause, and she felt sure that their numbers would be growing from what she had overheard earlier in the courtyard. But how?

'Horses, Benavente,' she ordered. 'Take me to see your animal park. If Philip is to enjoy diversions, then so shall we.'

155

Chapter 29

Juana rode between her two guardians and an accompanying guard of a dozen or more Austrian soldiers. The horses strolled lazily through the heat and dust, their pace gradually slackening until they finally halted in the shade of a small copse.

'Such a beautiful day. A beautiful Castilian day,' she steadied her horse, looking all around so as not to miss any of the sights. 'Gentlemen, I have wasted so many days depriving myself of such pleasures and delights. Why, look up there, on that branch ... no you must look much higher than that Benavente ... shade your eyes or you will never see ...'

A kick of her heels into her horse's side and they were off at a furious gallop across the park. A wide defence ditch loomed before her, but she drove him hard at it crying, 'Liberty or death!'

She grasped the reins short and with a commanding pull bad him leap the intimidating space, 'Come on, we can do it.'

Up went the forelegs. They flew as if on wings, a Pegasus carrying a desperate rider up and out and over. Juana's hood loosed itself from her head to blow away and leaving her hair to seek its own freedom from her gold mesh coif. Four hooves thundered onto firm ground on the other side and the horse snorted his foam-flecked satisfaction, stamping his pride.

'Oh, you magnificent creature. I am free,' she shouted leaning forward and hugging his sweating neck in gratitude.

She glanced back to see the guards in frustrated disarray, Benavente and Villena calling her to return, immediately.

'I think not, gentlemen,' she replied. 'Come, my beauty, we have far to go.'

She rode him hard and soon arrived at a small village only to have to wheel about smartly at the sight of several soldiers on horseback. She dared not let them recognise her. She headed for a group of cottages but was thwarted again with the appearance of yet more mounted soldiers.

'Is there nothing but cavalry in this country?' she demanded of her horse, having to change direction again.

They galloped off once more, 'Dear God, let there be somewhere, someone.'

❖   ❖   ❖

'God 'ave mercy on us.'

Juana leaned forward accustoming her eyes to the darkness of the little room thick with the smell of boiling salt cod and chick peas, and the bed's sour leftover odour of last night's sleep clinging to a straw mattress and covers. There was a plain wooden chest, a rough hewn table and bench; these and the bed were the only furnishings in the humble dwelling.

Stooped by the fire was the owner of the voice; a bundle of brown and grey garments. It remained motionless with ladle poised; startled eyes and gawping, gap-toothed mouth fixed on the intruder.

'Do not alarm yourself, good woman. I only need to rest here for a little while.'

The figure pulled itself up straight, a woman probably of middle age, somewhat on the plump side, her face round with cheeks and a mouth made for ready smiles and laughter.

Juana watched as reddened and calloused fingers fought to free skirt hems caught up in a waistband to let it fall over grubby petticoats.

'Please, would y' care to sit m'lady?' the woman offered, not knowing what to do or say to this person who should never have been here in the first place and certainly not here on her own.

With her skirts she wiped a place on the bench ready for this unwanted guest, then stood back making awkward rearrangements to her nearly white cap before nervously pushing her sleeves now up, now down; waiting.

Juana accepted the seat gratefully and sat quietly contemplating the fireplace with its fire irons and the huge black pot steaming contentedly above the licking flames.

'Are you lost m'lady? Maybe you want a message taken? I'd be happy to do so.' She would be more than happy to do something, anything, which might make some sense of this lady's presence in her home.

'I need only a little while to rest and to think, thank you.'

The peasant woman stole furtive glances at the stranger, taking in the black brocade skirts with their woven floral design, as yet not daring to raise her eyes above them.

'I could give you a drink?'

'That would be most acceptable, if it is not too much trouble. Do you have water?'

'In the shed. I keep it there because it's so much cooler. Mind you not as cool as when I get it straight from the well. But I only go there mornings ...'

'That from your shed will be perfect.'

'I'll fetch y' some of that then, shall I?'

She tied on a large apron, thinking this to be the right thing to do, then made a small curtsey to the person sitting on her bench and who she wished wasn't. No good was going to come of this, that was for sure.

After opening the door but a few inches she slammed it shut falling back against its wood, 'Oh my God, there's soldiers out there! We 'aven't done no harm to nothing nor nobody, honest we 'aven't. We mind our business; my 'usband works as 'ard as any good Christian. He goes to the bakery every day while I keep his home and yard all proper for him. We go to church regular. We're good honest folk, 'elping friends and neighbours at seed time and 'arvest, they'd all tell you ...' She pulled her apron over her eyes to shield her from this terrible calamity that was befalling her.

'Please, do not be afraid, good woman. The soldiers have not come for you, or for your good husband. They have come for me. But be assured, they dare not take me for I am the queen; Queen Juana.'

'Oh my God!' The apron was lowered to mouth level, 'Soldiers outside my door and a ravin' lunatic at my table!' She sank to her knees making earnest prayers for her deliverance; unsure who to fear most the soldiers or this crazy woman and hoping against hope that her husband would arrive. Without moving, her eyes fixed firmly on the roof beam above her with its hanging bunches of herbs, and with her hands still locked in supplication she mumbled bits of half-remembered prayers.

Juana looked down at her dishevelled self. Her dress and boots, not very clean to begin with, were now covered with a layer of dust, with scraps of clinging twigs and dry grasses, with splashes of horse spume. They showed very little sign of the quality neither of the materials nor of the skilled workmanship in their making. Her hands went to her head, her hood was missing and her fingers discovered several windblown, wayward locks of auburn hair, and a tangle of fine gold mesh that was once her coif. She laughed, 'I do not make a very convincing figure of a queen I grant you. But be assured I am, and I promise you will come to no harm.'

'You talk like a lady, sure enough, and I see you have clothes made of good cloth,' she answered. Her eyes were still gazing roofwards and now following the hesitant progress of a mouse, 'But I know that proper high folk 'ave jewels; rings and things like that. Even our magistrate wears them kind of things.'

Juana smiled, 'Yes, you are right, of course. It is just that I do not care to ...'

There were sounds of heavy footfalls and both watched the door, waiting.

Philip stepped into the room but would venture no further. He first held a pomander to his nose and then a handkerchief.

The baker's wife whimpered into swollen knuckles pressed against her mouth, 'Oh my God.' Who? What now? Purple brocades, a glittering gold chain with its pendant sheep across this gentleman's chest, gold fastenings on bonnet and coat, rings on gloved hands; it was unreal.

'This is Philip, the king consort,' Juana announced as though to a visiting ambassador.

Philip ignored her. 'Wait outside,' he commanded the trembling wretch still kneeling open-mouthed at his feet.

'Oh my God, I'm being sent to me death,' she wept and stumbled to the door convinced of the worst.

Philip unleashed his rage. 'You have done well Juana. News has spread of your "escape". You have stirred the emotions of many who are already rallying to your cause, whatever that

159

may be. And it has certainly painted a very poor picture of me. This has put me in somewhat of a quandary as to my next move, I shall have to be careful.'

'The next move is mine, my lord, not yours,' she replied, reasonably convinced she was completely safe provided she remain on the outside of any castle walls. 'You will return to Benavente's castle. There you will arrange everything for our journey to Valladolid. I, meanwhile, shall await your return. We can then travel together.' Her voice sounded as if it belonged to that other Juana and its strength was impressive.

'Valladolid? Valladolid?' A veneer of warmth stole across his face and into his voice. 'Do my ears deceive me or have I finally convinced you it is time for us to be sworn in as king and queen by the Cortes at Valladolid?' He took care not to sound jubilant. Were she to do this, as soon as they were sworn in he would produce the signed document drawn up by Ferdinand and himself disclosing her mental incapacities. And it would be farewell Juana.

'Sworn in, perhaps, we must wait and see.' She would not remind him that if there were to be such a ceremony, it must take place in Toledo. 'But I shall be nearer to friends, and how I have longed for that.'

Chapter 30

'Oh, ma'am, I don't know if there's enough time to get you prepared,' wheezed the old lady bobbing a curtsey and patting her ample bosom as she bustled to Juana's side. She set about smoothing the skirts and sleeves of Juana's black dress, then arranging her black hood and finally the heavy black veil that hid her face.

'Prepare me for what, Marta?'

'For the many important visitors ma'am, they're arriving all the time from all parts.'

Visitors; the word started a wave of alarm. Who might these visitors be? What was Philip scheming? Was it connected with her retiring to these rooms? She felt she had had no alternative. Their journey to Valladolid had come to a halt with Philip refusing to go further, offering no explanation, deaf to her demands they continue. She was still being treated little better than a prisoner so there had been no other recourse than to retreat to this sanctuary. But now this.

'Marta, what kind of visitors?' the question forced itself free.

'Not the kind to worry about, bless you. But I have to tell you some things before they get here.'

Since Maria had been sent back to Flanders (it was part of Philip's continuing plan to deny Juana anyone who might be supportive) she had come to rely entirely upon this dear old servant. Marta had always been an excellent laundress and most recently was quickly learning the art of dresser to her mistress; she was also proving to be her one source of information.

'Quickly then.'

'Well, King Ferdinand wrote to King Philip, saying that if Philip wanted to take any action against you he would have to do it alone.'

'Philip is determined to have me locked away. I knew I

161

could rely on my father not to let me down. If only I could get a message to him. How much time have I left? But there is more?'

'Oh, ma'am, if you would only let me finish. I don't want you getting into a nervous state. If you let me get to the end of what I have to say you will see that everything is all right. Now this part is disrespectful.'

'Tell me.'

'King Philip wants you declared mad ...'

'There is nothing new in that, he has endeavoured to do so ever since the death of my mother.'

'But he means to do it now; today, if he can. Oh ma'am, he wants to get the Cortes to sign an order saying you are mad and then declaring him king. But have no fear,' Marta hurried on, 'because the *Procuradores* will have nothing to do with it; so there you are. Cisneros and Juan Manuel have been trying all manner of bribes and threats to persuade them with no luck whatsoever. The grandees, mind you, well they're a different kettle of fish, they are. Some of them fair fell over themselves to sign at the first sniff of money.'

'But not many?'

'No not many, not by a long way, praises be. Anyway, Juan Manuel has summoned the spokesman for the *Procuradores* to question you, his words not mine, right now, and to report back to the others who are waiting below. He thinks that when this gentleman sees you sitting all alone like this he will be convinced that you ... that you are ...'

'I understand, Marta. So, Philip cannot wait until we reach Valladolid. His impatience is bound to lead to mistakes. I feel better than I have done for days. Is it Padilla who is to question me?'

'That's right ma'am, and what about this bit of excellent news; your uncle the admiral is coming too.'

'Wonderful; he will help me, I know he will. I feel even better.'

'Actually, King Philip is greatly put out because the admiral insists on seeing you before the grandees even meet to discuss this whole disgraceful business.'

There was an authoritative rap at the door.

162

'You were right Marta there was indeed so very little time.'

'I hope everything goes well for you my lady,' Marta whispered, crossing her large bosom in prayer and then, for good measure, crossing her fingers for luck.

Three men entered the room and made their bows; Cisneros, Juan Manuel and Padilla. Padilla was shaken for a moment by what seemed to be a black spectre huddled on a chair.

'Welcome Don Padilla,' the voice came from behind a veil that completely hid Juana's face 'How good it is to see someone from the city of my birth. I hear that you protect her pride with fervour, refusing to allow Burgos to usurp her position and rank of First City of our country.'

He was astonished; she had recognised him, she knew of this latest infighting! Padilla looked suspiciously at the other two. They had said she was totally incapable of showing any comprehension of anything, let alone politics, preferring to hide away from the world. This young lady, his queen, sitting here in the gloom dressed in black, heavily veiled, with only one attendant, and a wizened, ugly, old woman at that, was not the crazy person they had described. But something had happened to her. Why did she live this way?

'Your highness, I am here to bring the good wishes and all respect from Toledo who, as you say, continues to maintain her rank; and to bring you the good wishes and respect of every city in Castile.'

'My deepest thanks for such heartening news, I had begun to doubt that I would ever see or hear from faithful friends again.'

'Your highness, we are all your loyal countrymen, let no one doubt that. But we are concerned that you deny us your presence.'

What was she to answer that could not be misinterpreted? She grasped and clutched at her handkerchief.

'The reason my friend is this. I wished to mourn my mother; I wanted to be reunited with my father. These things should come first, but they were denied me. Then I was refused contact with any of my friends.' She leaned towards him, now whispering, 'And there have been so many plots and plans against me; I have been imprisoned and am threatened with

163

worse. So you see I find it difficult to trust anyone. I only feel safe with my own company and my servant Marta.' Her voice lightened, 'It comes as such a joyous relief at last to find myself close to one of my own people and to be actually permitted to speak to you.'

'Then I humbly request that you see your faithful subjects who are come to greet you.' Padilla knelt before her unable to believe what she had just said, it was too incredible.

For Juana this was much too quick, too great a challenge. She began to fidget nervously, studying him warily, no longer trusting him, wondering why he was in such haste. Would she be putting herself at risk? Could she really be sure he too was not in the pay of Philip and that this was not a trap?

So she shook her head, 'No. You see my enemies are there and they are seeking to destroy me. No, I shall stay here where I am safe with the memories of my family for company. If only my father could be here; what can I do when he has been sent away leaving me alone and unprotected in the clutches of Philip and his evil followers? Philip, oh Philip, I do not deserve this.' She looked down at her hands on her lap and sang,

> *'I suffer your disfavour*
> *Yet do not complain*
> *And still will I love you*
> *Though there's only disdain.*
>
> *I suffer your disfavour*
> *Yet do not complain*
> *And still will I ...'*

'Ma'am. Your royal highness,' Padilla was desperate to release her from the song after the fourth or fifth time and watching her carefully plucking at something she imagined to be lying on her skirts.

Juan Manuel took his elbow, 'Seen enough? Satisfied? You can see she is quite mad.'

Padilla turned angrily on him, shrugging himself free of Manuel's hand, 'I grant you that my queen is not well. But things are not right here; someone, something is at the root of all this. There are those around her, Don Manuel, who should feel shame and who one day shall be held to account. This is no way to treat the Queen of Castile. God, but I wish that I had been blind that my eyes would not have witnessed this, deaf that I would not have heard ... You can be sure of this, whatever malady does afflict my lady Castile will remain loyal to her. We shall not be persuaded otherwise. She is our queen. My lords, I bid you good day. I must speak with my colleagues. Something must be done.'

He bowed to Juana and left the room, taking with him the haunting words of her lament and an indelible picture of a tragic recluse.

Cisneros watched him go before speaking, 'So, Don Juan Manuel, the cities are against us; a problem for the moment, but not an insurmountable one. The next hurdle is Don Fadrique. I feel we can win him to our cause. His joining Ferdinand was only motivated by sentimentality, nothing more.'

'I am most reluctant to allow this interview with the admiral as you know,' Juan Manuel replied, 'since he refuses to sign until he has had visual proof of her insanity. I just pray that she keeps up this perfect exhibition in his presence.'

'Your attitude is offensive Don Juan Manuel. Show more respect for Queen Juana. My only concern, which should also be yours, is for Castile. We need to appoint the one best suited to govern our country. We both agree that that person is not Ferdinand, whose priority is Aragón, so it has to be Philip. We must, however, be extremely careful how we handle the delicate problem of Juana or we may push Castile into civil war.'

'A civil war holds no fears for me, archbishop, the sooner the better, get it over with, put the power into the appropriate hands ...' he stopped short.

The Admiral of Castile, the Constable of Castile, and the Bishop of Malaga entered.

'Your highness.'

Juana looked up and was delighted. Three of her old friends were here at last! She could scarcely believe it. She threw back her heavy veil and almost ran to Don Fadrique.

'Uncle, uncle, I had begun to think I would never see this day.'

He kissed her hands. She took his and would not let them go.

'Dearest Juana, my Juanita; how pale.' He was saddened to see her once sparkling hazel eyes so darkly ringed; her lovely mouth too readily pulled down in misery.

'It is nothing uncle. I never look well when I am with child. How many times was it rumoured in the past that I suffered consumption when it was nothing more than a pregnancy? Be assured I am well.'

The admiral took a long look about him, 'Juana this room is unfit for you, especially when your condition is so delicate. Why black hangings on the walls? Why no tapestries? Why no silver and gold plate? Why no ladies to attend you? And you, my pretty Juana, why dressed in plainest black with your precious face veiled and hidden deep inside your hood?'

'I am in mourning.'

'The time for mourning our late queen is past now. The time has come to look to the future.'

'Dear uncle there is much to mourn. I mourn for those dear to me, but I also mourn for myself for the misery and hurt I am made to suffer.' She tightened her grip on Don Fadrique's hands as she commanded Juan Manuel and Cisneros to stand aside that she and her visitors might have some privacy for their conversation. How she enjoyed this new strength drawn from her uncle.

'Constable Bernardino, we have not met since your wedding in Toledo two years ago. How is my half-sister?'

'You are most gracious to remember. My wife is well, I thank you.'

'And my lord, Bishop of Malaga, you too are most welcome. I feel I should pinch myself to make sure this is not a dream. Am I awake, are you real?'

'We are all real.'

'Then tell me, uncle, for I have heard that you have been with my father; where is he now? Is he well? Philip sent him away without ever letting me see him.'

'He is well, and yes, he is soon to set sail for Naples.' Don

166

Fadrique wanted so much to stop the tears he saw filling Juana's eyes.

'Then I must write to him immediately. Come with me. As I write you must tell me all about him, what you talked about, how you are now reconciled.'

Don Fadrique laughed, 'It would seem that there is probably little to tell, you know so much already. Someone keeps you well informed.'

'Indeed, uncle. There is my informant,' she whispered nodding in the direction of Marta standing in the shadows.

The letter was finished, hurriedly sanded, and given to the bishop, 'It would be best if you hid this until you leave the palace, then see that my father receives it before he leaves for Naples.'

She rushed to the constable and asked too loudly, 'How do you and your wife find your new home in Burgos? Is it to your liking?' Philip's footsteps announced his arrival and she was alarmed that he might discover the letter.

Juan Manuel and Cisneros standing by the door exchanged a few words with Philip as he entered. He went directly to the writing table.

'An idle pen and spilled sand. Writing letters again, Juana? And who is the bearer of your tidings this time? It has to be the bishop. Hand it over good man. No? Then I shall find it myself.'

Juana held her head, dismayed, the bishop bore the indignity of Philip's hands searching inside his clothing until, 'Ah here we are, tucked away in its little nest, keeping warm, thinking it would be quite safe, thinking only the bishop himself would ever put his hands there. Would you believe it, Juan Manuel, the bishop has a letter in his codpiece. Such imagination for a Spanish priest! You do surprise me,' he dropped his sarcasm. 'Get out! You will not be permitted to enter this court ever again.'

He read the letter. 'Another little note from a loving daughter to her dear father; how touching.' He tore it and flung the pieces in the air.

Juana wept. The admiral fumed.

'So, admiral, in the light of our queen's obvious stupidity made patent by writing to the enemy Ferdinand, do you not agree that it is dangerous for her to be involved with the governing of these lands? Would it not be in everyone's best interests to keep her out of the way?'

'Not so, sire,' the admiral controlled his anger, 'Queen Juana is in good health and remarkably well informed. We have just enjoyed a most interesting conversation, following which I can only conclude that you have done my lady grave injustices in allowing the spreading of untruths. And, goodness me, a letter of filial devotion hardly warrants such censure. Yes, I am of the opinion she should be sworn in as the Queen of Castile, with you as her consort. I would go further and suggest you advise your followers to forget any attempts of denying Juana her rights; they would run grave risks of angering too many of my countrymen.' He knelt before Juana, 'Queen Juana of Castile, the members of the Cortes are here and await your presence. Ma'am, did you hear?'

His voice was the one voice that could persuade her despite any misgivings. It was the voice of a man who had never, would never, betray her.

'Philip,' the decision was made. 'I am of a mind for us to be sworn in. Uncle, the Cortes may be informed that I intend to be sworn in as queen with Philip as my king consort. Now if you will all retire I shall prepare myself.'

Chapter 31

Juana entered the antechamber brimming with resolve. She would not be intimidated by anyone because that other Juana was here with the courage, as her brother once said, to fight for what is right and what is justly hers.

She still chose to wear black but her robes of satin and velvet had jewelled brooches and clasps running down the length of her bodice and holding the open fronted sleeves together at her wrists and elbows. And as it was a most special occasion she had decided to wear the necklace inherited from her mother, the broad chain of exquisitely crafted gold arrows. Her mantle of black brocade was edged with ermine, and her hood had a border of delicately embroidered gold flowers. Walking towards Philip she felt content and comfortable with her appearance; and confident.

Philip, who had arrived earlier, looked quite magnificent. Juana drank in every aspect of her handsome husband. He was in a scarlet jerkin and breeches. His knee-length gown was also scarlet with a broad ermine collar and lined with cloth of gold. Her eyes followed the heavy chain of the Golden Fleece that rested on his shoulders, nestling into the collar's white fur and crossing that strong chest she knew so well. And his long golden hair that she had so often caressed, the tresses sliding silk-like through her fingers, today bore his ducal coronet.

And still will I love you
Though there's only disdain.

For an instant the song came back to try to haunt again.

Four trumpeters announced them, rescuing her. The doors to the audience chamber were swung open. First to enter were the Kings-at-Arms wearing their tabards of office: Toledo, a gold crown on a blue field; Seville, an enthroned St. Ferdinand on a black field; Córdoba, four red bars on a gold field; Murcia, six gold crowns on a red field; Granada, a green pomegranate with its red seeds on a white field. Juana and Philip each walked behind their own quartered standard of Castile and Leon; the golden castle with three crenulated towers on a red field, and

169

the red lion rampant with its golden crown on a white field. Juana's standard was adorned with a collar of golden arrows, Philip's with the collar of the Golden Fleece, and both were surmounted by a crown and the eagle of St. John.

The members of the Cortes bowed to them as they passed. Juana looked at the grandees some of whom, possibly many, had sided with Philip. The others were for her but most probably as an act of defiance against Philip and the hated Flems; if that were so it was reason enough for the moment for it bought time for others to be persuaded. And she had all the city representatives on her side.

She remembered a scene very similar to this from the distant past, an assembly of lords, ladies, priests, her mother and father, and she had been terrified. But that was long ago and this time she was not afraid; at least she earnestly hoped she was not afraid.

She mounted the steps of the dais and quickly began to address them. 'Honoured sirs, do you know and recognise me as Doña Juana?'

'Your highness, we do.' They answered, puzzled.

'You accept that I am the legitimate daughter of Her Serene Highness Isabel the Catholic?'

'Your highness, we do,' they all affirmed still wondering.

Her heart thundered, she was nearly there, 'Then why are you here and not awaiting me in Toledo?' Her voice strengthened, 'You are all aware that Toledo is the only place where I can be sworn in as your sovereign. Toledo is the city where all our laws and the very constitution of the kingdom are formally sworn; fie on you sirs for coming here!'

It was done. Congratulating herself she descended the steps and passed down the room, bidding adieu to the assembly.

Philip turned to Cisneros to hiss, 'This is enough. I am sick of this woman. But I tell you I *will* find the way to have us sworn in and then have her locked away.'

'Sire, I am as desirous as you to have you crowned as soon as possible,' Cisneros whispered, anxious because delays were already aiding Ferdinand, but annoyed at the blatant callousness of Philip. 'Quickly, have Juan Manuel ask those questions.'

Philip prompted his accomplice who stepped forward hushing the assembly, 'Gentlemen, a moment longer, if you please.'

Everyone looked from him to Juana.

'With permission, ma'am, would you be generous enough to answer three questions?'

She faced the despicable challenger undaunted.

'One: do you intend to govern this land, and are you disposed to share this government with your husband, King Philip? Two: do you intend to dress appropriately and be accompanied by ladies? Three: do you intend to comport yourself as befits your state, and to end your isolation?'

Head held high she returned to the throne on the dais. She had hoped to have had more time, to wait until they were in Toledo before revealing her true intentions, but the moment had come so she must speak.

'Sirs, it appears that I must remind some among you that it is completely unacceptable for Castile to be governed by foreigners; read Queen Isabel's will and testament, clause twenty-five. A thousand shames on you, if you are one of those choosing to forget!'

Gasps and murmurings of shock and incredulity passed from one to another.

'However,' she silenced them, 'you may not realise that in Flanders it is inappropriate for a wife to hold precedence over her husband and I would never dishonour my husband by doing so. While on the one hand it would be in compliance with my mother's will for me to reign with Philip as my consort, on the other it would be unacceptable to Flemish custom if I did. Now perhaps you understand my dilemma. You must appreciate therefore, that under such circumstances, it is preferable by far that my father reign until my son Charles is old enough to assume the responsibilities of the throne. That is the only way to rid us of this dreadful impasse.'

A mixture of sounds of agreement and dissent filled the room.

Again she silenced them. 'Gentlemen, in response to Juan Manuel's second question, to which I take great exception, as it is of a personal nature — I do intend to discard my mourning when the time is right. However, I refuse to have any ladies in

171

my court; we all know my husband and his ways, and I tell you I fully intend to be saved the indignity of having any of his mistresses near me. I think it also advisable for me to distance myself from those who deny me respect and honour. I think you will find I have answered the third question regarding my demeanour and desire for solitude. You must respect my wishes to continue in this manner until the ceremony at Toledo.'

Don Fadrique had to restrain himself from applauding, whispering instead into the ear of Don Bernardino. 'Aye, the girl can still rise to the occasion, bless her. It is such a damned shame the devastating effect this blackguard has had on her. What will it take to help her fully recover?'

Padilla muttered to those nearest, 'If there was any doubt in anyone's mind, they must now be convinced that our queen is sound of mind.'

Philip was livid and pulled Cisneros aside, 'Could things get any worse? It was a stupid mistake to convene the Cortes here. Now what am I to do?'

'Calm yourself, sire,' Cisneros was losing his patience with the petulant Philip. 'Admittedly her highness gave an excellent performance, but we both know from past experience that it will not last. A change of tactics is called for. I suggest you follow my advice and not that of Don Manuel. Make a display of your reconciliation with your wife. Start immediately by ridding yourself of your sour countenance; escort the queen from the chamber showing her deep affection and devotion.' He stayed Philip's frustration, 'Trust me; this will be a far quicker and easier method to gain the crown.'

Chapter 32

Several weeks had passed since she had been tricked into the swearing in ceremony. (She was furious with herself for her incredible naivety, deceived by the warm affections of her 'loving' husband.) In those following weeks she had been held in seclusion under close guard. Then two days ago she had been brought here, to Burgos. She and Philip had apartments in her half-sister's home, the Casa del Cordón. She had been naïve once again in assuming her sister would still be here to befriend her, but Philip had "invited them to leave" and go to their country home.

September mornings can be very cold in Burgos and Juana and Marta were wrapped in fur lined cloaks as they strolled around the upper arcaded gallery. Down below men and horses were gathering in the courtyard. The shuffling hooves, the hearty camaraderie with calls, jests and laughter drew her to the balcony to look down.

Someone caught sight of her, 'Why don't you get back to that other crone; just the sort of company you need,' he called up.

'One thing is certain; they won't wear each other out talking!' another guffawed.

'Maybe the idiot wants to go riding on a mule again!

Now they all laughed; laughing at her, laughing at their blatant disrespect for her.

'My God, yes, the lengths the stupid will go to! No one in their right mind would do what she did, riding about the countryside all night,' another shouted up at her. This was grand sport.

'More like two mules, you should say, one a four legged dumb beast, the other a crazy and stubborn woman. Not forgetting the hag who never leaves her side.'

'And round and round and round she went, the old hag or nag hobbling alongside; what a picture.'

'You put on a fantastic show for the villagers,' someone else called up to the arcade to where Juana had last been seen

173

standing. She was still there, half hidden behind a pillar, unable to tear herself away.

'They thought you were a travelling fool come to entertain, your ladyship. They lit fires and made torches, not wanting to miss a moment. They cheered for you and booed the soldiers if they came anywhere near, a regular comedy.'

Marta held Juana's arm. 'Come away ma'am. Don't you fret yourself about them lot down there, ignorant they are, the lot of them. I feel like leaning over this balcony and telling them it was all my idea, and a clever one at that.'

'How right you are, Marta,' Juana replied not taking her eyes off the scene below. 'But for you the soldiers would have led me into that fortress and I would simply have disappeared; lost to the world. I thank God I have you for my eyes and ears.'

'And we sharp put an end to their little game didn't we, ma'am; us and the villagers. We all played our parts well. I say none of that lot can get the better of us. Always bear that in mind my lady!'

The jeers and taunts grew more feeble and weak as the men lost interest, their conversation turning to their eagerness for the chase, to have other defenceless creatures at their mercy.

A final taunt reached her, 'Anyway it's only a matter of months and Philip will be rid of you. He says he's only waiting for the birth of this last child then it will be adieu crackpot.'

Juana shuddered and clutched at Marta who held her firmly, 'Now don't you go paying any heed to a word they say. I knew we shouldn't stay here listening to this nonsense. Come away.'

'Not yet, I want to see Philip. I must see him.'

Marta threw her eyes heavenward and shook her head in despair, 'Dear Lord above!' Here was Castile going to rack and ruin: decimated by famine and plague, hundreds dragging their starving bodies from one city to the next; the royal coffers empty, the country bankrupt; Juana not only unable to do anything for her ravaged homeland, but threatened by that brute of a man who had already caused her all kinds of pain and distress and all she could think of was catching a glimpse of him!

Echoing calls of 'my lord' drew Juana back to the balustrade. And yes, he was there, a magnificent young king, a god, astride his white steed. The colours he had chosen to wear today declared him beyond doubt the most handsome of men. His mulberry half-cap had a gold coronet revealed in the openings of the upturned brim. His green velvet cloak had a wide border embroidered in gold, its two silk tassels lying on his breast. The gold of his doublet showed at the neck and between the slashed sleeves of his mulberry fur-lined jerkin. He pulled his cloak tighter about his shoulders; how she ached to hold those beautiful hands with their long slender fingers. She watched as someone offered him a gold pomander to ward off disgusting smells and the plague which apparently was not too far from Burgos.

'Where to, Manuel?' he called calming his wheeling, impatient horse.

'Hunting first, and then to my castle for lunch and ...' Manuel glanced up and saw Juana. 'How can you bear to have her sneaking about the place like Death come to invite you to join in the Dance?'

'Quite simple; I ignore her.'

It was then that he glanced up, just briefly, and the pain of her love and longing for him struck her so deep she almost cried out; to beg. Their eyes met but there had been no word, no smile from him, no recognition.

Chapter 33

'Just get out of my sight.' Juana grasped the arms of her chair lest she be tempted to strike Philip's insolent steward, 'If Philip is in desperate need of money I suggest he ask his friend and adviser, Juan Manuel, I am certain he has more than enough.'

'As an obedient wife you dare not refuse.'

'Out!'

'There will be repercussions when my master returns.'

'No doubt. Now please leave.'

Marta was bursting with indignation. 'The cheek of him asking for your silver to pawn. Mind you, things have come to a sorry state when the servants haven't been paid.'

'But not my problem. Continue about my uncle.'

'In spite of all the threats he won't budge, nor will Alba, nor their followers. More than half of the grandees are on their side now, and he said Philip needn't try to confiscate his lands, because he would only ever surrender them to you, and he told Juan Manuel he has an army strong enough to defend himself against him or anybody else who dared try.'

'Reliable, dependable uncle; but it is all very disturbing; the famine and plague might yet be the least of Castile's worries.'

Doctor Marliano, Philip's personal physician was announced.

Juana couldn't resist, 'Not another one with an empty purse!'

'Nothing of that nature. I came out of politeness to inform you that my master is suffering from a chill, and I thought it best to have him brought from Juan Manuel's home to his own bed.'

'When did he become ill?'

'Thursday morning. On Wednesday as you may recall he and his friends went hunting. They followed that with a rather fine lunch and a little while later my master took on a Spanish guard in a rather long and difficult game of pelota. The following morning King Philip felt unwell. I told him that after the game he should not have drunk so much cold water, and the water here is very cold, nor should he have sat about in his sweaty clothes.'

'Nor, more like, should he have gone cavorting about with some "excellent *muchachas*" who were provided, as I am told, for his evening's entertainment.'

'I shall continue. For two days he was determined to carry on as normal before finally conceding he was not well.'

Juana was almost at the door before he had finished. 'I must go to him.'

'Quite unnecessary. My master will soon be returned to full health. I have administered bugloss to purge the humours of his lungs, plasters of mallow root for his painful side, and pearled sugared lozenges for the fever. He will be better in no time at all.'

'Nonetheless I shall go to him. Marta, come.' The heavy veil was thrown off along with her lethargy and she rushed along the gallery to Philip's apartments waving aside the courtiers who lingered at his door.

She looked down at the patient, lying so pale and helpless under a scarlet coverlet bearing his coat of arms. 'It is always the same, my poor darling, you fall ill every time you are overburdened with troubles.'

Philip tried to mutter something, but all that emerged was a hoarse whisper as he clutched at his throat.

Doctor Marliano leaned over him, 'Cisneros's physician, Yanguas, has come spying, so I refused to let him see you.'

Juana was furious, 'How preposterous, two heads are better than one! Show him in.'

Philip nodded a weak, acquiescent nod.

The young Italian doctor leaned, eyes narrowed in criticism, over the shoulder of the wizened and stooped Yanguas as he examined the royal body of his master.

Eventually, following much beard tugging and knitting of brows, Yanguas gave his recommendations, 'What is needed here is; write this down: a paste of bran mixed with milk and lard for the side; quince and sugar for the inflamed throat, or possibly purslain with honey; and the sooner you start the vinegar drinks to stop the diarrhoea the better.'

177

Doctor Marliano sneered, 'What kind of quackery is this I am listening to? I will not allow any of it. You either intend mischief or you know nothing. My lord Philip, I want him gone from here.'

Yanguas had heard enough, 'I am leaving; I am certainly not staying to listen to insults. Archbishop Cisneros, whom I have served for years, was magnanimous in offering the wisdom of my many years of experience, and he will not be best pleased with this affront. Quackery, indeed; young upstart whoever you are, I will have you know I was a famous doctor when you were still wet behind the ears!'

'I shall settle all disputes.' Juana stepped between them, setting them apart with her hands. 'Marta, pen and paper, immediately, I shall send for my son Ferdinand's doctor.'

❖   ❖   ❖

'I have sat too long.' Juana moved stiffly away from her chair, her fingers comforting her back as she walked about the room. It was the first time she had moved since sometime the previous evening. A figure in black cap and gown sitting at a table in the corner raised his eyes momentarily from his book then returned to his studies.

Juana returned to Philip's bedside, 'At last you are getting better,' she gently traced the lips, the cheeks, the eyelids she had kissed and caressed so often, wanting so much to do so now as a mother comforting her child. 'Yes, since yesterday when Doctor Parra came, and not a moment too soon I might add, I have noticed a big change.'

Just prior to Parra's arrival they had all become alarmed. Philip was coughing up blood; and a dreadful rash of large, dark red spots appeared all over his body. And he had become delirious.

'But that is all behind us now. Yes, my love, you are in the capable hands of our son Ferdinand's doctor; a physician who brings with him not only all the wisdom of Galen and Hippocrates but also his years of experience at the University of Salamanca.'

178

Juana looked across at the old man in his black robes huddled over his many books and she thanked God for the change this man had wrought. Following plasters of linseed and fenugreek mixed with goose and duck fat, the humours in Philip's lungs seemed finally to have been scattered. Leeches, which should have been used in the first instance, had rid him of excess blood. The new medicines of honey with oregano and plantain were helping too; and they tasted better than some of the others. Juana knew this to be true because she had insisted on sampling every medicine herself before offering any to Philip. She had to be sure that he would like them, that they would not upset him.

'And today you are at last able to sleep. The fever has gone. You will get well.'

She took a fresh napkin, dipped in cool lavender water, to replace the one on Philip's brow. His eyes flickered as if to open, his lips moved as if to speak.

'Sh. You must not tire yourself, I am here. I will stay by your side until you are well. Have some of this it will help your throat,' and she poured a spoonful of an elixir.

'Asleep again? No matter, I shall still be here the next time you wake.'

A grumpy old voice scolded from across the room, 'Ma'am, I beg you not to continue taking all these mixtures. They are for someone who is ill not for someone who is with child. I fear for your safety and for that of the baby.' The doctor's eyes further admonished her from over his spectacles as he came to his patient's side.

He began to study him minutely, starting with the pulse at Philip's temples and wrist. Then he opened Philip's chemise to carefully examine his chest, his stomach, his armpits. He turned to Juana, 'Ma'am, will you come this way?'

She followed him curious and eager to know what new information he had for her, what new suggestion he may be about to make. She would agree to anything after the wonders he had performed in just two days.

He whispered, 'It is time to call for the king's confessor.'

This could not be. This was some terrible mistake. She must have misheard. She had fallen asleep during her long vigil and

179

this was an ugly dream.

'No, no, you must be wrong, Dr. Parra. He has stopped shivering ... he had that enormous sweat ... those are good signs ... the fever has gone ... the danger is over ... see, he is sleeping peacefully ... everything to indicate a full recovery.' her words fought their way through her choking panic. 'Did you not say so yourself?'

'I did, and normally this is so, but it pains me to say that the king is falling into a profound sleep. I am afraid it is the kind which can only get deeper leading inevitably to ...'

'No! No! No! I will hear none of this, not another word!' She put her hands over her ears, weeping her refusal, hurrying back to her seat by the bedside. She willed Philip to get well, willed him to prove the doctor wrong; he had to be wrong. She would make Philip better if no one else could.

Dr. Parra beckoned the gentleman of the bedchamber to his side and gave whispered instructions to summon the confessor and on his return to inform the members of Philip's household that their master's health was deteriorating.

Philip was anointed with oil, accompanied by the priest's prayers, 'By this holy unction, and by His most tender mercy, may the Lord forgive thee ...'

Juana continued her vigil, silently urging him to waken that his eyes might see her, that he might be strengthened by her and despite the doctor, despite the priest, he would recover.

At seven o'clock the following morning Dr. Parra took his leave. There was nothing more for him to do.

Shortly before two o'clock that afternoon, Friday the twenty-fourth of September, 1506, King Philip I of Castile, Archduke of Austria, died in his sleep.

Some time elapsed then the priest knelt before Juana, whispering, 'My lady, King Philip is ...'

Startled, Juana turned to him putting a warning finger to her lips. 'Sh, Sh,' she whispered. 'No noise; there must be no noise. The king is sleeping.'

She leaned across the bed to brush Philip's forehead with her lips.

'Rest, my darling, rest and get well.'

For another three hours Juana sat by the bedside. She had stayed close by his side for days and nights without any rest: his constant companion, his loving wife, his nurse and at times mother to him. Now this was all finished; ended.

Marta took her and held her, then led her slowly from the room. Every part of Juana was numbed. Her Philip was dead.

Later that evening the Admiral Don Fadrique and the Constable Don Bernardino, both hurriedly summoned, walked with Juana to join others who had come to pay homage to Philip for the last time.

The audience chamber was lit by only a few candles. At one side stood a small group of monks chanting the psalms and intoning the services for the dead.

The walls had been hung with the richest of Philip's tapestries, and a dais had been placed at the far end of the room.

Juana made her way towards the throne, supported by the two gentlemen; they steadied her as she curtsied.

Philip was holding his final audience, according to the long-held custom of France and Burgundy. On the steps to the dais were the shields of Burgundy, Flanders, the Low Countries, and Austria: lions rampant, eagles, fleur de lis, all on fields of black, silver, or blue. Other shields, also with various coloured fields carried his device of the cross of St. Andrew and a sparking flint, the flame of faith. The canopy above the throne bore the embroidered coat of arms of Castile. Philip's King-at-Arms held his lord's personal standard showing an ornate crowned helmet, the collar of the Golden Fleece encircling a many quartered shield, and a green ribbon at its base declaring his challenge; *QUI VOUDRA.*

Philip looked down from his throne on this his final court. He had been robed for the occasion in a knee length black velvet jerkin, with a full length black gown lined with ermine

181

and bearing the embroidered coats of arms of Austria, Burgundy, Castile and Leon. There was just a glimpse of scarlet hose above the black velvet Flemish-style shoes. A cross of rubies and diamonds lay on his breast. His black velvet bonnet bore a single large ruby.

Juana drew close to him for the last time. She kissed his hands, then his lips whispering, 'Oh, love of my life.'

She left the dais, walked back to her uncle and out of the chamber.

Tears of compassion rolled down Don Fadrique's cheeks to nestle in his beard. This was surely too soon to be the end, he prayed.

It had to be the time for a new beginning.

WIDOWHOOD

Chapter 34

'Get out of the way! Move aside!'

The column of riders escorting Juana to Burgos had come across pitiable straggling groups of starving peasants stumbling their way towards hope; anywhere, nowhere. Blank faces on heads almost too heavy for feeble frames stopped to stare.

Juana drew back the curtain and pulled her fur lined cloak tight across her breast to fend off the chill of a bitterly cold December day and the bleak picture of helplessness.

Further on her cavalcade passed groups of city folk, their hired carts laden with goods and chattels, standing to one side before continuing their flight from the plague and the possibility of civil war.

Juana's Castile was in chaos. It had taken three months of isolation in her sister's country home where she could grieve privately before she could find the will to pull herself free of her pain and anguish and address the problems that beset her beloved country. At last, following several days of intense consultations with counsellors, she was returning to the city, ready to meet the Cortes convened at her request.

Within minutes of her arrival at the city gates she was in the courtyard of the Casa del Cordón and two pairs of strong arms were helping her from her litter.

The stairs up to the gallery were almost too much of a challenge and she fell against Marta and the balustrade.

'I swear this child will be the death of me,' she gasped.

This time below her in the courtyard there was no handsome Philip magnificent in mulberry and green about to ride out with his friends, all extravagant peacocks; only a scattering of stable lads and her small guard. But she would not dwell on that, or on Philip's death, there would be time enough later for all her sorrows. Today she would remain positive, would be deterred by nothing and no one. There were to be no distractions.

She passed directly to her retiring room where ladies awaited her with a pitcher of steaming water, bowls and towels.

'Marta, I shall take some light refreshment before I meet with the Cortes.'

The salon chosen for the audience chamber was cold despite the efforts of a fire and several braziers. Her secretary rose as she entered, which she acknowledged with a smile, motioning him to resume his work. 'Do not let me interrupt you, friend, unless you wish for some time to warm your hands by the fire.'

'I am almost finished, my lady.'

On the dais a canopied chair looked singularly imposing, she thought, and would definitely assist her in her task. She settled her awkward bulk into its velvet seat.

Her sister, and Doña Ulloa, a recently arrived lady-in-waiting from the court of King Ferdinand, arranged her black velvet skirts and hood.

Marta, never very far from her mistress, cast horror-stricken eyes about the room, muttering, 'It's a sin, it is. A sin!'

It was but a few weeks since Philip had held his court here; the walls lined with Flemish tapestries, chests groaning under displays of silver and gold plate. Today there was nothing to gladden the eye or cheer the heart. Cold air issued from every stone of the bare, unadorned walls and moved unchecked about the room furnished with her throne and a simple bench for the bishops of the Cortes. Everything had gone; stolen, pawned, or sent back to Brussels.

Similar thievery had been taking place throughout Castile. No action had been taken against this and many other wrongs; but Juana could not be held responsible, she had been too ill. However, the situation would not be tolerated a moment

187

longer. Since her recovery she had been tireless in her efforts to begin the process of setting things to rights. Her task was almost done. After today's meeting she would leave the remaining details in the hands of others; and that included Cisneros.

She chuckled to herself, delighting in the thoughts of his having to carry out her bidding. There was no doubting he still found her wanting and was moving heaven and earth to have her father govern Castile. But he and the Cortes were about to be surprised.

The members entered, Juana noting by their faces that here there was uncertainty, while over there curiosity, elsewhere suspicion, and everywhere shock that it was she who had summoned them; and she rejoiced for she had heard the rumours regarding her poor mental state.

'Welcome, my lords and procuradores. Let us proceed. I do not intend to waste your time nor mine. Archbishop Cisneros, do you continue to keep my father informed of events here?' She knew there wasn't a day went by that messengers weren't scurrying to and fro between the two of them.

He bristled, furious with her for continually refusing to sign a declaration making him regent in the absence of King Ferdinand, causing him unspeakable aggravation.

He glared at her then addressed the assembly, 'I do keep King Ferdinand informed, and repeatedly entreat him to return. But a request from his daughter would lend more weight. Is that not true, gentlemen?'

And he would try that ploy too, Juana thought, 'No, I think not. I leave that kind of letter writing to others.' After some very bitter experiences she would never be persuaded to put pen to paper on the subject of regencies, and in any case she had something quite different in mind. 'But please do emphasise that I am anxious to have him here.'

Cisneros changed the subject, he knew of another way to

wrest the control of Castile from Juana; and with her help. 'May we turn to the subject of vacancies in the church; there are many sees without their bishops. It is unwise to leave so many sheep without their shepherds.'

'Archbishop, I would not know who to consider, having been absent from this country for so long.'

'That is where I can be of service.'

'And what if I still chose poor shepherds? Think how serious that would be for the sheep.'

The admiral with a 'Bless me!' stroked his beard to hide his amusement. Padilla nudged his fellow procuradores to his left and right.

Juana waved the archbishop back to his place on the bench, 'We digress.' She was determined that there should be no further departure from her agenda. 'The document, please.'

Her secretary held an enormous roll of parchment complete with royal seals.

'This edict that I have had drawn up will go far in returning Castile to its former self, to the Castile of Queen Isabel,' she raised a hand to quell the whisperings. 'I felt it incumbent upon me to have these Doctors of Law, the most trusted counsellors to Queen Isabel, attest to it. It is a lengthy document, but a necessary one. It states that no office, tenancy, nor church appointments may go to anyone not a Castilian born and bred. It also revokes all land grants given by King Philip; you will find that all are named.' There was no resisting a glance at the worst offenders, Benavente, Villena, Juan Manuel. 'All monies will be returned immediately to the Royal Treasury.'

There were a few ripples of objection, but a great wave of approval. Cisneros did neither, he was preoccupied with Juana's obvious intention to govern Castile and this had to be avoided at all costs. King Ferdinand must return, the country would not be safe in this woman's hands.

'Archbishop, I shall leave it to you to see that my orders are executed with the utmost urgency.'

'Then may I suggest that meanwhile you should retire to a place untouched by the plague, Arévalo, perhaps?'

'I thank you for your concern, but I have other plans.' Her answer was polite but inside she was fuming to think that he dared suggest the town where her grandmother had spent years as a prisoner in its ugly fortress. 'I intend to take the King Philip's mortal remains to Granada. That was his wish. Now I need to speak to the Papal Nuncio, my father's ambassador Ferrer, the Archbishop of Burgos and the Bishops of Malaga and Jaen. The rest may leave. I am sure you will all support the archbishop in every way you can.'

Don Fadrique tugged on the constable's sleeve as they left, 'She's as good as she ever was, she's nobody's fool; I can tell you. By Jove, she knows how a lot of us feel about Cisneros.'

According to Flemish custom, surgeons had prepared Philip's body for burial. The brain had been removed, the heart placed in a gold casket and sent to Flanders to be placed above his mother's tomb. The entrails had been burned while all parts of the body had been squeezed dry of blood to prevent rot. The cadaver was then filled with perfumes, sewn up and placed in a double coffin, the first of lead the second of wood and taken to the cathedral for the Requiem Mass. Later it was taken to the Carthusian monastery only five kilometres away at Miraflores.

Since then there had been many rumours of plots to return the body to Flanders and Juana had begun to fear that this would inevitably come to pass if she did not take action.

'Sirs,' she informed the remaining gentlemen, 'I intend leaving immediately for Granada taking my dear departed husband to his final resting place.'

'Your highness, might I counsel you that this is not the time for travelling, it is winter and your condition ...'

'Archbishop I thank you for your concern, but there will be no postponing my departure. It is essential that I carry out the wishes of Philip. I also intend to place myself amongst friends in Granada. You know as well as I that Granada has always been solid in its support for me. I will stay there until the feuding in Castile is over.'

'Then you must go alone,' came the stern reply. 'I will not give my consent for the body to be moved. This is Canon Law; it must not be moved for at least six months.'

Juana panicked, thinking the worst. Someone had already taken the body. These people now sought to delay her discovery of the truth. Her voice was an explosion of fear. 'This is untrue! My mother's remains were taken from Medina to Granada within days of her death. We must go to Miraflores immediately. You will all attend me. The coffin must be opened. I have to see if his body is still there. You will be my witnesses.'

She tried to hurry towards the door, speed was vital. The Bishop of Malaga sought to restrain her with gentle words, 'Do not distress yourself unnecessarily. Nothing has changed. You will see exactly what you saw on All Souls Day when we had the coffin opened for you. Our dead king is embalmed; his face heavily covered with the very same bandages soaked in unguents and lime showing nothing more than a shape.'

She screamed at him. 'Do you think I will not know if it is not Philip? We will delay no longer. My escort of soldiers is ready. I have thought of every essential for my journey. I have clerics, doctors, and nurses. A cart with four strong horses is standing prepared for its precious burden. And I tell you this; I pray for your sakes that you have not tricked me and that King Philip's remains are still there awaiting their final journey.'

Trying to sound calm, she spoke to her ladies, 'Sister, I cannot thank you enough for everything you have done; you have been more than generous, I shall not ask more of you.

Doña Ulloa and Marta you shall accompany me.'

Doña Ulloa was triumphant, impatient to tell King Ferdinand of her success in becoming Juana's first lady. Everything was going to plan.

Chapter 35

In a small manor house in a village a few days travel from
Burgos Juana and three young ladies, sitting on large floor
cushions, were laughing and chatting, while occasionally
turning their attention to their sewing. The gentle strains of a
lute competed with the bird song that tumbled into the room
down rays of summer sunshine.

'Ze vezzer here, she is so kind.'

'Not "she",' Juana laughed, 'the weather is not a lady.'

'He is so kind,' another offered.

'Not even a gentleman. In England you say "it", the weather
is neuter.'

'How can you neuter the weather? Is he an animal?'

Needles and their threads were dropped into laps and
laughter reigned.

More than a year had passed, and Juana was at last on her
way to meet her father. The charm of the huddle of homes in
this peaceful setting had tempted her to stop to rest here for a
few days.

Her recently appointed ladies were taking the opportunity to
improve their knowledge of England; its language and its
people. A widowed queen only twenty-seven years old was
extremely marriageable, reasons of state virtually dictated it,
and Henry VII would not be an unacceptable husband. This
English marriage presented marvellous opportunities for
Castilian ladies to marry into the English nobility, and so many
a young beauty had sought the privilege of being a part of
Juana's court. These were the lucky few.

'What do you remember most?'

'It was spring, colder than here. There were enormous

expanses of green, the most glorious emerald green, and with sheep so big and round I am sure they could roll down the hills. And swans, I have never seen so many. And there were miles of deep, dark forests.'

'We want to hear about the people!'

'You wish to hear of the gentlemen! Then let me tell you that they tend to be taller than in Castile, more robust, the peasants most certainly were; quite the opposite of our starving folk. I pray God sends us better harvests this year. English lords are very rich.'

Sighs of delight, longing, expectation interrupted her. She continued, 'But that is because they do not have to spend their money on wars and bribes.'

'And the most handsome and wealthy gentleman of all is King Henry,' said one eager to hear anything at all about this story book king.

'He is handsome, wonderfully so, especially in word and deed,' and Juana told again her memories of their times together. Her small audience hung on to every word.

'Do read us one of his letters again, they are so romantic.'

Juana was only too happy to oblige for she found them romantic, too. She had been a widow for about eighteen months and this "courtship" was a much needed antidote to the black and heavy sorrow that sought at times to crush her. One, perhaps her favourite, was chosen from the many similar treasures in her jewellery box.

'This one, ... *I remember when we met how you spoke with grace and eloquence, how you took such interest in everything around you and with a delightful enquiring mind. You moved with elegance and dignity. You are everything a husband could desire.* Yet, perhaps Henry is somewhat too old. He is almost fifty.'

'I do not think that old for a gentleman. He will probably lose all his teeth before he runs out of seed,' someone dared.

'Sh. Sh. Sh.' Juana covered her ears but laughed as merrily as the rest at the outrageous remark.

Marta beamed from her chair close to the door at the far side of the room. She was as content as a mother hen with her brood of chickens. It did her heart good to know that her mistress was happy at last. Juana had gone through some very rough times: months of struggle against being locked away, the shock of Philip's death. The birth of baby Catalina had been a grave worry, too, the delivery being such a complicated business leaving Juana so desperately ill. All her other children had come into the world so easily, and just when she needed every bit of strength, this last one had been awkward. The doctors had had to use some fearsome looking instruments. And all the while the plague followed fast on their heels, striking folk down indiscriminately, showing no respect. Marta had ensured that neither sickly people nor strangers got anywhere near her beloved mistress. That had been no mean feat; there were far too many folk crowded into this small town. It was all too ridiculous! Whatever possessed the lot of them! Her mistress could barely breathe for lords, bishops, soldiers. She found it a bit intimidating herself, but she hadn't said anything to Juana, deciding it was probably an overreaction because she didn't like most of the people involved.

But this was soon to be put behind them. King Ferdinand had returned from Naples, and soon he and Juana would meet. They would talk about what had to be done about Castile, about Philip's remains; and then Juana could start her new life in England.

The door burst open and Doña Ulloa walked briskly towards Juana, leaving Marta thinking how some folk could never walk nicely into a room, convinced it had something to do with their characters.

'A fire has broken out in the church!'

'Dear God in Heaven; quickly Marta,' Juana ran to the door

reaching for her faithful servant's hand.

It was only a short distance to the village church. This was one of the advantages of staying here, the other being that most of the lords and their followers, including soldiers, had been forced to seek lodging in other villages; although some had still insisted on taking over local homes, however humble, the owners simply thrown out to fend for themselves in barns or hedgerows.

Tongues of flame licked around blackened yawning windows, burning wood smoke filled the air. A chain of villagers passed water-slopping wooden buckets towards the door, getting in the way of soldiers trying to keep the entrance clear for the emerging eight strong men bending under the coffin's weight.

The cleric Ferrer, Ferdinand's ambassador, was calling out instructions, battling against the confusion. He saw Juana and shouted, 'Now see what you have done! I warned you, but you never heed my advice.'

Juana's heart pounded with indignation; his manner was insufferable, 'I give the orders. I wanted fifty candles around the catafalque.'

'And I reminded you that thirty is the number set down.'

'And you think it was one of my additional candles that caused this?' She wondered why she was even arguing with the man; Philip's remains were safe and the fire would soon be put out and she would pay for any damage. 'The soldiers will take the coffin to my lodgings. You will have one of the rooms prepared as a chapel.'

'Your home is not the place to house the king's mortal remains.'

'Do you suggest instead that yet another villager be thrown from his home to house an outsider, this time a dead one?'

'There will be some very raised eyebrows about this,' he

called over his shoulder.

Juana grabbed Marta's hands and growled her frustration through gritted teeth, 'That is the second time he has dared to criticise me; you remember when he tried to insist I order prayers throughout the country for the swift return of my father? He wanted me to make it public how useless I am without my father at my side. Just who does he think he is, this jumped-up little clerk, giving orders?'

'Never you mind, you'll soon be rid of him,' Marta comforted; and, she hoped, Ulloa, too.

'True, my father can have his ambassador back. In fact that is the first thing on the agenda. The second is to be rid of Ulloa. I shall offer her to my father's wife with my blessing.'

Relief flowed through every vein in Marta's body. She had heard enough of Ulloa's vicious and evil whisperings, and she suspected that the contents of her many letters carried the selfsame lies about Juana. Lies that fed on themselves, growing fat with distortions and downright untruths of Juana's always opening Philip's coffin so she could kiss his feet. Of course it was all poppycock, but all the same it was worryingly difficult to fight folk who are devious. She thanked God that they would soon be far away from it all.

Chapter 36

So, the marriage with Henry had come to nothing, after all; the English king had died, Juana mused strolling down the long salon. In truth she knew it had never been feasible. How could she possibly have reigned over Castile while living in England? She would have had to have made her father regent, and she would have none of that, it didn't accord with her plans.

Two years had passed, the happiest years she had ever known, two years spent with her children; Ferdinand now six and Catalina a darling two year old toddler. She was more than content to continue this family life by leaving most of the day-to-day government of Castile in her father's hands. All the necessary terms and agreements had been drawn up and simply awaited two signatures; hers and her father's.

They had finally met yesterday after an interval of six years, the formal kneeling and kissing of hands quickly becoming loving embraces with the two of them on their knees holding each other close, Juana holding on to shoulders still as strong as any valiant warrior's. Ferdinand tossed his bonnet aside and Juana's widow's veil was flung back. Seeing her father again completely overwhelmed her and she cried unashamedly. Through a mist of tears and with trembling fingertips she was reacquainted with the handsome, rugged features of her beloved father.

Today their meeting, for a moment or two at least, would be more formal but once the documents were signed they could turn their thoughts to choosing a convenient home for her and her little family. It was sad that Maximillian would not allow her other children to join her (that was hateful politics interfering again; he was determined to keep Charles in

Flanders).

Suddenly she laughed, 'Well, Ulloa, the remaining few Flems should soon be in Maximillian's court, having made good their escape from Castile. What ridiculous figures they must have cut dressed as poor Franciscan friars but with a train of forty mules laden with the rich spoils of their thieving.'

'King Ferdinand has done exceedingly well to rid Castile of the last of its enemies. He has always had the good of Castile in his heart and it grieves me that God could only reward him and his new wife with a sickly boy child so soon to be taken to Heaven.'

Juana bit her tongue so as not to say she was angered by her attendant's boldness in offering unsought opinions and that she had not asked for a lecture on her father's attributes.

But there he was! It still seemed nothing short of a miracle to have him near. Cisneros, now Cardinal thanks to her father's successful negotiations with the pope, and Ferrer were almost tripping over their master's heels they hovered so close. It was such a comfort knowing that soon she would never have to face either of them again.

After welcoming her father she accompanied him to a table prepared with quills, ink, candle, seals, and the precious document. Juana's secretary and four Doctors of Law stood behind the thrones. Juana had to force herself to remain dignified when all she wanted to do was skip and dance; she was about to take the most important step in her life. That piece of paper was about to determine her future, a future without uncertainty, anxiety, or fear.

It was going to be exactly as it was when her mother was alive;

two monarchs ruling. Her father, with his many years of experience of dealing with the day-to-day government, would come to her to discuss any decisions and to seek her signature on all documents. She was to be queen with all the rights and authority to make the final decisions. Moreover, anything less than this would be unacceptable to her countrymen, many of whom had little regard for Ferdinand.

Her father held her hand, 'So now we must determine the best place for you to live. I have in mind the small town of Tordesillas.'

'Whatever made you think of such a place with its history of imprisoned queens?'

Ferdinand tapped the tip of her nose, laughing, 'That was well over a hundred years ago, silly!'

'But it is rather remote.'

'Not at all; it is precisely what you prefer; small and quiet. But it is conveniently situated, reasonably close to Valladolid where I shall convene the Cortes, making it easy for me to visit you. I grant you it is a little out of the way, but that has its advantages for the moment. There are still pockets of unrest, and my heart would be at ease knowing you are safe while I am in Granada dealing with the rebels down there.'

Juana closed her other hand over his, delighted that she could be of use; it would make Granada's acceptance of her father as joint monarch so much more palatable if she were by his side. 'I shall accompany you. They have always voiced their unwavering support for me, they will listen to me,' she could barely contain her excitement, 'and I could take Philip to his final resting place.'

'It has to be a military operation. Cisneros and I are taking an army down there; that is the only language rebels understand.'

'But that would be unnecessary if I were present,' Juana reassured him.

200

The voice of Cisneros cut across hers, 'Do you have no regard for filial duty? How dare you contradict your father? A daughter should listen, not speak.'

'You may have spoken to my mother like that, but I will not allow it. I am the queen of Castile and I am discussing matters of importance regarding its security and development with the king. I would ask you not to interfere.'

'Hold your tongue daughter, you offend the cardinal!' Ferdinand warned.

'I am sorry, father, but his presence has shadowed me like a bird of ill omen for years; always implying retribution should I dare spurn his advice.'

'Enough, Juana!' Ferdinand then softened his tone, 'Granada is out of the question. From the deep love I bear you I cannot permit you to further embarrass yourself with regard to the funeral cortege.'

'Meaning?'

'It breaks my heart to think you have been opening the coffin lid to gaze on Philip's body, to kiss his feet ...'

'Lies, all lies!' She looked from Cisneros to Ferrer then to Ulloa; which of the three was the source of such offensive lies, and for what reason?

'And there was the incident at a convent.'

Hurt and anger caught at her breath, 'Stop! This is infamy! A malicious mind has been at work. In Burgos I insisted on his coffin being opened that I and other witnesses would know that Philip's body had not been stolen; but that someone should suggest that I ever did this again, and to make their lies disgustingly ghoulish is unforgivable.' Her voice grew loud, too loud. 'The convent episode was quite straightforward. It was the sanctuary of nuns and I was determined to protect their innocence, and probably their virginity, from the lusty guards accompanying the cortege. That is why I ordered everyone to rest outside its gates and not to take shelter indoors before

201

setting off once more. That is the truth of the matter!'

That other Juana came to her aid, and she cautioned herself that by explaining her actions she was surrendering her authority, she was allowing herself to become the victim. A queen is not called upon to offer reasons for anything. She stood tall and thrust her chin forward and in a quiet voice announced, 'This will never be mentioned again. I have also decided that this would be the best moment to offer Doña Ulloa's services to your good lady wife, Germaine, and to return your ambassador, cleric Ferrer. Your need for him is greater than mine. Now I shall make my preparations to travel to Granada.'

Chapter 37

Juana stormed into her apartments hurling abuse at Doña Ulloa. If her hands were free she would surely throw something at her or scratch her deceitful face, but they were otherwise occupied frantically tearing and pulling at fastenings at the side of her bodice and at laces attaching the sleeves at her shoulders.

'You vile wretch, you knew!'

'I ...'

'Do not dare speak,' she hissed the words from between clenched teeth, hot tears scalding her cheeks. 'Marta, help me. Find me a gown and robe, a mantle, a hood, something, anything, but quickly. And bring my jewellery casket.'

An astonished Marta launched herself into action; curious yet anxious not to know why her mistress should want to change into royal robes after months of total disregard for her appearance. If only Ulloa hadn't forbidden her to wander far from this area at the rear of the palace, she would have had some idea. As she rummaged in the solitary chest she heard Juana demand Ulloa bring a mirror, and she swallowed hard.

'Shall I send for some hot water? I think that might be nice.'

'No time for that, Marta.'

Marta's fingers succeeded where Juana's had failed, and the soiled and filthy woollen sleeves were freed and then the stained bodice. The chemise came off next, bringing with it a reeking odour of stale sweat. The fouled woollen skirts and stained petticoats carried an even worse stink of stale urine.

Juana pulled a loose robe over her shoulders and stared at the pile of discarded clothes. A few moments ago she had considered them embarrassingly ordinary, totally unsuitable, and that was serious enough.

'Marta, how long have I been like this?'

Marta's unease deepened, she had no desire to open old wounds. For months she had done everything possible to nurse and comfort her mistress, and together they had learned to cope with adversity, but she had failed miserably in helping Juana retain some pride in her appearance, to look after herself properly. She continued fussing and fidgeting with Juana's robe.

Juana snatched the mirror from Doña Ulloa, 'Get out, wait outside! Dear God, no!' The image staring back at her was covered with a layer of grime, smudged rivulets hinting at an unhealthy skin beneath, huge eyes set in a gaunt face, and the hair, that once so attractive auburn hair that Zayda had washed and dressed with perfumed oils, was nothing more than a dull and dirty thatch.

'Marta, what has happened to me?'

'My lady, you've not been well for some time. And, I might add, it's because there's some as have got too much authority and no common decency,' she flung the words towards the doorway, knowing that Ulloa would be listening.

'Why? When?'

Marta busied herself washing and dressing Juana, 'It was when King Ferdinand took your little boy away. But we don't want to go over all that again, it will only upset you.'

'But I got him back?'

'Only when you said you would come to Tordesillas. That's when he was brought back. But once we were here he was taken away again, because this place wasn't good enough for a little prince so they said. That's when you got really poorly.'

'I did? I was ill? When was this?' She had to make some sense; some order of forgotten days.

'Maybe a year, maybe more, but you put up a wonderful fight. You showed them, my goodness, so you did, refusing to come out of your room, not going to Mass and all the rest.'

'But I failed?'

'Well yes, but they couldn't stop you shouting about Ferrer; how he treated you, how he wouldn't let you do anything, not even permit you to visit your husband's tomb in the convent. That scared the lot of them. So they brought you here to the back end of the palace where no one would hear you.' And she had had to watch helpless as they dragged her mistress along the corridor.

'So the battle was lost.'

Marta wept as she completed her work, 'Not entirely. We've got through many a bad day. But then, after a while, you didn't care any more about yourself. You seemed to have given in. I'm sorry.'

A year or more had passed by? What had she been doing all this time? Reading perhaps, or playing her beloved vihuela, or sometimes her harpsichord, sewing; or sitting doing nothing, absolutely nothing for hours at a time. It was only if her father came to see her, and that was rare, that she ever got to know and talk about events beyond this room, this palace, Tordesillas or Castile.

'Marta, we must never let this happen again, I must be more positive. I have some awkward explaining to do first but then everything should be fine.' Juana studied herself in the mirror, 'Marta, you have done wonders.'

She looked regal in her black velvet with her mother's gold necklace of sheaves of arrows. Rubies and pearls on brooches sparkled on her bodice and skirts. Her lifeless tresses had been securely tucked away under a fresh black hood.

Marta folded her arms in satisfaction, 'I don't know who has come to visit you, but they'll never guess you haven't been well.'

Juana closed her eyes and said nothing; hoping.

She hurried along the corridor passing the guards placed there for her "safety".

'Hurry, Ulloa.'

She turned the corner and headed for the Grand Salon where about an hour ago she had entered with her father. The enormity of that disastrous visit now hit her hard.

Yes; earlier she and her father had entered the salon, he in his jerkin of black and gold brocade, a long gown of crimson velvet lined with ermine, on his head a black velvet bonnet trimmed with gold; and she ... not in a simple woollen dress, as she had thought, but wearing those disgusting, indescribably filthy, clothes now lying on the floor of her room.

There, waiting to greet her were ambassadors from France and Austria, archbishops, bishops, the admiral, the constable, the Dukes of Alba and Medinasidonia, counts too numerous to remember. A glittering display of power: Spanish power, Europe's power.

She had not been told of the audience or she would have changed into something more appropriate. She had frozen with shame. Her shame had become disbelief; that her father could have done this to her. With a supreme effort she had spoken, 'My lords you must excuse me. I had not expected you. I was not prepared. I request your indulgence for a few moments then I shall be happy to grant you an audience.'

And then she had fled, snatched remarks following her, 'Good God, she must be ill ... slovenly ... lamentable ... her mind must be ... cannot be fit to ...Ferdinand must ...'

The admiral had followed her, urging her to listen to him, but she would not stop, 'Not now, uncle.' She couldn't afford to waste a single moment.

The doors were opened and once more she entered the Grand Salon.

The room was empty. The room was empty, except for Ferdinand who stood at the window enjoying the view of the river and the meadows beyond.

'Where is everyone?'

'Gone, my dear, all gone.'

The battle was lost; they would not come again.

Without shifting his gaze he continued, 'They were overcome with shame or pity for you. They left after offering me their fullest support; recognising that sadly you are unfit to be considered as queen.'

'I cannot believe this of you.' She was bewildered, confused, frightened. 'You were here just yesterday and we talked of many things, detailing your meetings with envoys from France and Austria to form a league against Venice. Not once did you mention my appearance, nor did you say there was to be a royal audience today. But now I know why, I see it all. You were not content with all the power I willingly devolved to you!' Her voice was raised, she was shouting, and she couldn't stop herself. 'It was not enough, because you were afraid! You had to ensure that those who only tolerated you because you are my father would see me in such a light they would give you full authority! So you put me on display! You used me. You did not return to Castile to comfort and support me, today you proved that beyond doubt; you brought the fool to the feast and rubbed your hands with glee. A loving father would never treat his daughter so!'

'Do try to control yourself. Being a king is my first responsibility. I told you that, years ago.'

'To be a king, do you have to be a cruel father?'

She blotted her tears with the back of her hand, moving towards him, her heart breaking, her arms outstretched begging some compassion. 'I loved and trusted Philip. I loved and trusted you. A husband and a father; both have betrayed me.'

'You women have such strange notions about love. You make it your whole existence. We men have other driving forces to fill our hearts; love, when it exists takes a poor second place.'

'My uncle loves me, where is he?'

'Gone.'

'You have left me with no one to turn to. I have no means of redress.'

'None whatsoever; I now have Castile in the palm of my hand. There will not be one lord to side with you or your son Charles. I leave tomorrow for Granada to deal once and for all with those rebels. You will remain here withdrawn from the world. Very soon that world will cease to have any interest in you. Ferrer will govern this house and if you try to prevent him or his servants from carrying out my requests, then he has my authority to use whatever force is necessary.'

She was struggling to make sense of his words. What was he threatening? Why? What would he request Ferrer to do, and why might it require force?

'Am I to be treated as some wild creature to be tamed, to bend to its master's will? Is that all I am to you, a worthless animal?'

'I would not go so far as to say worthless. In fact you are quite valuable, inasmuch as I need you alive so that I can continue as regent of Castile; it is important I have her power and wealth to further Aragón's causes.'

How was she to fight this; and who was there to support her? At least she had Marta in whom she could trust and there might be others.

'I must have some of the ladies who served my mother,' it was always possible that they might be of some help.

'We shall see,' Ferdinand answered with indifference. It was of little consequence who was placed in Juana's service for they would be his appointees, taking orders only from him and answering only to him.

Juana was to be kept alive but kept out of the public eye.

People would soon forget her but so long as she lived Castile was his.

Juana had lost a crucial battle but she was determined the

war was not yet lost. It occurred to her that she did, in fact, have one weapon left in her armoury and she intended using it immediately.

She would refuse to eat.

Chapter 38

The year 1516 was a significant one for Spain and the Franciscan friar wondered if it would be equally significant for Juana. Brother Juan de Avila glanced about the miserable room; no better no worse than the rest in these apartments he assumed. The April sun only visited this part of the palace via a dank courtyard accompanied by the stink of refuse thrown into heaps outside the kitchens below and steadily rotting.

He had visited Juana's apartments every day since his arrival in Tordesillas as Juana's spiritual guardian about a week or so ago and his embarrassment and anger increased on each occasion. Neglect hung in the air as if this room had been long forgotten. It was his understanding that Juana had been restricted to these rooms for at least five years. His attention passed from a small table with its solitary candlestick to the humble woman standing in attendance before returning to Juana in her grey wool dress sitting at his side on one of the two chairs which along with the table were the only furnishings. He had to remind himself yet again that she was Queen of Spain and not something more akin to a nun.

They had finished their prayers but instead of leaving he had lingered, 'Your royal highness, I am to inform you ...' He straightened his coarse grey habit, 'I wish you to prepare for ...' He could not bring himself to utter the words, not yet. Instead he beckoned Marta, 'You must find suitable attire for your mistress. There is to be an audience in the Grand Salon.'

Juana raised her head. 'An audience?'

'Yes, my lady, a messenger from Cardinal Cisneros.'

This was odd; she never received visitors in this room let alone the Grand Salon. She would have to consider this most carefully. 'No one comes here, no one sees me save those who …' She held first one wrist then the other.

'The Bishop of Mallorca, the messenger, is the bearer of important news from Cardinal Cisneros.'

'Cisneros. I remember him. Why Cisneros? Why does this bishop not come from my father? In any case it cannot be good news,' she reached for Marta.

'The cardinal is regent of all Spain. My lady, King Ferdinand, your father, is dead.' There, it was said, he had done as the bishop requested.

'The king is dead; Cisneros regent. It seems to me he was regent of Castile once, but that was long ago. He was no friend of mine then, no doubt his opinion of me is still the same.' She nodded her head agreeing with herself; her father was dead, Cisneros was regent, therefore nothing had changed.

Brother Juan waited; it was said that she had never shed a tear for her husband, so perhaps she would not for her father. It was most strange.

'The bishop, my lady, the messenger from Cisneros; the audience?'

Juana jumped up. 'Of course, I must change,' she announced as if this was a daily occurrence. 'How marvellous it will be to rid myself of these filthy rags.' As quickly as she had stood she sat down again. 'But who is to say the messenger will still be in the salon when I get there?'

'My lady everything has been arranged.'

'All the same I am afraid that he and anyone else will be gone.'

'The Bishop of Mallorca is a gentle man and will have much good news for you, and have no fears for I shall be there. I will retire now and await you in the corridor.' He left the room to stand a few feet from the guards at Juana's door.

Marta found black velvets, brocades, and gave them a thorough shaking. The skirts were beginning to show signs of

211

age, but they would do.

'How strange that Cisneros should send a messenger. Do you suppose he wants me to govern Spain? I doubt it and, Heaven knows, Ferrer would never allow me to govern this house let alone give his permission for me to rule Spain. What do you think?'

'It's all too complicated,' was the only reply. Marta was determined not to enter into any discussion that might be deemed controversial; that was how she had managed to retain her position as the queen's servant. She saw what she saw, thought much and said very little, and it hadn't always been easy.

'Best to wear this chemise, for it buttons at the wrists and will cover those nasty marks.' How many times had she gently applied the warm mixture of olives, fat and egg white to the cruel wounds on that delicate flesh? It made her so angry that anyone should even dare to think of treating her mistress so, let alone actually doing it. Fancy, those poor wrists all scarred with fresh red welts and older browner ones where leather thongs had strapped her to her chair.

In the Grand Salon the Bishop of Mallorca was organising his papers and letters. Following the king's death there had been an uprising in the town of Tordesillas as well as a rebellion in the palace. Over the years many had been stirred by the stories of Juana's ill treatment and felt this was an opportune time to rescue her from Ferrer. The captain of the town guard and the chief magistrate had been the first to move, trying to gain entrance to the palace only to be repulsed by Ferrer and Ferdinand's Royal Guard. And then the bishop had arrived with unquestionable authority, detaining Ferrer, putting him under house arrest.

A clerk handed him a letter still smiling at its contents, 'You have pleased a lot of people with Ferrer's detention.'

'While he finds it all so unjust. How dare he talk of justice? He complains of malicious lies, insists he has never held the queen prisoner, that the only reason he force fed her was to conserve her life, and that above all every action he took was at Ferdinand's bidding.' He threw the letter on to the table, 'He writes seeking congratulations from Cisneros, in the form of a substantial pension, for running this house like a convent.'

The clerk sighed, shaking his head, 'The queen's lack of commitment to her religious duties is a cause for concern, but could never warrant the use of the lash; and possibly Ferrer's insistence on her attending several services every day may have prompted her rebellion.'

'I agree. Ferrer should consider himself fortunate not to be subjected to a public whipping alongside the others found guilty of the brutal treatment of Queen Juana. The confirmation of the appointment of the new palace governor is here?'

The clerk shuffled through the papers, 'Here, my lord. Such a wise decision; by the time King Charles arrives this house will be in such good order there will be no need for him to consider seeking elsewhere for someone of his own choice.'

The doors to the Grand Salon opened; the bishop quickly rose to welcome Juana. He bowed low, then knelt before her and waited to kiss her hand. He was shocked at what he saw; a lady in her thirties, old before her time and in clothes looking just as aged.

She looked bemusedly down at him.

The bishop began, 'Your Royal Highness, Queen Juana of Castile, Aragón, Navarre, Naples, Sicily …'

Juana looked about her, 'My, such a huge room. I had quite forgotten its size; the windows, the sunlight, so many beautiful things.' She marvelled at the tapestries, every chair, each table and the lustrous silverware.

She was led to her throne. It had a canopy above it bearing her coat of arms.

She was afraid to breathe lest this wonderful dream shatter. It was as if she were someone else watching as she entered this exquisite room, saw herself greeted formally by a bishop then make her way past treasures to a throne.

With timid fingers Juana traced the carved wood then lowered herself into a luxurious velvet cushion, carefully resting her back, its wounds still tender from the last whipping. She gazed down at her lap for some time before finally venturing to look at the others in the room.

They were all still there!

'Your highness I am here on the cardinal's bidding. He hopes to bring you his respects personally very soon. Meanwhile much has happened, and I would wish to share the details with you. Your governor, Ferrer, has been dismissed along with his servants.'

Juana asked the friar, not believing. 'Brother Juan, has he truly gone? For ever?' Her fingers sought out the scars on her wrists. 'But who is to take his place?'

She dreaded the thought of renewed lashes of the scourge, of a repeat of yelled insults and threats, of having to protect her face from stinging slaps, of further struggles against biting and burning leather straps tying her to a chair, and food pushed into her forcibly opened mouth. 'Who is to take his place?'

'It is Hernan Duque. At one time he was in the service of Queen Isabel and King Ferdinand.'

Juana clapped her hands with joy; he was someone from a distant happy past. 'I know him, my lord bishop. I know him. He was such a gentle, sensitive man.'

'He is here now. May I bring him to you?'

'Why is he not here already?'

'It would not be protocol to have him here before you have given permission.'

Protocol! She loved the very sound of the word. This was exciting. She would soon remember all the protocol with a little practice.

Hernan Duque, tall and handsome in his tawny robes, a brown velvet bonnet in his hand, approached the throne. Juana leaned forward to peer at the face of this man, now in his early forties, with those dark, honest eyes the same as they always were.

'You are most welcome, sir.'

He raised his eyes to the lady who spoke. She was so thin and weak as if made of paper. This lady had survived years of unmentionable terror, imprisoned like a common convict in a cell. He vowed that he would spend every waking hour seeking to lead her from the past horrors and guide her carefully through what must now be a confusing world.

There was an awkward silence. Juana could think of nothing to say. She smiled. Her smile saddened him immensely; it was a vacant smile, the smile of a simpleton.

'My lady I have issued orders for rooms to be prepared for you on this side of the palace.'

'This side, overlooking the river,' she played with the thought for a moment or two. 'Wonderful. And may I use the outer gallery?'

'This is your palace. You make the decisions and we, your servants, will do as you command.'

Juana hated that word, decisions. 'I do not care for decision making. That is what I told my father. I need someone good at day-to-day governing who will keep me informed, to bring the necessary papers for me to sign. Then I can live happily with my child. That is all I ask.'

Hernan Duque doubted she would ever again be capable of making any serious decisions.

The bishop changed the subject, wondering how, in truth, Juana and Cisneros could possibly cooperate. 'The cardinal will discuss these matters with you. Meanwhile, we must attend to your apartments, your clothes ...'

'I have little interest.'

'With respect,' her apathy shocked the bishop, even angered him, 'you must have everything that befits a queen. There has been gross neglect, of you and your apartments.'

Juana looked down at her worn skirts. His words had sparked a memory. 'I begin to feel this is some malicious sport,' she began. An ice cold grip of dread was taking hold. She must prepare herself for the bitter truth; it was like that other time, these people were only here to taunt, to mock, to ridicule.

'My lady,' Hernan's voice was kind, 'it may take some time for you to be convinced but try to believe we are here as your faithful servants. Your household is free of everyone who would wish you harm. All those dreadful times are banished for good.'

'Then I shall test you. I wish to take a walk outside,' Juana challenged.

'Whenever it pleases you; but there is no reason to ask. You will tell me what you wish to do or when you wish to do it. I am at your command.'

'Ah, but supposing I wish to walk as far as the convent, what if I ask to go to see my husband's coffin? What will you say then?' She waited for a resounding No. It never came.

'I shall be honoured to escort you, ma'am.'

She laughed, 'I must be in heaven.' She drank in everyone and everything in the room and it made her dizzy. It was too much and she began to tremble. 'I must go; I need to be on my own for a while.'

Catalina, her nine year old daughter burst through the doors, running. 'Maman, Maman,' she called, jumping up and down.

216

'Maman, we are to have new rooms. I sneaked along to peek at them. They are as lovely as this. You must come and look; the tapestries, furniture and most of all the bed hangings, I have never seen anything quite so ...'

'Yes, my dear, but first our manners. These gentlemen are our newfound friends, the Bishop of Mallorca and Hernan Duque our new House Governor. We owe these gentlemen many thanks.'

'Oh sirs, I thank you. I truly, truly thank you. The rooms are so big and so perfect and this one ... I could dance for joy.'

They were all touched by the little one before them in her black bodice and skirt, her hair pulled severely back into a tight braid. How had she coped with the years of isolation? What damage might have been caused? And who could even think of incarcerating such an innocent?

Hernan asked, 'And are the rooms truly perfect, my lady princess?'

'Well, I would love to have another window, a window that looked down on the street. I often heard children passing by in my old room and I expect they will go by this one and I would dearly like to see them and talk to them. All I ever see is grown-ups.'

'I shall see that it is done immediately. And there is more. DoZa Beatriz de Mendoza, of your age, will be taken into service as your companion.'

'Do you hear, Maman? I am to have a friend!'

Catalina skipped and danced her way out through the door singing, 'I am to have a friend. I am to have a friend. Wait till I tell nurse.'

'Catalina and I have much to learn or relearn in courtly manners. I think I shall take a little air out on the gallery before retiring.'

Hernan offered his arm to escort her.

She stepped out into air so pure, so redolent of liberty it

217

made her gasp and fall against him. Here were sights she had thought never to see again: the flowing waters of the river, trees swaying in the breeze, and people, ordinary people, working in the fields.

'This last struggle has been a lengthy one. Too long! Do you remember my brother? He was right. He told me to fight for what I thought was right. But there is something else too,' she moved away to look up at him. 'There is goodness in this world and good people to help me in my fight. Wrongs have been righted and I have finally got justice. I am free. I am Queen Juana once more. And this time I am queen of all Spain.'

'My lady, you are the monarch of the largest and richest nation in all Europe.'

The Franciscan, Brother Juan, was the first to speak as he and the doctor strolled up and down the anteroom, 'We live in very similar times as those of years ago.'

The doctor pulled his black cap tightly over his ears as if to shut out the evil of those days when Philip was king. 'Those damned Flems; leopards that don't change their spots!'

'True, doctor, anyone wishing to retain his official position must buy it from Chimay.'

They stopped for a moment to take advantage of the warmth from a brass domed brazier in the centre of the anteroom. The September day could not be considered cold but they saw no reason to deny themselves the luxury.

The bishop entered, muttering, 'More problems. Chimay has proposed a Flem as regent knowing we Spaniards would prefer Cisneros!'

'Truthfully,' Brother Juan commented, 'we would have almost any Spaniard as regent as opposed to a foreigner. And Juana's second son, rather than the Archduke Charles, or should I say King Charles, would be far more acceptable to many of our countrymen.'

Deep in thought at the dangers this posed they took several turns about the room.

The doctor reopened the conversation. 'I believe King Charles is unhappy about the queen's signature appearing first on documents.'

'Most unhappy,' replied the bishop. 'He is unhappy about that and to swearing that if one day God returns our queen to good health, he must revert to being prince.'

Brother Juan cleared his throat, warning his friends of

approaching footsteps.

Juana acknowledged them as she passed, on the arm of Hernan Duque, making her way into the Grand Salon. Her small court of ladies and gentlemen followed her. The three men joined them.

'Hernan, you have worked wonders.'

'Not a difficult task with so many magnificent furnishings to choose from. Those from Flanders are amongst the most beautiful I have ever seen.'

'My lord bishop, doctor, and Brother Juan, do draw near and listen to what I have to tell you.'

Juana had been transformed, changed beyond their wildest hopes in the last year and a half. She was no longer emaciated or sickly looking. Despite her thirty-eight years, many of them spent under intolerable conditions, a newly born youthfulness about her gave a fresh bloom to her face and added lightness to her step. The news that her children Charles and Leonor were coming to Spain had lifted her spirits even higher. She radiated joy.

Although preferring still to dress in black, red satin flashed at times from within the slashes in the sleeves and amongst the folds of her skirts, and she had begun to wear more jewellery.

'Gentlemen all the rooms are incredible. This one gives you some indication of the splendour.' She looked about her as she spoke; at the long table, the many chairs, the chests, all in dark oak; at the silver and gold plate and candlesticks on every available surface. 'As you see these tapestries from Flanders have replaced the others since my son apparently prefers biblical scenes. In his dining room there is a sideboard positively groaning with gold and silverware and all resting on the richest cover of crimson velvet. The floor has a carpet made of gold and brightly coloured silks.' She barely paused for breath, 'The walls in his private apartments are hung with cloth of gold, a tapestry of gold with several figures in red while another is completely of gold and white. Gentlemen the splendour is breathtaking.' Her eyes sparkled with delight as she hurried on. 'The rooms for Leonor have tapestries depicting woodland scenes. I like those very much for they so remind me of Almazán. The canopy over her chair is of crimson velvet and cloth of gold. Her sleeping chamber is all cloth of gold, quite perfect for a young lady.' Now she did pause, 'And this is most interesting. Prepare yourselves.' She put her fingers to her lips as if to conceal her smile. 'The rooms for Chimay have such entertaining tapestries.'

She leaned towards them beckoning her conspirators closer, 'The tapestries are all scenes of the miracles of Our Lord. It does make one think, might God even yet work some miracle on the dreadful man.' She could not refrain from laughing at the remote possibility of a reformed Chimay eating and sleeping at the feet of Him who sees all.

'My lady I am sure you did not intend to mock the scriptures and are truly hoping that God will offer guidance to Chimay and perhaps make him acknowledge the error of his ways in Flanders?' the bishop suggested.

Juana had already begun to think of making a similar lighthearted comment about the tapestry in this room since she found it quite enchanting. John the Baptist was preaching to an earnest group of listeners gathered round, but one small boy in the bottom left corner had found a wooden whistle to play with finding it far more interesting than a chronically dull sermon. But, obviously, the bishop was in too serious a mood and would not be amused.

'All these wonderful furnishings make our apartments seem quite ordinary by comparison.'

Hernan felt he had disappointed her and made to offer some changes.

'I tease, ours are good enough. The tapestries are to our liking and we do not require cloth of gold. Our plate is of

221

equally good workmanship, it is just not so abundant and quite rightly so. I do not seek ostentation.'

Juana had enjoyed every moment since Hernan Duque had become the Governor of the Household.

She was treated at all times with the honour that befitted her as queen. He had always ensured she had those about her to attend to her every need. Her meals were always served on sparkling silver. All her rooms were kept sweet smelling with rosemary and lavender. Her bed was made up with crisp fresh linen every day, and she was always carefully and elegantly attired. She had had the pleasure of holding frequent audiences. There were always musicians present to play for her or to accompany her whenever she wished to play. A newly arrived gold-inlayed clavichord had been a wonderful surprise. Her fingers for so long idle soon relearned their skill to transport herself and her listeners into the pleasantest of reveries. Whenever she wished Hernan would escort her to the Convent of Santa Clara where she offered prayers for the soul of her husband. Hernan had organised picnics, banquets, and tournaments, nothing of the scale of those in Flanders but just as exciting. Then there were those evenings when Catalina and Beatriz danced for them.

To add to this idyllic life she was soon to see two of her four children she had had to leave behind in Flanders twelve years ago.

'Your highness,' announced the Captain of the Guard, 'I have received the news that King Charles, your son, is on his way to Tordesillas.'

Juana scowled at the kneeling figure, 'Be it known that I stand alone as monarch. I am the queen, and my son Charles is the prince and nothing more.'

Juana may have sounded haughty, but immediately beneath the surface lay a fear, a heart-sinking suspicion that a struggle lay ahead.

Chapter 40

In the dusk of this late afternoon in December Charles entered the Grand Salon followed by his sister Leonor.

'Your highness,' the Bishop of Mallorca, Brother Juan, Hernan Duque and a small group of courtiers bowed low. Eyes were then lifted to discover a spindly framed youth with a face of corpse-like pallor with bulging eyes and a heavy, protruding lower lip and jaw. However, whatever he lacked in physical splendour was more than compensated for by his attire. He positively glittered in his outfit of red, yellow, white and gold, outshining the dozens of candles lit for this occasion. The high, quilted collar of his shirt was covered with precious stones. His long gown of crimson velvet was lined with cloth of gold. His white satin jerkin sparkled with gold and yet more gems.

Leonor, walking two steps behind, shone like the summer sun in her yellow brocades twinkling with jewels. She was an attractive young woman with the fairest of skins and bluest of blue eyes, and happily she had been spared the Hapsburg jaw of her brother.

'Hernan Duque at your service. As governor of the palace, may I say we are greatly honoured to welcome our king and his sister the Princess Leonor.'

A gentleman from Charles' entourage stepped forward, 'I am Prince Chimay, Chief Advisor to His Majesty King Charles. As yet my royal master has no understanding of your language therefore I shall translate for him.' Chimay gave a swift icy glare at Hernan, the person responsible for Juana's improved health; a threat to his plans.

The chill wrapped itself around Hernan. This man's manner and tales of his cruelty towards Juana provoked immediate

223

distaste.

The bishop and Brother Juan prayed for guidance in quieting their wrath against a man who, before Cisneros was even cold in his tomb, was seeking to have his young nephew made Archbishop of Toledo.

'*Je veux visiter la reine. Tout de suite.*' Charles had no time for tiresome introductions, he was impatient to have his interview with his mother over and done with so that he could assert to all, and in good conscience, that he had kept God's commandment and had satisfied the common people's wishes in honouring her.

'His majesty desires to see his mother.'

Hernan bowed, 'Yes, I understood. I speak several languages having spent some time in various foreign courts. French is not unknown to me.' What he did not say was that he had found it excruciatingly difficult to understand a word that Charles had said. His speech was dreadful: his tongue was too big for his mouth; words were left incomplete because his lower jaw jutted so far forward it prevented his mouth from closing.

Drawing himself up to his full height he addressed the king, determined not to speak through Chimay. 'Whenever it pleases your highness to visit the queen I shall be honoured to escort you.'

'One moment, Hernan Duque,' Chimay raised a finger of admonishment. 'King Charles has the title of majesty and we would be pleased for you to remember that.' He turned to Charles, 'Your majesty, a word in private.' He walked him some little distance away, 'I think it best that I see your mother first. I will plan your entrance as a surprise. We can talk about Brussels, you and your sisters when you were very young, your grandfather and aunt caring for you. Then I will announce your arrival; *et voila!*'

'*C'est nécessaire?*'

'*Je crois avoir raison.* By the time I have finished she will be confused to see two adults instead of two children. And I also expect her to be overcome by your splendour. It will undo some of that governor's splendid work we have heard so much of.'

'*Eh bien, excellent, Chimay.*'

Hernan Duque would have liked to know what Chimay was up to, but could hear nothing, 'If you would care to follow me.'

He led them down the corridor at the end of which was a door covered with a wall hanging. The guards stood to attention and servants drew back the heavy cloth.

Chimay motioned for Charles and Leonor to wait in the small anteroom. 'If you wait here with the door open you shall hear all.'

Hernan could not make sense of this. Why were Charles and his sister not going directly into the room to see their mother? A ploy by Chimay; but why, to what purpose?

Juana was sitting, as usual, with two or three ladies for company and with only the softest lighting from a few candles.

Hernan bowed, 'With permission, your highness, you have a visitor.'

'At this late hour?'

'Prince Chimay. Do you remember him? He wishes to present himself.'

She rebuked him with her eyes telling him she could never forget Chimay. 'I should be pleased to receive him.'

Juana felt so confident. Times had changed. She was queen. Not only was she queen but she was queen with many loyal supporters. She was in her own country and not in Flanders.

'Your royal highness.'

Here was the man on his knees before her (and about time she thought).

'Ah, Prince Chimay.'

'I hope I find you in good health.'

'Your wish is granted, I am in excellent health.'

'I bring you greetings from your sister Margaret of Savoy.'

'Poor Margaret. Life has not been too kind to her. Still, she has had all my darling babies to care for as though they were her own: Leonor, Charles, Isabel and Maria. I was not allowed to bring them with me.'

'The Emperor also sends his greetings.'

'Good. You will be able to send both of them mine. And at the same time you must let them know all about me. I am sure you would find that a most pleasing task. Writing letters, spreading gossip, is almost a national pastime in Flanders as I recall.'

Chimay was greatly surprised; surprised and disappointed for this was not what he had hoped for. This Juana was far different from the one he had expected. Her memory was good, her French perfect. She had that same old hint of sarcasm in her voice, she was arch and most decidedly not unnerved by his presence. It was that damnable Hernan Duque!

'My other happy duty is to tell you all about two of your children, Charles and Leonor. The way the Spanish have received your wonderful children could not have been bettered. Wherever they have gone the crowds have been jubilant.'

She smiled and nodded, 'I am sure you are right.'

'The Emperor Maximilian, of course, has ordered and monitored their excellent upbringing and education. I cannot praise your children too highly. They cannot be faulted; their tutors find them to be excellent students. You will never come across their betters. They are so virtuous and prudent, they have such good manners ...' He was floundering. It was the way she just sat there smiling; it exasperated him. 'What they desire most is to see you and do you reverence. And if you would be so gracious as to command me to go find them I will do so with great pleasure. I am sure that you would be happy to see them.'

226

'Chimay, I would be delighted to see my children.'

As he left the room she beckoned to Hernan, 'What is this all about? Where does he have to go to find my children? Are they in Valladolid, or here in the palace, and why do they not come directly to me? Are they too young to present themselves? I am confused.'

'They arrived, unexpectedly, a short while ago; and they are quite old enough to present themselves.'

'Then why all that nonsense from that odious creature? I did not need to listen to all that when I am about to see them. And when I do see them I can judge for myself as to their being prudent and virtuous and all the rest.'

Chimay re-entered with some five or six others and started to make the introductions but Juana dismissed him with a wave of her hand.

A young gentleman and lady emerged from the group and made their way towards her making three deep reverences every two or three steps. The gentleman approached her to kiss her hand, but instead she rose and took him in her arms and hugged him. She then welcomed the young woman with open arms, drew her in and kissed her. Stepping back she took a long look at them, from head to toe, up and down, taking in the elegance of their clothes, the gold, the jewels. She scrutinised their faces desperately trying to match them to the faces of a seven and a five-year-old of so long ago.

'And are you really my children?' Was it possible?

'I am Charles and this is Leonor,' Charles struggled his way through the introduction. A memory of her dear brother flickered across Juana's mind, for his speech problems had been the same.

'Charles and Leonor. How lovely for me just to hear you speak your names. But you were so tiny when I last saw you, little children playing with their toys, and here you are a young man and a young woman. This is quite amazing. How old are you now?'

'I am seventeen and Leonor is nineteen. I must say your French is astonishing. I did not expect you to have remembered.'

'Oh my son I never forget a thing and I have had many more things to remember than the French language. But here you are. It is incredible. I hope your journey was better than any of mine. There always seemed to be storms and shipwrecks. Twice I had to seek shelter in England; precious cargoes got washed overboard and so many drownings; all quite dreadful.'

Leonor replied, drawing an angry scowl from Charles as she had not sought his permission to speak, 'There was nothing quite as bad as that, but we did have some excitement. We were blown off-course and arrived at a small fishing village instead of the port of Laredo. The whole militia turned out to challenge us. Imagine it! They thought we had come to invade! And then there was such a dreadful delay because our clothing had been taken to another port!'

'That surely was adventure enough. But nothing was lost? That is good. Oh, but that reminds me of ...' All this childish chatter of tales of adventure, it was Flanders all over again, more unwelcome memories. 'Enough of all that for the moment, I am sure you will wish to retire after such a long journey. I have personally overseen the arrangements for your rooms. You will find they have been prepared to perfection. But let me look at you again. Hernan, here are my children, quite grown up.'

'We expect to be here for a few days, Maman.' Charles was tired of the fuss.

'Of course; and you will want to rest now. I suppose I must let you go. Forgive your mother's foolishness.'

'But not quite yet, Maman,' Leonor had spoken out of turn again, her eyes pleading with her brother for a few more moments. 'May we not see our little sister Catalina?'

'Why yes, of course,' Juana replied not waiting for Charles' opinion, 'and some time you must also arrange to see your brother Ferdinand.'

Charles answered coldly, 'We have seen Ferdinand. We said farewell to him before he left for Brussels.'

'Ferdinand has gone to Brussels?'

'Yes, it is best for him. I am here now to help you. He will be far better occupied in Brussels.'

'Gone, and never came to say goodbye?' Ferdinand must have been snatched away from her once more but this time to be sent to a hostile country, amongst her enemies. Juana feared for his safety. She needed to know more. 'Tell me who ...'

'It was important he leave immediately,' Charles answered sharply.

Catalina appeared before the glittering party.

Leonor could not believe that first her mother and now her little sister too should be dressed in such plain, ordinary looking clothes. They looked no better than peasants.

Catalina stood dumbfounded at the splendour before her. She had never seen so many jewels in all her life and certainly never thought to see so many on just two people. The colours of their clothes were astonishing.

Leonor thought her the prettiest and perhaps the saddest little child she had ever met. 'Catalina, I am your sister Leonor and this, my dear, is our brother, King Charles.'

'Prince,' bristled Juana.

Catalina's attire, the plainest of grey, made Leonor suspicious and she had to know if she spent her days as a princess should. 'Tell me my dear what did you do today?'

'My lady,' Catalina curtsied to this beautiful stranger, 'I had my lessons. For a little while I played with Beatriz, my companion. Later I watched the children playing in the street below. They play such pretty ring games and I so love to hear them sing.'

'And these street children, do they come often?' She forced a smile, inwardly shuddering.

'Oh yes, because I throw money down to them. That makes them return.'

Catalina was not a princess after all, she was a tiny caged bird, and Leonor was not prepared to allow this to continue. Something must be done; she would start thinking about it immediately.

'It is late and I am weary. We must talk more tomorrow dear sister.'

'Then you must retire,' Juana decided, still reluctant to let them go, 'there will be plenty of time for chatter when you are all rested. Goodnight dear children.'

She watched them as they left, two elegant adults and her sweet innocent one. It was almost too ridiculous to believe they were all hers.

Chimay eased his way back to her, 'Did I not say what perfect children God has granted you? And Charles is such a wise and intelligent king.'

'Prince, not king.'

'I am sure you feel most fortunate that your son has arrived.'

She did not know what he meant by fortunate. It was only right that Charles should be here, for this was his inheritance and it would take some time to learn all about the lands, their peoples and more importantly their language. It annoyed her to think that it had taken some people a long time to realise where Charles should be and that had he been here much sooner he could have protected her from many wrongs. Those wrongs however had been set to rights without him. She had enjoyed almost two years of blissful freedom without his aid.

'No, fortunate would not be my chosen word for the arrival of my son.' She looked at Chimay, 'Sir, I am fortunate in that all my babies have been healthy and that after so many years I finally see two who are now healthy adults. They and I are fortunate too that their hazardous sea journey has been completed safely, although it is my belief that royals never drown.'

'Then perhaps I should say you must feel relieved that your son has arrived?' This woman was irritating.

'I am relieved inasmuch as I said before that he has arrived safely, although it has taken many years for him to come to my side. Why do you not speak plain instead of in these silly riddles?'

'I am saying that it must be comforting to know that he is in Spain at last. Since God has granted you so many kingdoms, to be the sole monarch must be a most arduous task. Now that your son is here you need no longer tire yourself with their government. He is here to assist you. You should rest after so many difficult times; the knowledge of which, by the way, has been a heavy weight on your son's heart. Let your son take the burdens on his shoulders, he has wisdom enough and more importantly, as well you know, Castile has many wise and excellent counsellors. You would be left to enjoy the pleasures of a private life.'

Warning bells sounded. Her father had offered her this, and yet everything changed so quickly. It hadn't taken long before she was not regarded as queen in retirement. In fact she became a prisoner, or something worse, to be subdued and forced into submitting to others far below her rank. She had had to suffer the cruelties of torture. Might this not happen again?

But that would be absurd, she reasoned. Why would her son wish to treat her in such a way? Times had changed. Those days could never be repeated. Charles would honour her as a good son must. It was his duty before God.

Chimay waited, wondering how she could hesitate after his eloquent speech. He had other problems to deal with and wanted this one out of the way. The Cortes would be a rather more difficult matter. They had agreed that Charles should

231

have the title of king but with restrictions, not least of which was that Juana was still named as sovereign with Charles's name always appearing second. As chief advisor he saw it as his responsibility to have his master's name appear first on all documents. He was, after all, the king.

'I shall discuss this with my son. What you say does indeed sound acceptable. Charles will be my strength. I feel I should put my trust in my son in the full confidence that he will dedicate himself to the honest service of my country.' Juana looked at Hernan to see if he agreed.

But Hernan was in no position to say anything.

Chimay knew he had won. 'That is a most wise decision and may God grant you many years of peace and contentment.'

He congratulated himself on achieving two of his objectives; Prince Ferdinand was out of the way and Juana was being manipulated nicely. There was still much to be done, the funeral of Philip and the question of Catalina were trivial and easy to deal with; of major importance were the Cortes of Castile and Aragón, but they were not beyond his capabilities.

Chapter 41

Marta could not move. The morning of March 13th, would be engraved on her heart forever, would go to her grave with her; and that might be soon enough she thought holding her fist tight against the pain in her chest.

'Marta. Marta, what is this? Am I to be kept waiting?' The calls came at first from the adjoining room, now the voice and Juana appeared before Marta.

'Oh, m'lady, m'lady ...' She hung her head weeping tears of anguish, smearing her red eyes and wet cheeks roughly with the back of her hand. She sobbed, 'I don't understand.'

'Where is my daughter?' Juana panicked.

'M'lady I don't know.'

'What do you mean, you don't know, she must be here. The only way into the corridor is through my apartment. She must be here.'

She tore the covers from the bed. 'She must be here!' she screamed, 'People do not disappear. Look, damn you, look!'

'Please, m'lady, I have looked and better-looked. Her two maids of the bedchamber are gone too.'

'Go for Hernan Duque.'

Marta picked up her skirts and waddled off in the fastest waddle her old legs could manage.

Juana turned about the room wildly. Her beautiful and most precious daughter was not here, could not possibly be here, there was nowhere to hide. The large chest stood open, but it held nothing but disordered clothes tossed about in Marta's alarm.

'The window then,' but she saw it was still shut, the latches in place. She opened it to look down into the street. There was nothing to be seen. 'This must be witchcraft. She has been spirited away. What have they done with you, Catalina?' Panic tore at her heart, her thinking.

She patted the bed hangings between her two hands as if hoping to find her child amongst their folds. She lifted pillows and cushions as if expecting to discover her hidden beneath. She lay on the floor peering into the space under the bed. She searched the chest, the bed again, then back to the cushions weeping, 'Catalina, my Catalina.'

Her last hope was the tapestry and she tugged at it, pulling it away from the wall, Catalina may yet be behind it, teasing; but she knew Catalina would not tease.

A howl escaped her. 'What is this? Who has done this? My God, someone has come in here and stolen her! Dear God, somebody, anybody, come here and tell me what is going on! Hernan, where are you? Someone must know about this! I want my child! Here; now! Do you hear me? Someone must get her back for me!'

Her screaming and howling became smothered in one of Catalina's dresses that she pressed to her face.

Her new chamberlain strode in quite nonchalantly to enquire, 'My lady what is the cause of this distress?'

'Oh my God, Bertrand, someone has robbed me of my child,' Juana sobbed.

'Robbed, my lady? I cannot believe that she is missing at all,' his voice inferred she was completely mistaken. 'But we will soon find out.'

'I know she is missing,' screamed Juana pulling at his sleeve. 'Come, see here. Someone came through this opening behind the tapestry.'

'Why, my lady this is … this is …'

This was the hole he had made so carefully over a number of days. This was the hole he had made as part of the scheme Charles had devised on his last visit to Tordesillas. This was the hole he had quietly climbed through in the middle of the night. This was the hole through which he had escorted Catalina and her two maids to have them whisked off to Valladolid and to her brother, King Charles.

Catalina had taken a great deal of persuading. He had tried at first with tales of riches, fine clothes, servants, feasts and fiestas but all to no avail. It was only when he began to talk about disobeying the king and the wrath this would bring down on her head that she had finally agreed. She had cried and cried about her poor mother, trying his patience to the limit, so he had promised her faithfully that he would see to it that Juana was told the moment she awoke. The maids had been an easier proposition, they had either to comply or go to prison. They did not need reminding that it is treason to disobey a king, and treason brings its own special punishments. A litter waited in readiness at the bridge, with Leonor's ladies-in-waiting and a full mounted guard. The whole process had gone completely to plan.

All Bertrand had to do now was to act his new role of incredulity and indignation.

'My lady this is dreadful, unbelievable. I shall send for Hernan Duque. He will have some explaining to do.' The lies just tripped from his tongue.

'I have sent for him already. He should be here immediately.'

Marta had disquieting news. 'Hernan cannot be found,' she wheezed from the doorway.

Bertrand knew that Hernan Duque could not be found because yesterday, sensing foul play, Hernan had refused to leave the palace doors unlocked and for this insubordination had been dismissed and despatched to a monastery.

'No sign of him? So, the plot thickens.' Bertrand stroked his chin.

'Something evil is happening here,' Juana sobbed.

'Summon everyone, now. Oh, sweet Jesus help me find my daughter.'

'If I may suggest, my lady, there are too many for all to gather here.'

'Bertrand, do not suggest anything. I shall decide what is to be done. I will question them one by one until I get the truth. I must have my Catalina returned safely to me.'

Juana asked each and everyone who worked in the palace, from the highest to the lowest. She demanded information; she begged information. No one had seen or heard anything. Their lack of alarm irritated her. They said she must be patient as there was bound to be an explanation, and she was furious.

'Can you not understand, some kind of robber has crept into my child's room and has stolen her away? How dare any of you stand there and not be worried sick about my Catalina! Why are you not starting an immediate investigation, why are you yourselves not searching?'

At that moment she realised the truth. It had happened before, when her little boy Ferdinand had been taken from her. They all knew; they knew why Hernan could not be found. They had no doubts as to the whereabouts of Catalina; and they had no intention of telling her anything. That was the only possible way to account for their strange behaviour. Whose plan was it to torment her this time?

'I warn you, I will neither eat nor sleep until Catalina stands before me. Do you hear?' she shouted, and to emphasise her determination she repeated it several times throwing dishes, bowls, and anything else that came to hand.

'Your highness,' Bertrand dodged the missiles, 'I will go directly to the king for you. He will send messengers to every city and port in the land. Have no fear, he will find Catalina and have her returned to you.' He calculated that these further lies ought to calm her for a while.

For several days not one drop passed her lips, not one bite was taken from the meals left for her. She would neither wash nor change her clothing. She refused to go to bed and would not sleep. Bowls, dishes, ewers and pitchers were flung at the walls and at the floor. Marta remained at her side; waiting, praying, and trying to be of some comfort.

Bertrand, who had made no effort whatsoever to contact Charles, dared not delay any longer, he was worried and he wrote to his master. Within hours Charles arrived at the palace with Catalina.

❖   ❖   ❖

Charles awaited his mother in the Grand Salon preferring to save himself the discomfort of his mother's apartment where he was sure she would have the advantage. He would feel much more confident in this room seated on his impressive chair.

Juana had not wasted a moment. As soon as she had been told of his arrival she had run to find him.

She faced her son.

'Where is she?'

'My lady, I bring you good news of your daughter.'

'Where is she, I said,' she screeched.

Charles flinched. 'I have brought her back. Believe me this has all been a dreadful mistake. You see it was members of my court who accompanied me from Brussels. They were the ones, I'm afraid, who ordered her abduction. It was because they felt so sorry for her. They did not like the way she was being brought up here; with no one of her own age, passing so much of her time alone in that small room, unable to go out walking or riding. They felt she should have a court suited to her

237

station.'

'Lies, lies, lies! All pathetic lies and you know it! And, in any case, your people saw kidnapping her as the answer? Tell me why did you not return her to me immediately, from the very instant she was brought to you? You must have known how worried I would be, and yet you kept her with you. Everything is such a transparent tissue of lies, and you expect me to ...'

'No matter, for it shall not occur again. At the time I was so angered that my sister's plight had become the subject of such common gossip amongst my courtiers that I ...' He knew that another weak lie would do nothing to convince her. 'However, I have decided to provide her with a suitable court here.'

'Well how good of you! Surely that was all you had to do in the first place. There was never a need to steal my child away. How could you be so cruel? And did no one stop to wonder how I would feel? Did you not stop to think of the torment this would put me through, the anguish I was made to suffer for days? Or did you, I wonder? Every word I have heard you utter would sound dishonest to a fool, and believe me Charles I am no fool.'

He ignored her, 'I have brought a court of two hundred which should be sufficient for you and Catalina.'

'I am sure you know well enough that I do not care for large courts.'

'I am doing this for Catalina, and let me advise you that if you wish to keep her here with you, you will accept.'

'Then I have no option in the face of such a threat.' She knew she could not bear to live if she were to lose her daughter, her sole comfort.

'And you will also agree to Catalina having her own apartments some distance from yours, and the freedom to go in and out as she pleases without you. She is also to have children about her, young ladies and page boys.'

238

'I have never prevented her from … But I have had to be careful lest anyone, lest anyone try to take her … just as has happened. How can I be sure I can trust you, trust your wicked countrymen? You must swear to me that she will always be safe even when I am not with her.'

'Maman I am offended that you appear not to trust me, your son. Of course she will be safe. And I insist that she go out and enjoy the fresh air of the countryside.'

'We both enjoy that already. We go out together quite frequently with Hernan Duque. But if Catalina wishes to go out without me, although I am not sure she is old enough, and you can assure us of her safety why I am sure that it can be arranged. I shall speak to Hernan.'

'He is no longer the head of your household. I found him to be unreliable.'

'How can you say that when for two years he has been …'

'Enough,' he did not care to involve himself further. 'I have appointed the Marqués de Denia. He is the new Governor and Administrator of this house. I have also given him full control over the town of Tordesillas.'

'That seems to be extraordinarily unnecessary; the town already has a captain and a magistrate.'

'Denia will take his instructions directly from me, for the palace and the town. It is for the best. You will live here in comfort with your court as my honoured mother, with nothing to concern your dear self save any pleasures you desire.'

Chimay had assured him that in this way he was fulfilling to the letter the duties prescribed by the Cortes of Castile. He was assigning his mother a residence which was more than suitable for a queen. By removing Tordesillas out of Castile and making it his own private domain he ensured that any news of the queen coming from the town would be from one source only, Denia.

Charles clapped his hands, 'Now, here is the new Princess

Catalina.'

Catalina entered slowly and shamefacedly in her new outfit, a dress of lilac satin edged with gold.

'Maman, I am back with you. I intended no hurt. I am so sorry you were caused such pain. Some people lied to me, made me follow their orders, I had no choice. But now I am here and I promise I will always be here.'

'It was no wrong of yours my treasure. The wrong sits firmly on the shoulders of those who deceived you and stole you from me.'

Charles shrugged off her criticism. 'My work is finished here. I have important business to attend to. I leave you in the capable and secure hands of the marqués.'

Juana hugged Catalina. She was back.

'So, we are to have a grand court of two hundred. It sounds exciting; we will be able to do even more than we did with Hernan. If only I knew why he was dismissed. But come, we must go to Marta. This whole business has made her quite ill.'

Juana hurried down the corridor only half listening to Catalina's stories of the brilliance of Charles's court, of Leonor's preparations to leave for Portugal to marry King Emanuel.

'The last I heard he was married to my sister Maria,' she replied quite matter-of-fact.

'Aunt Maria died some time ago, Maman.'

'Well, there you are you see, no one tells me anything.'

They rushed into Juana's apartments calling for Juana's faithful servant. They didn't see her at first, only a bundle of skirts on the floor.

'Oh God, no. Catalina, go and call my doctor.'

A weak voice begged from the bundle, 'No, let me see the sweet child.'

They managed to place cushions under her head and Juana

held her hands, 'Marta, dear friend, what ails you?'

'Nothing, it will pass in a moment or two. I've been having twinges these last few days. But here is our Catalina safely returned to us. God has answered my prayers. I only hope he answers the others about punishing those who were wicked enough to do such a thing.'

Marta pulled her hands free to press them against the pain in her chest, gasping, her face contorted. There was a hint of a smile then Juana's devoted friend and confidante quietly died.

Chapter 42

'I swear you would sorely try the patience of a saint!' The Marqués de Denia, a thin and spiteful looking man, slammed the door shut behind him, folded his arms and glowered at Juana.

'And what would you know of saints and their patience? Very little, if anything, marqués. But you are making a fuss about nothing; I simply sent for you, as I have on so many occasions, God Himself only knows how often, to accompany me to the convent. Perhaps this time you would oblige me? Please do not use poor weather as an excuse again, it is a beautiful day.'

Juana walked to the window and looked down at the kitchen maids scurrying about their chores throwing waste onto an ever-growing pile of rotting refuse. Even this sight was preferable to facing her "gaoler".

Two years had passed since Denia had replaced Hernan Duque. Far from having her own court Juana had been forced to return to the apartments at the rear of the building to live in virtual isolation. It was true that her daughter Catalina now enjoyed a better life. She had her courtiers with young ladies-in-waiting and pageboys. There were banquets, balls, riding out into the country; all of which she merrily recounted to her mother, if and when she was permitted to come to this part of the palace.

Juana had no privileges, indeed had no freedom. There were no reasons given, no explanations.

She was dressed for outdoors, wearing her cloak and outdoor hood and, because she felt today was rather special; she was also wearing her freshly cleaned and pressed dress.

Without disguising his impatience Denia answered, 'How many times do you have to be told that it is I and not you who decides if and when you may go outside. You will not be going anywhere today.'

'Then I order you to send for the grandees to come here as soon as they are able, to see how I am treated. I want them to witness for themselves how you hold me prisoner.' How often had she commanded the presence of the lords, any of them, and yet nothing had come of it.

Denia snapped back, 'It is none of their business. They can do nothing for you. I grow weary of repeating myself, but let me remind you once more that I am following your father's instructions, and the grandees are in no position to question his authority.'

Juana knitted her brows, puzzled, forcing herself to look at him, her eyes searching his face, looking for clues, trying to make sense of what he had just said, wishing that Marta was still alive, and able to confirm that King Ferdinand was dead.

'You say again that these are the commands of my father?'

'If I must repeat it, yes they are.'

'Marqués, we both know that my father died some time ago.'

'Not so. Your father is alive, and that is the truth.'

'My son Charles came here because ...'

'Because,' Denia interrupted, wanting this package of lies over and done with, 'he wanted to personally intercede for you. He was most desirous to plead with your father on your behalf.'

'And where is my son now?' Juana asked, trying to comprehend.

'Your son is in Aragón. But why are we wasting our time discussing this. I have had to leave my work, important correspondence, to come here this morning.'

'Then return to your writing, marqués and, while you are

243

about it,' doing her utmost to fight her dejection she removed her cloak and hood; still holding them close lest there be any chance of a last minute change of mind, 'write to my son letting him know that his mother, the queen, insists that he or his representatives come here to … to …' to do what, she wondered.

'The reason I am here, the reason I have had to leave my work, has nothing to do with your going out, nor indeed about your treatment. I am here because of your behaviour towards the servants. They have been coming to me with their complaints.'

Juana looked at him, incredulous. 'I never heard the like! Servants complaining about their mistress; what is this?' This was all most difficult; first the confusion about her father and now being called to account by vassals.

'You have behaved in a disgraceful manner. You have dared to throw dishes at them.'

'What do you mean I have dared? Who "dared" to question my actions?'

'You ought to feel a thousand shames. I can imagine what your mother would say if she only knew. She would never have debased herself in such a manner.'

'Marqués, my mother had the luxury of having her own servants about her. I am denied that. Instead I have to suffer your servants. It is their behaviour you should question.' Her voice grew louder and harsher. She was furious at having to justify herself. 'They are insolent, refusing to obey even a simple request. They speak to me as though they were my equal. They turn their back on me and ignore me if it suits them not to listen. I have every right to be angry. And, I ask, why should I have to explain myself to you? Everyone seems to have forgotten that I am the queen.'

'Then the sooner you begin to act like one the better.'

Juana made a huge effort to control her temper; she would try a different tack. 'Here is a simple solution to all my

244

problems.' She smiled and spoke softly, wheedling. 'You will allow me one servant of my choice, to replace the irreplaceable Marta. You will escort me to the convent once in a while, and especially this week as it is Holy Week. With these two little favours, marqués, you will see in no time at all how content and amiable I can be. Life will be so much easier for all of us.'

But neither would be acceptable. The Marqués de Denia had had to dismiss all the servants chosen by Hernan Duque because they gossiped openly in the town when visiting with their families. As he had written to King Charles at the time, ... *they talked about things that they should not and carried tales that they should have left behind in the palace.* They had also been found guilty of bringing back news of the outside world to tell the queen while he was doing everything in his power to keep her in ignorance.

And as for allowing Juana to visit the Convent of Santa Clara, that was quite out of the question. She would come into contact with the townsfolk and who could tell what might be said or done? The people of Tordesillas were already highly suspicious of the circumstances surrounding the queen and her apparent lack of freedom, accusing Denia of keeping her his prisoner. Her presence could be used to dispel such thoughts, but the risks were too great.

'You know that I can do nothing other than obey your father's orders until such time that he either chooses to come to visit or he responds to a written request from me ...' in his anxiety to overcome her guile, he had magnified the lie.

'Then write to my father.' Her voice remained soft and gentle. 'Say that I want to go away from this place where I am held prisoner, allowed to see no one. Tell him I wish to go to Valladolid, to have the grandees visit me to keep me informed and to counsel me.'

'You write; he is your father!' Denia shouted.

'I command you, marqués.'

He changed the subject. 'You will be pleased to know that as from today I am allowing an altar to be placed in the corridor.'

'I am overwhelmed by your kindness. You are to allow me to leave my room for a short while to hear Mass in the corridor. And will you give me some money for the alms box? It would be a rather splendid gesture if you did. Do I need to remind you that it is my money I am speaking of?'

'For goodness' sake,' he railed, 'I am tired of this continual whingeing!' He reached for his purse, took out a few coins and tossed them on the table.

'I wish to see my treasurer about my money.'

'Not allowed. The subject is closed. I have wasted far too much of my valuable time. I should be attending to important matters.'

'I want to see Catalina.'

'This is ridiculous! I have told you she is safe and well. You surely can hear her and her courtiers from here. Just because your father has taken your son Ferdinand away to Flanders,' he swallowed hard over this, yet another of his lies, 'it does not necessarily follow that he would steal your daughter. When there is time I shall send her to you.'

'And what of my toothache? How much longer do I have to suffer? Are you doing anything about it?' Juana despised herself knowing how she sounded increasingly childish reaching out here, there and everywhere for some minor bequest, just one, granted.

'Good Lord. Everybody has toothache,' he called over his shoulder as he left the room.

She was alone. She stood for quite some time, still holding her cloak and hood.

'You may have won the battle today,' she said eventually, raising her chin in defiance at the closed door, 'but the war is not yet over.'

❖   ❖   ❖

The marqués was back at his writing table, wrapped in the luxury of his fur-lined gown and the importance of his role as sole correspondent of Tordesillas to his master King Charles I of Spain; the Holy Roman Emperor Charles V. All letters had to be written in his own hand and usually in code.

He scanned the few lines he had written before his visit to Juana, *In Valladolid and Medina and elsewhere everyone is saying that the queen is a prisoner and there are some who are thinking to free her and take her to Valladolid. She, of course, continues to complain of this place incessantly ...* He dipped his quill in the ink and continued, *I was interrupted because she sent for me. She wants me to write to her father immediately (I had repeated it was her father's will she remain here and that no change could be made until he said so). She keeps asking for Catalina, thinking her father might kidnap her. She had been begging for money for so long that I finally gave her some today. That should keep her quiet for a while. I have decided she can hear Mass in the corridor, she had ranted and raved about it for months, her language beyond belief, that I had to concede. That is not to say that I will not have it removed as a form of punishment if need be. Today she was artful as well as angry. She was so disarming at one point that I was almost tempted to allow her to go out. I really do have to keep my wits about me, as she can be so cunning. In town they are saying more often and more loudly that I keep her prisoner; you had best give that some thought.*

He signed, sanded, folded, and then sealed the letter before sitting back well pleased with his morning's work.

Chapter 43

'Ana, the French would probably call this *déjà vu.*' Juana's mouth twitched nervously as she shook her head.

The servant; Ana, a sullen, middle-aged reject of the marquesa, put the finishing touches to her dress. 'I beg pardon?' she enquired, cutting the thread to her sewing and smoothing the bodice at the side where she had completed the stitching.

'Nothing, nothing; only a myriad of thoughts,' she sighed, not wanting to admit that some of those thoughts frightened her.

Jewelled clasps were placed at intervals down the fronts of the sleeves then the chemise sleeves were carefully coaxed and puffed out between them. The only other jewellery she wore was her ruby, her mother's gift, on its gold chain.

Her fingers fidgeted with the clasps and the necklace then traced the gold edge of her hood. Then suddenly the words were out, 'I am afraid. I dare not think what is going to happen. Too often it seems I have dressed in preparation for ...'

The Marquesa de Denia entered in a swish of expensive brocades. 'My husband, the marqués is waiting, are you not ready yet? Hurry up.'

Juana steadfastly held her tongue instead of making some sarcastic remark in retaliation. She would not invite a confrontation, nor would she allow herself to be the one guilty of spoiling what might yet still be a day of pleasant surprises; she willed it to be such a day, a special day. Unbelievably, and after so long a time, someone had come to see her.

She studied herself in the mirror. It was an old lady who returned her gaze. She was forty-two and the last year or so had taken their toll. Her hair, where it showed at the margin of her hood, was almost grey and quite lifeless. Age lines ran deep and rampant across her forehead and cheeks. Suspicion and mistrust filled her eyes; her lips were pulled down in a curve of anger and bitterness.

Juana addressed her image, 'Denia must consider it an important occasion to allow me to wear my best dress and to permit a visitor; a visitor, at last. Oh, but I have lots to say and ask. But then again it could be something awful, something worse than ever before. Or it may be some tragic news. No not that, for surely Denia would have taken delight in delivering that personally.'

The marquesa tapped her foot with impatience, tempting Juana to linger an extra moment or two contemplating her appearance, and wondering.

She touched the ruby at her breast, thinking of it as her talisman and seeking courage from it. 'I am ready.'

Deciding not to wait any longer, the marquesa had disappeared; the days being long gone when she would have deigned to wait for her queen or curtsey as she passed.

Juana walked slowly, enjoying the luxury of her full and heavy skirts, savouring the sheer freedom to stroll down the corridor, unguarded, knowing she was not going to be dragged forcibly back to her room. She was finally doing something denied her for how long?

There had been those other times when, attracted by the music and happy voices or laughter from the Grand Salon, Juana had sped over these very tiles desperate to catch a glimpse of Catalina and her young courtiers dancing. If luck was with her she did manage to watch the rows of dancers, all in such dazzling colours, executing the stately movements of a pavan or, better still, she saw Catalina with her partner dancing a galliard, her dainty feet carrying her, light as a feather, through the rapid steps. But Juana was always discovered and bundled back to her apartments. Nevertheless, the treasured images of her beautiful daughter sustained her through the following days of harsh treatment and meagre rations of bread and water; and they were still there when the interminable days of solitude became almost unbearable.

But even now, as she was savouring her liberty, the fear that had never been very far away came flooding back. Whoever had come had come simply to mock, to ridicule. The marqués had had her dressed up like this for some evil purpose, of that there was no doubt. He was no longer content with his usual regime and was seeking entertainment of a different sort.

She grasped at the ruby, her talisman. 'Dear God, I do not know how much more of this torment I can take.'

There was an archbishop and his small court of clerics awaiting her in the salon, along with the marqués and marquesa and their full entourage.

Everyone bowed low then the archbishop approached and knelt before her, 'Your royal highness,' said a deep and mellifluous voice. He reached for her hand to kiss it.

'Please stand, archbishop.' She was unnerved by all this show of deference and looked about her with trepidation. 'I see by your robes,' her voice was ridiculously high, 'that you are an archbishop.' She was cross with herself for saying something so foolish.

'I am the Archbishop of Granada. The regent, Adrian of Utrecht, has sent me with this Council of State for Castile,' he indicated the others in the room, 'to beg for an audience.'

Adrian of Utrecht; yes, she knew that name, but what was he doing as regent? And what had the archbishop said about

250

her giving an audience?

'I am perhaps a little deaf, I would ask you please to repeat what you said.'

'We have come to beg an audience at the behest of the regent, my lady.'

She closed her eyes to ponder this. They had come to beg an audience with her. She was the one who begged for audiences; had done so for years. This didn't make sense. Still, since someone was here to listen, there was no time to be lost, she must speak. There were wrongs that needed to be righted, but she must be cautious and not appear too eager.

'Your highness,' the voice of Denia broke into her thoughts. 'It is procedure in a royal audience for the Council to be seated. On your behalf I shall send for some chairs.'

Juana coolly replied, 'Marqués, must I remind you that protocol demands a chair for the archbishop and benches for the councillors. It has always been thus since the days of the Catholic Queen, the Lady Isabel, God rest her soul.'

As Juana made her solemn and dignified way to her chair she was faintly amused to see that someone had been able to find its canopy bearing her coat of arms, and for an instant cherished the unlikely possibility that perhaps Denia had guarded it carefully in readiness for such a moment.

She smiled, enjoying all this play-acting, this dream-like world in which she was both a player and a spectator.

'My lady,' the archbishop was impatient to begin, 'Castile is in a perilous state and we come to beseech you, as our queen, to sign this decree putting down a dangerous revolt that is gathering momentum even as we speak. If you would simply put your signature here,' he motioned for the necessary paper to be brought to him, 'then our task will be made so much easier. We must not delay.'

'I cannot. You must ask my father to issue such an order, his word would carry so much more weight than mine,' she chided him.

The archbishop, who had been about to present Juana with the warrant, was unsure what to do. Denia had informed him that although she was totally demented, as long as she was treated as a queen; and they all kept up the pretence that this royal audience was a quite usual and regular affair for all of them, then everything would go smoothly, the warrant would be signed and he could leave.

But now they were talking about a dead man being called upon to sign, an indication of Juana's madness no doubt, but somehow or other he had to have her realise that he was no longer alive and that she was the only one able to issue orders. He had to get her signature.

'My lady, it is my sad duty and with great regret that I must advise you that your father died quite some time ago.'

'That cannot be so. Denia will tell you himself that he still lives. He has told me so on so many occasions.'

All eyes were on Denia. The marqués bowed, smiling a benevolent smile, 'I did indeed tell you so but that was because I thought by so doing I would calm your spirits.'

'That is not the way I remember it at all. And you do surprise me inferring that you have ever held any concerns for me whatsoever. But enough of that; if as you say my father is dead then the archbishop must send for the prince.'

'It is not Prince Ferdinand that we require,' replied the archbishop.

'Obviously not Ferdinand,' Juana fired back, angry that they all seemed determined to confuse her, 'I refer to Prince Charles.'

'I beg your pardon for the misunderstanding. It is just that Charles, your son, is our king and not a prince.'

Juana looked from one to the other trying to remember if she should have known of this. She was convinced that she was still the queen and therefore he should still be a prince, and wasn't he with her father, interceding on her behalf; or was her father truly dead?

The archbishop continued, 'King Charles is in Austria, my lady, following the death of his grandfather, the Emperor Maximilian, God rest his soul.'

'Marqués we must speak.' Her mind was in turmoil; where was the truth for her to cling to? 'I think you have been deceiving me for some time. Now, before these gentlemen I wish you to speak honestly. First, is my father dead, and do you swear it?'

'Your father is dead. I accompanied his mortal remains to be laid alongside those of your mother.' He bowed his head and sighed.

His obsequiousness nauseated her. How she loathed the man. But she must concentrate.

'When did he die?'

'Four years ago ma'am.'

'And the Emperor Maximillian, he is dead too?'

'He alas is also dead. King Charles has been elected ruler of the Holy Roman Empire.'

'And Maximillian died when?'

'Last year ma'am.'

'And yet, marqués,' the very words were choking her as they rushed to publicly confront her tormentor with his infamy, 'for years you have consistently tried to persuade me to write to two dead men, my father and the emperor. What kind of cruel trickery was this?'

There was not a sound, there was no movement, everyone, everything focussed on Denia. The archbishop and his councillors waited in silence. A heat of embarrassment hung about them that equalled that of the August sunshine on the plains around the city; a still, heavy heat before a gathering storm.

'There was no trickery. I assure you I only sought to divert your attention.'

'You sought to prevent me from seeking justice, marqués.' Turning to the others in a trembling rage she tried to explain. 'Believe me, archbishop, everything I see and hear today is like some strange nightmare. It must be at least … oh, so many years … I forget. No matter, it was long ago in Flanders when it all started. That was when people first started lying to me and since then I have been surrounded by liars. No one has been truthful with me. And here you see before you the very epitome of all liars, that man.' She pointed a long thin finger towards Denia her eyes never leaving the archbishop. 'And for the same length of time I have been mistreated; and once again no one has been more expert than the marqués. He has proved himself a master of deception and of cruelty.'

The archbishop, while finding this all most distressing and probably demanding further enquiry, hoped to return to his urgent business, quickly, before it became completely lost in this thickening morass of difficulties which was quite outside his remit.

Juana sought to clear her mind desperate to make full use of this audience while it lasted, for there may not be another. She must concentrate.

'My lord, tell me once more why you have come here.'

'There is a revolution in Castile. We are living in most dangerous times.'

'I remember now. And you wish me to sign a royal decree demanding it be put down.'

Prayers of gratitude flew heavenward from the archbishop and his followers. They were back on course; they had almost achieved their mission. The warrant was called for once more and it was offered to Juana.

Juana glanced at it for only a moment before rolling it up. 'Gentlemen I would point out to you that for years I have not been able to command the unlocking of the door of my room. It must, therefore, appear as ironic to you as it does to me that I should now be asked to order thousands of men to lay down their arms. Before you answer, I must add something else, and the marqués knows this well enough. For years I have been asking him to write to the nobles or any of the members of the Cortes bidding them to visit me, to tell me what was taking place in my beloved country. The marqués always responded to my requests with excuses or downright refusals. The grandees, I was told, were not here, they were ill, they were too busy, they were with the king, there was an epidemic. I therefore have no idea what this danger or peril can be of which you speak, nor who is perpetrating it. You say there is no time for delay and I have much to learn. Let us set ourselves to the task immediately.'

Denia was furious. His plan had failed miserably. He had thought to humour Juana; have her all dressed up, allow her to sit on her throne, experience the power of signing an important document and then have her escorted back to her rooms. Instead she was making him look a fool; have him appear a blackguard. How dared she!

The archbishop was embarrassed. This was to have been easy. He had been led to believe that Juana's mental state was such that she would sign any piece of paper put in front of her. Instead he had stumbled on and disturbed a hornets' nest; and there was more to come for he was now obliged to reveal all in his explanation. And he would have to choose his words carefully for the queen had shown that she was, more than likely, capable of understanding the situation.

'Ma'am, for some time there have been some minor problems between the people of Spain and the officials of the court of King Charles; those who accompanied him from Flanders.'

'I would imagine there would be more than minor problems, especially if the Flems hold high offices in government.'

'But your son needs those around him in whom he can have most confidence.'

'Such as Chimay?' That was a name she had not thought of for some time.

'And his chancellor from Bruges, Monsieur Salvagio, and Chimay's nephew the Archbishop of Toledo.'

Juana's eyes widened in disbelief; everything her mother had stated in her will was being flouted yet again.

'Enough. Name me no more names. Instead tell me of the wrongs these people have committed to cause such distress to my country.'

'No wrongs ma'am. They only act as any sovereign's advisers would. Taxes have been set, monies have been raised to pay for the royal household including servants, army, officials.'

'This is not sufficient to stir my countrymen to rebellion unless of course the sums were to be excessive.'

The archbishop decided to avoid answering that. 'There was also some strong ill-feeling when Adrian of Utrecht was made regent.'

'Why should his appointment cause more resentment than the others?'

'Some say that the king had made a solemn promise not to offer any more posts to foreigners.'

'And a king must keep his word!' She was bitter, thinking that every king she knew, including her father, never had done so. She leaned towards him, 'Yet there are much more serious affairs?'

He had not wanted her to ask questions, he only wanted her to listen and agree where necessary. 'It is really to do with timing, unfortunate timing. You see, with the emperor dying, King Charles had no option but to start his election campaign and elections are a costly business.'

'What you are saying is that Spain had to pay some hefty

bribes.'

The archbishop winced at her directness, 'These transactions are not viewed in that manner. Also, the king had to travel to Flanders. He needed the necessary ships and men at arms and these are items of enormous expense.'

'And you are telling me that Spain had to pay for all this, or did Flanders share the costs?'

'Spain on her own, my lady.' This interview was not going well.

'And what of the government of this country? I wonder if since the death of my father anyone has addressed the needs of Spain.'

'Much has been necessarily put in abeyance until the return of King Charles. Meanwhile Adrian of Utrecht and others ...'

'You need go no further, archbishop. I see the problem as two-fold. One: we have my countrymen smarting with broken Spanish pride, being trampled on and robbed by foreigners. Two: we have lost control of our own destiny, foreigners hold all the power. It is no longer Spain for the Spaniards. Little wonder there is unrest. This is not a rabble of common people, is it, archbishop?'

'Ma'am they are a group of misguided procuradores and grandees. In any case, it matters not who they are,' he flared, 'it is still treachery. Naturally they have a rabble of all kinds of malcontents under their command. The rebels met in Avila last month to declare that Adrian and his Council had been deposed and that they, this group of traitors calling themselves the Holy Alliance, is the only legitimate government.'

'And Avila is theirs?'

'It is.'

'Is this the only place they hold?'

The archbishop was furious at possibly having to reveal the full extent of the rebellion, so limited himself to the situation in Castile. 'No, the revolt has spread; to Toledo, Madrid, Segovia,

Salamanca, Zamora, Leon, Valladolid, Burgos. The only reassuring part of these worrying circumstances is that their decree declares that you are the only sovereign of Spain and that it is to you that they owe their allegiance. That is why I am here. We need you to sign this warrant to put down their revolt. They will respect your signature. Your name is sufficient. The salvation of the country is in your hands. Your signature would cause a miracle far greater than any of Saint Francis himself. I beg of you, please sign.'

Juana unrolled the paper and studied it this time.

'Archbishop you have given me much to think about. I agree with you that we face some very difficult times, but yet we are not in any immediate danger if, as you say, they have sworn allegiance to me. We must, I think, take more care with the wording of the contents of this document, we must be more specific as to what our intentions are and as to the manner in which we intend achieving them; it should not be a vague statement such as this. Have another one prepared and bring it to me tomorrow. You may go.'

Even before the archbishop left the room Juana had gone to the window to look out over the river, over the plains shimmering in the heat to the distant horizon, towards Medina del Campo, hiding behind the summer haze. She gathered the warmth and freedom of the land, her land, with every breath.

Without turning she spoke to Denia, 'Medina was never mentioned. Who has Medina allied herself with?'

'With no one. Medina is lost.'

'For once speak plain.'

'We needed additional ammunition to fight the rebels of Segovia and sought to take some from the arsenal in Medina. The citizens stupidly refused to hand any over, saying they would not have Spanish weapons used against Spaniards. We had no alternative but to set fire to some of the buildings as an example of what happens to traitors. Sadly the fire went out of control and more than three quarters of the town has been destroyed.'

The news brought with it deep sadness both for her mother's beloved town and for Spain. Medina was an international market. Much of Castile's wealth was held there: gold, silver, silks, brocades, pearls; all would have been lost.

The marqués interrupted her thoughts, 'It is very grave. And all brought about by rebels.'

'We shall see where the blame truly lies. You may go.'

She had dismissed him! She congratulated herself. She was free until tomorrow.

Advice was necessary before the return of the archbishop for the situation was complex and dangerous. There was no one to turn to other than her confessor and confidant, Brother Juan. And, in the absence of lawyers, who better; the Franciscan friar was honest and his judgement sound.

Chapter 44

Four days had passed since the archbishop's first visit and on each successive meeting he had brought a freshly worded warrant. None would satisfy Juana, not one fully addressed the grievances of the Spanish people. Brother Juan had been of enormous help but she deeply regretted the absence of doctors at law.

She stood on the gallery looking out at the plains bathed in the morning sunshine, stretching out towards Medina del Campo (poor, ruined Medina) and mused on her audiences with the archbishop and his black-robed clerics hovering like crows eager to snatch up the warrant and carry it away like some piece of carrion.

She didn't know whether to laugh or cry; this was the most ridiculous scenario imaginable! It was bizarre that she and the archbishop should be discussing Spain's future. Here they were in a tiny, nondescript, out-of-the-way town, the archbishop representing a powerless regent and she, so recently freed from her incarceration, ill-informed and unsure.

However, this new role was quite to her liking. There was immense satisfaction to be had in having people fawn over her, to watch their earnest strivings to please; these, after all were what monarchs should enjoy.

In the distance a dust cloud grew. Then from its midst a huge line of riders emerged, galloping towards Tordesillas. It was a veritable army!

There was a polite cough behind her.

'Are you ready to hold an audience?'

Juana turned to find her confessor who, she was convinced, had he not been a solemn man of the cloth was surely grinning from ear to ear.

'Brother Juan, I see we have more visitors coming to seek favour,' she pointed out the horsemen.

'Your highness is very popular.'

'I wonder what the archbishop suggests today.'

'We may never know; it is the town magistrate who begs an audience.'

This was impossible. 'But Denia would never allow the magistrate to enter the palace!'

'Precisely, my lady.' And yes, he was grinning.

The magistrate was on bended knee, his tired, old face a mixture of fear and elation, his voice faltering, 'Your highness, the townsfolk of Tordesillas have freed themselves from the yoke of the king's ministers. May I ask you to come to the courtyard to see and hear your people.'

There was no need to be asked twice; her people were here, in the courtyard.

When she stepped out on to the upper gallery she was greeted by a burst of trumpets and tambours and a frenzy of cheering. Colours danced and flashed: women were waving bunches of flowers or gaily patterned shawls, steel glinted and shone from beribboned halberds — and it was all too much. After so many silent, drab and colourless years in gloomy apartments she was shaken and she stumbled against the wall, closing her eyes and covering her ears to shut it out.

The crowd below fell into an uneasy silence; they looked up nervously, waiting.

Then Juana moved.

The magistrate knelt before her. 'My lady,' his voice rang out, 'would it please you to receive Don Juan Padilla, the leader of the Holy Alliance?'

The waiting was unbearable.

Juana was choking with indecision. Decisions were not for her to make, she hated them. This decision was the most

261

serious ever demanded of her. If she said no, would she be denying the people of rights they were struggling for, would she be aiding and abetting the hated Flems? If she said yes, she would be taking an extremely bold step, openly siding with rebels, all those opposed to the regency, the government. There was no one to advise. Where was her uncle or the constable? A voice from the past told her what to do, reminding her of that other Juana.

She decided. She nodded her approval.

Fervent cheers raced and chased around the pillars, bounced from the walls, surging upwards, engulfing Juana on their way.

A gentleman from a small group that had gathered at the foot of the stairs approached and knelt before her initiating a fresh wave of jubilation. 'Your royal highness, I appear before you to bring you freedom and to accord you all honours as Queen Juana. We are here to be of service to you for as long as we have breath in our bodies.'

'You are most welcome Don Juan Padilla. May Spain and I find you as loyal as your father; God knows we have need of such men. So, Don Juan Padilla, determine which of your group shall accompany you to the Grand Salon where I shall be most pleased to receive them.'

The air was rent once more with rejoicing cries and cheers. Never had Juana felt such floods of warmth enfolding her. As she turned to go she took a long look at all those who had come to wish her well. This moment would never be forgotten. All the misgivings she had had about coming to Tordesillas were swept away. She was at home here. She was amongst good, honest, and decent people in this brave little town on a hill.

The room had been hurriedly prepared. No one had been sure just how many people would be involved in the audience so several benches had been arranged along the walls.

Juana was once more seated on her throne with its royal canopy, quite revelling in this new state of affairs, savouring once more those moments on the steps, hearing again the adulation of the crowds.

Padilla led the line of gentlemen in solemn procession.

'Your highness, these gentlemen are my colleagues in our alliance. I pray you receive them.' He introduced them, 'Don Bravo, Don Zapata, Don Maldonado, and Doctor Zuñiga. We are here to defend you, to carry out your orders.'

It was all quite astonishing and so wonderful. Juana looked beyond the four leaders at a room filled with loyal subjects, her loyal subjects, every one of them wanting to serve their queen. She could not disguise her happiness. 'Gentlemen it pleases me greatly to have you here!' But it was time to be serious, and a huge effort was demanded to focus on the matter in hand. 'You must explain the circumstances which caused you to create this Holy Alliance. And then you must make plain your intentions, for you have taken extreme measures, which could be seen as treacherous, and yourselves branded traitors. It is only your loyalty to me, your queen, which saves you from such accusations.'

Padilla knelt before her, 'My lady, the problems began soon after the death of King Ferdinand. With respect, ma'am, your son Charles has allowed his Flemish ministers full rein. These foreigners have plundered our country; money has been going to Flanders like a river racing to the sea. More recently the burden of taxes has become unbearable. Also Spain finds itself these days with too small an army to protect itself. King Charles is not here to listen to our concerns and, worse, he has put the government in the hands of a complete stranger when we have Castilians suited to the post; like the admiral or the constable. Many cities rose in anger. My friends and I felt it essential to organise all the disaffected as quickly as possible. It was vital that we controlled the passions of our countrymen, to bring the cities together to act as one in pursuing a common end. We are not traitors, we are bound by solemn oath to live and die in the service of the king.'

'Then your fight is only against the Flems, Don Padilla?'

'Our fight is against those foreign leeches bleeding our country to death. Our fight is against those who deny us government by our own people. Our fight is against those who deny us our self-respect. Our fight is against those who set their guns against Spanish people.'

'And there was the disaster of Medina del Campo.' She was glad to show she knew something about recent events.

'You know of that?'

'The Marqués de Denia told me.'

'And did he tell you it was the Archbishop of Granada who was responsible?'

'Dear Lord, no he did not! Nor did the archbishop; and he has been here every day for four days! But the regent, he must still have an army?'

'Dismissed; he could no longer pay them. The Treasury is empty because the cities finally withheld their payments. My lady, Spain awaits your orders. Everyone will obey you, would be content to die for you.'

'Gentlemen, you are the true defenders of Spain.' Once more Juana had to strive to control her delight. Those enchanting words speaking of freedom and loyalty; the knowledge that they shared a common enemy; that they regarded her without question as queen thrilled her beyond words.

'This, my lady, is how we propose to keep Spain safe.' Padilla offered her a scroll of parchment.

She read its contents aloud.

264

'The king must return to Spain and live here.
If he leaves the kingdom it would be unlawful to
appoint a foreigner as regent.
On his return he must not bring more Flems.
There will be no foreign troops on Spanish soil.
Only Spaniards are to hold office.
No foreigners may be naturalised.
Each city is to have elected representatives.
Sending gold, silver and jewels out of the
kingdom is to be made a capital offence.
The present regent must be replaced by a Castilian.
The king must pardon all irregularities
that the cities might have committed
through excess of zeal.
The king must swear to accept all these
articles and never seek the Pope's absolution
from this oath.'

These were virtually the same grievances as a generation ago when Philip was king. Juana rolled up the parchment then paused, searching for a way to begin.

'After the death of my mother I always obeyed my father, because he was the king. From the beginning I wanted to be involved, wanted to know what was happening. But then my father put me here. I cannot remember why. And then, later, the foreigners had arrived. I was led to believe that the sole reason they were here was because of the visit of my children, Charles and Leonor, and that my father was still alive. I have had wicked people about me telling me so many lies, deceiving me.'

She shook her head to rid herself of the muddle always ready to return. 'I have a great love for my people and it pains me greatly that they have been treated so ill. I marvel that you have not already taken vengeance on those who have done such wrong. I would have tried harder myself but I was always afraid that some harm would befall my children here or in Flanders if I insisted too much. In any case there was no one ever to listen to me. I have no idea if those enemies are still prepared to injure either my children or me. Perhaps we are safe now that I am the queen, and you are all here to protect me. At the very beginning I was unable to involve myself with government because I was trying to come to terms with my husband's death. And then I did for a while, but that stopped when I came here …'

Juana knew she wasn't expressing herself coherently but it was all too complicated, impossible to explain. She pressed on, 'Gentlemen, I am relieved to see you here for you understand the wrongs which have to be righted, and I can tell it would rest heavy on your consciences if you did not attend to them.' This was much better; she was on safe ground again. 'Therefore I charge you with this duty; name four of the most knowledgeable and wise amongst you to come here every day to keep me informed. I will listen and speak with them and I will do what I can as it becomes necessary.'

Zuñiga took Padilla aside, 'There are two things yet. First, we need more than the queen's word assuring our authority, we must have her sign those Articles, and then we must have Charles relegated to prince. How can we be taking orders from the queen and her son still the king?'

'Quite simply,' answered Padilla, 'because the Cortes have always insisted that should the queen be restored to full health then that would automatically be the case. It is obvious she is well. The Cortes is not in session but I do not see anyone in Spain objecting to Juana as queen and Charles as prince. Nonetheless, I will obtain the signature although I think you are being over-cautious.'

He approached Juana, 'We are at your bidding. The four

men shall be chosen immediately. I also think it would be better if we were to move our headquarters here to Tordesillas.'

'An excellent idea Padilla, see to it.'

'And may I ask you to sign these Articles? It would prevent anyone doubting our authority.'

'That is a most sensible idea. When you come tomorrow with your committee I will have a secretary here and we shall attend to it. Brother Juan, my confessor, will arrange that. One last item before I retire; I wish to have some ladies chosen for me from the town. Oh, and do you know what has become of Denia?'

'Denia is not allowed anywhere near the palace.'

Denia is not allowed anywhere near the palace. How sweet those words were. 'Good day gentlemen, we shall meet tomorrow.'

The room emptied and she was left alone with the priest. 'Would it be blasphemy to call this a miracle?'

'Perhaps the hand of God has been in the making of these things.'

'At last I am free. I may go to church again, in fact, do anything I wish. I can choose my own ministers. We will make this my palace instead of my prison. We will hold our meetings here. There is so much to be done.'

'You have honest, brave men working for you and Spain to set things to rights. It will take some time and a great deal of patience. You have made an excellent start in suggesting a committee of four. I would suggest that at tomorrow's audience you advise them that you will restrict their attendance before you to once a week. Time will be needed to consider their information before communicating it to Castile and the rest of Spain.'

'Dear Brother Juan, of course you are right. Thank you for keeping my feet on the ground; I confess I feel like an over-excited child. The Articles of the Communes, should I

267

sign them? I agree whole heartedly with every one of them, they are my sentiments exactly; but I would not want to do anything that would suggest I am taking action against my son.'

Chapter 45

The admiral tugged at his snowy beard, pursed his lips, thought a moment or two then looked across the chess table to his friend. 'I still find it difficult to believe the success of our campaign against the rebels, Hernando.'

The board had been set up close to a brazier to offer them comfort from the icy January draught that wandered freely about the rooms of the palace. The admiral pulled the collar of his lynx-lined gown more tightly about his neck, 'Too bad it had to happen in winter. I have never cared much for Tordesillas at this time of year. It may be my age but I think this is the coldest it's ever been. Your move, Knight Commander Hernando.'

'One moment, I have lost my concentration. Let me see.' Following some deliberation the commander moved his white knight up the board to join the queen, and sat back. 'You know, that business of suggesting Queen Juana marry the Prince of Calabria was a rash move.'

'That is where the Alliance lost the focus of their argument, Hernando. That would have denied Charles his throne. That had never figured as one of their Articles,' replied Don Fadrique moving his black king out of check. 'It's all very sad; there are many of their concerns that I would go along with; but, having said that, I still feel more comfortable in my bed with the royal standard flying over the town.'

'A good six or seven hours work by our determined fighting men, eh? It was intelligent of the constable's son to march his men here by night ready to make a surprise dawn attack, and clever to find the weakest part of the wall just waiting to be breached.'

'It was too bad that Juana was unable to persuade the guard to order the gates be opened to us.'

'Impossible, of course, too many of them by then feared retribution,' commented Hernando moving his castle to the top of the board to take the admiral's which had been left unguarded.

'Damn, I must be getting too old, the poor brain is fuddled.' The admiral looked at his remaining pieces and saw it was simply a matter of time. He moved his queen back, furious at having played so badly.

'Glorious from our point of view; pouring through the broken wall, climbing above the gates to set up our pennants and banners.' Hernando studied the board. 'The cannon, the gunfire, hand to hand fighting, then trumpets and drums joined by the clamour of church bells. Then setting the houses afire ...'

'Perhaps it was a grand sight for a soldier but not for Juana and Catalina. It must have been terrifying. Imagine, all alone and deserted amidst that dreadful confusion, rushing through the dangerous streets jostling with frantic townsfolk, finally getting to the convent only to discover there was no cart to carry Philip's coffin if they were pressed to flee. Then a frightening dash back to the palace.'

'And then, so I'm told, the constable's son came riding into the courtyard to leap down from his horse and fall on his knees before the queen to say he was her protector. Oh admiral, if only I had been there. That is the very stuff of romances.'

'If only that were the case, my friend.' The admiral removed his cap and scratched his balding head.

'If only what were the case?'

Don Fadrique placed his hands flat on the chess board and leaned towards him, 'If only the lad could have continued as her protector instead of this damned Marqués de Denia.'

'Too true, too true. It's quite dreadful.' The commander

tut-tutted, 'I know of no one, not one single grandee who can stomach the man. For months many refused to rally to our cause because of him. If King Charles hadn't made you and the constable regents and offered rewards to the waverers I don't know where we would be.'

'In a terrible mess!'

Hernando lowered his voice. 'Fadrique, I have written to the king. I told him that Denia has come back here to renew his duties without any authority and with far too much vigour. I said that this is viewed very badly and that many of us are worried. I asked him to write commanding the marqués to temper his behaviour, to consider his approach towards our royal ladies and their servants, and I also said that he and his wife should be ordered to treat the princess with more consideration.'

'Good man. I wrote too but I doubt if the king will heed my words.'

'He surely must; after all you are kin. And besides he must know the great debt he owes you as Castile's great leader.'

'We shall see. However, I told him much the same as you, saying how unpopular the man is not only here in the palace but in the town itself. And I pointed out that it would be extremely unwise to have him govern the queen's household without someone to keep a check on things. It should be a shared responsibility.'

'Good thinking.'

They lapsed into silence, the game of chess forgotten; then the admiral got to his feet. 'I must tell you, friend, I cannot keep it to myself any longer. I fear I have done the queen a great disservice.'

'Is that what has been playing the devil with your brain? I knew something was wrong. I have never seen you play such a weak game. But come now you must be mistaken. Our queen is, well, like your own child, you have been her protector for

271

many a year. You could never be the cause of any injury.'

'Yet most things I have done seem to have been of little consequence.' He wiped his eyes with his handkerchief, coughing and fidgeting with his gown. 'Forgive me. You are right; I have always regarded her as my ward. She has had much to contend with, a damn sight more than most, what with Philip, Ferdinand, and now with Charles ...'

'Then, dear friend, with all the love you have for her what makes you think you might be the cause of any trouble?'

'Unwittingly, Hernando, unwittingly; a simple thing, or so it seemed at the time. Remember, she never signed anything for the Holy Alliance, even when they threatened her, correct? But she did sign something for me. That, I am afraid could be her undoing.'

'Come, friend, what could be so serious in that?'

'She signed a decree commanding the Comuneros, this Holy Alliance, to put down their arms and send their men home.'

'I would warrant any man would welcome that.'

'My immediate reaction; but I hadn't thought it through properly. The fact that she signed any document would persuade Castile that she is of sound mind thereby making Charles no more than a prince; just think of it! The other two regents insisted that I destroy it.'

The entrance of Adrian of Utrecht and the new constable interrupted him.

The admiral was first to speak thinking how much easier it had been for him to work with the last constable, this fellow's father. 'What news of the Alliance?

Constable Iñigo was eager to report its disarray, 'It is split. There are those still eager to rob all the nobility of their lands and rents, and offer them to the king in exchange for their so-called rights. Most have fled after this latest defeat, while others have returned to their estates, weary of it all. Padilla, Bravo, Maldonado continue to fight, the necessary monies being raised by Padilla's wife, who has stolen the plate from the churches and the cathedral of Toledo. Most cities and towns are welcoming our armies. Be of good cheer for our enemies are dejected, they will lose. So will those in Aragón, Navarre and Majorca; of this there is no longer any doubt. It is infuriating, however, that many still plunder and run home with their spoils.'

Adrian added, 'The excellent news is that more and more nobles are joining our cause. But I would speak of that other matter, admiral. Has it been destroyed?'

'I tore it up with my own two hands and burned it. It is gone. It no longer exists,' he raised his gnarled hands as if to prove by their emptiness he had complied with their wishes.

Adrian and the constable nodded their satisfaction.

'Unfortunately, admiral, we still lack funds. The Treasury is empty.' Adrian had no other recourse but to mention this although he knew it would invite a reprimand from Don Fadrique.

And the admiral was swift to attack, enjoying a moral upper hand. 'If you and the rest of the king's ministers had not been so busy in wanton spending, in appropriating funds for the coffers of Flanders, or for his majesty's campaign for the Imperial Crown, we should not be in this sorry state. And, by the way, have you taken into account what it is costing us, the lords, individually? We have called our vassals off the land, leaving farming to limp along as best it can. We have had to provide the arms, pay for all provisions. Such a burden cannot be borne much longer, I assure you, not at the rate we are having to sell off our plate.'

Adrian and Iñigo were well aware of how indebted they were to the admiral for bringing about the much-needed rally to the royal cause, and for how deep he had dug into his own purse. He was also the nobles' favourite, while they themselves were not popular. They needed him.

Adrian looked to the constable who was not inclined to speak, leaving it to him to make the announcement. 'The time has come to sell the queen's plate and jewels.'

'Over my dead body!' Don Fadrique growled.

The commander, who had sat silently throughout, spoke up, uncomfortable with the thought of touching Juana's personal belongings. 'It is surely to the king that you must turn. He will know best where to seek finances. Also, no decisions regarding the queen's property should be made without his knowledge. Ah, speaking of the queen ...'

Juana could still look elegant and, in her black velvet dress with its red and gold trim, her black hood edged with pearls and gold, the admiral thought her as lovely as ever.

Catalina followed behind, a charming vision in green velvet with red satin linings to the turned back sleeves and panelled skirts.

'Don Fadrique I could wait not a moment more. Tell me has the Alliance responded to our decree to lay down their arms?'

'My lady I have been unable ...'

Adrian interrupted, 'With respect, the rebels are gradually returning to their homes.'

'Not rebels,' she wagged her finger at him, 'but men who sought to right many wrongs and were neither against myself nor my son. But we shall not argue the point. What is the present state of Castile?'

'Most cities have opened their gates to our armies without fighting and are now returning to normality.'

The constable added, 'And this is good news. It should not be too long before we can summon a full meeting of the Cortes. It has been a dangerous time for our country to be without proper leadership. There has been too much disorder and violence.'

'True constable,' Juana agreed. 'My poor country. And the Cortes; shall we summon them here?'

'When the Cortes is convened it will be in Valladolid.'

'Even better; Catalina and I would prefer that.'

'Maman,' Catalina clapped her hands, 'I would dearly love to go there, to leave this place with its marqués and marquesa.'

'Catalina, this is not the time.' Juana was shocked by Catalina's outburst in the presence of the regents.

Iñigo was taken aback, 'I am surprised to hear that you are not content with the master of your household. I would remind you that it was your brother, the king, who made the marqués governor of the palace. I have written to Flanders that I intend putting all the responsibilities back in Denia's hands just as soon as it suits his majesty.'

Juana's blood chilled, 'Oh dear God, I do not believe this. It cannot be. Sweet Jesus let it not be.'

The admiral was furious. 'Nor can I believe that you would make so rash a decision in this atmosphere of distrust. Why did we not discuss this? Why did we three together not consider a new appointment? Good God man, we should be seeking harmony not discord.'

'I could do no other, the man still lives, he is here; and as I said it had been the king's pleasure to appoint him in the first place.'

Don Fadrique went to Juana and bent to kiss her hand, 'You know that your confessor and I have been most careful in selecting your servants and we shall continue to do so. My wife and I will make it our prime concern to oversee your household. I am awaiting a letter from Flanders which should clarify matters.'

'And am I to remain here?'

'It may be here, it may be Valladolid.'

Images of dark rooms, isolation, threats, beatings, and more from Denia, who would now be seeking his revenge for the indignity he suffered during the last few months, ran rampant, relentless in their assault until she crumbled and staggered beneath them.

A chair was hurriedly brought and she was assisted into it. Catalina knelt beside her, 'Sirs, nothing must be changed here. Everything must remain as it is now. Don Fadrique, please, I beg you.' She urged her mother not to give way to pessimism, 'Maman these gentlemen will not permit a return to the old regime.'

'I came into this room for an audience with the regents.' Juana's voice shook, forming a stream of unsteady and disjointed words. 'I came to seek information about my country. Now everything is turned upside down.' She struggled to be free of her confusion and fears but was their prisoner, 'I cannot breathe, I cannot think. I must have air.'

On her return to the salon she saw that Denia and his secretary had joined the company.

Everyone bowed; all except Denia. Juana gripped her cloak with alarm.

The others had noticed too.

'What have we here sir, that you do not show respect to the queen?' the admiral rounded on him.

Denia hushed the admiral, 'Let me advise you that because of recent circumstances, it is only King Charles to whom we are now answerable.'

'I hear what you say, and later will take you to task on that. Right now I say have some respect sir.'

'And I say I will pay respect where respect is due.'

Adrian interposed himself between the two, 'Denia, I know that our king would not countenance this behaviour for one moment. Apart from the honour he must show as a son to his mother, he must indeed be grateful for the love she has demonstrated for him throughout some most difficult times. Under great stress and with extraordinary courage she has given complete and unwavering support for our king. Let us not forget that were it not for that very support we would be in a very different situation today.'

'But we are not in a different situation. Oh, I refuse to waste time with useless words.' He unfolded a letter. 'This is from his majesty. By his orders the queen and the princess shall once more be under my care. There will be no further audiences here for the nobles. The king recognises that everything I have ever done was always to his satisfaction and he urges me to take up the reins once more, continuing along the same road as before, and to endure as much as is humanly possible the taunts, the gibes and the slander as may come my way. Your services, admiral, as co-administrator of this house, are no longer required. You may give your wholehearted attention to the regency and its demands. This is my domain, and mine alone.'

'This is not finished yet Denia!' the admiral stormed.

'Marqués, you will think to treat my mother, the queen, in a way suited to her station, for I shall not hesitate to inform my brother, the king, if it should be otherwise.'

'I think, young lady, that at fourteen years of age you must learn when you may and when you may not speak to your elders, and that when you are allowed to, you speak in an acceptable tone. You will now go to your apartments.'

Juana could not move. Had not the Comuneros warned her that this would happen? And she had taken their words as threats.

Philip had once wished to have her imprisoned because he wanted her crown. She had offered to share the crown with her father, but that was not enough. He had wanted it all for himself. The Comuneros freed her, yet she turned from them to put her faith in the nobles and her son. Did Charles really mean to have her treated this way? Was he another not prepared to share the crown but would rather have her somewhere far from the world as though she had ceased to exist? This was a possibility; how often had the Alliance said that she was preferred to him? Yet every time she had heard this she had leaped to her son's defence, would have none of it. And her reward? Denia.

She asked herself, wearily, if she had enough spirit for another fight. She was forty-three years old and tired of these conflicts. She glanced at those gathered about her who appeared as helpless as she. But the admiral was giving her an encouraging raising of his eyebrows and that was all she needed.

'The battle has not yet even begun, Denia,' she hurled at him as she strode towards him as firmly as her shaking legs would allow. 'Take me to my prison cell, you disgusting, snivelling little rat, you liar and torturer. Oh, you have a long struggle ahead of you, both you, you bastard, and your evil wife.'

Strong words had made her sound far braver than she felt. She could feel herself sliding and sinking down, deep down into a terrible despair.

'Uncle, do everything within your power to come to visit me,' she whispered kissing his cheek, touching that dependable beard. Then, head held high, she left the room without looking back.

Chapter 46

This was the second year of Denia's new, and stricter, regime. The door to Juana's apartments opened and closed quickly and silently. From her chair opposite that of Brother Juan, in the darkened room with only a solitary candle and the dying embers of the fire to offer meagre illumination, she knew it couldn't possibly be Denia. He would have slammed it shut, shattering the surrounding plaster and sending pieces flying everywhere, before hurling invective in her direction. He certainly would this evening because earlier in the day she had escaped to the gallery and screamed out to passers-by to summon soldiers to come to kill him and his fellow torturers and set her free.

She and the priest exchanged puzzled glances. For a moment there was nothing to be heard except the sound of someone trying to catch their breath, and then; 'Maman, Maman.'

Catalina's whisper fell like the most beautiful music on Juana's ears. She could barely contain her joy, 'Catalina, at last; can you believe it possible, Brother Juan?'

'It does my heart good to see her here with you.' The old priest's cheeks puffed out at the margins of a joyous smile.

'Uncle has found me a new maid, and she is so helpful. She discovered that the marqués and his wife are entertaining a nephew, about to be appointed as chaplain, I believe, and most likely will not stir from their rooms,' Catalina announced, struggling to remove her mantle while keeping something tucked under one arm. The garment was made into a rough and ready bed and the tiniest of dogs made comfortable in its velvety billows. This done, Catalina kissed her mother's hands then sat at her feet.

279

'Brother Juan,' chuckled Juana, 'did you ever see the like?'

The priest peered down at the shivering little creature, 'What will it be when it grows up?'

Catalina laughed. 'Not much bigger; that is all I know. She is my lap dog.'

'Then let me have her on my lap.' Juana reached out towards the dog, gathering the little bundle in her hands. 'My goodness there is not much to you. Where did you get her from?'

'From my brother. She is such wonderful company. If only you could have one. She loves to beg from me when I eat; sitting up so daintily with her front paws held up just so.'

As Juana stroked the silky coat an image, hazy at first, took shape in her mind. It was of her brother's dog, Bruto. 'When I was about your age my brother had a dog, not a toy like this, but a big hunting dog, white with black smudges. The dear thing was not in the least handsome, he was such a mixture of breeds, but he was so very, very clever. We would hide things and ask him to fetch them.' She laughed, 'One day we were standing in a logia looking down into a street, when a man went by holding a beautiful pair of green gloves. My brother sighed aloud to have them for himself. No sooner said than Bruto, that was his name, hounded off and within minutes returned with them, leaving the poor man speechless and not knowing where to look, towards the door where the dog had disappeared, or up at us squealing and giggling.'

Memories came and went before she was held by one more important than the rest. 'When my brother died, Bruto refused to leave his side and followed the cortege to the lying-in. A black cushion was placed next to the bier and Bruto remained there night and day for a week, leaving only to attend to necessities.'

'That story is too sad,' insisted Catalina. 'I brought my little pet to cheer you not make you miserable.' She reached across

Juana's lap to fuss with her little companion's satin collar, 'I made this especially for her, sewing on each diamond button myself.'

'Diamonds, on a dog's collar? How did you come by them?'

'Later, Maman; listen, I have so much to tell you. I have finally been able to write to my brother. I absolutely had to reply to a very cross letter he sent me about my alleged disloyalty when the Holy Alliance gentlemen were here. Denia has implied that I was in league with them; but what he did not say was that it was he who insisted that I wrote or gave them an audience to ensure he did not lose his position as governor when they came into power.'

'That sounds like the duplicitous person we have come to know so well. But you said you have finally written; Denia told me you were in regular contact with Charles, wherever he might be these days.'

'Yes, but never writing my own letters. When my brother writes to me Denia whisks the letter away, barely giving me time to read it, to prepare the reply which he later dictates to me. I am then made to sign without adding anything of my own. This time she added with excitement, 'I have written my very own letter. Denia knows nothing of its existence. It will be on its way tomorrow.'

Brother Juan sought to temper her exuberance, 'My child, how do you hope to get your letter out of the palace? I have never known so many eyes to scrutinise, so many ears to listen, so many hands to search.'

Juana felt a rising wave of concern; letters never did anyone any good, causing nothing but misery. How often had she herself been at their mercy? But, the deed was done and she must hope.

Catalina considered the priest's words. 'You are right, of course. My other courier was discovered carrying a letter of mine to Don Fadrique's wife, and it has taken me until now to be sure of the loyalty of this new girl. Meanwhile the marquesa searches not only my rooms but me, in the hopes of finding a hidden note.'

Juana knew her worries were justified. 'Is there no limit to these people's arrogance, their insolence? Brother Juan, the regents must be informed of this outrage against my daughter.'

'Maman, please, I must continue. I have begged my brother to allow us to keep you, Brother Juan, as our confessor and counsellor. He must agree when I have told him how much we need your support and comfort.'

'I thank you for your kindness. I asked the admiral to speak to the king on my behalf. But I must admit to having little confidence in the outcome. The marqués is uncomfortable with my presence here. He has not paid me in over a year and I am now reduced to begging for scraps to keep from starving. Forgive me, I had not meant to mention that. More importantly he puts every obstacle possible in my way to prevent my visiting you,' Brother Juan sighed. 'I fear our requests will be denied.'

Catalina was cross with him, 'You must be more positive. This should cheer you then; Regent Adrian has written to the king speaking very highly of you. Unlike you, I am very hopeful.'

Juana smiled at her daughter, this child fast becoming a woman because of harsh circumstances; beautiful, sensible, sensitive, caring. She reached for her hands to clasp them to her breast. 'Here we are, a small group of dear friends: ourselves, Adrian, the admiral, the admiral's wife and we are the only ones who know what is right and what is just. Equally curious, we are the very ones whose voices for the most part go unheard. It is a strange world that God has made when wrongdoers are rewarded for their actions and the innocent ...'

She sighed and Brother Juan looked reprovingly at her. 'However, never let this dampen your enthusiasm, Catalina, or cloud your optimism, ever.'

'You two cannot be much consolation for one another. You are such pessimists. Maman, I have mentioned you several times in my letter. First, I have explained that the reason you led me from the service on Christmas Eve was because Denia had not allowed you to join us, forcing you to worship on your own in your rooms. I am convinced he will give a different version.'

It appeared that Catalina was determined to court trouble with her letter-writing, but presumably her youth and innocence would protect her. Juana smiled, 'That is most kind and thoughtful, although I fully expect him to have the king's ear in this case. You know, Denia and I have fought so many battles over the years about where and when I may be allowed to worship that, to be honest, I forget now whether I have always been justified in my actions or if I am indeed simply being provocative.' She chuckled, 'May God forgive me for enjoying such a war.'

'God would surely forgive you anything, my lady, knowing how you are made to suffer.'

'Please may we return to my letter?' Catalina grasped at her mother's hand, 'It is still possible that someone may come before I am finished, and I want you to know everything. I have also spoken of your linens and jewels. Denia has told my brother that they were taken from you to give to me. This is a lie; it is his wife and daughters who wear them.'

'I know; they flaunt everything they have stolen from me.' And, just for a moment, she pondered on the source of the diamonds on the dog's collar.

'They have started taking my clothes, too. They wear them until they are soiled then return them, often without the jewelled fastenings.'

'The things that are going on out there on the other side of the door!'

283

'That is something else I have asked for; that you are allowed to walk in the gallery and the corridor and visit the Grand Salon whenever you wish. In fact I hope you will be given the freedom of the palace.' Catalina waited for her mother's reaction to what indeed might turn out to be the best gift she could ever procure for her; remembering happier days they had spent together arm in arm in those very places, before the marqués filled the palace with numerous members of his family and locked her mother in her room that she would not disturb them.

Juana thought that after her escapade in the gallery that morning such a move would never be countenanced. 'Too late for that, Denia and his offspring with their spouses treat this as their home, with me the unwelcome intruder.'

'Well, well, well, do I hear my name being mentioned in this cosy coven?' Denia walked from the darkness to the edge of the light.

'How unlike you to sneak in; no torrent of rage, no arms flailing with exasperation, you do disappoint me.' Juana was determined to remain strong when she saw her daughter's confidence ebb away. 'We have been enjoying one another's company and had rather hoped to have had more time together while you were otherwise occupied.'

'I ask you, would a good father sit all evening at the table and neglect others in his care?'

'You came to spy.' Catalina fought back tears.

'I would have you guard your tongue, young lady,' snapped Denia. 'It is as well I have decided to replace all your ladies, they have taught you bad habits. You have given me no choice but to inform his majesty of your blatant disrespect. I know he will not be best pleased reading of your attitude towards the marquesa and myself. The sooner you learn your place, the better. Only then, I would add, will I permit you the extra allowance his majesty wishes you to receive.'

Juana gripped the arms of her chair to prevent herself from leaping up and striking him, 'Who do you think you are? Let me remind you that you are a marqués; my daughter is a royal princess.'

'While you, ever since those damned Comuneros were here, have become insufferably haughty. You will never know the extent to which you nauseate me with your airs.'

Catalina shook with anger, 'You have no right to speak to my lady mother, Queen Juana, in such a manner. I shall write to my brother to tell him.'

'In another letter or as a postscript to this?' He held out the letter, her letter, the one she was so confident would be delivered safely into her brother's hands.

Juana saw it as history repeating itself; important letters, concealed letters, causing pain and anguish to the writer.

Denia continued, 'Have no fear, I shall send it, but it will be accompanied by my own; to clarify one or two points, one might say.'

'May God forgive you,' Brother Juan shook his head. 'Many a poor mortal would find it difficult.'

'And you, priest, may gather your belongings, you will not be here much longer. Just as soon as King Charles replies to my demand for your dismissal I shall personally conduct you to the door.'

Catalina looked from her mother to Brother Juan, then to Denia. 'This cannot be! All three regents have spoken on his behalf.'

'You appear to know too much for your own good, and you are very slow to learn when to speak and when to remain silent.' He turned from her to Juana. 'I will not tolerate this continual interference from the regents any longer. I refuse to have my authority undermined. I have told the king I cannot possibly carry out his wishes with them constantly snapping at my heels.'

The sickening realisation of the extent of this man's power filled the air. Juana raised her chin, 'I thank you for informing us. I realise it must be very difficult for you, after all they are nothing more than mere regents who are in charge of governing the country.'

Denia brushed away the sarcasm; there were witnesses in the room. He satisfied himself on this occasion by ordering Catalina, as he would a servant, back to her apartments.

Juana had heard enough. She rose from her seat, handed the puppy to Catalina then prepared to make her speech. With her hands loosely clasped before her and with quiet, measured delivery, she said what had to be said to this dreadful man. 'Denia, unlike Brother Juan, I do not think God will forgive you. For my part I hope He damns you to Hell. You have not one ounce of goodness in your body. You deny me the smallest of freedoms, not even permitting me to leave my apartments. You treat my daughter as if you were her wicked stepfather; you have the audacity to insult her. You also seek to rob us of our dearest friend and adviser. Let me assure you, you have not heard the last of this, I will find a way to make your behaviour made public. Do not think for one moment that the ensuing violence against me, under the guise of "people of her frame of mind deserve it" will lessen my resolve.'

She had to stop there for Catalina would be devastated to hear the many ugly truths about her treatment at this man's hands. She turned to the priest. 'Brother Juan, if you must leave, where will you go?'

'I shall go to the monastery at Avila. We have a friend there who will speak well of me should there be any stigma attached to this dismissal. I am more concerned about leaving you without support and companionship.'

'I am a survivor. Who is this friend we have?'

'Hernan Duque is one of the brothers there.'

'Hernan Duque, Hernan Duque; how I loved that man. Had

286

we been of the same station in life I would willingly have become his wife.'

'Maman!'

'My lady?'

'Typical!' sneered Denia. 'Complete lack of religious discipline and obsessed with lascivious desires. It is little wonder the king fears for your soul. As God is my witness I do my utmost to keep you on the straight and narrow path of virtue.'

'Pish; you have no idea of the meaning of the word virtue, nor of love, nor of respect for that matter. Hernan was a man of intellect and learning, cultured in the arts. We spent many happy hours together; the days were often not long enough.'

And he had been a gallant escort; so attentive, desperate to please, ensuring everything was to her liking, compassionate and sympathetic when doubts and mistrust reappeared from time to time and made her angry with the world. But she would not mention these things, they would only be sullied by a man determined to tarnish something good and pure.

'Another reason for keeping you isolated, away from dangerous influences. Education is not for women, it is an evil to be avoided at all costs.'

'My mother, Queen Isabel, gave her daughters the same broad education as her son that they might stand shoulder to shoulder with any man.'

'Precisely; therein lies another of your problems I am trying to rid you of. You do not know your place. Queen Isabel, let me inform you, would have made a very poor monarch but for your father, King Ferdinand.'

'The grandees should be here to witness this arrogance.'

'Far from anyone coming here Denia announced, every inch of his mean frame exuding authority, 'I have decided it best that you are moved to a more remote and secure place. The

287

fortress at Arévalo is my preferred option. There would be no gossiping townsfolk and it is decidedly more difficult for prying visitors to find their way there. I have informed the king of my intentions and hold everything in readiness for our departure.'

Juana swallowed hard but it didn't help. She had maintained her composure throughout but now it deserted her completely. Starting with a chuckle which grew to unrestrained laughter, she reached for the hands of Catalina and the priest and spluttered, 'This is such a delicious oversight on his part. This power-crazy fool so full of his own importance forgets that it is only in Tordesillas where he is in charge and everything is kept secret; locked inside the town walls, behind palace doors. Once outside the town of Tordesillas I would be in Castile, where he has no jurisdiction whatsoever! Thank you Denia, I think I would like that very much.'

'Damn you!'

During the next three years Juana's gaoler nursed his fury that his plans to leave Tordesillas had come to nought, and he made her life more miserable than ever.

She was standing over a small domed casket of inlaid ivory she had brought from her treasury, a seldom visited dusty storeroom leading off from her bedchamber: a room of caskets, chests and coffers filled with jewels and gold and silver plate; of rolled up tapestries piled high; of bolts of exquisite velvets, brocades, satins, and silks; of trunks packed with every shape and size of furs: ermine, fox, squirrel, marten.

'Here boy, put those things down and come here. I need help with this.' The particular jewellery box she had sought out now stood on its own on the table, its contents awaiting inspection.

The young chamber boy looked about him for a suitable place to set down the silver ewer and basin brought for her retiring room, wishing he could have passed through the room without Juana noticing. He turned this way and that, consumed by indecision, still hoping he would be allowed to continue with his errand.

'My lady?'

'Open this box for me; my fingers are too stiff to turn the key.'

He panicked; his face colouring. He stammered 'My lady, it is not my place. Shall I tell the treasurer he is needed?'

'No, you shall not tell the treasurer anything of the sort. You will open the box.'

The lad's face was crimson; he wiped his shaking, sweating hands up and down the front of his tunic, he knew he faced a whipping if Denia were to discover him doing something he shouldn't.

'Good God, boy, I would hate to have to rely on you in an emergency and you standing like marble scared to death because it might be someone else's job! Grasp the key, and turn it in the lock; a simple enough task.'

Juana would have done it herself but dared not. She still found it strange that almost two years should have elapsed before she was plagued by recurring images giving her no peace: the marquesa's "borrowed" rings and bracelets, the diamond buttons stitched on to a dog's collar. So, to rid herself of her suspicions, she had brought the jewellery box here that she could check the contents to convince herself that all was well; having done that she would return it to the storeroom.

There was a click, and the chamber boy scurried away to the ewer and basin, relieved his work was done; and just in time. He prayed he had not been observed; he didn't want any trouble.

'What have we here?' Denia's voice, thin and needle sharp, pierced the air. 'You boy, you know you are not allowed ...'

'He is when I say so. In any case I have no further need of him, so he may go. Do I read consternation in your face or something more sinister?'

'Neither,' he replied. 'His majesty will summon you within the half hour.'

'Charles is here? Why was I not told? So, he has finally decided to grace us with his presence.'

Denia ignored her. 'These ladies are here to assist you.'

Two of Denia's daughters with their accompanying maids stepped forward.

'Do you know, Denia, I had actually forgotten that you have found positions for all your family; most enterprising of you. I shall be interested to discover which of my jewels they suggest I wear inasmuch as they have had personal experience as to their suitability for different occasions.' Juana's fingers idly traced the decorated lid as she and the daughters exchanged glances of mutual loathing. 'There is very little that escapes my notice. Go find me my best grey dress. Goodness me, how long has it been since I gave an order; I quite like it. I will need warm water. Off you all go.'

❖　　　❖　　　❖

King Charles sat on his canopied throne in the Grand Salon. He was impatient, twisting and turning the rings on his fingers then playing with the short hair that curled about his ears. It was a new hairstyle recommended by his doctors as a cure for his insufferable migraines, a short style tapered at the neck and sides and exposing the ears. It seemed to be helping and it was certainly proving very popular, most men deciding to follow his lead, setting a new fashion.

After an interminable wait two priests were announced.

'The General of the Dominican Order, my lord, and the General of the Franciscan Order.'

Charles glanced up at them as they entered; the first robed in black and white cradling a sheaf of papers close to his chest, the second in grey his arms lost in the generous sleeves of his habit.

'You look wearied, my lord? I pray we do not find you unwell,' the Dominican remarked.

'Financial burdens are both irritating and exhausting, Father, as are other matters until they are resolved; so, to business.'

The Dominican priest began ordering his papers, shaking his head, sighing ayes of frustration as he arranged and rearranged an assortment of letters and notes.

Charles watched, anxiously stroking his recently grown

beard that helped disguise the unfortunate Hapsburg chin and lent him an air of maturity and experience. 'I am waiting.'

'I have investigated the case thoroughly for months and my conclusion is that Princess Catalina is at liberty in her conscience to marry whomsoever you choose.'

'You are certain of this? There must be no doubts whatsoever.'

'This betrothal to the Duke of Saxony has been annulled.' He proffered one of the papers but it was waved aside. 'And as for the other marriage contract with the Marquis of Brandenburg, it is not legally binding because the princess had no knowledge of the facts, was unaware of ...' He fussed with a number of other papers, hesitating.

'Meaning?'

'The marqués and marquesa had her sign the articles without allowing her to read them. She therefore had no idea that she was putting her name to a marriage contract.'

'She knew nothing of it?'

'Absolutely nothing, and she is therefore free to obey your majesty with regard to the contract with Portugal. All the statements and necessary documents are here. To my mind the greater difficulty lies in getting her to leave her mother.'

'That is not a difficulty, she will do as I command,' Charles growled.

'And Queen Juana? This demands some careful thought. The parting must be done gently; and if I may suggest, with the consent of the Cortes.'

Charles leaned forward, thrusting out the neatly trimmed beard, 'It is essential we keep all information regarding the queen out of the public domain. If we are to maintain peace and stability the nation must be responsible to me alone. I will not allow her to be the subject of open discussion in the Cortes; to even mention her name could stir ...'

'With respect, my lord, if you have the consent of the

Cortes, you have the consent of all Castile. Then should the worst happen, for example the shock of Catalina's departure endangering the life of the queen, you are blameless.'

'A good point; and I see no reason why the Cortes should not welcome this marriage; after all John of Portugal is the grandson of Isabel and Ferdinand.'

'It demonstrates your desire to strengthen the bonds between the two countries. Further, might I advise you to have the Cortes meet in Valladolid; its proximity to Tordesillas and the queen would add to a sense of openness?'

Charles smiled his satisfaction. 'Good, good. I thank God this can all be dealt with immediately. I am most grateful for your diligence.'

'On a lighter subject; I have a letter here. Would it please you to read it?'

'What is it?' He read aloud, '*I kiss your majesty's hands. If you remember we met recently in Burgos and it was then that I asked your permission to return to Tordesillas to see the Princess Catalina before she leaves for Portugal. I respectfully repeat my request.* Who is this? Ah, I should have known; Brother Juan de Avila, a meddling priest if ever there was one. I will not have him anywhere near.'

He took the letter to the fire and lit one corner of it, watching as the hungry flame greedily devoured the pleadings of Brother Juan. He dropped the charred remains into the fire, rubbed his hands and returned to his chair. 'Send for the Princess Catalina.'

Catalina and Leonor, the youngest and eldest of his four sisters, equalled one another in grace and beauty, but there all similarities ended. Catalina, now eighteen and quite grown up was radiant in her blue velvets. Leonor, twenty-six and widowed, wore black.

Charles studied his sisters; they would both make beautiful brides.

'Draw close, Catalina. You wrote me several letters of complaint. I wonder if you would remind us of their nature.'

His abruptness and coldness shocked; Catalina was taken aback. She had not expected to be interrogated like this, had never considered this as the reason for the audience. Leonor had hinted at the possibility of hearing exciting news from their brother, hence his unexpected presence in Tordesillas.

'Sir, do you doubt my word?'

'The marqués spoke with justification when he said he thought you forward.'

Leonor was surprised but delighted that her sister should be so outspoken with her brother, if only she herself dared.

Catalina bobbed a curtsey, 'I beg your pardon, sir. I do not seek to anger you, far from it. As I told you in my letters mother and I were suffering many indignities and I wrote to you seeking your support. My lord it is you and you alone who has the power to set things to rights. If you choose not to then mother and I are lost.'

'Such drama! Do you not suppose that I might find your tales somewhat exaggerated?'

'I must risk that in telling the truth.'

'Oh, we urge you always to speak the truth, do we not, Holy Fathers?'

His sarcasm stung. Catalina was hurt and angry that he should mock her earnest words. 'I wrote telling you how I had nothing that was mine; that clothing and jewels taken from my mother were not for my use but for the satisfaction of others. I told of my mother not being allowed to use the rooms of the palace because it would upset the marqués and his family, who view this as their own home. I spoke of being treated without respect as though I were no more than a servant ...'

'Yes, yes,' he snapped impatiently at her revelations, wishing now that he hadn't encouraged her to speak. The priests were obviously intrigued and Leonor was not disguising her eagerness for more details.

'But this has all changed, has it not, Catalina?' Charles smiled, anticipating the disclosure of the hugely increased allowance he had sent her.

'Things have certainly changed. Matters have worsened. The admiral's wife, my great aunt, was my friend and confidante; and sometimes I wrote to her. That has been stopped. These days I have guards about me watching and the marquesa searching me for my letters; the names of those to whom I do speak or give letters are reported to the marqués. And then my darling nurse, the nurse I have loved all my life, was suddenly dismissed. I am not allowed to speak to my mother or her servants. Sir, I have no one to share my confidences; even my confessor Brother Juan de Avila has been sent away. The marquesa and her daughters walk into my rooms unannounced whenever they please. I hear that if my mother grows close to any of her servants then the marqués ...'

He would hear no more from this outspoken young madam, the revelations were embarrassing. He applauded, 'A wonderful performance, Catalina, yet here you are looking from head to toe a veritable princess.'

She made to explain but he would finish, 'In the near future there will be great changes for you.'

'Mother and I will be forever grateful.'

'Speaking of our mother, does she attend to her religious devotions?'

He sat forward, one elbow resting on the arm of his throne, the bearded chin of authority wedged between thumb and forefinger. He was ready to examine the young witness before him.

The priests and Leonor had to make a swift adjustment to this new subject.

Catalina swallowed hard, 'That is a very difficult question to answer. Situations can be complicated and so affect our desire to do what is required of us,' she looked nervously at her brother and the priests. What did they want of her? 'When Brother Juan was here mother always confessed. Yes, she confessed and would sometimes attend Mass. But Denia dismissed him.'

'You say that sometimes she would attend Mass. Does that mean there were times when she could not or that she would not?'

She hesitated, fearful of giving the wrong impression; and if he wanted these questions answered, why did he not ask their mother? 'It is all very complicated. First, as I said in my letter, the marqués would often insist that mother attend Mass in her own apartments, not allowing her to participate with other celebrants in the palace. That made her very angry, and then, and then ...'

'And then?'

'That was when she refused to hear Mass. I cannot explain! This is all so unfair!' She looked in desperation to the others. But there was something positive she could mention in her mother's defence. 'Mother has always been a great benefactress to the Franciscans and the Little Grey Sisters of Santa Clara. She often dresses in a simple grey dress, spending hours in private devotion, to come close to their way of life. What more can I say?'

'I have heard enough.' It was now Charles's turn to look anxiously in the direction of the priests. What they had all heard suggested heresy: no confession, no Mass, dressing like a nun. Was his mother a heretic? If so and nothing was done about it, then every one of her family's souls would be dragged down alongside hers to perdition, and that included his.

Juana was sent for. The priests muttered earnest, priestly whispers to each other.

Chapter 48

They waited and waited for Juana, the delay weighing heavy over them all.

Catalina and Leonor talked of this and that, neither interested in what the other had to say. Catalina feared the worst, almost ill with worry, trying to remember exactly what she had said about her mother and just how damning it may have sounded. Leonor still guarded her happy secret, her good news, but was anxious that it might be forgotten again should Charles continue this religion nonsense with their mother; it was obviously all a misunderstanding.

The priests solemnly discussed the many problems of heresy that beset Spain and much of Europe, frequently casting glances towards the empty doorway where Juana of the errant soul still failed to appear.

Charles leaned back to rest his head and close his eyes. He had two important considerations on his mind, each one outweighing the other in turn: his plans for his family and the pressing need to restore his mother to the paths of righteousness. Which should be dealt with first? The priests would be impatient to see with what degree of rigour he would address Juana's serious lapses. But how would he then turn from that to the equally important family matters?

At last Juana's arrival was announced and the dreaded confrontation could be played out.

The priests bowed their heads, Catalina and Leonor curtsied, Charles resumed his regal pose.

The lady they watched as she made her way across the room bore no relation to a royal figure, and looked as unlike a mother as any woman could. The lines on her face were a record of pain and conflict. The mouth was turned down in a tight curve of bitterness. Strands of straw coloured hair had escaped her hood and veil to lie in lustreless tangles on her shoulders. A tired grey velvet dress reflected the creeping age of its forty-five years old owner. She was an old lady, a stranger, a nuisance.

Juana planted herself before her son, rigid with determination. Her chin thrust forward, her eyes and mouth narrowed in anger.

This was going to be more difficult than Charles had supposed. Juana looked defiant. He tried to clear away his unease with a sharp cough; to shake off his embarrassment by rearranging his short red velvet gown. After some hesitation he stepped down from the dais to greet her.

'Dearest mother, how good to see you.'

'Not so fast, Charles; dearest mother, indeed!' In a thin voice trembling with rage she began, 'Let me remind you of the time you allowed your friends to steal away my darling Catalina. Oh yes, I know you had her returned but only after causing me great pain.' She raced on, 'Let me also remind you that you have stolen my kingdom and left me here a prisoner of the evil Denia.' She turned towards the door where her gaoler hovered with his daughters, the "ladies-in-waiting".

Charles was about to speak but she silenced him, she must finish. 'Please do me the courtesy of not attempting to deny it; do not even begin to make excuses. So I am cast aside, an unwanted encumbrance. So be it. But now this,' she beckoned for the small casket. 'Tell me, Charles; tell me, your own mother,' she stabbed at her breast, 'why you have ransacked my apartments!'

The priests were nonplussed.

'Sweet mother,' he implored.

'Do not dare speak until I finish!' she screamed. 'Tell me why, after stealing my gold, my rubies, my sapphires and

299

diamonds; you went to the trouble to fill their place with these?'

She took the casket and emptied its contents onto the floor. Thirty or more small stones and pebbles rattled and clattered their way across the tiles.

Juana pointed to them, continuing to scream, 'What cruel deceit was this? Why would a son treat his mother so? What treachery! Dear God I must sit.'

Her heart battled against her ribs making a thundering in her ears. She stumbled towards the throne, pushing Charles aside.

Leonor, Catalina, and the priests stared at the floor, eyes searching out here a stone, there another pebble.

Charles stood beleaguered, the evidence of his guilt spread about his feet. He had to swallow his fury, 'Let me explain, although I need not if I so choose. Ever since I inherited the throne there have been some extraordinary expenses. Monies have been necessary to settle unrest in Germany and Flanders, for securing the Imperial Crown, for putting down the civil unrest here in Spain and latterly for the wars against France. The country's purse was quite empty and I needed more money. I did not wish to burden you with affairs of state, mother. In any case I felt justified in taking what after all are Crown Jewels. I have every intention of replacing them when Spain is at peace.'

She stared at him digging deep into his soul, shaking her head at his lies. He felt unmasked; she knew he would take anything and do anything he pleased; that he saw it as his right.

'Your words do nothing to excuse your duplicity. And as for replacing them, you will never have enough to match your endless needs. How much more do you intend to steal from me, and what will the excuses be?'

Charles had regained his composure, 'Money had to be found and there's an end to it. I need even more than I could possibly raise with your jewels, much more. Fortunately I have finally found the solution. I have at last secured one million ducats.'

This was an incredible amount; Leonor and Catalina exchanged wide-eyed disbelief, Juana shook her head, questioning such a preposterous figure. Only the priests, who knew of its source, remained unmoved by the disclosure that such a sum could have been found when every big bank of Europe had denied him.

'I am to marry the Princess Isabel of Portugal. Her dowry you must agree is considerable.'

Juana struggled with her memory. There had been so many suggested brides and betrothals. Had she ever heard that this princess, her niece, was a possibility?

'One million ducats! Royal houses; they are all moneylenders, or borrowers, or merchants, all seeking out the best offer and nothing more; where will it all end?'

'With marriage settlements.'

'Settlements; there are more than one?'

'Leonor is to marry.'

Leonor stepped forward, her hand to her bosom, calming her leaping heart, smiling as finally her mother and sister were about to hear her happy news. She was to marry her childhood sweetheart, Count Federico.

'Leonor is to wed a prisoner of mine, Francis, King of France.'

'Not true, not true; it cannot be! You promised me I would marry Federico!' Her brother had gone back on his word for the second time. 'You reneged on the marriage contract with John, making me marry his disgusting old father Emanuel; a hunchback, a dribbling invalid. I did my duty. You said his death left me free to follow my heart; those were your very words. I trusted you. You have no right to treat me like this.'

'I have every right. Remember your station, madam. I will govern this house as I do the nation. I am the king; I decide for

301

all.'

'I will not do it!' She had taken courage from her young sister.

'You know you will. You have no choice, nor does Francis if he wants his freedom. If it is of any consolation your husband-to-be is only four years older than you, and handsome.' He bestowed what he thought was a warm fraternal smile, full of understanding, on his romantic sister then turned to Juana. 'Leonor will become queen of France and as a wedding gift she will receive Burgundy. Burgundy will at last be returned to our family; are you not impressed?'

Juana glanced at her two daughters both looking completely miserable. 'You can see that we are all delighted beyond words.'

'Well, at least I know I shall cheer Catalina. She, unlike her sister, will not be ungrateful. I told you earlier there would be great changes for you, Catalina. You, too, are to wed. You are betrothed to King John of Portugal, brother of my intended wife, Isabel. You will no longer be obliged to remain here suffering all those terrible discomforts you were complaining of earlier. Now, what do you have to say? What, not even a smile?'

Catalina was overjoyed. Freedom; how often had she dreamed that one day she might be free of this prison? It was wonderful news. It was more than that. She would be going to Portugal to become the bride of a king! It was all too good to be true. But what of her mother? Could she abandon her so easily? Who would there be to protect her?

'No! No! No!' Juana's howls rent the air. 'No, you cannot do this to me! She is all I have! Dear God she is my life!' She stumbled down from the throne on its dais, moving distractedly about the room, trapped in her anguish, staring wildly, wringing her hands, biting at her knuckles. She stopped, resting on the sideboard. Two candlesticks were in her hands, and she turned, hurling them at Charles and screaming, 'You have taken everything else but you shall not have my Catalina.'

Silver dishes, gold plates and pitchers followed, clattering against furniture, crashing to the floor as she sobbed, 'She shall not go!'

Juana's screams lost nothing of their intensity as she flung everything she could lay her hands on until at last there was nothing left on the sideboard save the velvet cover. She tore it from its place, collapsing with it to the floor.

Leonor led a tearful Catalina from the room; there was nothing they could do.

As soon as Juana lay still the Franciscan priest came to her side and knelt down. He urged Juana to be joyful for her daughter. He admonished her for her selfishness in standing in the way of her daughter's happiness. He called on her to seek forgiveness as a true daughter of God for her unseemly behaviour.

Juana quickly dried her wet cheeks on the cover then fixed him with an angry, incredulous stare. 'Selfish? I am being selfish when Catalina is all I have and I have just been told I am to lose her forever? Catalina is my solace, my only joy in this hellhole. You dare to judge me, knowing nothing of me and the way I am treated, having no idea of the conditions here. How presumptuous of you to criticise. I tell you now, priest, I will never, ever confess again. No, not while I have breath in my body,' she hissed at him. 'Nor will I seek forgiveness. Where, in God's name is your compassion? Where is your sympathy? Where is your charity? Where are the words of comfort? Get out of my sight! You disgust me!'

'I must warn you that you invite excommunication,' the Franciscan's voice was loud and harsh; but having heard Catalina's evidence and now this outburst, matters were indeed serious. 'It would appear that you need reminding that confession is an absolute obligation imposed by divine institution. You must humbly ask pardon of God, and absolution from our Heavenly Father. If you refuse to hear the Church, you are a heathen and outside the Church. Outside the Church is the devil. My lord, King Charles, has every justification in fearing for you.'

Chapter 49

The years 1525 to 1533 had passed over the palace at Tordesillas without stopping to look or care. One dark day followed another, adding to the misery and age of the inhabitants, and it was an enfeebled marqués who now shuffled his way along the corridor. He came to a halt, catching his breath, at the door to Juana's apartments. He was thinner than ever, his white hair sparse and forming a ragged fringe under his black bonnet.

A guard held the door open for him. He still paused, waiting until his eyes became accustomed to the poor light. First he made out the shapes of two serving girls, who had stopped their cleaning the moment he appeared and backed away deeper into the room, then he noticed the silhouetted figure of Juana standing by the window.

'Someone is here to see you,' he wheezed.

There was no response.

'We have not improved our manners in the last eight years, have we?' It was delivered with weary sarcasm.

Juana whirled round, snatched a broom from one of the girls and began jabbing it in his direction to drive him away.

'You know I cannot allow this kind of behaviour.' He took a step towards her.

Juana dropped the broom, closed her eyes, and raised an arm to protect herself from the coming blows. But there was no need, for these days Denia was incapable of administering anything other than verbal punishment.

And, of course, nothing happened, as so often these days. She lowered her arm. 'Where is Denia?'

'He's gone, my lady, just turned and went. But he's right,

you do have a visitor. We'd heard, but didn't want to say; you know what the master is like about us telling you anything. There's been a proper commotion, I can tell you.'

'Is it friend or foe; and does it matter,' Juana began giggling nervously.

'It's an admiral; your uncle, he says. Said something about how he hasn't seen you in eight years.'

'Eight years? Denia was just talking about eight years.'

'What we were thinking was that it has been ages since anybody at all came to see you.'

Raised male voices tumbled down the corridor; old, crackling, angry voices.

One of the girls ventured, 'You see what I mean? It was like this all day yesterday; such arguments as you wouldn't believe.'

'And I say I will go to the queen's apartment to see her! If she is too unwell to leave her room I know she will not take it amiss if her old uncle comes to her.'

'I insist that you wait for her out here!'

'I am here on the king's business. I am family. I have come for a family visit.'

'Whatever you tell the king will be of no consequence, his majesty only heeds my words. I will tell you anything you want to know, there is no need for you to go in there. In fact I refuse to give my permission.'

'You, sir, are probably the most exasperating man I have had the misfortune to meet, and I have met a few. Now let me get on.' The admiral shepherded him aside with his stick.

Don Fadrique, his stick returned to its intended use, limped his way into the apartments of his niece. Through dimmed rheumy eyes he peered at the figure who had once, decades ago, been his beautiful, tender charge; a young girl with hazel eyes and

306

auburn hair, a lass with a zest for life. Now she was in her fifties, a wrinkled and old woman, with grey unkempt hair that neither brush nor comb had been near in years. An ugly grey dress, or robe, or whatever it purported to be, clung to her thin frame. It took all his determination not to weep.

If his eyes, poor as they were, didn't deceive him that woollen dress was unwashed and spattered with months of accumulated stains. There was a heavy, foul odour in the room, and it emanated from Juana. When had she last bathed or changed her undergarments?

He advanced a step and bent one leg very gingerly, 'I should kneel, I know, but then I might never get up again.'

Juana studied him as he raised her hand to kiss it. Who was this old gentleman with kind eyes and comfortable beard? Was it who they said it was; her uncle? And then it happened. It was like the arrival of a new dawn, the early sun bringing warmth after the cold of night. The old face was calling up scenes of other times, other places; there were ships and high seas and shipwrecks, there were palaces with banquets and balls, huge rooms flooded with candlelight and music.

A hesitant smile; then, 'I do know you! I was so afraid of being unsure. I rarely see anyone and people and places get all mixed up. But now I know it is really you. You are my uncle; my dear Uncle Fadrique.'

'And you my favourite niece.'

'We must have so much to talk about. Will you be here for long?'

'For a few days.'

'Even so,' she frowned, 'there will probably be so little time. She pointed over his shoulder towards the door, 'that man, may not permit another visit.'

'Rest assured that will not happen.'

Like a happy child she introduced him to her two servants, 'Here is my uncle come to see me. Find him a chair.'

'Would you not prefer to take a stroll?' He had no wish to stay in this room a moment longer than necessary and had a ready excuse. 'I find if I sit too long my knees turn to stone and forget how to move.'

'Why, of course, a stroll. That sounds splendid. Usually I am not allowed to leave my apartments, although sometimes I do sneak out and I rush to the far end of the corridor. Then I scream for someone to come to rescue me. But no one ever comes.'

The delivery was flat, emotionless, and Don Fadrique doubted it was true. But supposing it was and his frail niece was desperately seeking help and there was no one to offer succour; what then?

'Denia gets so angry and ...'

'The marqués gets angry and what?'

Juana glanced about her, putting a warning her finger to her lips, 'Shh. But I am too strong for him. He will never win, you shall see.'

'What is all this Juana, are you telling me that the marqués is violent towards you?' Don Fadrique knew this must be sheer invention; the marqués would scarce put fear into the heart of a mouse.

'Oh yes,' she was quite dismissive. 'All the same, not a word; promise.'

Although unable to put much faith in Juana's words, they and everything he had seen and heard since his arrival formed a terrible picture. Juana was a prisoner; she certainly looked like one. This room was her cell and she could not set foot beyond the door without being punished.

He remembered that time, all of twenty years ago, when King Ferdinand had been determined to prove that she had lost her reason, she had been in bad shape. But she had looked positively radiant years later, when Hernan Duque was here, and again after the routing of the Comuneros. Had not all the reports buzzing about Spain and beyond spoken of her grace, her intelligence, her charm, and the excellence of her gowns?

He had never forgiven himself for being one of the regents who had freed her from the rebels only to deliver her again into the hands of that villain Denia. These last eight years of confinement without the support of Catalina had possibly broken the last threads linking her to ... he could not bear even to think of the word. Hopefully the letter he would write to the king would bring about some changes here; something must be done, and quickly. He stopped, clapped his hand to his forehead muttering, 'But wait, you old fool, Charles has been here, has seen how things are. Dear God, how could he allow this?'

'What did you say, uncle?'

'Oh nothing; just moaning my frustration with the aches and pains that old age has thought fit to bless me with.'

They wandered slowly down the corridor and into the anteroom of the Grand Salon, making their way towards a neglected chess table with two chairs, the pieces arranged and standing waiting, as they had waited for many a year, to welcome players.

'Shall we, Juana? Do you still play? You were quite good once.'

Perhaps she had not heard. Her eyes rested on the white king. She picked it up to study it carefully then replaced it. Next she examined her wrinkled fingers with their long nails filled and edged with all kinds of nastiness. She would try to remember to do something about that.

'You have news for me, uncle?'

'Nothing of great importance, I came to chat about this and that. Did you know you had a grandson and two granddaughters?'

'Ah, yes, they came here once. Charming little children; DoZa Maria and Don Felipe, and the baby named after me.

Their mother is quite a beauty. Do you know how I remember?' She smiled and beckoned him closer. 'I remember because she was wearing one of my favourite gold chains.'

The admiral wanted to hear no more of the plunder of Juana's jewellery.

'And your dear Catalina, she has given you another granddaughter.'

The agony tightened about her once more, the picture so vivid, of those hours watching the entourage bearing her child away over the bridge and across the plains until there was nothing left to see. For two days she had remained at the window refusing to move, willing Catalina to return, never allowing her eyes to leave that point on the horizon where she had last seen her.

'They took her away from me.'

'She had to go to Portugal, Juana. That is the way of things. But you must rejoice in the safe delivery of her child.'

'Catalina never came back. I am alone with my tormentors.'

'What is it that you suffer at these people's hands? What is it that Denia ...?'

Juana pushed herself up from her seat. 'Do not speak his name. He is vile; a slimy, disgusting reptile. May God curse him, the foul heap of dung. I spit on his name, on his wife's name, his sons' and daughters' names, and all those who follow his orders.' She spat on the floor for everyone's name she could remember.

Her vehemence rocked him. He was at a loss to know what to say, so decided to say nothing, to wait until the storm abated. He left her cursing and spitting and walked to the window to look out at the route Catalina had followed and to contemplate those ensuing years that Juana had had to endure, alone.

Eventually there was calm and silence behind him. He turned to find Juana smiling at him as if nothing unusual had occurred.

310

He would try a different topic.

'Did you hear of Charles's coronation as Holy Roman Emperor? It was evidently splendid beyond words.' Don Fadrique groaned as he lowered himself into his chair.

'It would have to be. And whose jewels did he steal to make it a glittering occasion I wonder? It would certainly take many more than those he stole from me.'

Don Fadrique laughed and slapped his knee. 'Juana,' he chortled, 'you are still the same. You were never one to be afraid of voicing your opinions.'

'I only speak the truth, uncle.'

'Well, it is a fact that he has taken most of his wife's jewels, to the value of ninety thousand ducats; promising to pay them back, of course.'

'Ha! I could tell her that he never gives back he only takes. He is no better than a common thief.'

The admiral put his finger to his lips and pointed towards the door. She nodded. She understood, Denia was probably listening, and she smiled. This was exciting; they were conspirators, sharing secrets.

'Be that as it may,' continued Don Fadrique, 'his cape and crown were made of so much gold and so many precious stones it would be impossible to calculate its cost or its weight. And, would you believe it, following the ceremony gold and silver coins were thrown to the crowds.'

'I believe it; he would enjoy playing the role of a great emperor. He probably thinks himself greater than Charlemagne. He is the most conceited and selfish man I know. And I can tell you something else; it would be other people's money that was thrown away, not his!'

'Tut tut, Juana.' It would be best to avoid further stories of Charles. 'Did you know that Leonor is married?'

'She married the Portuguese king.'

'He died. Catalina married his son, the newly crowned King

311

John.'

'Catalina never came back and I waited and waited. That was a knife straight to my heart; my only child, taken from me.'

The admiral had no intention of going over that ground again. 'You do have five other children.'

'Really? All strangers except for Catalina; she was mine, all mine.'

Don Fadrique hastened the conversation on. 'Leonor married King Francis of France.'

He watched her knit her brows and struggle through a mist of confusion, having to substitute the French king for the ancient Portuguese monarch; all excusable really and damned difficult, he thought, when days had melted into months then years, and all news had been deliberately kept from her.

Finally she nodded. 'Ah, yes, so she did, so she did, I remember now. It was politics; it was Charles striking a bargain, using his sister.'

'You are right, of course. Burgundy was returned to you and your family and Charles returned Francis's two young sons.'

'He steals children as well as jewels! How did he come to have them?'

'Francis had been Charles's prisoner but was released in exchange for the boys. They were held as hostages until all the negotiations were completed. They were then set free; Leonor accompanied them to France.'

'Men can be the cruellest of creatures. Imagine, two little ones, with no one to love or care for them, in a strange country, terrified. I expect the French would not look too kindly on Leonor.'

'Wars are very complicated.'

Juana interrupted, 'Do you remember Margaret of Austria, my sister-in-law? They gave her my children.'

'She certainly cared for four of them.'

'Does she still look after them?'

'No. They are all grown up and married.' There would be no point in elaborating. 'Alas, Margaret is dead. It was a stupid accident. A glass goblet was broken in her bedchamber. They say a stray fragment had found a hiding place in her slipper. She cut her foot and it became infected. A sad business; I know you had a great affection for her.'

But Juana was travelling with her memories to years long gone. 'She was married to my brother.'

'You remember!'

'Oh yes I remember some things.' She played at making pleats in her skirts then gave her undivided attention to the stains on her sleeves.

'Dear Juan. Mother always called him her angel. When we were little I called him Juanito. He was so very special. I have a picture of him right here,' she tapped her forehead. 'He once said that I was a fighter and should always fight for what is right, what is justly mine. And I have fought, uncle. I have fought many a battle; I am not sure if I ever won any outright but here I am still fighting.' She sat up proudly, 'Who knows I may be victorious one day.'

'There is no one who can match you for spirit; that is for sure.' He stroked her hand.

Juana laughed wickedly. 'Spirit, yes, but what of my soul? Did you know that everyone here is obsessed with the fact that I rarely confess and often refuse to attend Mass?'

The admiral was alarmed; this was far too serious to be treated so lightly. 'Juana you must take care. I am not afraid for your soul, but we do live in difficult times. The Inquisition has not ceased its Holy War against heretics and it would be dangerous if those around you were to imply that by these actions you ...'

'Do you suggest that I should be a hypocrite; only pay lip-service to my duties while doing nothing to have things set

313

to rights?'

'No. Oh Juana, I do not know the answer. How am I to advise you? If only you would find another way to protest. Could you not seek some compromise?'

'Would you have me surrender so readily? As Juan said, I must continue the battle.'

'Then God be with you.'

Their conversation had found its natural end. There was nothing left to discuss, today or any other day. He knew as he uttered those few words they were his valedictory blessing on Juana. They would never meet again. There would be little point in his returning. Also, he was old, far too old, to get involved in religious affairs; and in any case he lacked the heart and stomach for the struggle. He despaired at his failure, the more so as he recognised that any report he sent to Charles would be set aside, unread. The marqués was right.

This visit had amounted to nothing more than one of self-indulgence, assuaging the longings of a sentimental old man to see his niece just once more before he died. Following his departure Juana would continue alone and unaided.

'Juana, shall we have something to eat?'

'No, I usually eat alone. I have little appetite, and I am sure you would want more than bread and cheese. I get tired of them day after day. Still, I find they save better than most things if not eaten right away.'

This revelation of another outrage against his niece, being given nothing better than pauper's fare, was unbearable. He accompanied Juana to her apartments and watched as the door closed behind her. He sank on to a nearby stool, setting his cane between his feet and dropping his chin onto his bony knuckles. Silent tears rolled down over his cheeks to lose themselves in his snowy beard.

A kitchen maid came along the corridor carrying two earthenware bowls, one on top of the other, and a pitcher. She

314

put them down on the floor near the door. Don Fadrique shook his head at them: one bowl with its slab of dried and cracked cheese, the other its hunk of bread, the pitcher full of water.

His old heart was being torn asunder, his ancient body one huge angry protest. 'What is that?'

'The queen's meal.'

'Who ordered this?'

'The master says seeing as how she doesn't seem to want much it would be sinful to waste good food, so she gets the bread and cheese and we eat what was cooked for her. And very welcome it is too, even if I shouldn't say so.'

'So while the queen gets nothing more than this, you dine on beef, chicken, pork?'

'As I said, sir, it's because she doesn't always like to eat.'

'And why put it here on the floor, for pity's sake?'

The woman squirmed, reluctant to reply, 'Sir, if you please, it has been done this way since before my time. You see, you never know what sort of mood she might be in. Sometimes she can get very bad tempered when she sees her meal and when she does she throws things. So we just leave it here outside the door. If she wants it she gets it herself. It saves a lot of bother, you know, like somebody having to punish her if she has hit anyone in her temper ... I've said too much.' She curtsied and dashed away.

So this was how they saw Juana; an animal, a wild beast, or something worse, to be fed from a safe distance.

He thought of the Juana he had just spent the last hour with. Yes, she had shown spirit, but of the kind that would never invite censure were she a man. In any case she was the queen and therefore at liberty to do and say as she pleased. At liberty, he chided himself, was an unfortunate turn of phrase to chose. Juana had also shown confusion at times, but that was not so surprising after years of confinement.

What had happened to all those promises to treat Juana as a

queen?

Ignored; instead they had deliberately set about making her into a monster so that now appropriate measures could be taken to deal with their own creation.

And where did Juana fit in with all this? After many years of experiencing nothing other, she had grown accustomed to filling that very role.

'Dear God in Heaven he wept, 'please show her some mercy and justice, for there is no one to offer it here.'

Juana was seventy-four years old (she must be because someone had said that this year was 1554) and she congratulated herself once more on her remarkable stamina. Many might have been broken by the years of ill-treatment at the hands of the Denias, but not Juana. She wouldn't allow her enemies that pleasure. If only the admiral or some other long-lost friend could be here to share in her wry satisfaction.

She closed the lid to her casket with its remaining trinkets then manoeuvred it with deliberate precision alongside an oblong leather box holding perhaps her most treasured possession. Ferdinand, her favourite son, had sent it from Vienna a few years ago, wishing to be remembered to her on her sixty-ninth or seventieth birthday, she couldn't remember which.

The casket and box accompanied her wherever she went in the palace. Her apartments were being repaired and decorated so she had been transferred to this more spacious accommodation. It had happened before so she knew that her stay here would be nothing other than temporary.

Having positioned the casket to her liking and caressed once again the leather box she settled herself into her chair and was ready to speak to the middle aged gentleman standing at the other side of the table.

'How is your father?' she enquired as a ritual of Don Luis, the new Marqués de Denia.

'He is no better,' Don Luis lied, as he did every time, having inherited the title on his father's death almost twenty years before.

'What kind of lingering illness does the man have that it

should last so long? Not that I miss his company. It seems to me that he has never been well since that time he took me away from here. A threat of plague, he said. Serves him right for lying; saying I was to get all new clothes when we got to wherever we were going. And to think I believed him and threw out so much. But I stopped the servants from helping themselves to my things which I intended to have burnt.'

'Yes indeed,' Don Luis replied, bored with the tale so often repeated, 'because you threw dishes at them as they sorted through the bundles lying in the yard below.'

Juana was disappointed, she would have preferred to have enriched a story she enjoyed retelling.

'And your father was too mean to allow me my own mule. I had to be content with being hoisted up to ride with him; undignified and uncomfortable I would have you know.'

The marqués knew full well that the reason for her travelling in this manner was because his father had been terrified lest she went galloping off on her own to seek sanctuary.

She continued, 'As it turned out we went nowhere, spending a few nights of aggravation wandering aimlessly about before returning here.' She laughed, 'He said that the inconvenience to me was unfortunate but that he was acting solely for my safety. Now, does that sound like your father?' She raised her arms to emphasise her rhetorical question.

Don Luis was sorely tempted to tell Juana that their exodus from Tordesillas was to protect his father and his family, not her, and that he had had no option but to take her with them. But he refrained as he had on all other occasions.

Juana concluded, 'You may tell your father not to concern himself over hurrying back to his duties on my account since I have found in you a man every inch as bad.'

The marqués was impatient to be gone, he found visiting Juana an irritating waste of time. It was rare that he came to see her, and then only when necessary. Today he had come to inspect the room before Francisco de Borja was allowed in. No, he wanted no part of these boring conversations with the crazy old hag of seventy and more years, wizened, hollow cheeked and toothless, who for some reason refused to die and liberate him from his obligation to King Charles.

'You have a visitor.'

Juana stared blankly at him.

'You have a visitor,' he repeated, admiring the rings on his fingers, the gold chains about his neck. They had all found their way from Juana's treasury, some into his father's possession and thence to him, others he had selected himself.

He and his family had fared well for many a year under the generous auspices of King Charles. Their loyalty had been repaid bounteously. They each had a more than generous personal allowance. The number of Juana's servants, soldiers, and guards, in reality Denia's, had reached the grand total of three hundred and accounted for at least one quarter of the town's population. The palace was sumptuously appointed, as indeed it must be, in readiness for important guests, especially the king, although his visits were infrequent. In the meanwhile everything was at the disposal of Don Luis and his family. It was of no consequence to him whether Juana ate, slept, changed her clothes, did or did not do anything provided she was held secure.

As Juana continued to ignore him he turned on his heel and walked out, muttering about the patience of Job.

Juana hadn't responded because she was preoccupied. She was wondering who might be coming to see her and why. She was determined not to criticise anything or anyone. She had learned that lesson long ago when her complaints to her own son had exacted nothing but brutal punishments from the Denias.

Denia returned accompanied by a black-robed priest. They bowed, the marqués announcing, 'With permission, your

319

highness, this is Father Francisco.'

Juana cackled her reprimand, 'Such deference! You hypocrite; and in front of a priest, no less!'

The Jesuit priest was unaware of all this. He was transfixed. The last time he had seen Juana she was still an attractive woman. Admittedly her beauty, even then, had begun to fade and her choice in clothing and a lack of interest in her appearance had done little to help; but this, this was too much of a shock. This Juana looked like a work-worn ancient nun, little more than a skeleton dressed in coarse grey wool, left to spend her remaining days sitting by the fireside dozing and dribbling while the rest of the community went about their business. What had he expected? She was very old and most people died long before reaching her age. He talked himself out of his disquiet and focussed his thoughts on the reason for his being here.

'Your highness I have been sent by the King of Naples.'

'Oh, really,' she squinted up at him. 'I had no idea there was one. My father used to be the King of Naples but he died and I inherited the title. I suppose you mean Charles; he steals everything.'

'King Charles thought it best your grandson, Felipe, should now have the title. It is King Felipe who has sent me.'

'You can assure him that I want nothing.' She would keep to her word, holding her own counsel on conditions here.

'I think it is rather what he wants of you, my lady.'

Juana disliked his tone, 'I find it exceedingly remarkable that anyone could want anything of me; whatever I once had they all took without asking.' She reached out to her casket and the leather box to protect them, 'But they shall have no more, these stay with me night and day.' She paused, 'Come to think of it, I saw him recently and he never asked for anything then.'

'His majesty told me he had stopped here before leaving for England. He is to marry Queen Mary Tudor. More importantly he is also on a mission for God.'

'He mentioned something about getting married. He was married before, you know. Such a pretty little maiden, a bit on the plump side, but then none of us is perfect. Poor girl died within days of giving birth to a son, and from what I hear he is most odd and grows increasingly strange every year. So, I imagine Felipe has gone to another bride to see if he can do any better.'

Father Francisco was not here to discuss the trivia of marriages, brides, nor procreation. 'King Felipe has gone to save the English people. He will guide them back to the Church. He lives and speaks as a true Catholic.'

'Bravo!' She applauded, 'I am happy for him and his crusade!' She then dismissed the subject with a flick of her hand.

Father Francisco came straight to the point of his visit. 'Can you say that you are a true Catholic, my lady? Are you not perhaps living somewhat like the English: without Holy Mass, without the blessed icons and statues, without the Sacraments?' He thought it best she had a gentle chastisement, a reminder that she was failing her family in neglecting these very duties herself, especially when death might come rather quickly and unannounced at her advanced age; unless, of course, she was not of sound mind as many would have it, that would be a different matter. 'King Felipe is hardly in a position to accuse others when the same fault lies here within his own family.'

A toothless grin suddenly lit up her face, 'I have it! You were here many years ago, as a child, a pageboy.' This was something far more interesting for them to talk about. 'Yes you were a little page boy to my daughter Catalina. You are Francisco de Borja, a grandson of my father. Your mother was conceived on the wrong side of the sheets,' she wagged a reproving finger in his direction.

This was a fact, although a somewhat indelicate one to raise,

321

but it made him think about her ability to retain and recall facts. First Naples, Felipe's son, now this; her mind might be sound after all. Felipe could well be justified in his concern for her soul.

She inspected him thoroughly, 'But how is it that you are now a priest?'

'That happened years ago when I accompanied the cortege carrying the mortal remains of Felipe's mother to Granada. Before the body could be interred the coffin had to be opened and the body identified.' He paused recalling that harrowing moment. 'It came upon me then, the certainty that the purity and readiness of the soul for God's Heavenly Kingdom was far more important than all the ephemeral grandeurs of this earth.'

'So you gave up everything to become a priest.'

'Yes, for this is what God desires of me. And now King Felipe desires that I set you on the road to piety, bringing you back to the Mother Church. He is afraid for your soul; that it is not in readiness ...'

'Afraid for my soul,' she scoffed. 'I tell you there are plenty of others whose souls are in far greater danger than mine and much more deserving of his immediate attention.'

He would not be deterred, 'Can you tell me in all honesty that you do believe in the articles of faith, those prescribed by the Church?' This was of great concern to Charles and Felipe and the reason he was here.

She was astounded; offended. 'How could I not believe in them? Of course I believe!'

'And do you believe that the Son of God came to the world to redeem us all.'

'Of course I do!'

'Then will you be confessed?'

'Of course, Father. Good Lord what a great deal of fuss all this is.' But she had first to consider how much of her soul she should lay bare, and ought she to accept culpability for incidents that had been forced upon her by the actions of others, notably the Denias. How much blame should she accept? It might all be too complicated; the more so if she mentioned that she had talked about her misdemeanours directly with God refusing the assistance of priests for whom she had no respect.

In the end she decided to confess; admitting her stubbornness, her temper, her rebellious spirit, her wicked language.

This she did in all humility, humbly seeking pardon, and she received absolution. She sat back content, happy to have been of service to this kind priest. It must have made his journey worthwhile.

'There was a time when I confessed regularly and took communion. I attended Mass. I had statues of the saints and reliquaries in my rooms. Yes, all these things ...' Juana drifted into her own thoughts.

'And then what happened? Why did you stop?' The priest needed as much information as possible, be it reasons or excuses.

'It was none of my doing. Believe me, Father, I still wish to; but come close, listen.' She had him incline his head so she could whisper into his ear. 'The ladies in my service will not allow it. They are sinful witches, they mock me.'

Perhaps he was wrong after all about the state of her mind. 'Surely you are mistaken?'

Juana shielded the oblong box from possible enemies. 'That is why I will not allow them to see this. They joke about my crucifix held safe in here,' she whispered. 'They mock the reliquaries, the icons, my rosary and ...'

'This cannot be!'

But Juana had already warmed to her story and would not be stopped. 'They have even spat on my statues. On St. Domingo, St. Francis, St. Peter ...'

Father Francisco was convinced this was pure invention. 'I cannot believe this, there must be some misunderstanding.'

Juana hurried on; she had not felt so animated in ages. 'When I said my prayers they snatched my Psalter from me, or sometimes they turned it upside down. Other times they shouted to drown out my words of supplication.'

'You are mistaken, let us ...' He wanted to return to being her guide and mentor.

Juana hushed him, 'They even put filthy things in the Holy Water.'

This was preposterous. He must be firm with her. 'My lady, these sinful acts cannot have been committed by any of your ladies. No one would dare offend God in such a way.' Perhaps now he could resume his mission of saving her soul.

'On reflection, I think you are right, Father.' She leaned towards him as if in agreement. If he had come to save her soul she felt duty bound to give him something to battle against, to keep him gainfully employed; and it was a more pleasant way of gaining attention than not eating. 'It could be that they were the spirits of the dead. What do you think of that?' She eagerly awaited his response.

Father Francisco now wished he had accepted the stories of the serving ladies. 'I do not for one moment ...'

'Listen to this, then. One day when my granddaughter Doña Juana was here, and sitting right there where you are, they did the same to her.'

'Which they are we talking about?'

'They say they are the spirits of the Conde de Miranda and the Chief Comendador. It wasn't the first time; they often come in here and do some most disrespectful things; magic, just as if they were witches.'

Father Francisco thought of the young and beautiful widowed Princess Juana whom he confessed regularly and with whom he had grown very close, both of them sharing the same deep religious convictions. She would have sought his help. He shook his head. He was being led into difficult waters.

'You do believe me father?' Juana asked, giving him the most innocent of looks. 'What I would suggest is this, you get rid of these ladies or spirits and then I can attend Mass. That should please everyone. Felipe included.'

'Rest assured; one way or another I will get to the bottom of this. And, should it emerge that it is of your servants' doing, I will call upon the Holy Office of the Inquisition to deal with them as heretics. In the meantime I shall write to my friend Brother Domingo de Soto who is an expert in this field.'

Juana nodded and smiled her approval. At last she had someone who listened to her, who was at her bidding; even an expert was to be consulted! This was just the beginning; she had found the perfect stratagem; all she had to do was bide her time, and watch and wait. All those accusations levelled at her over the years, every action taken against her were now her ammunition.

Chapter 51

A few months later the Jesuit priest, Father Francisco, was writing his latest report to King Felipe when Brother Domingo de Soto, the eminent theologian, was announced. He set aside his pen and got up from his desk to welcome him.

'I thank God you are here, Brother.' Francisco clasped him by the shoulders.

Brother Domingo reciprocated the warm greeting, 'My friend, I had to come. Although I found your earlier letters intriguing, they were of no great concern. You appeared to be dealing with the problem admirably. I, like you, was convinced that the queen was making excuses, bizarre at times, for her laxity; it was ever thus with those who wish to deny their own failings. And, as you observed, her granddaughter, a most devout young lady, would have had no hesitation in reporting anything malevolent here. But then the letter arrived hinting at deeper concerns. I heard your cry for help, and here I am. How is her majesty?'

'Not well at all, and that is what makes this all the more worrying. Since her fall some while ago, when she injured her back and legs, she has shown a gradual decline.'

'How ill is she?'

'Not ill exactly, but it is rare that she leaves her bed. If she does it is to be assisted to a chair, where she remains seated all day. She can only take a few painful steps. The doctors have been unable to make any diagnosis since she refuses them anywhere near.'

'Then she might deteriorate quickly?'

'There is every possibility; that is why I feel we should not waste any time. By the way, I have had those supposedly offending women servants removed, and at King Felipe's suggestion, to satisfy the queen, I told her that they were brought before the Holy Inquisition, were tried, and subsequently imprisoned. It seems to have worked, and I am sure that God will forgive my lying on this occasion. But now to the serious matter which I dared not put in writing,' he lowered his voice to a barely audible whisper. 'Just prior to her accident I had persuaded her to join us all for Mass, but the moment she saw the altar cloth, well, I can only say she went berserk; ranting and raving.'

'The altar cloth, you say, was the cause?' Brother Domingo looked cautiously about him.

'The altar cloth. It is an exceptional piece of Flemish workmanship; gold brocade with the Three Kings embroidered in coloured silks and gold thread.'

Brother Domingo took him by the arm and led him as far away from the doors as possible; no one but Francisco must hear what he was about to say. 'There you have it in a nutshell! They are not the Three Kings, they are three false Conversos. Moors; three of the many who pollute our land, who pretend to have converted to the Christian faith while concealing their continued worship of a false prophet, secretly adhering to their heretical customs and rites. And there they are on an altar cloth, come to mock God, to mock our Christian beliefs. Our problem is this; is the queen a staunch supporter of those daring to continue this heinous blasphemy, and was she afraid that her guilt had been discovered?'

'No, no, this is all going too far.' He found it absurd, but would not say so, not in so many words. 'However, I expressed my shock and dismay at the impiety of her actions only to be further disturbed by her refusal to accept any culpability whatsoever. She would only repeat, quite forcibly, that she was no different from the Poor Little Sisters of Santa Clara and was offended by such ostentation. She kept on insisting that an altar required only the simplest of cloths. This is what I find so disturbing; this has the foul odour of Lutheranism. Yet how could she know of Martin Luther?'

The only response from Brother Domingo was a patronising smile and the raising of learned eyebrows.

'Well then, Brother Domingo, shall we go to the queen?'

Juana sat in her bedchamber, her only company a lowly serving woman standing near the door, her face to the wall, as Juana had instructed, so that she would be unable to see whatever might be removed from the ever-present casket and oblong leather box.

The box was opened and the crucifix carefully removed. She held it fondly in yellow, cracked parchment fingers. A fleeting image of her favourite son Ferdinand (she often thought of him as her only son since Charles was a blackguard and had forfeited all rights) brought a moment's ease to the incessant pains in her back and legs. She recalled the time when he was a little boy, just six years old, how her stubbornness had forced her father into returning him to her.

Her thoughts then tumbled into a haphazard review of other strategies she had employed over many a year to fight for what was right and for what was justly hers. She chuckled and sometimes sighed remembering. It was true that her outbursts of screaming and shouting had all been failures, although they had given her some satisfaction at the time. Spur of the moment actions had been more successful. It was her stubbornness that had proved the most effective of campaigns to wage. But this latest tactic, to make them question her insanity, forcing them to renew their doubts regarding her obedience to the church; or conversely, to declare her mad after all, was the best ever. That was why it was so infuriating that just as she had begun to enjoy this new role she had had that damnable accident.

She had fallen, and fallen badly, and was now unable to move without suffering excruciating pains in her legs and lower back. Getting dressed was an agony. Attending to her personal toilet became such torture that she preferred at first to postpone it and then to abandon it completely.

Of course, she bitterly complained to herself, Denia was to blame for the accident. After years of seeing him and his family wearing her jewellery she was determined he would never have any of the few remaining pieces still in her possession or this beautiful crucifix, the loving gift from Ferdinand; the only gift to have been given her by any of her children.

If only Denia had not had the effrontery to open the box, to touch then lift out the gold cross with its Christ in His final hours of agony, to have his covetous eyes linger on it, she would never have tried to rush those few steps, would not have tripped as she reached to snatch it from his thieving hands.

Juana looked up and hastily locked away her treasured crucifix as the two priests entered. She felt quite gratified to have the attention of not one but two priests.

Father Francisco introduced the visiting priest. Brother Domingo bowed his head to hide his shock, nestling his nose into his praying hands to prevent inhaling too much of her stink.

'I am honoured to be of service,' Domingo greeted the lamentable figure before him.

Eyes set deep in a cadaverous face stared back at him, questioning. A claw-like hand scratched amongst the remaining wisps of white hair hanging forlornly from her mottled skull, disturbing the lice and sending a few of them down to join the community in the collar of her chemise.

Juana offered her hand for the customary kiss before withdrawing it quickly; these days she had a deep aversion to being touched. She beckoned to the woman to bring chairs, the extended arm revealing a further army of lice in her cuff, and around her wrist the evidence of their uninhibited feasting.

'We prefer to stand,' Brother Domingo was quick to suggest, and quicker still to get down to business. 'I am here about the ladies you complained of to Father Francisco.'

'Ah, yes, the ones in prison; and serves them right. And, I must tell you, Father Francisco, that since they left I have had no further problems of that nature.'

'It was no more than I promised, my lady,' Francisco smiled through his deception.

But Brother Domingo was not prepared to have his opinions go unheard. 'Let me put it to you that the ladies were guilty of nothing more than a lack of respect for their mistress whose gross and uninhibited behaviour had set a bad example and who, in doing so, has condemned them to the most severe of consequences!' He glared down at her, determined not to give any quarter. He would not allow her to shift her guilt on to others.

The room suddenly filled with Juana's cackling laughter. She clapped her hands, slapped the chair arms. 'Why, goodness me, but I am convinced! You are the grandson of my mother's secretary!'

'Yes, but ...'

'Thank goodness it is you who has come to deal with the dreadful problems we have here.'

'The major problem is you!' Domingo found it impossible to control his temper. 'We need to get you to recognise your obligations as a true daughter of the Church.'

Juana would not be spoken to in such a manner and pointed a filthy forefinger up at him. 'If I must remind you, it is your task to rid me of all those who are set against my carrying out those very obligations. You are here to do that and nothing else. Once you have fulfilled your duties in improving the situation here then I will be in a position to judge when the time is right for me to resume. I will not be hurried.'

'You do not seem to appreciate your position,' he persisted. 'I must ascertain ... Father Francisco tells me that you have professed the Catholic Faith, that you make the sign of the cross with Holy water, that you ...'

Juana was growing impatient, 'Yes, because those women have gone!' The man was a perfect nuisance, and he was making the pains in her legs and back worse than ever.

'Therefore we must discuss the matter of Mass.'

Juana had had enough. 'I am too ill for that. In any case I am too worried about the cat.'

She eased herself carefully back into her chair to watch and wait as her words took their desired affect. The priests exchanged all kinds of questioning glances.

Francisco shook his head.

Domingo closed his eyes and prayed for God's guidance, 'And what cat might that be?'

'A giant civet. It has already eaten a princess of Navarre. And I shall tell you something else; it has eaten the spirit of my mother. Just the other day I watched horrified as it tore the flesh from my father. I tell you I am terrified. It is lying in wait for me all the time. I have to be extremely vigilant. He could be anywhere; behind a door, under a chair, under the bed, even behind you.' She leaned gently sideways to peer around Brother Domingo.

The priests turned to check for themselves. Juana was pleased, encouraged that the cat and the spirits should keep them occupied for some time, and their subsequent reports would be something to look forward to.

Domingo lost his temper completely and shouted, purple with rage, 'Your parents have been dead for over forty years! Their spirits are in Heaven, quite safe from any animal which may or may not feast on spirits!'

Nevertheless this was something else to worry about. Was the civet an anti-Christ, a demon? Domingo knew that Satan had often taken the form of an animal to attack Christian souls. Had Juana actually witnessed the presence of the Devil, been in league with him? Or was she, as Francisco would probably have it, simply teasing? Or was she mad? How could he be sure of anything?

Francisco thought to test Juana, to play her at her own game. 'If this cat is so big how could it possibly hide under a chair?'

Juana was sublimely patient and gentle with the disbelievers, 'I have seen it, I would have you know, quite often. It comes and goes as it pleases, and more importantly changes its size at will. I am afraid, Brother Domingo, that until you have it destroyed there is no possibility of my ever attending Mass.' And, she felt sure, that would take some time.

Still seething, Domingo drew himself up to his full height, 'Father Francisco, you must see to it that the queen's apartments and her bed are sprinkled with Holy water, and you must insist that she attends Mass. These acts will prove her Catholicism, and protect her from the evil that pervades this place. By your leave, my lady.' He bowed and swept out of the room. Francisco followed.

They strode in an uncomfortable silence along the corridor until at last Domingo spoke. 'I can now appreciate the king's anxiety over her readiness to face God when the time comes. I must caution you, however, that under no circumstances is she to be allowed Holy Communion. Let me emphasise also that in the event of her approaching death you must administer nothing more than Extreme Unction.' He rubbed at his chin nervously, before offering his final piece of advice, a serious warning. 'If any Christian were to offer her the sacraments their own souls would be damned.'

'But is there not part of you that feels this is all posturing on her part, seeking attention, after years of loneliness?'

'Father Francisco,' Domingo would have him remember he was an eminent theologian, an authority on the subject of heresy, and would also have him know how very angry he was that such a dreadful state of affairs could have been allowed to exist in the royal house and that there had been no intervention before now; nor would he be made a fool of, 'on the one hand she is under the influence of heretical powers, or on the other she has the mind and soul of a new born babe and lacks all comprehension. In either case, you must not on any account, and that includes any weakening of your own resolve, offer anything other than Extreme Unction at the onset of death. There is nothing further to discuss.' He had to get back to his books; the answer must be there somewhere.

Chapter 52

Following the departure of Domingo de Soto autumn slipped quietly and uneventfully into winter; the worst winter in years. No one could remember one with quite such stinging blasts of icy winds, with leaden skies repeatedly hurling down frenzied, blinding snow enveloping Tordesillas in a thick, freezing, white blanket.

February of 1555 continued the bitter cold. The houses in the small town provided only minimal shelter against the storms constantly renewing their attacks.

The palace fared little better. Every part, be it room, corridor, or staircase, had its own particular chill or draught. Everywhere, that was, except Juana's bedchamber, where heavy curtains at the firmly shut window and a tapestry hanging across the door forbade entry to the merest suggestion of winter, and where a fire blazed in the hearth.

The door had been held open just long enough to allow a team of young lads to carry the many buckets of hot water necessary for the queen's daily bath; that done it was quickly shut tight allowing the small room to return to its former stifling state.

Four ladies of the bedchamber, chosen by Father Francisco for their exemplary Christian character in a climate of creeping heresy, four chamber boys, and Juana's physician, the wide and very round Doctor Cara, filled what little space remained between the bed, a small table, and the bath with its draped white sheet.

The ladies of the bedchamber waited, armed with snowy white towels. The doctor stood by the table with its bowl of ointment next to the casket and the leather box and beamed down his self-congratulation from thick, moist lips and shining red cheeks. This ointment, a mixture of bretonica and goat fat, was proving immensely effective, and he congratulated himself once more on having made such a wise decision.

With chubby hands clasped over his rotund belly he addressed the closed bed hangings, 'And how are the pains this morning, my lady?'

'Almost gone,' was the muffled reply from behind the brocades. 'I slept better, too.'

'Excellent!' But still he sighed because much valuable time had been wasted through her stubbornness, her refusal to allow him anywhere near to offer the benefits of his profound wisdom and expertise.

A whole year had passed since her fall and for almost as long she had been confined to her bed or chair. Eventually she had lost the use of her legs and they had become so swollen and unbearably painful that she finally had to concede defeat and permit Doctor Cara to examine her.

Remarkably his regime of daily baths and the application of generous amounts of the soothing ointments had eased the pain and controlled the swelling.

In fact Juana was beginning to feel well enough to entertain the idea of renewing Father Francisco's visits. They would most certainly brighten up the monotonous days. She was already planning the subjects for discussion. The first would centre on her granddaughter and her apparent desire to join Francisco's new sect, the Jesuits. Juana knew the princess wasn't the least bit serious; it was a ploy to prevent Charles from planning to marry her off a second time; and Juana applauded any stratagem, whatever it might be, to thwart men who felt it their right to dispose of women as they would a table or a chair.

A conversation of this nature would also discourage any further talk about her own continued determination not to attend Mass, and the huge threat of excommunication allegedly hovering over her. It was on everybody's lips. Hopefully Francisco would not bring that other dour priest who would pour his sour gloom over what could otherwise be a most pleasant chat.

Another topic she had in mind should provide her with some entertainment at Francisco's expense. She had discovered some while since, she couldn't remember who told her, that one of his daughters was married to a son of the dreadful Denia. She would dearly like to know why he had never mentioned it. Now might be the time to find out his reasons for not doing so, not that she was overly suspicious, but it would be best for him to be open with her, then she would know she could trust him. It was such a wicked world and some of the wickedest folk in it were those you would least suspect. Yes, perhaps later today after her bath she would send for him.

'Have the queen prepared for her bath.'

Accompanied by Juana's groans of discomfort and irritation — she so hated to be touched, hated anyone to see her nakedness — the ladies loosened her chemise and raised it above her head, a sheet laid over her to protect her modesty.

The bed hangings were then pulled back and the four chamber boys drew near. They each took a corner of upper and lower sheet and carried Juana in this hammock to her bath. She was slowly lowered into the steaming water.

Juana screamed; her arms flailed wildly desperately trying to be free of the wet linen clinging tightly to her.

Doctor Cara rushed to her, 'My lady?' He plunged his hands into the water to lift her. 'Get her out, get her out!' He bellowed at the boys, leaping back, pushing his hands inside his wide sleeves for comfort. 'Who, in God's name, was responsible for testing the water? Did no one add cold? This is scalding hot; get her out, I tell you!'

Juana was lifted out; the lads content to thrust their hands and arms deep into the hot water knowing that those responsible for this would probably experience far worse.

'Lay the queen on her front.'

Juana was too distressed to care about the indignity of being bundled and rolled; that her wrinkled, dried out breasts and her belly hanging as if ready to slide off her bones were about to be exposed for all to see. The wet sheets were removed and dry towels placed gently over her back and legs.

'Boy,' Doctor Cara collared the nearest, 'you get yourself down to the pharmacy as fast as your legs will carry you. Ask the pharmacist for ointment for scalds. Gum Arabic is best; but no, speed is most important, so ask for whatever he can prepare the fastest. Tell him it's urgent. Tell him it's for the queen.'

Juana was whimpering, clinging to the mattress, biting into the pillow with toothless jaws, praying that the pain would lessen.

Doctor Cara approached her. 'My lady, I must see your back to determine the extent of any injuries.'

'No! No! Never! No one must touch me,' she cried into her knuckles. 'I am best left on my own.'

'You must allow me, if I am to help; and you do need help.'

There was no alternative; she had to yield, 'Then be quick.'

The examination was completed. Doctor Cara was chilled and sickened by what he saw; the whole of her back from her shoulders down was red and inflamed; her buttocks and legs were worse than anything he had ever witnessed in his life. Leaning close and sounding as if he had all the confidence in the world he announced, 'Yes, well, there is a little scalding here and there which we will have cured in no time.' He beckoned one of the ladies, 'For the next few days or so you will ensure that the queen has goat's milk and butter at every meal; and will you send for the barber, her majesty must be bled.'

'No, a thousand times no! I hope everyone hears this; I am

337

not to be bled. Just look at me, I barely have enough blood to fill my body as it is.'

The boy returned from the pharmacist bursting into the room with a huge bowl and a breathless message, 'He says there is a better one but it takes longer to prepare but he's going to start on it right away, and he'll bring it himself as soon as its ready.'

'So, ladies, if you are ready; this must be smoothed on with the utmost care. You must ensure that every affected part of the lower body is entirely covered. Then take the towels and place them gently over the reddened areas. When this is done it is your duty to see that her majesty remains as still as possible.'

Juana laughed through her tears, 'How fortunate you are doctor that your patient is expert at remaining still for hours, even days. At least on this occasion I will not be judged as being crazy for doing so.'

'Shame on you, lady, for thinking such thoughts!' But it was true, nonetheless.

Juana was meanwhile bitterly disappointed; she would have to postpone her meeting with Father Francisco.

Chapter 53

The relentlessly painful days of February had become the relentlessly painful days of March. Doctor Cara arrived for his usual daily visit. Today he was followed at a discreet distance by two elderly menservants, their rickety legs looking more bowed than ever as they tottered under the bulky burdens on their backs.

He stopped in the antechamber, 'You wait here until you are called.'

He checked the position of his doctor's cap, tucking it about his ears, rearranged his gown at the shoulders then swept into the bedchamber. Looking neither to right nor left he marched straight to the bed surprising the ladies and the chamber boys more accustomed to his jovial greeting.

There was no time for pleasantries today. Doctor Cara was angry, very angry. He had had enough of addressing his patient through a wall of heavy brocade; he was tired of being denied access; he would have no more of it.

Without a moment's hesitation he threw back the bed hangings. He was met by a blast of hot, reeking foulness that made him reel. He held his sleeve across his nose and mouth and swallowed hard to prevent himself from retching.

It took him a second or two to compose himself and return to the indignation that had propelled him scowling along corridors and up the stairs.

'My lady,' he addressed Juana's back, 'why have you allowed all the good work to be undone so quickly?' He moved briskly to the other side of the bed and pulled aside more hangings.

Juana buried her head in the crook of her arm not wishing to face him. 'Go away.'

But he was not of a mood to go away, not any more. He was furious and he was going to have his way.

'The blisters were beginning to heal until you started this nonsense: when you stopped using the ointment, when you decided to ignore my instructions. I said that you were to have your position changed regularly; gently but regularly. You decided otherwise and refused to move, lying on this one side day and night. Today you shall be moved. I insist. I will also examine you. And another thing,' his ruddy cheeks had taken on a livid hue, his voice was tight with rage, 'your bed linen will be changed. How many weeks is it ...?'

A faint crackled refusal came from beneath her elbow. 'Go away. I will remain as I am. I command it. I am the queen.'

Doctor Cara exploded, 'You are my patient. I am the one who gives the orders!'

'I will not be touched.'

The thought of the indignity of such an event was too embarrassing to contemplate, and she could not bear it. She prayed that they would leave her alone in her filth; it was hers and she could and would continue to tolerate it. When she had had that first accident in her bed it had been a difficult decision to take as to whether or not she should ask someone to attend to her, but once taken there was no going back. But she hadn't counted on Doctor Cara overriding her orders. How was she to prevent the inevitable?

'My lady, I will hear no more. Dear God, I would not suffer an animal to sleep in such mire!'

He snapped his fingers at the chamber boys, 'Tell the servants to bring in the mattresses; they are waiting. I want two of you to lift her majesty.'

She raved and howled, but she was lifted from her bed and placed on a newly made mattress on the floor. Following weeks of inactivity the room was suddenly alive and busy. The fouled mattress, sodden with urine and faeces was bundled out of the room. Chamber boys held a screen of sheets as the ladies stripped Juana of her filthy chemise and bathed away the excrement from her buttocks and legs.

Never had they envisaged such a demand being made of them, yet they found the courage and the will. Juana was soon clean, in a fresh chemise and lying on the other new mattress, between sheets with their newly laundered fragrance.

Now that she was so clean and so much more comfortable she began to wonder why she had resisted for so long. What would that other Juana have done under the circumstances? Would she have wanted to protect herself from the indignity of being treated as an infant, to be turned this way and that in her cradle, to be cleaned from top to tail? Or would she have been ready to dismiss it as no more than a delicate situation? Juana knew the answer, and felt she had let herself down rather badly.

No sooner had she resolved to be more positive than the marquesa appeared in the doorway, elegant in green velvet and holding a silver pomander beneath her proud nose.

'You said my presence was necessary,' she complained from behind the silver ball.

'Ah, marquesa,' the doctor had returned to his more affable self having rid the room of all the gruesome evidence of neglect. 'I am this very moment about to examine my patient.'

He, the marquesa, and the ladies of the bedchamber surrounded Juana who groaned at this further embarrassment; that the marquesa should see her like this. It was going to take a huge effort, but then again the marquesa's embarrassment might be even greater than hers. A weak laugh escaped her.

Doctor Cara congratulated himself for Juana's return to good humour seeing it as a direct result of his intervention. 'It is good to hear your laughter again. Ladies if you would kindly turn the queen. This is the side her majesty has been resting on for far too long,' he explained to the marquesa who had no intention of allowing her eyes to rest on anything other than the engraved floral designs on her pomander. After the briefest of moments she retired to wait by the door.

She was joined shortly by the doctor who gave instructions for the fire to be built up and ushered off a chamber boy on a whispered urgent errand.

'Marquesa, as you witnessed, the blisters from the scalding never healed; in fact they have reopened and become infected. Both buttocks are covered in sores.'

'You may spare me the details.'

'There is also evidence of rotting flesh. There is no time to be lost. I have sent the boy for my irons.'

'Tell me, doctor, how soon will you know if she is responding to this treatment?'

'I shall do what I can but, truthfully, I see little hope.'

'Then why bother?'

He wouldn't allow himself to answer.

'Then if you must, you must. Meanwhile I shall send a message to Valladolid to ask the princess, DoZa Juana, to come immediately; just as a precaution, you understand.' The marquesa hastened off to deliver the good news to her husband.

'This will be painful, but necessary, my lady.'

Two ladies held her arms, another two her feet as the irons were applied. Smoke and the pungent smell of burning flesh filled their nostrils. Juana's piteous screams filled the room, the palace, escaping even to the narrow road that ran below the window. Passers by heard and covered their ears hoping someone would stop whatever was causing such agonies. Somehow or other the news of the gravity of Queen Juana's illness spread throughout the small town, and folk flocked to the churches to pray for their beloved monarch.

Juana's granddaughter arrived later in the day and went immediately to her bedside.

'Who asked you to come?'

'The marquesa sent for me, honourable grandmother.'

'How like her, she is probably on her knees right now praying for my death.'

'Grandmother! You do her a grave injustice.'

'What would you know?'

'All the townsfolk are praying for you.'

'And theirs are honest prayers; they are the only ones who have ever cared.'

'Your criticism of the marquesa is unfair. She has been an excellent servant to you for many years.'

'Speak only about those things of which you have an indisputable knowledge.'

'Perhaps this will please you; I have sent for other doctors.'

'I want to be left in peace. Doctor Cara has done everything there is to be done. There is to be no more meddling. Let everything be.'

'Well I shall certainly send for Father Francisco.'

'If you deem it necessary,' she snapped back wanting to be left in peace, wishing her granddaughter had never come; she had no need for anyone. Then she mulled the idea over, 'Yes, do that, send for Father Francisco. I have some unfinished business with him.'

Chapter 54

A month had passed by, day upon day of unspeakable agony.

'Where is Father Francisco?' Juana was barely audible, her voice tiny, breaking; her thickened tongue making it a huge and tiring effort to speak.

'I am here. I am never far from your side.'

'Father,' hot tears spilled over her cheeks and on to her pillow, 'will I be forgiven for what I said yesterday? My anger was meant neither for you nor the Church. I should not have ranted at you, you are a good man. I know I did say some wicked things. Can you hear me?'

'Yes, I hear you; your words were not wicked but most unjust. It was wrong of you to say that for years no one had shown any interest in your health and well-being, but now that the end is near everyone is making a tremendous fuss about your soul. You do many people a great disservice.'

Her tears continued to flow but now they were for all those friends she had forgotten by concentrating so much on the many who had sought to deceive or hurt.

'You are right I have committed many a grave omission.'

'We will pray together then I will hear your confession.'

Juana confessed, listing the recipients of her ill temper: her mother, father, husband, children, the governor Ferrer and last but not least the Denias. She had to fight against her still strong convictions that, in the first place, she would have behaved in an entirely different manner had they treated her with decency and with respect and, secondly, that it was patently obvious, for those prepared to accept the obvious, that after years of ignoring her very existence there were people now paying her all kinds of attention. These details she would only share with

God. She moved on to repenting her lack of appreciation for the many who had given their time and patience to aid and comfort her; most of all her Uncle Fadrique, Zayda, Maria, Marta, Hernan Duque, Brother Juan de Avila, her constant companion for years, and many more whose names she had forgotten. She thanked God for the love and wisdom of her dear brother, Juan, who had died so young and whose advice had helped her survive. She asked that God would forgive her for having ever been cross with him.

'God will show mercy on you. He will see that you are a true penitent. He will welcome you as a faithful daughter.' Francisco smiled down on her, delighted at such a lengthy and honest baring of her soul. In a rush of fervour, which he instantly regretted, he suggested Holy Communion, inviting her to receive the Body of Christ.

Juana's forehead became blanketed in an icy coldness, 'I am going to vomit.' A rush of stinging hot bile burst from her.

'Quick, a bowl and towels here,' Francisco shouted as Juana heaved and retched then fell back onto the pillows exhausted and sweating.

As the ladies pulled back the bed covers and bundled them to the floor, removed the stained chemise, Francisco walked over to Denia.

He had been sitting all the while by the fire oblivious to everything, his attention riveted on the magnificent gold crucifix in his hand.

The priest had to unburden himself, had to tell someone. 'I should not have allowed my heart to rule my head.'

'One moment,' Denia replaced the crucifix in the cushioned satin lining, closed the lid to the leather box, and slipped it into his buckskin purse at his waist. He smiled up at him, 'King Charles has not paid me my salary this last month or two, but this will compensate in some measure. You were saying?'

'I so want to help her majesty that I am allowing myself to

become emotionally involved. Fortunately it was the queen herself who saved me from making a grave mistake. I need Brother Soto de Domingo. Would you do the favour of writing to him?'

'If you feel it necessary. Speaking personally I think it a waste of time. You will only be going over old ground.'

'I want a letter sent post haste!'

Brother Domingo arrived two days later. He visited Juana, talked with her, and now after due consideration he was prepared to give Francisco the benefit of his conclusions.

'Her majesty does appear to have all her faculties. You say she has confessed and shown herself to be a true daughter of the Church. However, this may not be a lasting condition and it behoves us to exercise extreme care. She is gravely ill and continues to vomit; this in itself will help your cause. I dread to think of the consequences if something of that nature were to occur once she had received the Body of Christ. Yes, the queen, in effect, has resolved the situation. Your only recourse is to offer Extreme Unction. I might add that you should do this without further delay. Have no concerns for her soul or those of her family; they will all be safe.'

'I shall be forever indebted, Brother. And thank you for travelling here during Holy Week; I know you would have preferred to have spent these days in prayer.'

Brother Domingo bowed his head graciously acknowledging the gratitude of the other.

The room was put in order and the household summoned. Many stood in the shadows while others gathered in the salon and the corridor beyond. The marqués and marquesa stood close to Father Francisco.

Although Juana found little respite from the continued bouts of vomiting there was an overall tranquillity in the air; the tranquillity of resignation.

'Your highness, you have reached the end of your days on earth, the end of your travails, and you must be prepared to meet Our Lord God. You must now beg His forgiveness, with all your heart, for the many ways you have offended him.'

'I beg forgiveness for all my excesses,' her voice was faint, her breathing laboured. 'I desire nothing but that He will look kindly upon me, His erring servant ...' the words faltered.

Brother Francisco offered her his crucifix. She kissed it gently then tried to say the words of the Creed.

Her body was anointed as the prayers of the ritual were offered. Her eyes were closed and she whispered to a succession of unsummoned images. 'My handsome Philip, dallying with any pretty thing; you scorned my love, trampled upon it. You denied me any friendships, denied me my liberty. Ah, father, you too used me as though I was your property to do with as you desired. Why did you feel nothing but envy for me? You wanted all the power and had me imprisoned so that I would be unable to share. All I wanted was to be loved, yet you and Philip sought to hurt me. And Charles, I thought I would see you. Never once did you show me any compassion. One day you will realise that but for me you would have lost Spain, I wonder too if you might regret the way you and your friends have treated me, stolen from me? No better than villains, the lot of you.'

A new image appeared, much stronger than the rest. 'My beloved brother Juan; you were the sweetest, kindest person ever. Mother was right, you were an angel.'

She thought she saw him reaching towards her to put a finger to her pouting lips as he did once before so many years ago. He was right. She dismissed the other images with the strength of that other Juana.

Exhaustion engulfed her, pushing her into a deep sleep.

Dawn brought with it the first intrepid calls of a solitary bird bidding farewell to the night, welcoming the day. Others soon joined in until there was a full chorus of jubilation. The slow tolling of bells in their steeples also announced the beginning of the day, the day of the final agonies of the Saviour. It was Good Friday.

Juana's eyelids flickered then opened. Juan had brought her safely through her last battle and had left her to rest. She stirred and she felt no pain. She moved her arms then her legs; she discovered that she could move her legs again, and there was no pain! Gone was the nausea, gone was the foul bitter taste in her mouth and throat.

Her eyes had dimmed and she could barely make out the priest, 'Father Francisco?'

'I am here my child.'

'Please, the crucifix.'

'I have it here; I have been holding it over you as you slept. And here is something else.' He handed her a jewelled medallion of the Blessed Virgin.

Juana felt it then traced her fingers across the back of it to be sure; and there was her name. 'This is mine, my very own.' It was a gift from her mother, for her fifteenth birthday. She had worn it the day she was told of her marriage contract. How long had it been lying about somewhere, forgotten, until Father Francisco had found it?

She drew it to her, kissed it, and placed it on her breast; it would travel with her. She held the crucifix to kiss her Saviour's feet then freed it reaching up as if towards some helping hands and called, 'Sweet Jesus, who was crucified, be with me ...'

348

Queen Juana died at six o'clock on the morning of Good Friday, April 12, 1555.
She was seventy-five years old and had spent forty-six of those years imprisoned in Tordesillas.

Epilogue

Tordesillas

April 12, 1555
The Mayor declared ten days of mourning. Everyone was commanded to wear black and there was to be nothing of colour hanging in windows or from balconies. There was to be no music, no dancing, no shows of merriment and no singing in the streets.

April 15, 1555
In a solemn ceremony attended by a host of political and ecclesiastical dignitaries Juana's body was transferred to the Royal Chapel in the Convent of Santa Clara and placed in the same vault where her husband Philip had been interred forty-six years earlier. A wooden railing bearing twelve coats of arms stood around the vault and guards were posted at the four corners.

April 23, 1555
The full town council in their ceremonial robes and bearing their maces of office walked through the town in solemn procession to attend a Requiem Mass for Juana.

Valladolid

April 1555
Two of Juana's family attended a memorial service in the
cathedral; her great-grandson Prince Carlos with the Grandees
and Counsellors, The Princess Juana remained in the upper
choir; such was her pain and distress she would not be seen in
public.

Flanders

September, 1555
Juana was accorded full funeral honours.
A cortege was led by two horsemen, their horses caparisoned
in black velvet bearing a single red cross, edged with gold and
Juana's coat of arms in each corner. A jewel encrusted crown
was carried on a golden cushion. Heralds bearing the coats of
arms of Castile, Leon, Aragón and Sicily followed. An English
herald preceded Juana's grandson Felipe (Philip, King Consort
of England). He was on foot, in a full-length hooded black
cloak.
Finally came the ambassadors and grandees and then, hundreds
of poor attired in black carrying torches.

The Monastery at Yuste

September, 1558
On his deathbed, Charles expressed his desire to have his
mother's mortal remains brought to the convent at Yuste to be
laid alongside his own.

Madrid

October 1573

King Felipe ordered his grandmother's remains to be taken from Tordesillas to Granada.

Granada

1603

Fifty years after her death Juana finally recovered her status and dignity. She was laid to rest next to her husband Philip and her parents Queen Isabel and King Ferdinand in the Royal Chapel of the Cathedral of Granada.

Her effigy shows her in the bloom of youth; a young queen; beautiful, serene, at peace.